MW01298344

Praise for *Housemoms*

"An intriguing and compelling tale with complex characters . . . look[ing] at the sisterhood formed in sororities that extends to those who work in, and around, them."

—*Kirkus Reviews*

"The book shines in its emphasis on the power of women having each other's backs and rooting for one another . . . A witty, wild ride and an overall gripping read with unforgettable, wholesome moments."

—*Booklist*

Praise for Jen Lancaster

"Scathingly witty."

—*Boston Herald*

"Witty and hilarious . . . Jen Lancaster is like that friend who always says what you're thinking—just 1,000 times funnier."

—*People*

"No matter what she's writing, it's scathingly witty and lots of fun."

—*Publishers Weekly*

"Jen Lancaster is like a modern-day, bawdy Erma Bombeck."

—Lisa Lampanelli, *New York Post*

"Hilarious."

—*InStyle*

PETER PULASKI MUST PAY

OTHER TITLES BY JEN LANCASTER

Nonfiction

Bitter Is the New Black

Bright Lights, Big Ass

Such a Pretty Fat

Pretty in Plaid

My Fair Lazy

Jeneration X

The Tao of Martha

I Regret Nothing

Stories I'd Tell in Bars

Welcome to the United States of Anxiety

Fiction

If You Were Here

Here I Go Again

Twisted Sisters

The Best of Enemies

By the Numbers

The Gatekeepers

Housemoms

The Anti-Heroes

PETER PULASKI MUST PAY

A NOVEL

JEN LANCASTER

Little
a

This is a work of fiction. Names, characters, organizations, places, events, and incidents are either products of the author's imagination or are used fictitiously. Otherwise, any resemblance to actual persons, living or dead, is purely coincidental.

Published by Little A, New York

www.apub.com

EU product safety contact:
Amazon Media EU S.à r.l.
38, avenue John F. Kennedy, L-1855 Luxembourg
amazonpublishing-gpsr@amazon.com

ISBN-13: 9781662530722 (hardcover)
ISBN-13: 9781662530739 (paperback)
ISBN-13: 9781662530715 (digital)

Cover design by Sarah Horgan
Cover image: © TatyanaKar, © Ellegant, © Pics Garden,
© Uswa KDT / Shutterstock

Printed in the United States of America

First edition

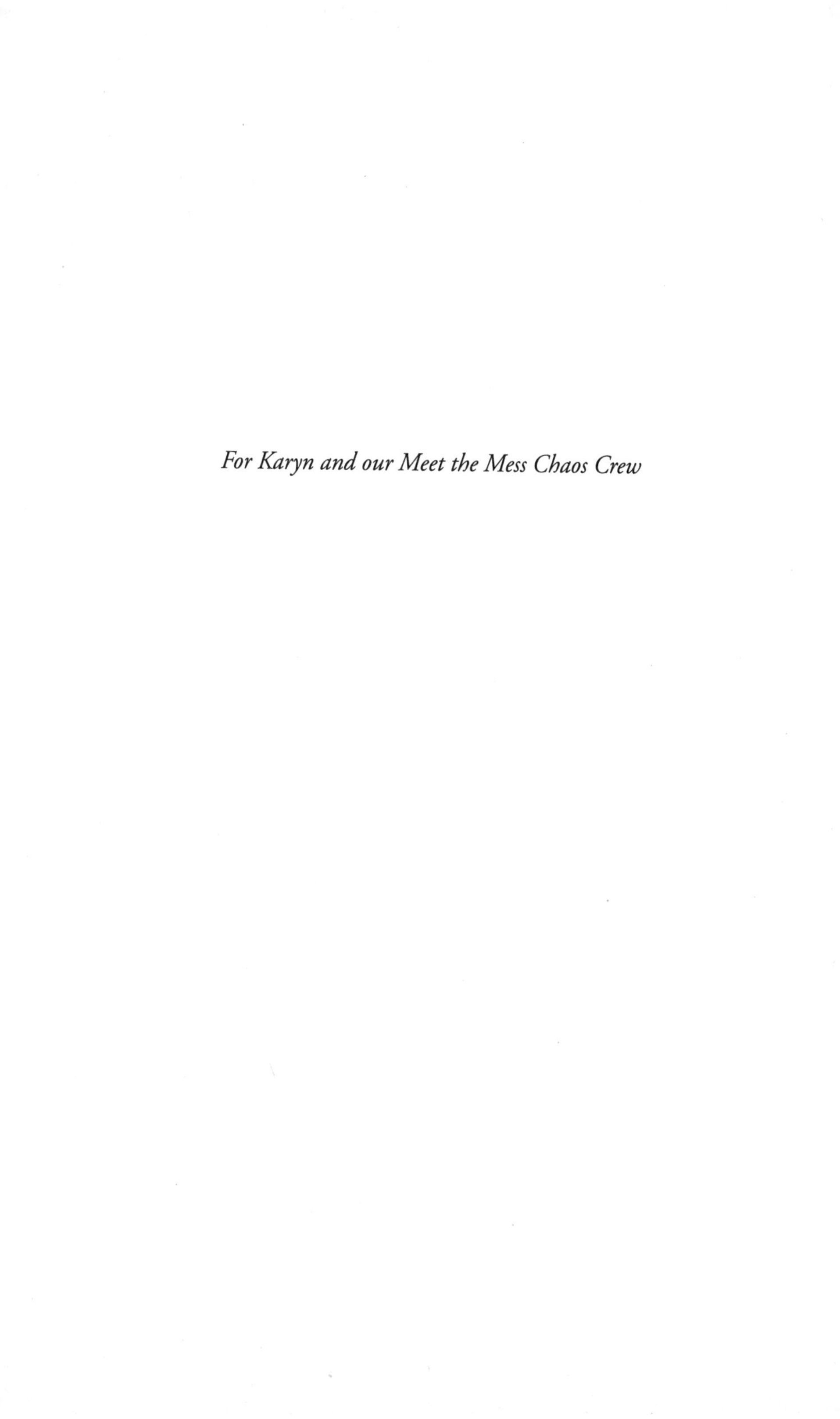

For Karyn and our Meet the Mess Chaos Crew

THE FRIDAY NIGHT DOOM CREW

EXECUTIVE BOARD

President: Elinor O'Neill
Our founder Eli isn't new to creating something extraordinary. She turned personal tragedy into triumph, going from being a young mother and widow to starting a billion-dollar management consulting company. Having retired early after taking her company public, Eli brings this same drive and passion to making our true crime community informative, empowering, and inclusive. Eli lives on the North Shore of Chicago with her lazy Tibetan mastiffs, Pee-wee and Herman, who do not share her zeal for long-distance running. Eli is one of our keynote speakers at DoomCon 2025, which will take place at Chicago's McCormick Place in November. **(Tickets still available—CLICK HERE to order.)**

Vice President: Carmen Delgado
Carmen is one of the most intuitive and insightful members of our club. She's a former forensic psychologist who has a deep understanding of the motivations and behaviors of criminals. Her analysis and expert commentary gives us all a better insight into the psychological aspects of the true crime cases we study. Carmen lives in Humboldt Park with her husband Juan and two of her adult children, whom she would be

delighted to help leave the nest. If you've joined us at our Chicago meet-ups, you already know her homemade *pasteles* are legendary.

Secretary: Diana Pulaski

Diana is a meticulous and organized individual, responsible for managing the club's administrative tasks, including overseeing moderation of our Substack, Facebook, and Discord groups; scheduling meetings; taking minutes; and managing member communication. Her attention to detail ensures the smooth operation of our club. But she's so much more than that; she's the beating heart of our group and of our community at large. Whether it's by volunteering with Habitat for Humanity (Diana swings a mean hammer!) or rescuing any animal in need or just being the friend who's always there, Diana has captured all of our hearts. She lives in the western suburbs with her children and her physician husband, Peter.

Treasurer: Stella Thompson

Stella is responsible for the club's finances, including membership dues, budgeting, and fundraising for our Justice for Victims charitable endeavor. **(CLICK HERE for our Annual Report and Form 990.)** Her financial acumen is essential for our club's sustainability and allows us to do maximum good. You may also recognize her from her popular **Instagram presence** touting body positivity and all things pink. She lives in the Printer's Row neighborhood of Chicago with her fiancé Abe in what she describes as her "Barbie Dream Townhouse" and calls herself a recovering pageant addict.

Historian: Frankie Sullivan

Frankie is a history enthusiast with a particular interest in true crime, and he's dedicated to researching and documenting cold cases, which often influence the art he creates. **(CLICK HERE to view his available work on Society6.)** He shares his extensive knowledge with club members through presentations and discussions, and on occasion, his vocal styling. **(CLICK HERE to sign up for his Chappell Roan karaoke night at DoomCon. Space is limited.)** He lives in Lakeview with his partner Gavin, their French bulldog Kevin, and their extensive collection of vinyl.

Website Manager Jazz Ahmadi

Jazz is responsible for maintaining the club's website and online presence. Her skills ensure that the club's information and resources are easily accessible to members and the public. When she was fourteen, she hacked into a *certain government entity*, which prompted a visit from the NSA, much to her Persian immigrant parents' chagrin. But as an adult, Jazz only uses her prowess for good as a cybersecurity consultant. She lives with her family on the northwest side of the city. Although IT is her passion, her dream is to be cast on the next season of *Love Island.*

Prologue

Dr. Peter Pulaski

I stare up at the night sky as I feel the blood rushing from my body. The pain radiates through all my limbs as the adrenaline of the shock dissipates, leaving a dull, spreading ache behind. The sodium lights that dot the parking lot begin to dim in my peripheral vision. The voices around me are muffled; my ears ring from the gunshot and I can't make out what's being said. Are they talking to me? About me? I can't say.

There's a metallic taste in my mouth and my skin grows clammy. With every breath, I can feel myself slipping away.

How did I get here?

It wasn't supposed to go this way.

I made some mistakes, but everyone makes mistakes.

I'm not the first person to take a shortcut. I'm not the first person whose questionable choice opened the door to more bad choices, causing everything to snowball once it was in motion. I'm not the first person to get in over his head.

If I'd known where it would lead, yeah, I'd have done it differently. Too late for that now.

I wasn't hurting anyone directly. The health care system was broken long before I came along and decided I was tired of being screwed over. Hell, half the country cheered when the kid took down that CEO on the street right before the investor meeting. His company's billions in profit came on the back of denying claims.

You know who doesn't get paid when a claim is denied and the patient can't afford the bill?

That's right, *me.*

I was writing off more and more debt every year, and earning less and less for the same procedures, while my costs skyrocketed.

I couldn't keep up.

So when I saw a chance to tip the scale back in my favor, I took it. Maybe I even enjoyed sticking it to the big dogs a little, making *them* pay for once. But if I'd known it could end like this, I might not have been so quick to succumb to the lure of easy money and a different life.

I exhale one last time and the world goes dark.

Chapter One

Frankie Sullivan

"I hate that we even have to make this a rule," Eli says with a sigh. She runs her fingers through her blunt-cut auburn bob. Her square, short nails are polished in a high-gloss Granny Smith–apple green. The contrast against her pale skin accentuates the freckles dotting the backs of her hands and trailing up her sinewy arms, every muscle toned and defined. Eli is always fretting about feeling like a little old lady, but not with those guns, babe.

Not by a long shot.

While Eli at sixty-three is almost four decades older than Jazmin, our youngest Doom Crew board member, I guarantee she could bench-press more than any of us. Lord knows she can outrun us all. She talked us into what she claimed was a "casual sightseeing jog" with her once on a Doom Crew retreat. Despite studying mixed martial arts at the time, Jazz had to call an Uber and Carmen and Stella peeled off to go to a bar. Obvi, I *keeps it tight*, so I'm the only one who made it the whole way. But then I fell asleep in the bathtub before dinner, doped up on extra strength Tylenol and Whispering Angel rosé, one gravy boat of olive oil away from going the full Whitney Houston. (RIP, queen.) Never again.

"I thought our members would have a modicum of sensitivity," Eli adds. Eli never stops moving. She frets with the strings around the hole in the knee of her barrel-leg jeans that I guarantee came that way intentionally from Bergdorf Goodman with a price tag that would have covered the rent at my old place. She lets me hang out in her walk-in (oh, the irony of wanting to be *in* the closet) every time we're at her house, and it's half wacky T-shirts and half quiet luxury, like some Siobhan on *Succession* shit. There's a wall of Loro Piana. An entire *wall.* I want to bury myself face-first in all that cashmere.

A word about my Eli? She is a *catch.* She's smart AF and looks like Julianne Moore. She's legit on one of those *Forbes* self-made women lists, but what she's most proud of is running a sub-3:25 marathon. We do not get it. Girl, you're rich; why run? Like when Oprah competed in that marathon—what was she trying to prove? You're Oprah. Just lean into it.

We're always trying to set Eli up, but she doesn't care about dating. Says she's never been with another man since she lost her husband Hank thirty years ago to an aneurysm, which left her alone with two small kids. But Eli did what Eli does, rising to the occasion. Out of nothing but grit, she created a management consulting company that went worldwide. *Of course* I'm obsessed with her. Then again, I'm obsessed with our whole Doom Crew executive board; I love us.

Stella and I tried desperately to get Eli to audition for *The Golden Bachelor*, but Eli just laughed when the casting people reached out. They were salivating over the idea of her! But she told them she already had one great love and that his memory still sustains her. (Hank does sound pretty freaking amazing.) What ABC doesn't know is that she and Jazz researched the first Golden Bachelor. Jazz has . . . ways of finding hidden info. Heh. A few ~~questionably~~ definitely illegal queries later, Eli decided she didn't want to risk half her fortune on some random guy who used to repair hot tubs for a living.

Like I said, smart AF.

Eli does seem happy and her social calendar is always full, so we don't push. Okay, that's a lie. We push. We push so freaking hard, but it's like trying to use a cannonball as a kickball—ineffective and painful for anyone who tries. Thus far, she's rejected every one of our offers to make introductions. She won't let us fix her up, yet she's the whole reason Gavin and I are a couple. She totally made us get together, not taking no for an answer because she was convinced we'd be right for each other. Now, every single one of us has our person, except for Jazz, who's saving herself for whomever she meets on *Love Island*. People laugh when Jazz shares her plan, but lemme say this—if she can hack into the Pentagon's servers, she can *for sure* break into the summer broadcast season on CBS. Sleep on Jazz to your own detriment.

"Um, yeah, you would think they have some sensitivity because *you* believe people are good at their core. I do not suffer from that misconception," says Jazz, never once stopping tapping away on her phone. She has the fastest thumbs in Chicago, plus the face of a Disney princess: perfectly symmetrical and beautiful, save for her perpetual scowl, which I think makes her way more interesting. She flips her heavy black French braid over her shoulder and it lands with a thud. "People are trash. Period. And when we throw the doors open to just anyone, we can't be surprised when *just anyone* wanders in."

Jazz is not wrong. We held our first DoomCon four years ago. This was a small event in a hotel conference room out by O'Hare in 2022, held for other true crime aficionados. The six of us Doom Crew board members had found each other in an obscure Reddit group a couple of years earlier, drawn together by our fascination with one particular cold case. We started to grow our membership from there. That lady boss Eli is running the show is the secret to our massive success, even though she's too modest to admit it.

We didn't know that anyone would even come to our con because we'd only just opened up our Facebook and Discord groups to outside members back then. We invited a couple of local true crime authors to host panels and we scheduled some workshops and seminars, with a handful of vendors stationed outside in the hallway. (Honestly, I thought it was overkill, but Eli swore she had *a vision*.) We had no idea how quickly the event would sell out, or that our growth every year would be exponential, especially since we don't even have an associated podcast, just discussion groups across a few platforms. DoomCon has turned into a bit of a scene or a circus, depending on your point of view.

The good news is, anything we earn from ticket sales goes directly to our victim advocacy charity, and we raised *a ton* last year. Our newest endeavor is building safe houses for human trafficking victims, and we've already broken ground on the facility on West Washington.

The bad news is, lately we've been attracting people who fetishize crime. Not ideal.

Plus, we've recently started to hemorrhage membership and we're trying desperately to slow the bleeding. We're losing people left and right to these for-profit crime podcasts, so our future is in question, and that is some bullshit. We exist solely to give back, so we have to keep on track with our growth because we're making bigger and bigger financial commitments.

Carmen and Juan had to attend a family wedding in Puerto Rico, so she didn't witness what happened at DoomCon 2024. Through a mouthful of goat cheese–stuffed, prosciutto-wrapped figs, Carmen says, "What, what did I miss?" She uses the back of her hand to brush away an ombré tendril that's escaped from her perpetually messy topknot. (Her hair is like a prisoner no bars can contain.) Her irises are so dark brown that they blend into her pupils. Her kids say that when she gets mad, it's like looking a shark in the eye. However, she's too mellow to ever get mad, so we'll have to take their word for it. Carmen has whatever the opposite of resting bitch face is. Her lips cant up in the corners, so she always looks like someone told her a joke and she's trying not to laugh.

Right now, Carmen's perpetual smile and intense gaze are fixed on the buffet that we're all sitting around. Whenever Diana hosts, everything she serves is legendary. She blows us all out of the water with her ability to channel Martha Stewart. Lilly, her daughter, showed her a TikTok of turning a kitchen island into a charcuterie board, and now there's nothing but cured meats curved into the shape of flowers and so many different cheeses directly on the quartz, bordered by fresh and dried fruit, dips, and assorted nuts. OMG. And do not even start me on the caliber of wine she serves. Even Eli buys wine from Trader Joe's because that's what *she* drinks (which is rare), but Diana scoops up cases of the good stuff she discovers on trips, and she's never afraid to share. Today's Barolo has notes of truffles and chocolate, with a hint of eucalyptus. I want to dive into a pool full of it and just float around.

We rotate where we gather for our weekly get-togethers so no one has to go out of their way cleaning or prepping more than once every six weeks. Every meeting has a different vibe. Not to brag, but everyone says coming to my place is like visiting the coolest, hippest café in the world, where the drinks are strong, where recreational drugs are always an option (that no one but me takes), and where the food is hit or miss. Listen, I have ADHD. Does this give me laser focus on my art or the historical research I do for the group? Yes. But often it means I whiff the little details, like dinner. Oops. Unless Gavin is there to manage the dinner spread, we'll get pizzas if I remember to order them. The girls say they don't care and being together is enough. I hope so, because this group is kind of my everything.

Carmen's home is festive and chaotic, with her kids and their friends always coming in and out. It's a perpetual party and that house is legit full of love. My girl Carmen *claims* she wants her adult sons Freddy and Tomas to move out of her basement, and yet she continually finds a reason that whatever apartment they look at isn't good enough, whether it's her suspicion of lead paint, black mold, too close to the L, et cetera. *Uh-huh.* Do I blame them for not wanting to leave? No. If it weren't for Gavin, *I'd* move into her basement.

Stella's town house has the kind of soft, flattering lighting that makes every one of us look ten years younger and ten pounds thinner, so it's selfie central. We always have the best delivery at Jazz's family's house because she refuses to learn how to cook, like the idea of it actually offends her.

And then there's Diana's home, which is a live-action Pinterest page.

If I'm obsessed with Eli, it doesn't hold a candle to how I feel about Diana who is just . . . *mother*. Goddess. Icon. Walking into here feels like stepping into a warm hug, and I'm not kidding. Truth bomb? I loathe the modern farmhouse style, but in Diana's case, it works. The neutral palette of walls and overstuffed down couches in the open concept living area doesn't feel bland, boring, or basic. Instead, the muted tone of the decor serves as the ideal backdrop to highlight all the bright Italian pottery jugs of fresh-cut wildflowers. Plus, she has a huge, gorgeous oil painting over her fireplace that I made for her last year.

Okay, I'm biased.

I was inspired by my research on the disappearance of Maura Murray, who was lost on a snowy road in New Hampshire after she'd had a car accident and was never seen again. If you're a true crime person, there's a good chance her story drew you in.

Something the group always says is that if you like true crime, don't be ashamed. There's nothing wrong with you. Hell, half of America consumes true crime content. It's my theory that anyone who's into the genre has an origin story, the case that sparked their imagination. I hesitate to call anyone in the Doom Crew "fans" because that implies that we support or admire criminals. Hard pass. But there's definitely a fascination, and everyone was sucked in by some event. Like, maybe you were a kid and you recall seeing JonBenét Ramsey's perfect little face on the cover of *People* magazine and you wanted to know what happened to that glamorous but tragic baby girl. (In my opinion, that former housekeeper knows more than she lets on, bet on that.) Or maybe you were a newlywed and you couldn't take your eyes off Laci Peterson's radiant smile and statement necklace in those Christmas party photos. Maybe you're an old Hollywood buff and you were vexed by the Black Dahlia murder. Or you're a college girl who was horrified that Bryan

Kohberger could violate what should have been a safe and sanctified place. Everyone has a gateway case, something that resonates so deeply or feels so personal that they want to know more.

For me, true crime inspires my art. It all started with a piece I did on Matthew Shepherd in my high school art class because his story resonated with my experience. My oil painting was selected to go on display in a local gallery because it moved my teacher so much. I'd captured . . . something deep inside me. That event opened a floodgate and led me to the conversation that ended my relationship with my conservative family back in Nashville.

You can't love me but hate my orientation, because it's part and parcel of who I am.

Not long after that, I ~~ran away~~ moved to Chicago and never looked back. I did what I had to do to survive and eventually was able to take more classes. I was so compelled by what I wanted to paint that I created my own momentum. I found a way.

I'd describe my style now as Fauvism, so my work is saturated with color and bold brushstrokes and it teems with energy. But my version of the scene over Diana's mantel is the alternative ending. In my painting, Maura is found and saved, and I made it so you can see the taillights of the emergency vehicle that rescued her on the moonlit night, almost out of frame. Rarely is there a happy ending to the crimes we discuss, but when it comes to my art, I want to give victims that better edit. One of my favorites is a mixed media piece I did about a grown-up JonBenét, backlit and dancing at her own wedding in a *Midsummer Night's*–type garden strung with fairy lights. It's just so hopeful.

I'm not crying, you're crying, shut up.

Anyway, Diana's house is totally our favorite, even though it's not nearly as bougie as Eli's palatial Frank Lloyd Wright–built home in Winnetka, which is a wealthy suburb on the North Shore. The problem with Eli's place is her dogs, although they're not a problem for me. Pee-wee and Herman are the sweetest boys, like two living, breathing teddy bears. But collectively they weigh about 350 pounds, not an exaggeration. Standing on their back feet, they're taller than everyone but me, and that's only because I bouffant my bleached platinum hair. (It's a lewk, okay?) Yet there's no convincing them they aren't lapdogs. Regardless of how well groomed they are, they pin us down to love us and we leave blanketed in fur. The first time we went to Eli's, she handed each one of us a hand towel when we walked in, the use of which became immediately apparent when she brought out the food. The second that appetizers were served, it was like someone cranking open a faucet. We're talking rivers of drool. Literal rivers.

Still, Carmen and I always roll around with them and Diana kisses their fluffy, jowly faces nonstop. Stella can't resist snapping selfies with them because they're just so rare and majestic. (She feels like the contrast of their dark fur really brings out the peaches and cream of her skin and her flowing strawberry blonde pre-Raphaelite curls.) Jazz is the only one who keeps a suspicious distance, although sometimes we'll catch her petting one of their stability ball–sized heads under the table. They sense that, deep down, she's a softie, and they're right, once you navigate past all the broken glass and the concertina wire of her personality.

"How did y'all not hear this?" Stella asks Carmen. Her voice still holds her Southern accent, which only intensifies with her wine consumption. Her brand-new cushion-cut platinum-and-diamond engagement ring catches the light and sends tiny rainbows bouncing all around the kitchen as she takes a deep draft of her Barolo. That rock is *major*. A few more glasses tonight and she's going to sound exactly like Foghorn Leghorn, and I am here for it. "Some people decided to show up in costumes, as though this were *Comic-Con*. Oh, my stars and stripes, it was vile. Vile, I say."

See? Foghorn Leghorn.

"When I saw that woman dressed like Casey Anthony carrying that doll with the floaties, I'm all, *Are you fucking kidding me?*" I exclaim. I was so disgusted. As I gesture, I notice I didn't get all of the blue paint out of the creases of my knuckles. Oh well. I guess I've just been extra inspired lately, and I can't keep my hands off the canvas. We recently covered Amy Bradley's disappearance from a cruise ship en route to Curaçao, so she's my subject. I'm working on this piece as a present for Stella's engagement party, so don't be surprised if I turn Amy into a mermaid or reunite her with Daisy, the bulldog she adopted before she left for her cruise. Whatever it is, Stella will love it; I'll make sure of it.

"She was all, *I'm sorry, and you are?* So officious! To me! And I was like, *Founding father, bitch.* I swear to you, these randos are acting like there's zero discernible difference between wearing a Princess Leia costume and putting on a clown suit in homage to John Wayne Gacy. No fucking decorum. None. Like, *I can't*," I say.

"Right?" agrees Jazz. "People *literally* came dressed as their favorite murderer. One woman was in drag, re-creating Jeffrey Dahmer's mug shot. I'm talking the blond wig, the aviator frames, the striped short-sleeve dress shirt, and the height chart on a posterboard behind him. It was repulsive."

"Oh, please," Stella replies, taking another pull on her wine. "Carmie, what's even worse? Some people came *as victims*, like the pair who dressed as Nicole Brown Simpson and Ronald Goldman with this sticky stage blood on their throats. Dis-gus-tin."

Carmen crosses herself and Eli winces and wrings her hands. "Ugh. We can't have this. We simply cannot have this."

"Is this why we're losing so many members?" I ask. "Are people just grossed out with us? If we don't keep expanding our membership, we're not gonna make what we've pledged this year. We need at least 5 percent more by the end of the year or we're not going to hit our next benchmark." This is an issue. We've made promises and everything; we have obligations. We are *literally* saving lives with some of our programming.

"Here's what we'll do." Diana pops out from behind the door of her double oven, where she's pulled out yet another tray of delectable appetizers. She sets the heavy baking sheets down on silicone hot pads at the corner of the island. I'm so excited about the idea of bonus snacks, I do a little dance in my chair. What's so funny is everyone says that when they met me IRL, they were all so intimidated by the intensity of my chiseled model-like features. (No! They actually said this, I swear!) But then when I opened my mouth, they realized I was just their Frankie and it wasn't weird.

"Pigs in a blanket, nom nom nom!" I exclaim. My mother never made anything but gin martinis, so anyone who cooks a meal for me is my idol. I think I fell in love with Gavin the first time I woke up at his place and he made me eggs Bene. I was like, *Are you for real?* Who makes homemade hollandaise?? Like, he's so great it makes me anxious. Lately, he's been talking about making our relationship government-official. And most of me wants this too, but a part of me is so afraid. I don't want to love anything too hard, because feeling such pure love inevitably leads to loss, in my experience. Gavin understands and lets me hold him at arm's length, but at some point, I worry he's going to need to know that I'm all in, and then what? Ugh, it makes me anxious just thinking about it, so I grab one of the piggies, giving it a quick puff to cool it off. Then I stuff it into my mouth . . . before screaming and spitting it back out into a cloth cocktail napkin. OMG, I never learn.

"Who could have guessed it was still hot?" Jazz says, shaking her head. "It was literally in an oven ten seconds ago."

"Noted," I reply with a look that could kill as I chug some ice water.

"You know what they call people who refuse to learn from their mistakes? They call those people *Frankie*," Jazz says with a snort.

"You know what they call people who are a massive pain in my ass? *Jazmin*," I retort. I'm sure she's quaking at my disapproval. The longest we've ever fought was for five minutes. While it turns out Jazz was actually wrong that time, she refused to admit it in so many words. (I guess because she's our youngest board member, she thinks we don't look at her as being completely credible, which is *so* not true.) Instead of an apology, she offered to ruin the credit of whomever I deemed my worst enemy. For a second, I thought about that football player who stuffed me in my locker junior year, but I decided to be the bigger person . . . for now. Sleep with one eye open, Thad Thibodeaux.

"Here, sweetie, this will cool you both down," Diana says as she retrieves a bowl from her glass-fronted fridge and sets it down between Jazz and me. "Almost forgot to serve it."

"Whoa, is that *mirza ghasemi*?" Jazz asks, phone and squabble momentarily forgotten. "Holy shit, did you make this for *me*?"

"What is it?" I ask, already plunging a flatbread cracker into the dish and shoveling up a heaping orange scoop. (It's not my fault I equate food with love.)

"It's garlicky ground smoked eggplant," Jazz says. She takes a bite and closes her eyes, nodding in ecstasy. "Oh, my God, don't tell my *maman joon*, but this is better than hers." Jazz's entire extended family found asylum in the US after fleeing from Tehran in 1979. Even though they've made movies about what happened when the Shah's regime collapsed, anything historical is of little interest to her. Jazz would prefer to discuss her passion for sneaking past the security systems at the local riverboat casinos after being categorically banned for counting cards. We always laugh when we say we'd rather have Jazz as a friend than an enemy, but we're not wrong. Also, the claim on our website about Jazz only using her powers for good is a bit of wishful thinking on our part. Like if we say it enough, we'll will it into existence.

Diana says, "Well, Jazmin, you said your favorite Persian place closed, so I thought you might enjoy a little taste of your heritage." One of Diana's three-legged cats has loped into the kitchen and attempts to hop up onto the counter, but she catches him so gently but quickly, it's like it almost didn't happen, save for the kiss she plants on his shoulder blades before setting him down on the couch. Not only is Diana bananas for animals, she always finds the ones who need a good home the most. Her pets are sort of like something from the Island of Misfit Toys, whether they're deaf, blind, or missing a limb, but that only makes her love them more. We always say there's a special place in Heaven for our sweet Lady Di.

Maybe that's why she's so special to me; she loves what's broken the most.

Diana removes her apron and washes her hands with soap that smells like geraniums and basil. Every touch here is so lovely, so *her*. "Anyway, we'll fix this, don't worry. I know exactly what to do. First, I'll send an email blast on Substack, explaining that while we appreciate people being excited about DoomCon, *we will not fetishize crimes*. If we're losing members because of poor taste, this should stanch the bleed. We'll say killer or victim costumes are on our no-fly list and they will not be allowed admission. I don't think most are trying to be insensitive; I bet they just don't know. I'll also send an email to all ticket holders explaining our position and I'll pin the same on Facebook. Eli, we'll have you make a TikTok about it too, to cover our bases."

Eli is TikTok famous, no joke. She can't do anything without making it ultrasuccessful.

Diana continues, "The way we'll sell this to those who want to grumble about us being 'no fun' is that we welcome them to come dressed as their favorite cop or sleuth or hero. If they want to make this a costumed event, they can dress up like the good guys. Maybe they'll come as Jessica Fletcher or Columbo or Sherlock Holmes. Does that sound like a plan?"

Of course it sounds like a plan.

Because our Diana knows how to fix everything, and that's such a relief. We can't let our group fail; it's too important to all of us . . . especially me, as I already lost my family of origin; there's no way I'm letting anything get in between me and *this* family.

"What are we featuring this week?" Eli asks as she sips her LaCroix LimonCello. I'm surprised we even got a single glass of wine into her, as she's not much of a drinker. She quietly believes that liquor should taste like candy, so it's rare that she finds anything sweet enough for her liking. She must have been so distressed about the costumes and our declining membership that she lowered her guard. Or maybe it's that the German Riesling that Diana offered her tasted a little like cotton candy grapes. Plus, she says there's no better buzz than endorphins. I'll never understand how someone considers a "runner's high" a better drug than alcohol. Carmen always tries to defend Eli's zest for fitness with technical explanations about dopamine and serotonin and neural pathways, but really, I just tease her because I adore her.

Deciding on the feature is one of our perennial tasks. The way the group works is, we post a story about a different crime each week on our Substack and Facebook page and in our Discord group on Monday morning, and everyone spends the week discussing it. We use multiple channels because different people gravitate to different platforms. Every day, Eli posts her *Elinspiration* while she takes her sunrise run on the lakefront, plus she'll often post video of our board meetings if someone says something funny. (Spoiler alert, it's usually me.)

And while of course we cover what true crime aficionados would consider the "greatest hits," especially when there are breaks in the cases, like with the Zodiac Killer, we also delve into the more esoteric stories. Our aim is to have fresh discussions each week. I always do the deep dive on the topic because I love to get lost in the research, but really, I consider everyone's suggestions.

Once in a while, we'll even post something lighthearted when it's feeling a little heavy, like the story of Michael Anthony Fuller, who tried to buy a vacuum cleaner and microwave with a fake million-dollar bill and then demanded the Walmart store give him his $999,524 in change. The GIFs everyone posted for that were superb, just top notch. So fun.

We all met on a Reddit thread about (alleged) family annihilator John Davidson Karlsson, also known as JDK. Although he one million percent did it, if you ask us. We all had theories about JDK, and that's how we connected. His story isn't that well known, probably because everything broke around 9/11. JDK was from Wisconsin. Eli was into the case because she grew up in Whitefish Bay and her parents lived there before they retired to Florida. The crime completely rocked their sleepy little community. Eli told us her mom was so interested, she even started keeping news clippings, which she pinned to a corkboard in her craft room. She said her mom's wall was a thing of beauty, like a scene from *Homeland.* She feels like if her mom had grown up in different times, she'd have been a detective.

I was drawn to the case because there were rumors that the oldest son was gay, which is what caused the super religious JDK to snap. That hurt my heart. Why is acceptance so GD hard for people?

JDK's entire family was found brutally murdered. All of them, including his wife, his three kids, and his mother-in-law. It was so terrible. At first, no one knew it had happened because the Karlssons often spent August at their cabin in Door County. They had a lawn care service, so the house looked normal from the outside, not overgrown or abandoned. Some of the drapes had been drawn and the lights were on timers. The mail had even been stopped. It all looked like business as usual for a family on vacation. Authorities didn't even discover the bodies until the school year began and a neighbor got worried when she couldn't reach Mrs. Karlsson about their carpool. The people next door finally alerted the police for a wellness check, and that's when they made the gruesome discovery.

What was so spooky was that the crime scene had been scrubbed before the police arrived. Every deceased family member was found neatly tucked in their bed. This was eerie because that's not the hallmark of a random act of violence. As Carmen explained it, when the murderer is familiar with the victim, they'll often take special care of the body, such as covering them with a blanket, so that's what caught her interest. There was evidence that the killer even stayed in the home temporarily, as they'd left sandwich fixings out on the counter before leaving. So cold blooded.

What was particularly odd was, JDK's body was missing, even though all the family's cars were there. Given the horrific nature of the crime and Karlsson's position in the community, everyone assumed he was abducted for a ransom. But there was no note, there were no demands. The math just doesn't . . . math, you know?

The more investigators looked into it, the fishier it became. I mean, the Karlssons lived in a wealthy neighborhood, so police thought the motive was a robbery gone awry. But once they got in there and looked around, they discovered that nothing was stolen. Except for Rusty, the family's Irish setter. Turns out, Rusty was discovered at a shelter in Chicago months later. The dog wasn't microchipped, but Rusty had been a show dog. Someone from an Irish setter rescue group recognized him because he'd been from a champion bloodline. The dog is what did it for Stella. To her, it just screamed, *The husband did it.*

Eventually, authorities were able to get into Karlsson's finances. Turns out, he wasn't the high roller everyone had assumed he was. He was a business owner, but it had gone sideways and he was deeply in debt, but no one knew. They also noticed that all the photos of Karlsson had been removed from the home. If JDK did it, he had up to a month's head start to get out of town. You can cover a lot of tracks in a month, especially if you have help. That's what attracted Jazz to the case. She lives for a conspiracy theory.

There were maybe thirty people who contributed to that Reddit discussion in the early days of 2020, back when I was living in a shitty studio apartment, after yet another devastating breakup, and decontaminating my Amazon packages with Lysol wipes. The restaurant where I waited tables was shut down and I was lonely and heartbroken and going stir-crazy, so connecting with other people gave me a reason to wake up in the morning. I think that's why Diana joined—between her kids homeschooling and her husband barely seeing patients and constantly being underfoot, she needed an escape.

At some point, Eli suggested we get on a Zoom call together, which was way too public and invasive for those on the thread who wanted to remain anonymous. Maybe fifteen or so people participated, including us six who had the Chicago connection. As spring turned to summer, people fell off until it was just us.

We don't know what it was, but the six of us just clicked.

On the surface, none of us had much in common. What did Jazmin, a computer science student finishing her college degree virtually, share with a fancy retired lady boss? Nothing . . . and yet everything. Jazz loved Eli's take-charge attitude and Eli got such a kick out of Jazz's foul mouth. The more we veered from the topic of true crime, the more we discovered our sameness. Carmen and I would have Netflix teleparties where we'd watch cheesy old '80s movies together, me for the first and her for the millionth time. (Although the one where the nerd takes the passed-out cheerleader home? *Problematic.*) Stella felt like the daughter Diana probably wished she had, as Lilly hit puberty like a brick wall and became megabitchy. We all fulfilled something the others needed. Obviously, I have mommy issues, with a side of sister issues, and suddenly having a whole new family who loved me *for* who I was, and not despite? That was major.

Our Friday night Zoom calls were as much about our lives as they were about true crime. (Thanks to a typo, we started calling them our Friday night Doom calls, a name that caught on and stuck.) We got to know each other in that profoundly intimate way that kids at camp experience, like we were just immersed in each other's lives. Because we came into it with no expectations or preconceived notions, all of our artifice was stripped away and we each brought our true selves.

Some of the friendships seemed more likely, like Stella, who's a fab, plus-size body positivity influencer, connecting with me because we're both from south of the Mason–Dixon Line. There's a lot of shorthand between us. And some made no sense whatsoever, like me and conservative Catholic Carmen, who won't even curse in English, yet I'm the one she relied on to talk her through perimenopause. Meeting online allowed us to collectively drop our guards, ironic because we came together talking about a subject that would put anyone else's guards up. It was sort of like a *Love Is Blind* kind of thing, only not romance based.

What mattered is that we were there for each other, like when Diana's mom had that cancer scare, or when Stella was dealing with an online troll who tried to reach out to everyone in her real life, including her sponsors. (Jazz took them down with staggering quickness; it was beautiful.) We were the best of friends for an entire year before we ever met in person. First it was Diana and Stella who got to have lunch together, as their vaxxes were prioritized, Diana because she works in health care and Stella because of her BMI. They were our canaries in the coal mine, and we were hoping if they hit it off in person, maybe we'd all jell as much as we did on Zoom.

Of course they did. We already knew each other's hearts. (What probably helped is that Jazz ran everyone's credit and criminal histories and she trusted us, although she didn't admit this for years.)

We didn't all meet in person until the summer of 2021, when Eli threw an outdoor shindig at her ~~palace~~ house overlooking Lake Michigan. We worried that it would be awkward, but what was weird was how natural it all felt, like we'd been friends our whole lives. (Also, those hand towels were freaking hysterical, though they weren't meant to be a joke. Carmen and I legit collapsed into each other's arms, laughing.) Now we're at the point where we joke that we're the kind of friends who'll help the others bury a body, so every time Eli mentions something annoying her kids have done (how did someone so great create two such entitled jerks?), or Jazz complains about her lazy Boomer bosses, someone will inevitably quip, "I'm bringing my shovel."

Right now, we have big fish to fry. Stella did the math and if our current burn rate continues, the Doom Crew is going to end up being just the six of us again, and then how are we going to do any good? There's just too many groups like ours now, between new podcasts and Substacks, and they're actually monetizing, which feels *icky*. We need a hot topic that brings people into *this* group. As the Crew's historian, I have just the thing. I pull a familiar picture up on my phone, readying it for the dramatic reveal.

"It's time to do it," I say. "Time to lean into our origin story." I hold out my phone and I'm disappointed when no one gasps.

"You think we should finally cover Karlsson?" Carmen asks. She looks thoughtful as she twirls one of the curls framing her face. "The anniversary is coming up, so it's timely. I like it."

Diana drops an empty pan as she tries to tidy up around us. "Oopsie, sorry! But JDK? Really? There are so many dead ends. At this point, it's just a sad story. I think it will make people feel helpless, like there's nothing we can do. I vote we do something else."

"Brf to berfer," says Jazz through a maw full of dip and chip crumbs.

"What was that in English?" I ask as she chews, swallows, and swats me on the shoulder.

"I said that I *beg to differ*. What if we took it to the next level—instead of just *discussing* him, we could make it a call to action. Let's try to find the fucker! He's probably still alive. Evil never dies, you know." Her eyes are already shining in anticipation of the cyberlaws she's about to break in trying to find him.

"Ooh, like the Reddit Websleuths forum? I sorta love that idea!" Stella says, referring to the group that actively researches cold cases. "Eli, whatchu thinking?"

Eli twists her giant gold cabochon ring as she weighs our options. "I'm leaning toward yes, but it seems like every time we discuss JDK, we always end up voting against him for some reason. On the plus side, my mother would be beside herself if we dug in. On the minus side, his story has never garnered much interest. Even with all the podcasts, all the documentaries, all the *Dateline* episodes, no one's ever touched him. Maybe we need something bigger to get the eyeballs back?"

Diana exhales loudly and I notice the sweat beading at the top of her lip and her hairline. "I vote that we save him for next year. It will be the twenty-fifth anniversary then and maybe we could get some media looped in." She surreptitiously blots at her lip, looking vaguely pained. I don't want to call attention to her hot flash, because she's likely to be sensitive about it. Our Diana feels everything so deeply. Carmen said hers were so bad, she'd actually have to blow-dry her hair afterward.

In an effort to take the attention off Diana, I offer a different suggestion. "Eh, doesn't sound like a consensus, so I've got a weird one we could do instead."

"Weird like a severed head in a freezer?" Carmen asks. (Jeffrey Dahmer, obvi.)

"Weird like senior citizens' bodies buried in the basement in order to steal their Social Security checks?" Jazz suggests. (Iva Kroger.)

"Weird like peeing in a grocery store aisle?" Stella says. (Joseph D. Chee. The silliest stories are her jam.)

"Weird like a bride lacing all the food at the reception with marijuana because she thought it would be funny?" asks Eli. (Danya Svoboda, and of course it happened in Florida. Of course it did.)

"Weird like smothering your husband in the middle of the night because he pushed your buttons one too many times?" Diana asks. We all look at her—wait, who committed *that* one? She gets flustered. "Oh, shoot, I'm sorry. I thought we were just making stuff up."

I offer a dramatic sigh. "If *you people* are done, I'll tell you. This is a good one to balance out last week's because, my God, I cannot deal with kids getting hurt. The Devonte Hicks story we discussed is giving me so much latent rage." This was particularly tragic. Devonte's lesbian parents would take him and his adopted siblings to protests where he'd hold up a *Free Hugs* sign. There's an iconic shot of this precious boy sobbing while hugging a white police officer. The photo made the rounds on the internet as a really positive thing, but the backstory is horrific. The poor kid was actually abused by his adoptive parents, who were under investigation. The story ends with the whole family barreling off a cliff in a minivan, with no evidence that the mother tried to hit the brakes. His passing presses on my soul and makes me struggle to breathe.

Carmen bares her teeth. "The system failed that innocent little boy and his siblings."

We all nod. That was a rough one with absolutely no closure and no justice. We debated about posting it, but ultimately thought it would be better for humanity if we studied what went wrong so we can all spot the signs of trouble sooner. It takes a village, you know?

I try to collect myself. "So, there's a group in Japan—"

"*All* the weird shit is in Japan," Jazz says with a knowing nod.

"Y'all, I love the expression *kuchisabishii*, which literally translates into 'my mouth is feeling lonely,' which is what people say when they're not hungry but want to eat anyway," Stella adds. "It's so fun."

"You would love Tokyo, Frankie," Eli adds. "They have these places that are called wax bars, and it's all music on vinyl with DJs. And don't start me on the ramen!"

I give every one of them the whale eye before I press on. As usual, we've digressed. "*As I was saying*, there's a group in Japan that you can hire for people who"—I make air quotes with my long, tapered, vaguely blue fingers—"'must pay.' Apparently there's a Japanese word for this expression, but it's all squiggles and intersecting sticks so I have no idea how to pronounce it."

Jazz says, "That's called a kanji, which is an ideogram that stands for—" Jazz stops herself when she notices my absolutely poisonous expression. "Go on."

"Anyway, it's a group run by some Japanese underworld figures, but no one knows who, exactly. The theory is it's the yakuza, but there's no concrete proof. Here's what's interesting about it. They're sort of like Robin Hood, only, you know, for crime. Okay, you guys look confused, so lemme give you an example. Let's say some bully has been picking on your son. Like, bad. Like *bad* bad. Like actually hitting your kid and leaving a mark and pantsing him on the bus and stealing his supercool SpongeBob lunch box that he used his birthday money to buy," I explain.

Gently, Diana lays a hand on my shoulder and says, "Frankie, that feels like a really specific example."

"Yeah. Maybe. I don't know," I say, allowing myself to lean into her palm. Fucking Thad Thibodeaux. He was a monster even at ten years old.

But they do know. I was born Franklin Vanderbilt Sullivan IV, a.k.a. "Quatro," of the Sullivans of Nashville, where I left my home at seventeen when my family didn't support me coming out, or if I really think about it, long before then. They aren't my *people* anymore—the Doom Crew is.

I continue, "So you do the adult thing and you go and talk to the parents, right? But instead of the parents grounding that little shitbag or taking away his Minecraft or whatevs, they're total a-holes and suggest that maybe your kid is weird and *should* be bullied. If that bullied kid had good parents, they would then get ahold of this group to administer a little *street justice*."

"I hate that I love where this is heading," admits Carmen as she inspects the tray of pastries Diana's set down. She goes for a wee shiny fruit tartlet and a fudge-topped mini cream puff that I just know Diana made herself. We've tried to get Diana to teach Jazz to cook, but Jazz has no interest. The only recipe Jazz wants to follow is for chaos.

"Precisely," I say. "It's an organization where they give back exactly what these bullshitty people put out. It's karma, baby. Like, if they discover you're cruel to animals, they'll kidnap you and stick you in a cage all weekend with no food and a dirty water bowl. Maybe even shove an electrode up your back door. If you let your kid beat up another kid on the bus just because he's fabulous, they will not only rough you up, but also humiliate you by, say, making your search history public. Like, on billboards in whatever the Japanese equivalent of Times Square is. It's a real eye-for-an-eye kind of thing. What's interesting is that this has been going on for years and they've never caught anyone in connection. The theory is that law enforcement over there isn't exactly trying to find a culprit because for those who've been subjected to this vigilante shit, they change their ways tout de suite. Losing face scares them straight."

"Again, I hate that I love how *Black Mirror* this is," Carmen says, brushing the crumbs she's dropped into her hand and then depositing them on her dessert plate.

"I am so down," Jazz agrees, cracking her knuckles, like all five foot one of her is just spoiling for a fight. For a while, she was into mixed martial arts training, but nothing ever keeps Jazz's interest for long, so I'm dubious as to whether she could truly hold her own against an opponent. But if she wants to believe she can, I'm behind her.

"I have about fifteen trolls for whom I would like to enlist these services," Stella says. She doesn't have the social media following that Eli has—who does?—but she's actually able to make a living as an influencer. All the selfies and videos she takes seemed weird when we first met her, but now we don't even notice. It's less vanity and more of a day job, but it does come with a side of vocal haters.

Stella arranges a tiny crème brûlée and raspberry and lemon curd tartlet on a little plate and takes a few snaps of them before she hands her phone to Jazz to film a reel of her eating them. If you want to see Stella go ballistic, ask her about the influencer event where everyone lined up to get these beautiful soft serve swirled rainbow unicorn cones covered in edible glitter. The other content creators took one bite and, as soon as they were done getting the perfect shot, not only dumped them in the trash, but spat out the bite. She said it was disordered eating and a crime against ice cream. The amount of animosity she generates by being unapologetically herself is not insignificant and is so unfair, all because she has the nerve to not hate her own body. In my opinion, *these* people need to pay.

"Yes, I love it. The must-pay thing sounds like the palate cleanser we need." Eli slaps the countertop to punctuate her point. "I love it and I think it's perfect for this week's topic."

"I feel like this could gain back some of the traction we lost," Diana says.

"Agree," says Jazz.

Carmen says, "All in favor say 'Aye.'"

We all say "Aye," having no idea the events we're about to set in motion.

Chapter Two

Diana Pulaski

"If you could make anyone pay, who would it be?" Frankie asks the group, after giving us a lengthy dissertation on all the ways he was wronged by his high school nemesis, Thad Thibodeaux. The last Frankie knew, when he was living out of his car in Chicago, trying to save up for the security deposit on a studio apartment, the former star QB was playing for 'Bama and living the high life.

"But karma is a real thing," Jazz argues. "I bet things went south for him." With the fastest thumbs in the universe, she has an update within a minute. "According to my . . . source . . ." We all exchange pointed glances. Jazz has a lot of "sources" that we simply do not care to question, lest we be complicit. "His football career didn't quite pan out. Seems that he had an ACL tear his sophomore year and he lost his scholarship. Ouch. And now . . . looks like Thad the Cad is currently selling used cars down in Baton Rouge, Louisiana. He appears to have a 520 credit score, a predilection for losing at online poker, and three ex-wives, all of whom cheated on him. Two of them with the same guy!"

There's a prolonged silence until Eli asks, "Should we be concerned about how you found that, Jazmin?"

"Eh, I feel like that's on a need-to-know basis," Jazz replies with a shrug.

"Guess the Tide stopped rolling for ol' Thad," Stella observes.

"Sounds like maybe he's already paying," I offer.

"Boo-hoo, what a shame," Frankie says as he tries—and fails—to wipe the victorious smirk off his face. "Eli, who would you make pay?"

We've been winding down for a good twenty minutes, but Frankie always wants one more bite, one more drink, one more conversation. He's like a little boy sometimes, begging for another story before bedtime. I always feel sad about his life in Nashville; I don't know how anyone wouldn't be thrilled to love him unconditionally.

Without a moment's hesitation, Eli blurts, "Elon Musk," and we all laugh. Eli has a long-standing beef with Musk, so much so that his name has become an automatic group punch line. But it only recently occurred to me that she may have actually had dealings with him and doesn't just despise him on general principle. Eli insists she's an open book. While this is largely true, she's also a downplayer, meaning she's awfully blasé when it comes to the details. Like, occasionally she'll mention her friend Sheryl and only later will we find out she means her friend *Sheryl Sandberg*.

"What about you, Carmen?" Eli asks as she fiddles with the raw edges of the place mat in front of her. We all laugh with Eli that she can't keep her hands still. I would suggest she take up crocheting, but when her daughter actually paid for a course for her to learn, Eli was apoplectic. Somehow in her kids' minds, her very young sixty-three is actually more like a decrepit eighty-three. Which is funny because Eli's mom *is* eighty-three and she's a demon on the pickleball court. Just an absolute demon. She and Eli beat the pants off Frankie and me the last time we played when she visited.

"I would make Alderman Stacia Mueller-Johnstone pay," Carmen says, referring to the former alderman who recently went to prison for extortion and racketeering after funneling almost two million dollars earmarked for her district into her own pockets. The alderman wasn't slick about it either, doing things like chartering private jets and taking all her friends to Vegas on taxpayer dollars, then posting it all over social media. Because it happened in her district, Carmen took it as a personal affront.

"Isn't she already paying?" Frankie replies. "They didn't send her to one of those country club, *Orange Is the New Black*–type places either. She went to legit prison."

Carmen's eyes light up and she offers a pleased nod. "I guess she is. So what about you, Jazz?"

Jazz frowns and starts tapping her phone. "Lemme consult my enemies list."

Frankie peers over her shoulder. "There's like a hundred names on that spreadsheet! And they're all Russian."

Jazz blinks at him. "What's your point?"

"Stella? Who's on your list?" I ask, interjecting, lest we go down that road. Jazz has beefs with *a lot* of people, but she has an odd prejudice against anyone from Russia. We thought this was some weird government secrets–type thing, because she has a knack for finding hidden info. But in this case, we discovered it's because a Russian kid named Dmitri—in her words—"stole a chess championship" from her. She insists there was collusion. But she always insists there's collusion.

Stella presses a polished nail to her glossy pout as she considers before looking me dead in the eye. "I would say the person who slaps the durn dishes out of my hands when I try to help her clean up."

"Not funny, Stella," I reply. I don't mean for my words to come out so forcefully. The volume of my voice startles little Luna, my newest foster. She's a sweet tuxedo cat with her right eye sewn shut in a permanent wink, thanks to losing a street fight in her former life as an alley cat. She dashes out of the kitchen and down the hall, banging into the door of the primary bedroom, as the poor dear's depth perception is lacking.

"*Chica*, please. We're not leaving you with this mess," Carmen says, keeping her equanimity. Her calm is almost preternatural. She levels her gaze at me as she pushes yet another stray hank of hair out of her face. I swear her wild locks can't be contained by a mere scrunchie.

Stella positions herself behind Carmen, as if to back her up, her second in case things go off the rails. Or maybe she just needs to lean on Carmen, as she's a little bit tipsy. I can tell because her eyes are not quite blinking in unison, a fact exaggerated by the thick mink false lashes she always wears. (The Barolo was particularly nice tonight, and I'm glad she enjoyed it.)

Frankie shakes his head at me. "Gurl, are we really doing this again?"

I've been keeping them from helping me with cleanup for an hour now. "Time to go," I insist cheerily, trying to herd them toward the door. "No, really, I *need* you to go."

"Please, it's five minutes of us helping. You're not being reasonable, Diana," Eli explains, as though she can change my mind through the force of her iron will, which she secretly believes everyone should bend to. She plants herself between me and Carmen and Stella, trying to mediate.

"I'm absolutely being reasonable. This is what I want, so please respect my wishes and do what I ask," I reply, squaring my shoulders like they taught us in that self-defense class so they know I mean business. I mean, it really *is* what I want and I don't understand how I can make them understand this is the hill I *will* die on.

"Miss Diana, this is ridiculous," Stella says. "And my mama would be jus' furious. I couldn't leave y'all in a state like this."

Jazz exhales sharply and shakes her head. "You know we end up doing this dance every time, right? She's not going to let us win; why are we trying? So, while you people waste your breath arguing, I'm gonna go see if Ethan wants to get in a quick game of chess before I go. I need a rematch after the last time. That little fucker keeps beating me and I cannot have that. Okay? I can't have it. How is this *The Queen's Gambit* for him all of a sudden? He up in his room?"

I nod but I don't take my eyes off Carmen and Stella, circling me like two incredibly polite bull elephants.

Jazz starts up the back staircase and then stops herself on the landing. "Oh, hey, do I need to, like, knock on his door first? Give him a minute because he's getting busy with Rosy Palm and her five friends? He's what, thirteen now? He's probably *all* up in his own business, like all hands on his deck. My brother Cyrus was a maniac at thirteen. One day he was so into Pokémon and then the next, he was pokey-*man*. Gives me the ick just thinking about those endless showers. There would be no hot water left, none. Like, the idea of running water traumatizes me now. I even set up parental controls on our home network because I was sick of taking cold showers, but these kids can find *anything* if they're motivated. Firewalls? Bitch, please. BTW, you're probably seeing a lot of tube socks in the laundry. *A lot.* Ugh, boys are so disgusting. However, I'm fine with that because *maybe* Ethan won't be thinking so many moves ahead this time. I swear he's Bobby goddamned Fischer." She shouts up the stairs, "Hey, Ethan, put it away, I'm coming up to whoop your ass!"

Wait, is my baby becoming a man? No!

The thought that I'm growing more and more irrelevant in my children's lives, that they're moving on without me, shuts me down for a full minute. Lilly's been flat-out rejecting me for a few years now. Of course I understand she's in high school and our matching mother-daughter outfit days are long past, but she won't even leave the door cracked an inch for me. Whenever she has a problem or a question, she goes straight to Peter. Of course I love that they're close, but I just wish I were included. I swear, when they're together, it's like the cool kids not letting me sit at their lunch table, which isn't even something that happened in high school. So the idea of Ethan not needing me gives me pause. It takes me a second to regroup and return my attention to the standoff, where Eli has the nerve to be laughing at my abject horror.

"Well, it is what they do," Eli offers with a shrug. "Anyone who's raised boys has been there. At least Peter can have the *your-changing-body* talk with him. I had to do it myself with Henry. Twenty-five years later, I still cringe at how awkward it was. I drank an entire bottle of peach schnapps afterwards and was queasy for two days."

Frankie rises from his seat at the counter and folds his napkin, placing it next to the decimated charcuterie spread. He claps his hands. "Ladies, listen up. As much as I would love to stay all night, I actually have to locomote now. Gavin and I are heading out to the Kit Kat Lounge when I get home. I promised him I'd be there by 9:30, so I must take my leave. You guys can continue to lose the argument with Lady Di over whether or not she'll let you help clean up, and I'm going to make my way to the door. Good luck and looking forward to your big party next week, Stell-Belle! Kiss, kiss, love ya, mean it!"

"I'll walk you out," I volunteer, before fixing each of the Doomers with a steely glare, shaking my pointer finger at them. "But don't you touch a single dirty dish while I'm gone!"

I can hear the elves giggle and spring into action the second I walk away. I have to grit my teeth. While they think I'm doing a *bit*, I actually do hate it when they try to help me clean up. That is not their job and it makes me feel like a bad host, like I'm lacking, failing. I can practically feel my parents' disapproval radiating from two towns away, and I'm suddenly right back there in time, wearing my cutest church dress and my hair in perfectly symmetrical braids.

"Don't you dare touch a single dish!" my mother would instruct everyone around our grand dining room table.

My mom was the consummate homemaker, and I wanted to be just like her when I grew up. Every Sunday without fail she made the most magnificent lunch after church, whether it was a beautiful rare roast beef with juices oozing onto her pretty floral china platter or a rack of lamb where the ends of the chops wore those little paper hats, garnished with homemade mint jelly. The oohs and aahs of our guests were so gratifying; I could see why she loved hosting these meals. And we always had such special guests at our table. Sometimes it was my dad's patients, sometimes it was our neighbors. If we were lucky, we hosted my grandparents, or better yet, my favorite aunt and uncle would come down from Milwaukee with my cute young cousins. Those days were the best.

I was always so impressed that what my mother said went. If you were an invited guest, you did not touch a dish in Dr. and Mrs. C.'s house! My mom even had walking pneumonia that one time and she still prepared a boeuf bourguignon that was so tender and rich that people still talk about it.

Without fail, my mom whipped up something complicated and delicious, and she positively threw a fit if anyone so much as brought a dessert spoon to the sink for her. Sometimes she and I would spend hours washing up afterward, and she never once complained. She'd say, "Diana, it's an honor and a privilege for us to be able to entertain the way we do." She was just so gracious that I promised myself to be the same kind of host in my home someday.

What can I say? My mom set a high bar and I do my best to meet it.

Frankie and I head out the double French front doors and down my bluestone pathway, and my humor immediately improves as I look around. The pavers are flanked on each side by lush decorative grasses and cheerful purple coneflowers in full bloom. When I glance back at my house, every light is lit and the whole place appears to glow from within. The scene just seems so cozy and inviting. The temperature out here makes it feel far more like summer than fall, which is always how it is in September. The air is warm with a touch of humidity, dampening all the sound. It's so quiet that I can practically hear us breathing.

All the homes on our sleepy suburban street have a college flag suspended from a bracket between their garage doors and subtle uplights illuminating the bushes and mature trees. Every sidewalk blown clean by landscapers and every flower box lovingly tended. I have to smile as I take it in because I grew up like this and it's exactly how I hoped my children would too. I have to pinch myself sometimes when I realize my dreams became reality.

Peter and I closed on this house two weeks before Lilly was born sixteen years ago. I was so worried it wasn't going to happen after our first deal fell through when our inspector discovered the sellers were trying to hide a mold problem. Peter was calm and businesslike, confident that we'd find something even better, but I was crushed. All I wanted was to bring my new baby home to a *house* and not the sad, stuffy rental condo we'd been living in during Peter's orthopedic surgery fellowship at Rush. I was so thankful when we found this place, especially as it's only a few miles from where I grew up. So when we pulled into the driveway with precious baby Lilly secure in her car seat, I thought my heart would swell and burst because I had every single thing I ever wanted. Or at least I thought I did until two years later when we had Ethan and I really knew our little family was complete. We did everything right and we were the ideal family unit . . . until lately. I can't put my finger on it, but something feels off a beat. As close as I am with Frankie, I've been meaning to bring it up, but the moment never seems quite right.

We stop next to Frankie's darling navy MINI Cooper convertible, parked behind Eli's ginormous SUV at the end of the driveway. Frankie loves having the top down so much that he will drive with the heat blasting practically until it snows. He must use industrial strength pomade on his hair because his coif never moves, despite all the wind. He even keeps extra blankets in the back seat in case his passengers complain. Personally, I think the fresh air is invigorating, but the first time Stella rode with him for a Doom Club meeting, she spent the entire night claiming to have been turned into a "durn Popsicle." She catches rides with Carmen now, since she doesn't have a car. I'm not even sure if Stella has a driver's license, honestly. I feel like it's weird to not drive, but who among us doesn't have something off about them?

Frankie throws an arm around my shoulder and I'm suddenly enveloped by the slightly sweet scent of Sicilian lemons and bergamot. "What are you wearing? It smells like heaven," I say, breathing deeply.

"Sunshine and lollipops," he replies. Obviously, he's kidding, but it's exactly how I'd imagine those scents would smell. "You outdid yourself again tonight, Lady Di. You put us all to shame."

I can feel the blood rush to my cheeks, as compliments always make me flush. "Thank you. I just want to make it nice for you guys." This is my chance to broach the subject, but I lose my nerve. I'm probably just being silly anyway. Carmen said she was hypersensitive when she was going through the Change, so I'm sure that's what it is, just the progression of life.

"Girl, you bypassed 'nice' about fifteen pounds of imported Italian pancetta ago. I'm going to feel bad the next time I serve us cold leftover pizza from Giordano's," he replies. "Especially when I insist you help with the dishes, which *will* be paper because I DGAF."

Frankie plants a noisy, vaguely garlicky smack on my forehead and holds my chin as he looks me in the eye. "When you go back in there, I need you to tell everyone, 'Thank you for your help.' That's it, just say thanks. And don't you dare reload the dishwasher the way *you* want it until after they leave. Got it, got it?"

I have to laugh. He knows me well. "Got it, got it."

❧

I can literally feel my eye twitch when I come back to find all my crystal stemware loaded into the top rack of the dishwasher, but I give everyone my brightest smile. Frankie's right—squabbling over something so small isn't worth causing hard feelings. Finding this group was so important to me. Although I have lots of mom friends and people I'm friendly with in the neighborhood, I'm not close with them like I am the rest of the Doom Crew. My other relationships are more surface level, like they never progressed past exchanging pleasantries, and that's totally fine. Sure, there's not a lot of depth when we're swapping Key lime pie recipes or talking about acidifying the soil around our hydrangeas to bring out the blue coloration, but we don't need to be deep. Maybe I always wanted to get more real with them, but I just didn't know how to make that connection. But I have it now and don't want to blow it over something silly.

Of course I have a wonderful relationship with my family, and I feel so blessed in that respect. My folks are the absolute salt of the earth, happily married for more than fifty years. What's funny is that I can't remember ever having seen them fight. Not once, even though my dad has *very* strong opinions. I'm sure they must have disagreed behind closed doors, but it's not anything they subjected my brothers or me to. My mother's motto is "Keep on the sunny side," so I try to be as positive and upbeat as she always is. Even when things did go wrong when we were kids, she didn't let us dwell or ruminate on what we didn't have. She'd urge us to look for the silver lining. Peter says my parents are basically both Ned Flanders, but I never watched *The Simpsons*, so I choose to assume it's a compliment.

The old expression was "You can count on the Carlsons!" and I swear my mother headed every school committee and organized every church potluck. There were no duplicate casseroles on *her* watch! She's a great role model. I particularly admire how she wasn't afraid to let herself age, never worrying about vain things like wrinkles or coloring her hair. She always says, "Diana, I earned every one of these grays!" and she's why I've allowed the silver streaks to creep into my own hair, even though Lilly is always photoshopping shots of me with blonde streaks instead. Some of her friends' moms look like the *Real Housewives of Hinsdale* and it's hard to tell who's the mother and who's the daughter. That's just not for me.

"Thank you for your help," I say, just as Frankie instructed.

"See? It's not so bad leaning on someone else," Carmen replies, pulling me in for a small hug. I guess she's not wrong.

Peter comes into the kitchen while I'm saying goodbye to the rest of the girls. It's rare that he even leaves his office on our board meeting nights because he wants this to be our time. (Also, he has zero interest in true crime.)

"Hey, Dr. Peter! Replace any good hips lately?" Stella asks as she collects her to-go bag, because of course I send everyone home with a little something. Of course I do.

"I'm living the dream, ladies, using the bone saw every day," he replies, his eyes crinkling as he gives each of them a megawatt smile that could rival George Clooney's. Even all these years later, he's still so handsome to me. Every time I look at him, I get the same butterflies I had the first time I spotted him when he started his residency at my hospital twenty years ago. He's deeply tanned from his time on our club's golf course and he keeps himself nicely fit, even though it means a lot of time in the gym. But I should want him to take care of himself. I'm aiming for a fifty-plus-year marriage like my parents, and his commitment to good health is a key piece of the puzzle.

Peter's pristine white oxford shirt is just as starched and crisp as when he left for the office this morning. A few years ago, he had a medical conference in London. I wish the kids and I could have gone with him, but it was such a short stay, I said it didn't make sense when he invited us to tag along. While he was there, he discovered a place called Turnbull & Asser. It's a *haberdashery*. Isn't that the best word? Now they make his shirts custom. They're not cheap, but he reasoned that no one wants their hip replaced by someone who looks sloppy.

Eli glances down at his wrist, as he's wearing a new watch. "Whoa, that's some major hardware there."

It sounds trite, but my father always said you could judge the caliber of a man by three things—his polished shoes, his clean nails, and his choice of timepiece. When I met Peter, he was wearing scruffy New Balances, but I let that fly because he was often on his feet for twenty-four-hour shifts. However, his nails were impeccably groomed and he had a fancy watch. It was years later when I'd learn that he'd won it in a poker game! There's no way he could have afforded it himself back then otherwise. Things were so tight in the beginning, and we really had to rely on my salary as an ICU nurse. I worked a lot of double shifts when we were starting out together, but we made it through and now we're very comfortable. As far as I'm concerned, he can collect all the watches he wants, which he keeps in a locked cabinet in his dressing room.

"Question—did you talk to my mother?" he asks as he thumbs through his texts.

I say, "One sec, hun, let me just say my goodbyes." I give everyone hugs and cheek kisses as we reach the front door. "So, Eli, I'll send you the minutes from tonight once they're organized. I feel good with the whole yakuza direction, like we're going to make up some lost ground with Frankie's idea. Carmen, you and I need to circle back offline to talk to the director about some programming at the shelter. And Stella, I cannot wait for your big party next week!"

"Y'all better bring your dancing shoes," she replies. Her engagement party on Saturday is going to be the event of the season. A couple of years ago, Lilly would have described Stella as "extra," yet I don't know what the newest slang for "over the top" is. But the night promises to be . . . something special. Not "skibidi," which I know is bad, even though it seems like it should mean "fun," right? What a happy word to say. Like "skipping" and "yippee" had a baby.

"Hello?" Peter calls from the other room, impatient.

"Sorry, Di, don't let us keep you," Eli says. "What's the opposite of the Irish goodbye? Because that's what we're doing." Some nights it takes a solid half hour for us to get out the door.

I wave her off. "Please, it's fine. Doctors always look at everything as a code blue, right?" I got used to this really quickly when I was working at the hospital with so many physicians, and now it just bounces off me.

"Did you get back to her? Yes or no?" he insists.

"We should go," Carmen says, stepping outside, followed by Eli and Stella.

"Are you even listening to me?" he calls, louder this time, which causes the girls to exchange *looks* and now I'm a little embarrassed. Peter can be pushy, but again, he's so much like my father that I'm used to it. Everything was life and death with my dad too. When he'd get bossy, my mom would give her eyes a good-natured roll and proceed with a placid smile, so that's what I do.

"Love you guys, bye!" I call, closing the door behind them before returning to the kitchen.

He's pacing the floor. "She said she texted you to call her. And she said you blew her off. What happened?"

I give Peter one of my mother's smiles. "Yes, she did text, about an hour before my guests arrived, and I had my hands full. I was making the kids dinner. I mean, I couldn't serve them a frozen pizza when I was laying out such a spread for my friends, right? So I whipped them up a nice veal piccata, although Lilly suddenly won't eat veal despite devouring a veal parm last week. When did she stop eating veal?"

"When she saw a TikTok about how the calves are treated," Peter says. I sort of hate that he knows stuff about our daughter that I don't.

As I pull the stemware out of the dishwasher and set it aside to hand-wash, I say, "Anyway, I had to make her chicken and that put me behind schedule. So I'm sorry, I wasn't able to chat with your mom, but I'll give her a jingle first thing!"

See? Problem solved.

People like to throw around the advice to never date anyone who's close to their mother, but what terrible advice that is. I love how close Petey is to his mom . . . although she's the only one who's allowed to call him that. (Peter says it's weird for me to call him by his childhood nickname, so I don't say it out loud. But he's Petey in my head.) He's close to everyone in his family, and that was a real selling point for me. His mom is like a second mother to me. I'm honored that she treats me like a daughter, trusting me to run all their important family events.

And she even has Kelty, her daughter who lives close, so I feel extra special that she always solicits *my* input.

"She wants you to coordinate with the vendors for my sister's twenty-fifth anniversary party coming up. Kelty says the florist is 'stupid' and she and Mom want you to fix it. You know how to get stuff out of people, so just, like, work your magic," he tells me. He opens our glass-fronted Sub-Zero and begins to paw through the leftovers, opening all the little containers I'd just stashed. "Seriously? Cheese? Cured meats? Stinky garlic dip? Do we have any *real* food?"

"Sweetie, go sit down and I can make you whatever you want," I say. Hopefully what he wants is veal or chicken, as I have both ready. I take a lot of pride in my home-cooked meals. For a while after I had the kids, I tried to keep working. But the family needed me so much that it made sense for me to be a SAHM till the kids went to school, even though I think Eli quietly finds the idea archaic. Now I pitch in once a week at my brothers' office, because it keeps up my skills, even though I don't let them pay me. I can't take money from family!

"How about grilled salmon, steamed broccoli, and brown rice. No oil. Use the Paul Prudhomme seasoning I like and please don't ruin it with all the fresh dill," he says.

"I picked up some of that nice wild-caught Coho today at Whole Foods. I'll bring it to you as soon as it's out of the air fryer," I tell him. I'm kind of tired, but I appreciate that he respects my request to stay out of my kitchen because I'd rather cook it myself. I have my way of doing things and that's how I want it to be. I pour myself the last of the Barolo and I get to work.

Peter eyes my glass of wine and purses his lips. "You know you shouldn't hold your glass like that. Your fingers will warm the wine. They told us that at the vineyard tasting room."

"Oh, I didn't realize I was doing it," I reply, setting down the goblet so I can grasp it by the stem. I used to drink it right until I watched the show *Scandal.* I felt like Olivia Pope always looked so glamorous the way she held her drink cupped in her upturned hand, so sometimes I catch myself holding glasses her way.

"Will you bring me some of the Barolo?" he says as he grabs his iPad and heads to the L-shaped couch in front of the fireplace. He flops down and begins flicking through the cable guide. I swear he'll spend a whole half hour looking at what's on TV instead of watching the TV, but he likes to know what his choices are.

"Oh, shoot, I'm so sorry! We finished it all at my club meeting tonight. Do you want this one? I just poured it."

"Ugh, no. And your friends are freeloaders."

I have to laugh to myself because that is *so* not the case. He didn't think they were freeloaders when Eli closed down the entire amusement park for our big summer party last year. I cannot even fathom how much that cost. And I know what's in the gift bags at Stella's engagement party next week, because I helped her put them together. She spent *thousands*. With an *s*. And the painting Frankie made me? His work is starting to sell for big bucks. Or how about how Jazz sat down with Lilly every week to tutor her in geometry out of the goodness of her heart? And Carmen for calling in those favors that helped his sister with her kid's IEP? I'd say offering decent wine is the least that I can do.

Like my dad, Peter can be a little bit of a terrorist after a grueling week, and everyone knows you don't negotiate with terrorists or toddlers. "You're much better off with a nice glass of Whispering Angel because it's still rosé season. Or we have that gorgeous Viognier we bought in Napa. Either of those would pair so much better with the fish, and the Barolo was too intense. Heavy on the truffles and much better in colder weather," I explain.

"Viognier actually sounds good," he admits. Of course it does. I get all the components of his dinner managed and cooking and then I bring him his glass of wine, presenting it with a kiss.

"Why do you smell like a fistful of garlic?" he asks, turning his iPad face down.

"Mirza ghasemi," I tell him.

"God bless you," he replies, and we both laugh.

Peter's not the world's greatest wit, and sometimes he can be a bit of a bear, but I will give him this—he's a man who knows how to keep my secrets.

Chapter Three

Elinor O'Neill

"Tell Grandmama that you love her," my son Henry says in the background of our FaceTime call as I gaze directly up my young granddaughter's crusty nostrils.

"Ooh, Hen, no. I thought we agreed the kids would call me 'Nora,'" I say. I really don't care for the G-word, and "Nora" sounds like a close enough hybrid of "Nonna" and "Elinor" to work.

"Ramona and I think 'Grandmama' has more gravitas," Henry says.

Of course Ramona thinks that. My son Henry's wife Ramona has a lot of big ideas, like "gentle parenting." In theory, gentle parenting involves remaining calm and not being reactive, validating the children's emotions. I very much like the idea of it. My Hank never yelled. He had the patience of a monk. On the rare occasion he'd get mad, he'd go quiet, leave the room, and compose himself so he never reacted in anger. I'm sure there were times when I raised my voice when I shouldn't have when my children were growing up. There were likely situations I could have handled with more patience. I own that. I guess if Henry believes in gentle parenting because he perceives he could do it better than I did, I should support him.

Aren't we all trying to do better than our predecessors?

However, in practice, Henry and Ramona's gentle parenting means their children Zephyr, Atlas, and Jupiter (no, I'm not kidding, and yes, I'm afraid to ask about their vaccination status) have zero boundaries because they've never heard the word "no." It's . . . problematic. This is why I've flown with his family only once. On that trip, I sprinted to the ladies' room when we landed in Maui because I thought every other passenger who was subjected to the worst travel experience since the Donner party was going to seek retribution and I wanted to disassociate. Justifiable homicide and all. That the kids' abhorrent behavior didn't end up on the news was nothing short of divine intervention.

I am not proud to admit I faked food poisoning on the way home and extended my trip a day to avoid flying with them again. I would worry that I was being intolerant, but my own mother has vetoed his family's every attempt to come stay with her and Dad in Vero Beach; it's not just me.

"Have you thought any more about our offer, Grandmama?" Henry asks, taking back the phone. Now I'm looking directly up his snout.

"To sell my house, get rid of my dogs, and live in the studio apartment over your garage? In Dallas? Which is in an entirely different state than my current life? It's tempting, but I'll pass," I say. I shoot a glance over at Frankie, who's dramatically pretending to vomit. Henry begged me to move down there to live with them, but let me just say this without delving into politics—I do not mess with Texas. Also, Henry can be a pill. I love him with my whole heart and I'd die to protect him and his family, but I can only handle about three days of his mansplaining and Ramona's tradwife-ing before I must exit stage left.

"But what if you need help on the toilet?" he asks, and I have to keep from screaming into the void. Why are my kids convinced I'm so frail and infirm? It's like they can't *see* me. I guess that's what happens when you lose a parent young; you become fiercely protective of the other one. Save for my genetic predisposition to high cholesterol, I'm in perfect health. I mean, I'm far more informed on pop culture and current events than either him or Margo. Case in point, they didn't recognize Post Malone when we ran into him in the elevator at the Four Seasons Maui last year. When I joked if he'd ever moved to Florida and bought the car he wanted, he barked with laughter, whereas my kids thought I was having a "senior moment." (Post and I chat in my DMs now. What a sweet man.)

"Hen, it's getting loud in here, I have to go," I tell him, as Stella's engagement party actually is getting louder.

"Mom, do you know how to get yourself home?" he says as Frankie face-palms.

"I'll be sure to ask the first man in a panel van I see if I forget," I promise him before disconnecting.

"Spoiler alert, your kids suck," Frankie says.

"He means well," I reply with a generosity I'm trying to feel. "Probably."

"Yeah, so did Mussolini," Frankie says with a snort.

"Eh, enough about Henry. Have you seen the traffic from this week's post?" I ask. "Wow. Amazing job, Frankie. You crushed it. This may be our most viral entry yet!"

Our post on the must-pay movement in Japan is breaking our previously set records, truly resonating with our readers, and bringing in new members. Whew! It's a good first step, but we've got to keep up the momentum or the group will have trouble meeting our commitments. And honestly, I *need* this group to succeed. I was at such loose ends after I took an early retirement. I thought unlimited downtime was what I'd worked so hard to earn while we were going public, and everything leading up to it. When I was deep in the throes of trying to wrangle expanding my business empire and arranging college tours for two surly teenage children as a single mom, I'd fantasize about someday getting more than four hours of sleep.

As it turns out, sleep is overrated.

I was bored to death. Retirement made me feel as old as my children believe me to be.

Not being useful or challenged dried my brain into a tumbleweed blowing forlornly across the once-fertile prairie. I had no idea how lost I'd be without a purpose, having gone from a million miles an hour for decades to a dead stop. I no longer had the community I'd fostered in the business world, and I found myself with far too much time on my hands. Then the pandemic hit and I was so isolated; I hated it. Forming our group allowed me to channel my talents into something meaningful again, and it's been so gratifying.

Of course, Henry and Margo think I should be in a rocking chair on a porch somewhere, quietly awaiting death, as though my utility ended when I had the audacity to turn sixty a couple of years ago. Maybe I don't put the "sex" in "sexagenarian," but let me remind everyone that Kim Cattrall is five years older than me. Is anyone calling *SATC*'s Samantha Jones old? I think not. I'm at my best, both mentally and physically. I'm in the prime of my life, especially now that I have the freedom to do whatever I want and I'm not cloaked in the mantle of anyone's expectations . . . which is a constant sore spot with Margo and Henry. They'd prefer it if I were a little *less* visible, starting with my wardrobe, which now trends toward interesting denim and Chucks and my favorite Basquiat tee with the cartoon mandrill on it. Margo accused me of approaching my "me so kooky" years when I tried out that green streak in my hair. She says I'm going "the full Iris Apfel." To which I say, amazing. We should all strive to be so stylish. Like Taylor says, when the world was black and white, I was in screaming color.

What bothers them most is that I figured out how to make technology work for me at a time when my Boomer peers are best known for getting scammed by phishing links. But again, I'm the gal who had the foresight to get in on MSFT at $3.50 a share, so . . .

"Of course we're crushing it," Frankie says, congratulating himself. He has to raise his voice over the sound of the band playing "Don't Stop Believin'" and all the partygoers singing along, united by the promise of love and the power of Journey.

Frankie's looking particularly fabulous tonight. Because this engagement party is a big deal for our Stella, he's gone all out, wearing his take on a three-piece suit. Only instead of trousers, he's sporting a knee-length pleated kilt, dark socks with contrasting stripes on one of the calves, and brogues. I absolutely adore this look—it's Thom Browne meets Daniel Levy.

"We can't be surprised that our members love justice," I say.

Frankie snorts. "No, our members love the idea of *Dexter*, only in real life. Everyone wants to make the bad guys accountable, especially when the law doesn't go far enough. It's so empowering. Did you read the one where they threw that illegal whaler in the orca's tank at that aquarium?"

"I didn't. Someone must have posted that one this afternoon, because I haven't checked since this morning. Was the orca okay?" I ask. I've been following an orca-attacking-yachts account on social media. What magnificent creatures they are! Apparently they've been sinking yachts lately, which shouldn't be funny, yet . . . I heard on NPR that orcas follow trends the other orcas set. Isn't that interesting? For example, years ago, one orca was wearing a dead salmon across her nose, sort of like a hat. Then the other orcas in the pods did the same thing. So now that a couple of orcas have attacked yachts, more of them are following suit. Marine biologists are saying it's a form of play when they ram the rudders, which causes the boats to fill with water, but I imagine those billionaires on the yachts are not so amused. It actually happened to my friends Mark and Priscilla while they were off the coast of Portugal, but their boat was too big to capsize.

Frankie swirls his festive melon-colored drink and plucks out a maraschino cherry, popping it into his mouth and chewing thoughtfully. When he's done, he blots his lips with a paper napkin displaying a swirly calligraphy *Stella & Abe* logo. You can't rush Frankie when he's telling a story. He's an artist with his words as well, which is largely why he writes our posts.

"Yeah, the orca attacked the guy but didn't kill him. Instead, he played so rough with the man he *wished* he were dead. He's hanging up his harpoon forever, I promise you that. Best part? The shady aquarium that everyone had been protesting was forced to move the orca to a protected sanctuary because the killer whale was, you know, trying to live up to his name. I guess the aquarium owners finally decided the orca was 'too dangerous for captivity.' They don't care about the orca's quality of life when it's making them money, but when they realize they could have some liability if he were to hurt someone? Game over. So, everyone wins. Except the illegal whaler. And the shitty aquarium. Two birds, one orca. Wait, I'm putting a pin in that—that whole scene sounds like a lot of fun to paint."

"Cheers to that," I say, and we clink glasses.

What a gorgeous party this is! The event space is in an old River North warehouse with huge windows, brick walls, and exposed ductwork. Instead of flower arrangements, the circular tables are covered with fuchsia-colored linens and topped with madras plaid runners and clear water-filled glass cylinders with candles floating on top. Because Stella wanted to emphasize the scope of the space, she went big with the florals. Not only did she do a fragrant rose arch in front of a step-and-repeat photography area, she rented dozens of ornamental tree roses with electric pink blossoms and California Honey mandarin trees in oxidized iron pots to showcase her pink-and-orange color scheme. Each one is adorned with plaid ribbons to match the runners and has tiny twinkling lights woven in, so it looks and smells like we're in the middle of an enchanted forest.

The band starts playing "Uptown Funk," causing the guests to cheer and more revelers to swarm the dance floor.

"What are we drinking, by the way? This is delicious." My cocktail is bright and tart but also complex because there's a distinct sweetness, sort of like limeade with a faint hint of carbonation. Every sip makes me feel warm inside. "I'm on my second," I admit.

Frankie raises a sculpted eyebrow, which has a new, thin vertical line shaved in the side of it this evening. "Woo, you're letting your hair down tonight, gurl! The little sign on the bar said some kind of punch? I was actually admiring my reflection in the windows, so I wasn't paying full attention. Do you like this business?" he asks, pointing to the brow slash, which appears to be freshly created.

"It's brilliant," I say.

"Gavin questioned it, but he also thinks flat-front khakis are the height of style. Ooh, look, there's Stella. Let's ask what these are," he says. "Yoo-hoo, gorgeous, get your dangerous curves over here."

Stella sidles up from the dance floor, absolutely ethereal in a flowy embroidered tea-length chiffon dress with full flutter sleeves and a neckline that plunges all the way down to the Empire waist. She moves languidly, like she's being filmed in slow motion or has a dreamy soundtrack constantly playing in the background. Tonight's engagement party look has her with bits of ivy and gardenias woven into a crown over her complicated updo and every inch of her skin glimmers, just so radiant. "You look like Mother Nature, and I mean that in the best possible sense," I tell her.

"Oh, my stars, I love that for me!" she replies, raising her glass. "And I love y'all! Thanks so much for making my night so special! And my painting? Oh, Frankie, you outdid yourself, darlin'!" We do a three-way hug and I have to avoid taking in a mouthful of her poufy sleeve.

"What is this heavenly concoction that we're drinking?" Frankie asks, swishing it around in his cheeks like he's approving the sommelier's pour. "Nectar of the gods."

Stella's face is wreathed in smiles. "That, my dear girls, is a family recipe for Chatham Artillery Punch. It was created in Savannah when the Republican Blues came back from battle."

"Is that a War of Northern Aggression thing?" Frankie teases. Unlike Stella, he has no pride in or ties to his apparently problematic Southern family heritage. His eyes sparkle in the moody lighting of the event space.

"Oh, honey, y'all know we don't talk about Bruno at family events."

"Who is Bruno?" Frankie asks.

"He's not family; it's a line from a song in a Disney movie," I explain.

Stella pointedly clears her throat and gestures toward her elderly relatives. "Anyway, Sergeant A. B. Luce, who is a distant, great-great-great-great-uncle, mixed up a ton of booze, fruit, and sugar and served it over crushed ice in a horse bucket. And lah-di-dah-di, every-freaking-body got absolutely shit-wrecked on it, like dancing in the streets and all. Years later, a journalist tasted himself a glass and he declared it 'a mortal enemy of despair,'" she tells us. "Isn't that the best? A mortal enemy of despair. What could be a better theme on a night like this?"

I'm not much of a drinker because everything is always too sour or bitter, but this cocktail is hitting on all cylinders. It's like a glassful of Jolly Ranchers—magical! "It's making my whole body feel effervescent, like I could float up to the ceiling the same way Charlie and Grandpa Joe did after that fizzy lifting soda in Wonka's factory." When I posted a shot of my glass on my Instagram, the likes began to pour in. I'll need to get the recipe and share it tomorrow. I always want to be in the moment, so anyone who's interested will have to wait till then, including *you*, Post.

"Gonna land y'all on your asses if y'all aren't careful," Stella says with a giggle. "If I were *smart*, my next drink would be water. But if I were me, I would have more punch."

Stella's fiancé Abe approaches, his phone out and filming. He has a long, angular face and a prominent nose with a curved bridge that Stella always says is his best feature. She insists you can tell a lot about a man's character by his nose and that she would never date anyone with a perfect ski slope on his face. His coarse brown curls are flecked with salt and pepper and tamed in a short, textured cut, capped with a yarmulke. He's not classically handsome, but the more we've gotten to know him, the more we see how beautiful his soul is, so he's Jude Law circa *The Talented Mr. Ripley* in our eyes. Although don't say that to Stella. She claims she just knew Law would cheat, based on the flare of his impeccable nostrils.

Abe absolutely beams when he looks at his soon-to-be bride, like he just won the lottery. Their relationship is a bittersweet reminder as to how it was between Hank and me. Stella says she's the lucky one, which is why she's in classes to convert to Judaism. Her Southern Baptist family had some palpitations at first, particularly her Mee-maw, but when they witnessed firsthand how he treated their sweet magnolia of a girl, they said "Mazel tov" and learned how to cook a brisket. As Jazmin says, their combined Thanksgiving is going to be *lit*.

Abe says, "She's not kidding. There's *so* much alcohol in it, like you wouldn't even believe it, but it sneaks up on you because of the sugar. It's going to take you out at the knees like Jeff Gillooly with a crowbar. This is a dangerous combo. Listen, Stell-Belle, let's film a quick boomerang. We have got to capture this lewk for posterity. Raise your glass and take a drink. Nope, hold up, let me fix this flower first." He adjusts the loose gardenia by her right temple, easing it back into place. Abe knows how important her social media feed is, so he learned her best angles and now he's the greatest content wingman ever.

After Abe finishes his impromptu photoshoot, he asks Frankie, "Where's your better half? I can't believe he's missing this. We ordered the Wagyu sliders just for him!"

Frankie sticks out his tongue in mock disgust. "Ugh. His firm is in the middle of an IPO and he's drowning in due diligence right now. But he promised he'd sneak away at some point, so we'll see him, especially if there are Wagyu sliders." Then he laughs. "He'll be here in his best Patagonia vest, I'm sure."

"How does he not share your impeccable sense of style?" I ask. I connected with Gavin when I worked with his company preparing for my IPO. All the other underwriters were sharks, and I wanted that, but something about Gavin struck me as special, like he wasn't the kind of guy who'd sell out his own mother for an extra couple of bucks. Maybe it's because he was kind to the assistants. He impressed me by making sure they got home safely after staying late. Plus, he actually seemed to care about *me* during the process, so we kept in touch after we went public. Then when I met Frankie, a light bulb went off in my head. There's something so intrinsically *similar* about both of them that I'd thought they should meet. They had odd commonalities, like how winter is their favorite season here. Trust me, winter is no one's favorite season in Chicago. When Frankie mentioned how much he loved the feel of the frozen wind whipping off the lake, I recalled having the exact same conversation with Gavin years before and I thought, *Why not?* Frankie fought the pairing at first, largely because he wasn't used to dating anyone with a job that didn't involve an apron, or who treated him kindly. He said Gavin felt too "grown up" but he eventually got past it. I do have a sense for relationships, at least for other people.

Frankie waves his hand. "I promise you it's his single flaw, so I'll allow it. Well, that and insisting we call our dog 'Kevin.' What kind of name is that for a dog?" They have a spunky little brown French bulldog with bulging eyes who does, somehow, manage to look like a Kevin. Whenever Kevin does something naughty—which is often, given his passion for pillow humping—Frankie always says, "We need to talk about Kevin." This also shouldn't strike me as funny, but again, it does. Exactly Frankie's intent.

"Where's the rest of the Crew?" Abe asks, scanning the crowd, which is an eclectic mix of influencers, crime junkies, former debutantes, and Abe's conservative Jewish family members, all mingling and making friends with the Southern Baptists. When the band starts playing "Come on Eileen," the younger people leave the dance floor and queue up at the bar, and the Gen Xers rush in, crying "Woo!" with their arms flung in the air.

"Carmie and Juan are dancing," I say. No matter where we are, if there's a dance floor, those two are on it. Salsa music is their favorite, but they'll groove to anything. Carmen can cut a serious rug in sky-high stilettos, which is so impressive. I'm wearing a pair of low, blocky heels with pointy toes and they already hurt so much that I want to hurl them out the window. My Chucks have spoiled me. I don't know how I ever put up with punishing shoes or constricting Spanx for so long. I heard that Stella has a basket of flip-flops for everyone later, and I am counting down the minutes.

I check my phone for texts. "Looks like Jazz is in an Uber—she's close—and Diana and Peter are running a little late. We'll all be here for the big toast." Abe shared that he has a special speech he wants to give later tonight, which is just like him. I predict there won't be dry eyes in the house.

"Well, if you'll excuse me, I have to check on my grandmother. She's complaining to the caterer about the shrimp cocktail," Abe says.

"Shrimp cocktail? Wait, I thought your family kept Kosher. I'm confused," I say.

Abe's eyes crinkle and he lets out a huge guffaw. "We do. That's Bubbie's problem. She's harassing all the servers about there being no shrimp cocktail tower. Apparently she's recently decided that our dietary rules don't apply at parties or Chinese restaurants. So we're seeing what we can do to accommodate her, even if we have to order DoorDash." He's still chuckling as he approaches a person in an apron and bow tie who's negotiating with his tiny gnome of a grandma. "Bubbie, we're handling it," he tells her as he gently steers her away.

An adorable little boy in a kippah and a suit coat runs past Abe—he must be Abe's nephew, because he looks like a miniature version of him. He's chasing Stella's niece, whom her whole family calls Bug. As they chase each other around a table, the boy almost plows into the tiny grandma. Instead of yelling, Abe swoops him up and places him under his arm, much to the boy's delight. He squeals with joy, especially when Abe picks up Bug and carries her off under his other arm.

"He is going to be the best father in the world," Frankie says, his voice wistful as he watches Abe lovingly sweep away all the chaos.

"Darlin', don't I know it?" Stella replies. "I sure can pick 'em. Now, speaking of meeting someone . . . I would love for *you* to meet someone, Eli."

Of course she does. But no one seems to understand that I am perfectly happy alone. Perfectly. My life is exactly what I want and where I want it, and I cannot imagine having to change everything around to accommodate some strange man after thirty years of making it on my own. Yes, a few years after I lost Hank, I thought for a minute that maybe I should be open to meeting someone, but Henry and Margo shut that notion down so effectively that even now, the idea of a relationship feels odd to consider.

"Yes, yes!" Frankie crows as he bounces up and down on the balls of his feet. "Let's get Eli laid!"

"Can we not and say we did?" I counter. I am uncomfortable about this constant pressure to "just have a chat with this divorcée friend of mine" or "maybe think about meeting this man from my church for lunch." I don't know how to say this so everyone understands that I mean it—the factory is closed. Shut down. Abandoned. The *No Trespassing* sign is hung. The premises are surrounded by a chain link fence and choked with weeds. Violators will be prosecuted. It's too late . . . right?

"I'm real excited for the two of y'all to meet," Stella says. "He's a snappy dresser and a great dancer and he even owns his own business. He's a bit of an environmentalist, and I know that's something you value."

Maybe it's the alcohol coursing through my system, or maybe my defenses are down. Or maybe talking to Henry put me in a *state* and I need to prove that I'm just beginning my third act instead of waiting for the final ovation at curtain call. In a moment of weakness, I find myself asking, "What's his name?"

"Well, his given name is Clarence Chester Fontenot. But we all call him Uncle Cracker," Stella replies, causing Frankie to spit-take, his sip of punch spraying out 180 degrees as he bursts into hysterics.

"Please, please, please meet Uncle Cracker, I beg of you," Frankie says, blotting at his mouth with the heel of his hand. "I never ask you for anything."

"Last week you asked if I would let you make my sweaters into a pile so that you could jump into them like the one golden retriever with the fall leaves on TikTok," I remind him.

"That was different. I need you to do this—'this' meaning 'him'—for me."

"Franklin, compose yourself. This here is a dignified occasion," Stella replies. Then a small burp escapes from the depths of her midsection, she claps a hand over her mouth, and she and Frankie crack up all over again.

Frankie tries to pull himself together, taking a deep, calming breath and wiping away a tear. "Okay. Question for you, Stella. Does Uncle Cracker have all his own teeth?"

"Frankie, baby, we talked about this," Stella retorts. "You of all people should know that is an unfortunate stereotype that we are not perpetuatin'."

Chastened, Frankie replies, "I'm sorry, you're right. My bad. I can't expect people to do better if I don't."

Stella continues, "Also . . . his dentures are bee-utiful, all big and pearly white like Joe Biden's. He spent a lot of money on them."

"May I please inquire as to how he lost his teeth?" Frankie asks, trying desperately to keep a straight face. "If it was from not flossing, you don't want any of that, Eli. The heartbreak of gingivitis and all."

Stella looks vaguely uncomfortable. "He had an accident."

"Oh no. A car accident?" I ask. "That sounds awful."

"Airboat," she says in a soft voice.

"Stell-Belle, is Uncle Cracker *a swamp boat operator*?" Frankie asks, bouncing again. "Is that why you say he's an environmentalist? Because he works in the bayou?"

"You know, no one gave Lana del Rey shit when she married that airboat operator a while back," Stella protests.

"Yes, they did, it was all over social media," Frankie counters. "It was a huge story. CNN covered it because everyone thought she lost her mind. Literally everyone. Tell you what, give me Uncle Cracker's

Instagram handle and Eli will meet him as long as there's not one shot of him posing with a gator of some sort."

I'm honestly not sure what to root for here.

"Bet," Stella replies, as though I weren't even a part of the conversation. I hate when my single status is a problem that needs to be "managed." If I wanted to feel like I should be managed, I'd spend more time with my children. The two of them furiously tap away at Frankie's phone.

"Profile picture!" Frankie hoots, raising the phone in victory. "Ha! We didn't even get past his profile pic without seeing a gator! Or a croc, I don't know the difference." He hands me the phone. I glance and nod, handing it back.

"It's an alligator. To be fair, Stella, his teeth really are lovely," I say. "I mean, Uncle Cracker's, although the gator's teeth are equally impressive."

The band announces they're going to take a quick break, and Carmen and Juan high-five their dance partners before they join us. They'd been dancing all night with Stella's "questionable cousins." (Her words. She's previously raised concerns regarding their whereabouts on January 6.) Yet the cousins clearly were having so much fun with Carmen and Juan that I wonder if their minds aren't a little more open now that they've celebrated with people who aren't from their same background. One can hope.

We all exchange kisses and hugs, as though we haven't seen each other in a lifetime and not just eight days. We skipped our usual Friday night board meeting because we knew we'd be together today, although we've been texting furiously about ideas to maintain our growth. The increased traffic this week is good, but we need to keep going in that direction.

"Frankie, you are a genius," Carmen says.

"Oh, I know . . . but specifically why do *you* think I am?" he replies.

Without Carmen asking, Juan pulls a clean cotton handkerchief out of his breast pocket and blots at a little bit of perspiration at Carmen's hairline in a movement as choreographed as any dance. Smiling, she tilts her head from side to side so he can get all angles.

Carmen tells Frankie, "People are *loving* the must-pay post."

The story Frankie selected was about a man who'd been terrorizing neighborhoods all over Japan as a Peeping Tom. This man was perpetually lurking outside in the trees, and he did it for years, but he moved around enough that he was impossible to catch. He was not only a Peeping Tom, but he monetized what he saw, because first he'd film people in stages of undress and then he'd stream the content from an anonymous account. His site's name translated to "Secret Naughty Bush Hidden Man" and it was hugely popular.

The National Police Agency there was never able to track him down. Plus he was a hacker as well as a pervert, so the cyber unit couldn't trace him either. Enter the yakuza. Or who we're assuming are the yakuza; it really is unclear. I know I shouldn't root for these vigilantes, but in this case I couldn't help it. They were able to find the guy. Instead of turning him in, they took him, stripped him naked, and placed him in a blast-proof clear acrylic box in the middle of Shibuya Crossing at rush hour (like our Times Square to the nth degree), plus they streamed a live feed of it on his own site! It took authorities hours to free him. That story has really gotten our members buzzing. The discussion it's spurring is even better. Apparently everyone has thought about how they'd make someone else pay. In detail.

I tell them, "Let me say this—I would not want to be someone who hurt a kid or a kitten around our cohorts."

"Amen to that, sister," Stella says. "From the sounds of it, our people would get positively medieval on their asses."

Juan surveys all of our glasses. "Who is thirsty? May I get anyone a drink from the bar? I am taking orders." Juan is one of the most jovial people I've ever met, just a genuinely nice man with a good word for everyone. A perpetual optimist. Not only is the glass half full, but it's full of the coolest, most refreshing water anyone has ever served, sure to slake any thirst. He has a bushy gray beard, a wide, flat nose

(Stella-approved), pot belly, and wears wire frame glasses. Carmen says he was born to play Santa Claus. You'd think that all his years spent as a marriage and family counselor would make him brittle and detached, but somehow he doubles down on spreading kindness wherever he goes. Strangers are just friends he's not yet met. Their relationship does give me a twinge here and there. If I thought there was even a chance I could re-create what they have, or what I once had, I'd join an app and swipe right (or is it left?) on everyone aged forty to eighty.

Frankie lifts his glass. "If you're offering, I'd take another glass of punch, please."

"Actually, I would too," I say. "Thank you so much."

"*Mi amor*, can you please bring a whole tray?" Carmen requests. "That might be easier."

He gives her a courteous nod and winks at the rest of us. "Anything for you, *mi reina*."

"Hashtag couple goals," Frankie says as he makes a heart shape with his hands.

"Is it just me, or is the love in the air tonight real thick?" Stella muses. Before any of us can answer, Jazmin comes charging up, in more of a state than usual. The elevens between her eyebrows are extra deep.

Frankie looks Jazmin up and down. "I'm glad you went with something black, rather than something . . . black." Jazz's newest obsession is dressing Goth, which is an endless source of amusement for Frankie. Tonight's outfit is a short skater skirt, fishnets, and a turtleneck made of spiderwebs (?), paired with studded platform combat boots.

"Jazmin, are you okay?" I ask. She seems more keyed up than her usual degree of keyed up, and that's saying something.

"Listen, we have a problem," Jazz says, completely letting Frankie's comment fly without countering with a retort. Whoa, that means we really *may* have a problem. Head on a swivel, she scans the party. "Is Diana here yet?"

"Hmm, haven't seen her. She texted to say she was running late. Why, is she not okay?" I ask, suddenly concerned. I do not like the expression on Jazz's face at all. Even her usual scowl is scowling.

"Pfft, understatement. Peter Pulaski is a *prick*," she hisses.

"Huh," Stella says, undeterred. "He's only ever been polite to me, and I am an arbiter of manners. Plus, he's got that li'l crook in his nose. I think he's just fine."

Jazz is undeterred. "Yeah, but how much time have you spent with him, like *really* spent? How much time have any of us spent with him? The only one who's really ever around him is Juan, when the spouses gather to get away from the true crime chatter. We don't get much time with him. Anyone can hold it together and be courteous for a short period."

"Hmm," says Carmen. "There was that weird moment when we were leaving last week. I didn't care for his tone with Diana."

"Now that you mention it, it was a li'l hinky," says Stella. "I was sort of tipsy, and I thought I was just being sensitive."

I think I was so wrapped up in trying to come up with a good hook for the page last week that his rudeness didn't really register until now. It was odd. I rack my brain trying to think of the other interactions I've had with Diana's husband. We haven't seen him very much at all. If we're around any of Diana's family, it's usually Lilly and Ethan, and sometimes her parents, brothers, and their families. We rarely see Peter more than in passing because he's always tied up at work. When we ask after him, Diana will laugh and tell us, "Oh, Petey's off saving lives *again*."

"When did we see him before then? Was it at the Christmas party last year?" Carmen squinches her eyes shut as she tries to recall.

"Was it at your place for New Year's, Eli?" Frankie asks.

"No, he's never even been up there. Don't you remember at New Year's when he was supposed to come? Some Chicago Bear had a complex fracture, so he wasn't able to make it," I say. As I'm the only one of us who follows football, that event sticks out for me. What was weird was that I didn't recall seeing any players on the injured reserve list after that, but it was right about the end of the season, so maybe it wasn't breaking news.

"Did we see him at DoomCon last year?" Stella asks.

"No, he couldn't make it—I recall Juan asking about him because he had that usual get-together in the greenroom for all the spouses and significant others," Carmen replies.

"Think about it," Jazz insists. "Anyone can be polite for a quick interaction. I mean, *Jeffrey fucking Dahmer* was able to lay on the charm long enough to convince the Milwaukee PD that poor little fourteen-year-old Konerak was actually his nineteen-year-old boyfriend and they were just having a lovers' spat. They left! They listened to him and they left, all, *Seems fine to me.*" (We're all still angry about that, by the way.)

"Now that you mention it, Peter's kind of a zaddy," Frankie says and then takes in our expressions. "What? We're all thinking it."

"Are we?" Carmen says, cocking her head. "I feel like you are having an entirely different conversation in your head right now."

"Eww," Jazz interjects. "What is wrong with you, Frankie? And the rest of you people, are you done with your bullshit?"

We shrug collectively—I guess we don't know if we're done with our bullshit? Personally, I have no idea where this is going, but seeing Jazz fired up over something small isn't terribly new. When not busy jumping to conclusions, Jazz obsesses. Whether it's a hobby, a habit, a style, or an idea, she will grab hold of something briefly and shake it in her jaws until the life goes out of it and she loses interest. I gesture for her to continue as I put all my weight on one foot to temporarily relieve the pressure on the other. Women would have started shattering glass ceilings far sooner had they been allowed to do so in flat shoes and nonbinding undergarments.

Jazmin is so mad that Frankie takes an instinctive step back, lest spittle begin to fly. "Because I am not fucking kidding. He is a monster, okay? A *monster*. You guys weren't there. I saw behind the facade. The mask was off. Criminals hide in plain sight all the time. Ted Bundy? The Beast of Birkenshaw? Donald Michael Santini? Happens all the time."

"Whoa, wait, are you saying you believe Peter is a *criminal*? That seems like a stretch," I say. "And why would you wait to tell us?"

"Because I was collecting information!" Jazz says. "You guys think I'm always mad about everything—"

"Show me the lie," Frankie says.

Jazmin says, "I was *trying* to collect proof because you rarely believe me! Like there's a credibility gap with me, which is so not true. You're always, *It can't be the Russians again, Jazz.* Even though it can. So, last week, everyone left and I was upstairs getting my ass handed to me in chess by Ethan *again.* It's getting to be embarrassing. I need to read a book or something. It's like the FSB are training him. I am tempted to put a keystroke logger on his computer because I do not know where he's learning these moves."

"A keystroke logger? Is that something you know how to do?" Frankie asks.

"Pfft, in my sleep," Jazz replies. I'd say we worry about Jazz, but she can take care of herself. My only worry about Jazz is that she occasionally acts like she's trying to prove something to us, but it's so unnecessary. We love her exactly as she is.

"So, this is about Ethan's chess prowess?" Carmen tries to clarify. "Is there something insidious there?"

If anyone in our group is prone to out-there conspiracy theories, it's Jazz. Her take on who may have helped JDK kill his family is why we connected with her on Reddit, because hers was a theory none of us had ever considered. She argued that the way the facts align, he had to have had some assistance. But from who? Spoiler alert: Jazz blames the Russians for a lot. *A lot.* And don't even start her on what she's convinced Ted Cruz's father did. (She should probably not share that theory with Stella's Texan cousins.)

"No! Ethan's become a worthy opponent and that is commendable because he's making me up my game," Jazz replies.

"That is one lovely boy," Stella adds. "I can't even hold his perfect button nose against him. But I feel like he'll grow out of it. Let's hope he takes up contact sports. Boxing, ideally."

Jazz lets out a strangled scream of frustration before stomping her giant boot and continuing. "Are you people going to listen to me or not?"

"Jazmin," I say, placing a hand on her shoulder. "The floor is yours."

"Then buckle the fuck up, cupcakes, because I have a story to tell."

Chapter Four

Jazmin Ahmadi

My whole life, my family's all, *Oh, Jazmin, you're a drama queen. You have such an active imagination.* But I know what I know and I've seen what I've seen. They don't understand the info I'm able to access, so they fail to realize exactly how far behind the curtain I'm often able to peek. I can find the unfindable, but do I burden everyone with what I learn? No. (Plausible deniability, and you're welcome.) Do not even start me on what goes on in the deep ocean per the National Archives and Records Administration; it would blow your goddamned mind.

But I'm not talking about what I've gleaned from my skill at classified data exfiltration.

No, this was witnessing with my own two eyes.

I tell everyone, "I was upstairs, hanging with Ethan." Maybe it's a little weird that my friend has a kid who's only ten years younger than me, but whatevs. He's a worthy opponent or I wouldn't give him the time of day. "So we were playing chess, and I failed to realize that Ethan was purposely showing me something funny on TikTok to disarm me. It was a video where two people fill their mouths with water and take turns slapping each other in the face with tortillas until the other one laughs. He was all, 'I promise this will make you crack a smile,' and I was like, 'Pfft, game on, kid.'"

"Ohmigod, I've seen that!" Stella exclaims. "It's hilarious!"

I nod. "Yeah, well, he got one over on me because I let out one little snort, and that threw my concentration. So then, taking advantage of my lack of focus, instead of defending the pawn, he sacrifices it by moving it forward to f5. I was like, 'Ha ha, dumbass, who's laughing now?' This move seemed counterintuitive as it gives up material, right? What I was too distracted to see is that little shit was opening up a diagonal for the white bishop to attack the black king. Naturally, black is forced to respond to the threat, and he counted on me making a mistake that allowed white to seize the initiative and win material or positional advantage. Classic example of a sacrificial tactic, where a player gives up a piece in exchange for a more significant advantage, and I should not have fallen for it. I didn't know that little wanker was capable of that kind of calculation and strategic thinking. But I underestimated him."

"Wow, Jazz, this is a riveting story," Frankie says, making a hand job gesture while he takes a big sip of his fruity drink.

"Keep your skirt on, Franklin, I'm getting to the point. Also, you're wearing a *skirt*. Wait, are you going *commando* under there? Don't tell me, I don't want to know. But really, no one else has thoughts on this?" I point to his kilt, look around, and I'm not getting any reactions. "No one? *Anyway*, doesn't matter, except God have mercy on you if there's not a pair of boxer briefs under there. So I was heading down the back stairs, and I was just going to slip out the side door because I figured if Diana saw me, she'd insist on coffee and a chitchat and it would be *a whole thing*. I didn't have it in me for one of her endless Midwest goodbyes. I was tired, I was cranky, and I wanted to just get out of there and lick my wounds over my loss. They must have thought I was gone because I ended up overhearing her and Peter when I was trying to creep out."

"They did have a weird little thing when the three of us were leaving," Carmen says sort of hesitantly.

"Yeah, Ethan and I heard that, but it was *nothing* compared to what came next," I say. "Trust and believe."

Legit, I was shocked.

"You guys cannot fathom the way he talks to her when he thinks no one's listening. I am not kidding. Condescension would be one thing—he was flat-out verbally abusive, and that's no joke. I guess she accidentally put dill on his salmon, and he lost his damn mind. For real, he snapped. He totally lit into her! Over a sprig of dill! You guys, *he threw his plate*."

"Are you sure?" Eli asks. "Could you maybe have misinterpreted something?" Eli is really steadfast on the whole "believe women" thing, but she's also big on empirical proof.

I say, "No! I saw it! He straight up smashed that shit against the fireplace like he was in a Greek diner, yet he didn't shout *Opa!* Frankie, remember when Gavin made us watch that movie about the old Hollywood star and she was all, 'No wire hangers!' It was that energy, no lie."

Stella's mouth hangs open in a perfect O while Carmen's lips are pursed into a thin white line. Eli just looks troubled. I'm not entirely sure they believe me because I'm kind of the baby of the group. It's like the whole youngest child syndrome, with the head pats and people saying "There, there."

"Are you sure it was 'threw' and not just 'dropped'?" Frankie asks me. Okay, I only came around the corner when the plate was already in motion, but from the angle of his hand, it was clearly a throw. Clearly.

I continue, "Yes! And *that's* not the most fucked-up part! The fucked-up part is that Diana didn't even react, she just did this weird little laugh and was all, 'Oh, my goodness, I can't believe I did it again, I guess I was on autopilot with the dill. Sorry, hon. I'll make you a fresh one in two shakes.' Like it was just any other day, like she was totally used to having to placate him. The scene was like something you'd see on that weird, repressed Mormon #MomTok. Like, *My husband is my king and that's it.* I didn't know what was going on, so my first reaction as a murderino was to GTFO. But when I got outside, I thought maybe I should go back, and then I heard the door bang open. As I turned around, I saw her foster Luna come flying outside like she was a sack of potatoes. What in the actual fuck?"

"Wait, did Peter throw *her*?" Eli asks and I see her hands balling into fists. "Is Luna okay?" she asks.

"I didn't see that part, so I don't know how the door opened, or if that's how the cat normally goes outside, but I have my suspicions. And the cat is fine because I took her home with me!" I exclaim.

For real, I am not a pet person, but I was not about to see someone be mean to a rescue, especially with only one eye.

"Then I had to text Diana some cock-and-bull story that my car window was open and Luna must have gone out the cat door and climbed in because I didn't know how to say, *You're married to a psychopath so I took your cat.* Because *that* is who's unkind to animals. That is *documentable*."

"She's not wrong," Carmen says, more to herself than any of us. "Henry Lee Lucas, Charles Manson, Albert Hamilton Fish—the list goes on and on."

"Exactly. Also, Luna is still at my house, by the way. I think she might be my cat now," I say. "I sort of love her. I filled out the paperwork; I bought her an electronic litterbox, a sweater, and a spiked collar with a buckle; and I've lengthened her name to *Lunatic*." Everyone's gawping at me.

The whole group seems to be in shock. Eli says, "This news feels like it came out of nowhere."

"What? Shut up. I'm allowed to love things on a long-term basis," I say.

"No, Jazz, I mean about Diana," Eli clarifies. "Were there signs? Were there indications? Have we all been too wrapped up in our own little worlds to notice that Diana's might not be quite as rosy as the picture she paints? Have we let her down?"

Juan approaches carrying a tray brimming with a variety of cocktails, from rocks glasses to champagne flutes to beer pints. Hold up, is he a *waiter* now? I knew that social work didn't pay a ton, but it's kinda sus that he's working Stella's party. Is their family in financial trouble? I thought they were doing fine. But there he is, plastic straws and lemon garnishes as far as the eye can see. He balances the tray on an upturned hand, like a real pro. I feel like he's done this before. I'd look into it, but I already know way more about my friends than I want; I can't handle any more bad news.

"I brought back something for everyone," he says. "I did not know who might want what, so I tried to plan for every eventuality." He stops distributing drinks as he takes in our expressions. "Wait, why does everyone look so serious?"

"Why did you wait a week to share this with us?" Carmen asks me.

"Well . . . ," I admit. "Sometimes it's possible that I get it wrong on the first go, and my instincts aren't always right. I may or may not jump to the occasional conclusion."

"You don't say," says Frankie, smug.

Listen, did I not offer to ruin his enemy's credit that time I was wrong about "irregardless" being a real word? Like, I'm admitting I can be fallible, okay? And yet the argument can be made that people use the word "irregardless" all the time, "irregardless" of it being incorrect. In which case it's so commonly misused that it's kind of okay, like how "whoa" is so commonly misspelled as "woah" that people totally use it now and it's fine. I mean, I've even seen it wrong in ads now.

I continue, "So I wanted some time to process it all before I went off half cocked. Like, what if I didn't know the whole context. What if he was acting fucky because he lost a patient that day? Stuff happens and I wanted to make sure I was covering my bases before I came to you guys with an accusation, because I knew you'd have your shovels ready."

"Why do we need to ready our shovels?" Frankie asks. "I'm not opposed, I just wanna be informed. Do you know more than you're telling us?" He leaves the *or are you just being a drama queen* bit unsaid, but I can practically feel it floating in the air all around us.

Carmen says, "People can act out when they're in pain, whether it's physical or mental. Were you trying to give Peter the benefit of the doubt?"

"I guess," I say.

"Doesn't it seem like if something were off, our Diana would tell us?" Frankie asks.

"I don't know. Would she?" I counter. Personally, I have zero faith in humanity, but I may be at the far end of the bell curve.

"Let's all take a breath," Eli says, doing her usual voice-of-reason thing. "Let's talk this through. Juan has probably spent the most time with him out of any of us, as we tend to group off when we have gatherings with our whole families. Juan, would you say you're a man who can find the good in everyone?"

He shrugs. "I do try."

"Then, what do you think about, say, Joseph Stalin?" Frankie says.

"Do you mean the general secretary of the Communist Party, or is Joseph Stalin someone here at the party I've met? Is that Cousin Joe Jack's full name?" Juan asks.

"The former," Frankie says.

"Well . . . while of course his rise to power came at a tremendous cost with repercussions that would last decades, Joseph Stalin did transform the former Soviet Union from an agrarian economy to an industrial superpower," Juan says with an apologetic shrug.

"That's my point," Eli says. "If the nicest guy on the planet can't find anything kind to say about Peter, we may truly be looking at a problem. So, what do you think of Peter Pulaski, Juan? As a person."

A pained expression crosses Juan's face and I see his wheels turning as he tries valiantly to say something positive. "Oh, yes, Peter. He's . . . I mean . . . you could say . . . the thing is, when you . . . um . . . he has great taste in watches."

I cross my arms over my chest and flip my braid over my shoulder. "I fucking told you so."

Chapter Five

Diana

I'm always excited when Peter and I have plans to do something special. Just being together as a couple and not as a whole family unit reminds me of the fun of the early days. I wouldn't say everything was easier back then, because we both worked all the time, but those definitely were less complicated days, when we only had to worry about ourselves.

I'd be lying to myself if I didn't acknowledge things have been a little *off* between us lately, so I'm really looking forward to just getting to talk and dance and socialize tonight, like we used to. Maybe he needs a little reminder of what we've always had.

I recall that when I woke up on the morning of the day we met, twenty years ago, I was feeling like something special was going to happen. Like deep down in my gut, I just sensed a new adventure on my horizon. Maybe part of it was because I was actually getting out of bed in the morning as the sun came up, instead of the late afternoon. I'd been working nights at Northwestern Memorial for a couple of years since I finished nursing school at U of I. But somehow I managed to get all of the weekend leading up to July 4 off—I couldn't believe how lucky I was, especially considering how busy the hospital would be. The damage fireworks can do is no joke. Long before I ever thought about having kids, I pledged to myself that first holiday in the ER that I'd never so much as let them hold a sparkler. (Those things burn at two thousand degrees!)

I was so grateful to finally be out of my parents' house, living with my college friends in Lincoln Park. Our three-flat had seen better days, plus there was no central AC and we had to take our dirty clothes to the laundromat, but I didn't care. It took two whole postcollegiate years of living in my childhood bedroom to convince my dad that I was ready for my own digs. The best part about the old place was that we were around the corner from the Burwood Tap, which was all about the pool table and the free popcorn. The music was always good and the beer on tap was cheap and cold, so it was our favorite place to go on my days off.

My roomies and I hung out at North Avenue Beach for a few hours that day, so I got a little tan, despite all my SPF. The plan was to hit the Burwood that night, as the fireworks weren't until the next day. My window-unit AC barely made a dent in the oppressive heat, and the air was still sticky when I was getting dressed, so I'd picked out a cute sundress with spaghetti straps and a handkerchief hem. I remember thinking how my mom was kind of a puritan about me showing so much skin, and then I laughed that she wasn't there to stop me.

The only downside of my outfit was that I'd had to be super cautious when I was playing pool. When I'd lean over to make a shot, I was afraid I'd show everyone at the back bar my unmentionables. Of course my roommate Dorie mocked me because I just could not get into wearing thongs. But I never wanted a patient to see a "whale tail" under my scrubs if I had to stretch to hook up an IV, so I stuck to plain cotton cheek-covering low-rise briefs or boy shorts. (Floral if I was feeling saucy!)

I remember every detail of that night and it plays in my head like a movie. "We Belong Together" was playing and I was sort of dancing by myself while I waited for my opponent to take her shot. And then Dr. Peter Pulaski walked in. I swear, it was like I sensed his presence before I even spotted him. Here's the thing—I'd seen him before. I knew exactly who he was because he'd just started his ortho residency at Northwestern. Back in those days, he was on everyone's radar, especially mine because he just took my breath away, like some dreamy combo of the best parts of Johnny Depp, Vince Vaughn, and Keanu Reeves. Swoon!

Peter was tall, so well groomed, so stylish. The other residents looked like they lived on Red Bull and cigarettes, but Peter appeared to have stepped right off Wall Street with his designer loafers and expensive belt. So polished! He actually reminded me of the character that Christian Bale played in that one financial movie I never saw, with his slicked back hair, piercing eyes, and expensive watch. I was so impressed. I was all, "What resident has the money for a fancy watch? Most of them have a futon and mid–six figures of med school debt!" Granted, Peter had that med school debt too, I'd find out later, but he didn't look like it.

So the whole night went by and I didn't think he noticed me, because he spent so much time chatting up Dorie (with her tiger-stripe highlights, tight layered tank, and jeans so low rise you could see the top of her butt crack), as well as a few other women there. But then when I was bent over, about to take my shot, I drew my cue back and I could feel the end of it connect with something solid. I heard an "Ooof," and I was annoyed. I was thinking, *Who walks behind someone playing pool? It's like you're asking to get a stick to the solar plexus, and now I have to apologize even though they were the one being careless!*

I spun around, ready to give that person a talking-to, and I came face to face with my victim—Dr. Peter Pulaski!!

He laughed, looked me in the eyes, and said, "Talk about your meet-cute."

Oh, my gosh! I melted! By the end of the night, it was *my* number he asked for, not Dorie's!

I suspect it's because he noticed how hard I worked to be demure. As my mother always said, "Men marry class, Diana." He kept calling me his English rose, which pleased me because I was named for the late, great Princess Diana. (Actually, I was born a little bit before they were engaged, so I'm not even sure if she was in the public eye. But my mother was so enamored with her that I never questioned it.) What's funny is, it wasn't until I got home (alone, because I was a *lady*) and undressed that I realized I was wearing vintage–rose print panties and I thought it was fate. But now that I think about it, I wonder if he was referring to seeing my underwear?

I go downstairs to ask him. "Peter, the night we met, did you see my underwear?"

He looks up from his computer. "What are you talking about?"

"You called me an English rose that night. Was it because you saw my underwear?"

He shrugs. "I'm sure I don't remember."

That's when I get a better look at him and I realize he's still in his gym clothes, with his hair smashed under his White Sox hat. "Why aren't you ready? I thought you showered hours ago when I ran to the market."

"No. And, sorry, I can't make it tonight," he says with a shrug, returning his attention to the screen. I suddenly feel like I've been sucker punched.

"What do you mean you're not coming?" I ask. I'm standing here, completely ready to go, pearls on, hair up, dress just right. "This is Stella's engagement party. Our Uber will be here in ten minutes. We agreed we were leaving at 7:00 and it's 6:45."

"I had a tough workout and I'm tired," he says. "My trainer did a number on me today. It was burpee after burpee. Plus, my tennis elbow is flaring up. I'm out."

"Peter, you promised! You can't be out! We RSVP'd for two; it's so rude for one of us to cancel at the last minute." I mean, Stella spent a mint on the guest gift bags! And not to sound petulant, but Peter gave me his word that he'd come with me tonight. He rarely attends our events, but he swore he'd find a way to be there with me, as he's missed so many other nights. "I was so looking forward to our going together. It's not just that I want this; it's that I feel like we *need* this."

"Diana, you're whining. You sound like one of the kids. And the truth is, I forgot. So you're going to have to go without me." He returns his attention to the screen, as though it's all resolved and our conversation is over.

Peter has never been a fan of women who yell, so I keep an even keel when we're having a discussion, lest he overreact, which does happen once in a while, but only when he's under a lot of stress. But I know he's always more willing to listen if I just present the facts. "Sweetie, I respect how demanding your schedule is, but I sent you a calendar invite months ago! And then I reminded you last week, yesterday, and this morning before you went to the gym, this afternoon when you got back, plus you received those notifications on your phone and there's a Post-it on your bathroom mirror. I guess I don't understand how you could forget."

"Didn't we just see these people a week ago?" Peter asks, neatly avoiding my question.

"You saw them for five seconds as they were on their way out," I say. "I don't want my friends to think that you don't like them."

He shrugs and begins to root around for something in his desk drawer. "Why would they think I don't like them? I actually don't think about them at all."

I just want to cry right now. Peter's always so busy. I thought we'd have fun being out as a couple, all dressed up in a festive atmosphere, surrounded by people who care about us.

How does he not want this too?

We used to have the best time together and we'd share everything, for better or worse. It meant so much when he was there for me, especially when I was at my lowest. But lately it seems like the demands of his job are getting harder, not easier. When we finally paid off his student loans a few years back, I thought we'd be able to do more as a couple, like in the early days when everything was an adventure. Yet now he's practically a vapor trail. I mean, I understand that he undertakes all of this to move our family forward, but what's the point if you never even see that family? We're comfortable right now, but I'd welcome a little discomfort if it meant he could have more free time that doesn't involve the golf course or the gym. He's not even on call today, so he should have no excuse!

"You're just going to have to go without me," he says, like this is the end of the discussion.

And that's when Lilly walks in.

We're not fighting per se, but I don't like her having to hear it when we exchange words. My parents protected me from their disagreements and it's something I try hard to do for my children as well.

"Hey, Li'l Bit, what's up?" Peter asks, brightening. I'm sort of bothered that he seems to favor one of our children over the other, which is why I baby Ethan so much. I never want him to feel "less than" because he doesn't have much in common with his father. My hope is that they grow into some shared interests, although when Ethan tried to teach him chess, Peter wasn't exactly a willing student.

"Why are you guys still here?" she demands. Lilly looks so much like her dad, with her thick, dark hair and light eyes, plus she inherited his height, which is why she's already playing varsity volleyball as a sophomore.

"What do you mean?" he asks.

"You. You're *here*. Like, *physically present*. You said you guys were going into the city. The whole team is coming over and we're watching *Wicked*. They're gonna start showing up in, like, half an hour. You assured me you wouldn't be *here*," Lilly says. "You said you were gonna be cool and let us have the house to ourselves since Ethan's at his weird nerd overnight thing. Yet *here* you are, about to ruin my parent-free good time."

Wait, what?

"I'm sorry, you're having people over?" I question. And for a *good time*? What does that mean?

"Uh, yeah. Dad said I could," she replies.

Peter gets up. "Oh, shit, I'm so sorry, you're right. Let me hop in the shower and we'll be out of your hair before your friends get here. Di, reschedule the Uber for more like 7:15. Love you, kiddo." And with that, he kisses Lilly on the cheek and sprints up the back stairs.

I'm confounded for a minute as Lilly glowers at me until I finally think to ask, "You're not planning on having a drinking party, are you? That is not acceptable."

Lilly lets out a disgusted sigh. "Oh, yeah, Mom, it's a 'drinking party,'" she says, making air quotes with her fingers. "I've invited the whole team *and* the coaches over for a kegger so we can all test the school's 'zero tolerance for athletes' policy together."

"I mean, I'm sorry, I didn't know. If you'd told me, I could have arranged something fun for you," I say. I feel hurt when I'm left out of stuff like this. I would have loved to make this nice for her, to put together a theme, to do something special.

"Dad gave me his credit card for pizza and sodas, so it's all handled." Then she sizes me up, head to toe. "Is that what you're wearing?"

I glance down at my outfit. I've got on a sage-green Mac Duggal cocktail dress that brings out the gold flecks in my hazel eyes. There's a high-low hemline and a sheer chiffon overlay with tasteful beading at the waist. My hair is swept up in a chignon. When I finished dressing, I looked in the mirror and I felt like I'd just gotten a makeover in one of those '90s rom-coms. "Um, yes? Good choice?" I ask, embarrassed that I'm so hopeful for her approval.

"It's certainly *a* choice. Byeeee," she says as she exits. I try not to compare my daughter to a viper who strikes out of nowhere and then vanishes back under the rocks, unconcerned about the damage it's caused.

I guess, if I look on the sunny side, at least Peter's coming with me to Stella's party.

Like my mom always says, a win is a win.

Chapter Six

Eli

I spend the whole night watching Diana like a CIA operative on a mission.

What's strange is how *normal* the party is once Peter and Diana arrive. Diana's laden with impeccably wrapped gifts for the couple and effusive greetings. She's totally business as usual. She apologizes for their lateness but doesn't explain, although nothing *seems* to have happened.

Diana is acting exactly like herself, just being the social butterfly we've always known her to be, floating around the party in the most exquisite green dress. For example, when Abe's cousin's zipper broke, Diana efficiently whisked her off to the ladies' lounge to stitch it shut with her emergency sewing kit. When everyone was doing the wobble, she was front and center, gettin' low and scrubbing the groun'. When Bug's French braid came loose, Diana showed her mom how to use a second elastic to keep it tightened up.

As for Peter, not only is he well behaved, he pours on the charm as he speaks to Abe's brother-in-law, who's a physician in St. Louis, inviting him to his club for a round of golf the next time he's in town. He does have movie star charisma, I'll give him that. Jazz can't stop staring Peter down—her poker face is nonexistent—but he doesn't seem to notice.

We eat, we drink, we dance . . . and one of us neatly avoids getting sucked into conversation with Uncle Cracker and his chompers. There's nothing that stands out about anyone's interactions that makes us feel like there's a thing out of the ordinary.

We all keep touching base with each other over the course of the evening. "Anything odd?" I ask Carmen. Given her training, she's the most qualified to assess behavior.

"Nada," Carmen replies, watching as Peter spins Diana around the dance floor to "The Way You Look Tonight." Diana beams as he twirls her, just pure joy.

"Does that mean Jazz misunderstood, or that his bad behavior is so frequent that it doesn't even register?" I ask.

"That's the question of the night, isn't it?" she replies, peering over at them. "I trust Juan's judgment more than anyone. Yet notice that their body language isn't showing any signs of duress. Their faces are relaxed, they're leaning into each other, they're making eye contact. Nothing's triggering any alarms for me. Look at how he is with her right now. He's coming across as the perfect husband."

"But you know who else came across as the perfect husband? Michael Peterson," I say, referring to the famous true crime case that's been the subject of a TV series and documentaries, as well as so many podcasts. Everyone's covered it, from *My Favorite Murder* to *Southern Fried True Crime* to *Crime Junkie* to its own dedicated podcast, *The Staircase Podcast*. Peterson was a novelist with what seemed like an idyllic life and relationship with his wife Kathleen. Yet one night, she was found dead at the base of the stairs, and what happened next devolved into a whole lot of nonsense (like blaming an owl for her death) and legal wrangling. "We don't *think* she's in danger, right?"

"We'd have seen signs. I can't imagine we'd miss them," Carmen says, but she doesn't sound confident, maybe because Diana never doesn't have on a happy face. When we first met, I thought, *No one could be this cheery*, but that's how she's been consistently this whole time. "I do believe she'd trust us enough to confide in us . . . right?"

"You're right," I say, but I'm not sure either of us entirely feel it.

As the night proceeds in an entirely normal way, I wonder if Jazz was mistaken about what she thought she saw and heard. It did take her a whole week to tell us, so I'm curious if she's doubting herself. I believe she saw what she saw, but again, it goes back to context. Yet the next day, when I texted Diana to see how her night went after we left, she talked about putting her feet up and watching a *Below Deck* marathon. She took two paragraphs to complain that it's never been the same since Kate Chastain and Captain Lee left.

If Peter had snapped, wouldn't she have mentioned it?

In fact, every one of us has gotten alone time with Diana over the evening and we've all been fed the same version of her usual domestic bliss. Now I'm not sure what to think.

Abe was right—the punch has crept up on me and I feel weak in the knees. Everything is a touch hazy, a bit swimmy. I'm not sure if it's the alcohol or the sugar, two things I normally consume in moderation. I should take myself home. I'm going to call an Uber as soon as he finishes his lovely speech. I was going to ride Metra back to Winnetka and walk from the station as it's only about a mile. But I don't trust myself not to stumble, even though I tossed my hateful shoes in the garbage as soon as Stella broke out the flip-flops. I suspect I will not be going on my usual run tomorrow morning. I'm sure the boys will be thrilled if I decide to stay in bed with them for once.

I wish I weren't quite so buzzed because I'm not focusing on Abe's speech. The good news is, I'm sure there will be dozens of recordings of it online tomorrow, so I can catch it again. He's standing there at the front of the room, holding the microphone with tears in his eyes as he describes—

"Goddamn it, you asshole. That is a *Submariner* you just spilled on."

Wait, what's happening?

In the corner of the room, behind a copse of beribboned trees, I see Peter gripping a terrified bartender by the bicep across the bar. He shakes his Rolex in the frightened young woman's face and growls in a low voice. "Do you see this? This watch cost more than you make in a year." He looks like he's about to punch her.

Whoa. I try to go toward them, but my brain won't signal my feet to move.

Diana materializes out of nowhere with a clean terrycloth bar towel and blots his wrist. "Listen, we're all just fine here. Sweetie, your watch is waterproof to one thousand feet. It's just a little tonic water. Tonic won't hurt anything." To the bartender, she offers a bright smile and nervous laugh, saying, "I'm so sorry for any confusion here over the spill, this is for you," and she stuffs a wad of bills in the tip jar as the bartender scurries away.

No. That was not confusion.

That was the threat of violence with a side of assault.

And Diana's acting like it didn't happen?

What is going on here? I blink hard, wondering if the punch is causing hallucinations, as the floor is definitely not standing still right now and the brickwork is undulating. I sort of feel like I'm standing on the deck of a boat on choppy seas, like I do need Captain Lee at the helm.

"Hope you didn't like this job too much because you're definitely not going to keep it," Peter spits at the retreating bartender as Diana placates him with little pats on the shoulders. He shoves her off him, and she stumbles back a few steps before righting herself, fixing her smile, and hurrying after him.

I crane my head back and forth to see if anyone else in the crowd has witnessed this scene, but it seems like everyone else's attention is fixed on Abe.

Did . . . I imagine what just happened?

Did . . . I see what I saw?

How strong is that damn punch?

I come to my senses and I find myself chasing after them, but by the time I reach the door, they're already on the street, climbing into a car.

Do I need a sanity check?

That's when I hear Frankie's voice on the other side of the lobby, staring at the taillights, saying, "No *fucking* way."

Chapter Seven

Frankie

Now that Eli and I have seen the way Peter can be with Diana, it's no longer just a single interpretation. *Of course* we trusted Jazz, however, my girl does tend to jump to worst-case scenarios. For example, the time she swore that Stella had oral cancer, yet it turned out she'd just stabbed the roof of her mouth with a blue tortilla chip and the embedded tip took a few days to loosen. Like, sometimes an AT&T van parked in front of a house is actually there to repair a telephone cable and it's not full of Feds surveilling a safe house where the occupants are actively plotting WWIII. Hell, even last night she took me aside to ask if Carmen and Juan were having financial issues, because she made a wrong assumption, assuming he was working at the party instead of attending it.

We meet for an emergency brunch to discuss a potential action plan, although none of us ever needs an excuse to get together. Luckily, the Cheesecake Factory is the most centrally located gathering spot. The five of us are here. Even Stella thought our putting our heads together was important enough to bypass sightseeing with her extended family.

"What'd her text say to you?" I ask Eli, who is looking more than a little worse for the wear. "Did you call her?"

"Of course I tried to call her. She didn't answer her phone. She texted back lots of emojis and said, 'I had a magical evening but now I have to deal with the aftermath of the volleyball team, but let's chat soon.' Then more emojis of cleaning supplies and the one that's just a person shrugging," she says.

Stella unrolls her napkin, placing her cutlery on the butter dish and her napkin in her lap. She's kind of dressed like a sexy pirate wench today, and I am here for it. "She texted me to wish me a lovely day taking my family around the city. I'll be honest, I didn't mind leaving them, because it was *not* gonna be lovely. I mean, it's a giant silver bean. While it's kind of cool to see it the one time, I do not understand why my kinfolk feel they need to pay homage to it each time they come into town. Oh, my stars, it doesn't change; it's just a durn metallic bean."

"Um, noted. What'd she say to you, Jazz?" I ask.

"She sent me a link to a discount code for the Blue Buffalo cat food that Lunatic likes," Jazz says.

I try to process this but it's not making any sense. "So it's all business as usual from her end? Because she texted *me* to find out what kind of pomade I use. I guess Ethan's thinking of updating his haircut and he'll need new product? And I was like, 'No, really, how *are* you, hun?' and she was all, 'Peachy keen!' followed by a bunch of peach emojis, which I should explain to her not to use. This is weird, right? We saw what we saw but she's acting like nothing happened. How deep does her denial run? It feels a little *Stepford Wives*."

"Never met them," Jazz replies.

A cheery server arrives to take our drink orders. Her brows knit briefly, likely as she's trying to figure out exactly what ties this disparate group together. I mean, *none* of these things are just like the other. Jazz requests a quad espresso, extra hot, and an iced café mocha (she has a minor caffeine addiction, at least this week); Carmen a sparkling black cherry cream soda; and Stella an iced tea with extra lemons and a side of simple syrup, and more of their brown bread, pretty please with honey butter on top, even though we haven't actually been served any of their brown bread yet. (But we will plow through it like a bear through a salmon, I promise you that.) I ask for a Tito's Bloody Mary, which causes sad little Eli to dry heave before croaking out a request for a ginger ale, no ice.

"Hair of the dog might help you, Eli," I say, tapping my copy of the extensive cocktail list, somewhere around page forty-seven of the Cheesecake Factory's dining menu/bible/catalog. "You look absolutely miserable, like you've been dragged along a mile of bad road. I've never seen you without your eyebrows drawn on. You're giving newborn baby mole."

"I didn't think Eli had that many drinks," Stella said.

Eli's eyes are red and rheumy and her hair is a rat's nest. Booze fumes emanate off her and her voice sounds like Batman's. "Your vibe is that of having crawled out of a dumpster behind Lululemon," I say.

"You have no idea how your body will betray you after sixty. No idea," she says.

"I say this with love, but did you sleep in those clothes?" I ask.

"No. I slept on the bathroom floor," she replies with a groan as she cracks her neck. It sounds like she's snapping a stalk of celery and everyone winces.

"I have three words that will change y'all's lives—*chicken an' waffles*," Stella says. "The salty? The sweet? The crispy skin of the fried chicken? Mmm-mmm, to die. Plus, we could all use the protein."

Eli appears to be considering vomiting in her handbag. I hate that she's suffering, but it's a bit funny to see our captain, oh captain, less than the million percent she normally is.

"I'm at a loss," I say. "What's our game plan?"

"I *told* you people," Jazz says, throwing her hands in the air. Today she's sporting the more casual look of a sleeveless baby doll dress over a lacy bodysuit, an inch of sooty eyeliner behind severe cat eyeglasses, Wednesday Addams braids, and about seven hundred black rubber bracelets that stack halfway up her forearm. "Didn't I *tell* you people he was bad news? I feel like you guys never believe me."

"We all believed you," Carmen assures her, rubbing Jazz's shoulder. Carmen is also fresh today as she danced off all her drinks last night. She's dressed in her pretty church clothes and little hat, having attended an early mass before meeting us. "The question isn't 'Did it happen?' but instead 'What do we do about it?' Because doing nothing is not an option. We do not stand idly by."

Eli has her face cupped in one hand while she blots at the back of her neck with a damp napkin in the other. "Is no one else sweating? Why am I sweating? And tell us again what Diana said when you called her this morning."

Carmen says, "I told her I missed saying goodbye to her last night. I wanted to give her the space to tell me what happened, to explain her rapid departure. She laughed and said that her Petey was tired and they didn't want to make a big deal out of ducking out because Abe was in the middle of his speech. She acted like she didn't have a care in the world and talked about how she might go apple picking in Wisconsin later with the kids."

"That is *so* not what happened," I say. Today I'm doing a fitted black-and-white striped boatneck shirt with a little silk scarf tied around my neck, a pair of baggy white jeans with the cuffs rolled halfway up my calves, and red espadrilles. I couldn't look more French unless I were carrying a baguette or miming being stuck in a clear glass box. I guess I can understand why our server was confused. Each of us appears to have stepped out of central casting for five entirely different films.

"He pushed her. That bastard pushed her. I don't know if it was intentional, but it happened. And that was after acting like he was going to punch the bartender in the face for spilling a little bit of a drink on him," Eli says. "Frankie saw it too. It was a real Dr. Jekyll and Mr. Hyde moment, as he was Mr. Wonderful the whole night up to that point."

"I told you so," Jazz insists, pounding her fist on the table.

In her calmest therapist voice, Carmen says, "Yes, *chica*, we have all established that we believe everyone. The issue is, what do we do about it?"

"Oh, he needs to pay," I insist. "This aggression will not stand. I hate seeing anyone take advantage of Diana, and it happens all the time. We all know that if someone wrongs her, she'll just apologize instead of making waves or demanding what she's due. I'm still furious about when her awful mother-in-law foisted off Thanksgiving on her the day before the event and then she had the nerve to bitch that Diana didn't make a wide enough variety of side dishes. The Pulaski didn't fall far from the Pulaski tree."

"She was up for thirty-six straight hours and no one even thanked her! All they did was complain," Carmen says.

"This is it," I declare. "This is my line in the sand."

"Abso-fucking-lutely," Jazz adds.

"If I could wish *this* feeling on him right now, I would," says Eli. I can tell she's absolutely miserable. Her skin is the color of an oyster.

I put a protective arm around her, then I catch a whiff and I gingerly remove it. "Hun, I ask this with love—did you take a shower this morning?"

"I took a shower. I was sitting on the bench seat while I took it, but I did take one," Eli replies.

"If you took a shower, your shower didn't *take*," I reply, and I very casually try to shift upwind of her.

"You're perfectly illustrating my point, Frankie. We share unpleasant truths with each other," Jazz says. "That's how we operate."

We look to Stella for her opinion. "Does anyone want to split the brûléed French toast as a side?" Noticing all eyes on her, she says, "Wait, what's with the faces? Of course I vote for him to pay. I'm happy to march right down there and make him pay myself. I just reckoned we had moved on to the decidin' what we're going to order portion of the day. I need to eat. I can't let my blood sugar drop; I'll get the dizzies."

"Carmie, level with us. Are we way off base here?" I ask as my anxious fingers tap out what's probably Morse code for SOS on the tabletop. "Are we being terrible people for wanting to make him pay?"

"Maybe, especially if that is the plan and we don't even talk to Diana first. I don't like not having this conversation with her. That's not how we should operate as a friend group. Shouldn't we try to sit her down and have a brutally honest convo with her?" Carmen says. Of all of us, she seems to be wrestling hardest with this moral dilemma. "That feels like the most expedient, mature, rational, professional solution. Then again . . . she's so conflict avoidant, I am concerned she'd shut us all out, like she did when she shared the story of her sister-in-law ruining Easter. Remember how we tried to help her express herself using 'I' statements, like 'I feel sad when you mock my family traditions,' and then she avoided us all for a couple of weeks? If we run this past her, she'll be alone, because we know she'll hide from us. We don't want that."

"It feels like if she wanted to let us in, she would," I say. "She will normally share ad nauseam. Remember when she had that weird cyst down by her ladyparts and she told us all about it? *All* about it. No details were omitted. I wish some details had been omitted." I shudder at the memory. "I'm guessing she's in deep denial, just trying to put on a happy face, but that is not a long-term strategy. And we know she didn't tell you anything on the phone, even though you tried."

"Oh, and she put a thumbs-up on the group text I sent. You Boomers have got to stop using that emoji. It's *very* aggressive," Jazz adds.

Eli says, "She's not a Boom—eh, forget it, I don't have the strength to explain generations today." She lays her head on the table and I tentatively stroke her snarled, damp hair as the server tries to place our drinks down around her.

Stella toys with her glass. "Truth? I do not feel like she would be open to a conversation. Y'all remember when Eli said to maybe not let Lilly talk to her the way she did and then Diana had 'the flu' for a month?"

One night at a board meeting, Diana mentioned that Lilly had instructed her to "go piss up a rope," at which, yes, I laughed, because it was funny. (Bless her heart, Diana does not normally have great comedic timing.) However, it was clear she was bothered by the interaction. The older that kid gets, the more Regina George she becomes. I wonder if she's not just trying to get Diana to push back? Like she's hoping for some boundaries?

"We thought she was asking for help in her roundabout way," Stella replies. "Yet when Eli tried to offer a direct solution with concrete consequences for Lilly's smart mouth, she absolutely shut us down in the most passive-aggressive way. If she really had the flu for that long, she'd have ended up in the hospital. If we even raise a subject she finds vaguely uncomfortable, she will 100 percent crawl into her shell and turtle her durn head. Remember? Said she was 'too sick to answer texts,' yet she was still chatting it up in the comments section of that *New York Times* au gratin potato recipe? So the question is, how do we proceed, if we're agreeing that we need to proceed with *somethin*?"

Eli tears off a tiny piece of bread and chews it slowly, pondering. It takes her a few tries to swallow.

"The last thing we want is for her to isolate herself with a man who isn't treating her well," Eli says. "And she's proven that she will run if anyone tries to help, regardless of us having the best of intentions. Direct confrontation is not the way to go. I say we go to the source and show *him* that there are consequences for his actions. Nip this in the bud, because it does seem sort of new and we don't want him to escalate. But not if we're not all behind it. Carmen, *you're* the mental health professional. You have the best insight into how she operates. Should we try to make him pay?"

Carmen takes a long, thoughtful pause and bites her lower lip.

"Okay," I say, slapping the table. "I'm making a management decision. No pressure, but we're going to put this on you, Carmen. You're the expert on human behavior, so if you're against the idea of retribution or teaching him a lesson, that's it. We're out. In which case, Plan B is staying extra close and hoping for the best."

We likely have no business trying to emulate the yakuza's moves. We're crime junkies, not criminals, and we wouldn't even have an idea of where to begin. Making Peter Pulaski pay is a bad idea wrapped in a mistake, then covered in poor judgment . . . right?

"Chris Watts," Carmen finally says.

She's referring to a Colorado man who'd been so distraught over the disappearance of his pregnant wife, Shanann, and their kids that he became kind of a media darling. But it eventually came out that they died at his hand. "For the longest time, everyone thought he was the ideal family man, that he checked all the boxes. That they were always so affectionate with each other. But in the few weeks leading to her 'disappearance,' Shanann had been sending her friends heartbreaking texts about how terrible he'd become."

"Imagine the guilt her friends feel every day for not having done more," Eli says. We all sit with that information for a minute.

"Hell is the truth discovered too late," Jazz says.

Stella says, "What if there's more to this we don't know and our Diana is really in trouble? Those people in Shanann's life have to wake up every mornin' with the weight of what-if just pressing down on their chests, making it hard to breathe."

"Then is that our answer? Are these our marching orders? Or do we just stand by and wait for Diana to ask us for help? What do we do?" I ask. I honestly don't know and I just feel sick about it.

We sit in silence for what feels like an eternity.

"I guess my question is, what would making him pay look like, exactly?" Carmen asks.

We exchange cautious glances around the table. "That wasn't a no," I observe.

"What if he's doing the whole Michael Peterson thing, the perfect husband act? Scott Peterson did the same thing," Carmen says.

"Hell, so did Drew Peterson. Wait, do you think there's some weird connection between people with 'Peter' in their name and a propensity to do harm to their wives? My God, that is chilling," I say. I feel goose bumps rise on my arms.

"I gotta ask, if someone intervened, would Laci still be around? And both Kathleens? And Stacy?" Stella says, referring to their victims. "Doesn't sound like anyone was ever onto any of them, ergo no one ever tried to stop them. What if it's *us* who's standing between Diana's safety and a murderer? What if his rope is fraying and he's a few strands away from snapping? What if teaching him a lesson yakuza-style is exactly what he needs to get back on track and start treating Diana better, yes? Then it's almost a moral obligation for us, right?"

None of us can argue with that logic.

By the time brunch is over, we have the inkling of a game plan. We don't know the details, but we absolutely know anything we try will be neither legal nor ethical, but here we are, all in agreement.

Peter Pulaski must pay.

Chapter Eight

Jazz

"This is not what I expected *at all*," Carmen says, looking around.

Yeah, she's been to my house dozens of times, and we've been on scads of Zoom calls, but she's never actually *seen* my bedroom. I'm pretty fierce about my privacy, so I always use a blurring background, or I'll superimpose a funny backdrop if I'm on my computer in here. I've Zoomed everywhere from the Roman Colosseum to the inside of a submarine, depending on my mood or the news cycle. (I was in the sub for a month after those billionaires imploded.) Lately, I've been using a lot of industrial scenes, like I'm at a rave in Berlin. Frankie hates that one. A lot of times, I try to figure out what will annoy Frankie the most and I go with that. I always tell people that if I don't harass you, then I don't really care about you. (Obvi, I am relentless with Frankie.)

"I just did not see all the pink coming. Wow. So much pink," she says, running a hand over the flocked floral wallpaper in every hue from Bashful to Blush. "And your plants! They're thriving! And there are so many!"

"Why, do you hate it or something?" I say, which makes me feel *some* kinda way.

"Oh, chica, no, I love it, it's so beautiful! I just didn't expect your space to be so soft or delicate. Honestly, I envisioned more 'prison cell' and less 'Pottery Barn Teen,'" Carmen replies. "This is the bedroom of every young woman's dreams. Your space is like a Pinterest page. I think you may have out-Stella'd Stella."

Okay, so my room is a little to the left of what she might have imagined me in. But the fluffy rug feels really good on my cold feet in the morning and I just sleep better under a chiffon canopy and a thick white hotel duvet. And, what, was I supposed to get rid of my teddy bear collection? They have *feelings* and I'm not a monster.

"Here, let me move the baby and you can sit." I gently lift my winking tuxedo cat from a pale green velvet tufted armchair. I place her on a mound of pastel pillow shams at the head of my bed. "She likes to be comfortable," I explain. "And stop looking at me like that—you're making it weird."

"Sorry, I won't say another word, except to ask for a link to where you found those gorgeous lace curtains," Carmen says.

"I'll text it to you. Anyway, if we're gonna do this, I need your insight," I say. "If I'm going to hack into Peter's computer, you've got to help."

Carmen barks out a laugh. "I can barely download an app. You expect me to hack?"

"No, no, I'll handle that part. I need your insight. Your criminal psychologist mind."

"How will this even work? I'd like for you to explain it to me like you're explaining it to your mother," Carmen requests. "Remember, I'm not technical. I mean, I'm old enough to remember when AOL came on a compact disc in the mail. And I keep my passwords on a little yellow Post-it next to my desktop because I always forget the password to my password keeper. This might be the one thing I do that annoys Juan."

I can feel my eye start to twitch at such lax protocol. "I would really like you to tell me you're kidding."

Carmen shrugs, sheepish.

"Jesus, it wouldn't even be fun to try to hack you. Like, zero fun. You've got to give people a little challenge." My cat hops off her bed-pillow throne and settles into my lap. She lightly bats at my nose with a gentle black paw and I respond with a kiss between her ears, because that's what she's asking for. "Carmie, do you think I'd even need a *Post-it* to figure out your password? Ten bucks says it's the first two initials of each of your kids' names, followed by '1234' or your birthday."

She tries (and fails) to hide her guilty smile. "You're completely wrong."

"Oh, okay," I say with a smug nod. "I forgot to add in an exclamation point before the numbers."

"No, smarty-pants," Carmen says, deadpan. "The exclamation point comes *after*."

"We're gonna put a pin in our talking about upgrading your security protocols later, Carmalita," I say. "We have business and I need your help. There's a lot of different ways to go about getting into Peter's network. There's password guessing and brute force, which is how I'd get into yours. That is shit-simple when there's poor security. But if he's logging into anything at the hospital, they'd require more protocols, so I doubt that would work. For him. For you, it would take even the worst hackers four seconds."

"Okay, okay, I get it. I'll change my password and lose the Post-it," she promises, clasping her hands together as if in prayer.

"Thank you. If Peter's not using encryption in his setup, even though he's stupid not to, then I could go with a password sniffer. If it's encrypted, and I'll be disappointed if it's not, then there's the whole Trojan horse method, or I could exploit a buffer overflow, which is when—"

"Wait, stop. Please, how about you simplify it for me?" Carmen suggests. "I don't see how I'm useful here." She pauses and looks around. "Wait, what is that smell? It's . . ."

"What?" I challenge her.

"Utterly enchanting!"

"I have a jasmine diffuser. But it's too floral on its own, so I also burn chamomile candles so it's not so aggressively sweet."

Carmen nods, amused. "Jazmin, you contain multitudes."

"Thanks. Okay. Whatever." I am not comfortable with compliments, so I push past her praise. "We're gonna do the same thing those hackers did to get the dirt from the RNC during the last election cycle. Remember how the Iranians got all those documents?"

"I recall that they *got* documents, but I have no idea how they did it. The explanation was Greek to me."

"Well, they were able to sneak in the back door and mirror that computer. In layperson's terms, what they were doing was coming in and sticking a rock in the doorway, which then allowed them to return and see stuff whenever they wanted," I say. I'm trying to explain this in a way that she understands. That was a piece of critique I always received in school—that I overcomplicate what should be easy. Listen, I'm working on it.

"I see. You're saying that our job is to wedge open the door. Let me ask you, where do we get the rock and how do we put it there?" Carmen asks.

"Great question. We go phishing. The rock is a simple link. We need to entice him to click the link. That's where you come in. We need to come up with something that will bait Peter."

"Is this the definition of 'catfishing'?" Carmen asks.

"You catch on fast. What would you say is most important to him?" I ask.

"His wife and children. And probably his patients," Carmen replies.

"Bzzt, wrong answer. Don't give me the bullshit Hallmark heroine answer, I need you to look into his psyche. We have to come up with stuff that will pique his curiosity. So dig deeper. What is *really* important to him? What makes him tick? Where are his soft spots, his vulnerabilities, because that's how we exploit him," I say.

"*Madre de Dios*," she says while crossing herself. "This is such an ethical violation."

I was afraid this would happen, so I have to turn the screws. Sometimes "ethics" and "the right thing" aren't entirely aligned. We are definitely in a gray area today. "Are you in or out? Because if you're in, I need you all in. Do you want to help save Diana from something potentially terrible or not? I can do it by myself, but not nearly as well."

Carmen sits with that for a minute, deeply uncomfortable. "I . . . wouldn't be here if I didn't."

"Then none of that political correctness shit, please. If you were assessing him as a professional, what would you see? Pretend you're back on the job. Psychoanalyze him. What are his weaknesses? How does his vanity play into his personality and how do we use that against him?"

Carmen presses her eyes shut, clearly struggling.

"Chris Watts," I say. From the expression on her face, I see that this blow landed.

"We hit him in his pride and we hit him in his wallet."

Yep, there we go. "Was that so hard?" I ask. "Now we're cooking. Let's do the first email. We'll appeal to his pride in being an acclaimed ortho. We'll write this one so it comes from, say, a fictional orthopedic surgeon. Like, really credentialed and impressive. Let's say he's in London, so Peter won't wonder why they've not met at a conference or something. We'll add a *u* to the word 'favor,' just Brit it up. We'll say he's asking Peter as a professional *favour* to review an abstract on new procedures. That would play into his need to be smarter than everyone else."

"I could see that working, but how would we write the abstract, even as a short description with an embedded link? I'm a psychologist, not a psychiatrist. I have quite a bit of medical knowledge, but not enough to write even the most basic orthopedic abstract."

"We use generative AI. Easy peasy. Okay, next."

"We need another?" Carmen asks.

"Yeah, we need more. We need a bunch. We don't know which one is going to appeal to him, so we send a flurry, spaced out over the course of the day. So what else motivates Peter?" I ask.

"He does tend to brag," Carmen says. She's still being kind, because that MF is a total blowhard. "Why don't we cater to his desire to be seen as important?"

"Ooh, nice one. Let's make it a . . . donation request from the Fraternal Order of Police in exchange for being honored," I say. "We'll say there's a ceremony and we'll make it seem like he's going to get a lot of positive press."

"What if he makes the donation?" Carmen asks.

"Then the FOP will get a donation. Who cares? But I like it and that's a great suggestion. We need more. What else?"

Carmen rests her chin in her hand, thinking. "He kept going on and on about his golf game last night. Juan couldn't get away from him fast enough, and Juan actually loves golf. Yet I notice that Peter didn't invite Juan to his fancy club."

"Pfft, that's because Juan can't do anything for Peter," I reply.

"He's really not a good man, is he?" Carmen muses. "Very opportunistic. How on earth did he land a woman as wonderful as Diana? She does not deserve this."

"Carmen, baby, that's why we're here. So let's write one from a golf pro offering a membership at a new PGA-level course in Hinsdale," I suggest.

Carmen nods and the motion makes a few of her curls escape from under her church hat. "That's good. It will appeal to his desire for exclusivity."

"But wouldn't he know if there was a new golf course being built in his town?" I ask.

She shakes her head. "Not if it's so exclusive that only the most special people are invited to know about it."

"Aha, you're right! Carmie, this is really helpful," I say. "I knew you would crush this."

"Oh, good, I'm glad I could be useful," she says as she rises from her seat, thinking we're done.

"Now all we need is, like, twenty more and we'll be all set."

"Should I get comfortable, then?"

"Yep."

She sits back down and kicks off her shoes. This could take a while, as we are trying to reel in a *very* big fish.

Chapter Nine

Eli

Deciding Peter should pay was the easy part.

Deciding what paying looks like? Less so. How do we go about it? What do we target? We don't want him hurt (much) and we don't want to take away resources from his wife and children or impact their lives in any way. However, we're not opposed to him being scared or embarrassed, especially if that experience makes him change his ways.

Ultimately, we want him to lose face, enough so that the nonsense stops.

We're gathered on a Zoom call, again minus Diana. It feels wrong not having the whole screen filled with all our faces, but that's how it has to be. The boxes containing our heads look like an ersatz opening to *The Brady Bunch*. Luna(tic) is joining us. She's sitting on Jazz's lap and they're nuzzling each other's noses. Yes, Jazz definitely has a cat now.

"Y'all got into his computer? Remotely?" Stella asks. She's cozy in a wicker egg chair that's suspended from a chain in her town house, lightly swinging back and forth, bathed in the light of the golden hour streaming through her oversized windows. "I cannot even fathom how."

Jazz cracks a rare smile from what appears to be the backdrop of Batman's lair and scritches the cat behind its ears. "Please. Don't ask me how I did it, I just did it and it *wasn't* hard. Gimme a challenge next time."

Fortunately, I feel vaguely less like death after a power nap, a second shower since the first one didn't take, and the restorative powers of the Cheesecake Factory's Mexican chicken and tortilla soup. I'm also comforted by mountains of fluff, as I'm leaning on Pee-wee and Herman is leaning on me. We are a literal dogpile.

"Teach us your ways, we are dying!" Frankie says. He and Kevin are lying on the couch together as Gavin prepares dinner in the background. A variety of fancy Le Creuset pots simmer on their industrial range. Gavin's trying to make the most of a rare evening not spent in due diligence. Frankie keeps saying how glad he'll be when that damn tech IPO is over and he gets his partner back full time. That he's even around for a dinner is a testament to how devoted Gavin is to Frankie, because I know the expectations on him right now. I'm not sure Frankie fully grasps how big it is that he's home, even though I've tried to explain. I wish Frankie would completely lower his guard. I worry that he's going to let a great man slip away because of his fear of commitment.

"No, not 'we.' You. *You're* dying. I'm not listening because I'm not an accomplice," Gavin calls, happily waving a silicone-tipped wooden spoon at us. "Hey, all. I'm not here! This never happened. And I am totally *not* eavesdropping, fascinated."

Gavin is just as wonderful as Juan and Abe. When I finally got them together a couple of years ago, he chartered a limo and took us on a Chicagoland gangsters and ghosts tour, led by a retired homicide detective who gave us the real dirt on our city's most notorious criminals. It was fascinating! I knew he'd win Frankie's heart, but winning everyone else's has been an added bonus. (I really am a great judge of character.) Frankie was gun shy after his last partner cheated on him, so I gave Gavin the inside scoop to treat him extra carefully and absolutely lean into everything Frankie loves. I just wish Frankie would fully lean into what Gavin wants to have with him; they're remarkable together.

While Gavin has little interest in true crime, he did the tour because he wanted to find a way to support Frankie's passions and include us. That's why I hate this for Diana. She should have what the others in the Doom Crew have. (Or will have, once CBS gets its shit together and casts Jazmin.)

Jazz explains, "The short of it is, I sent him a phishing email. That means I included a link and he clicked on it, abracadabra, some background magic happened, and now I can control his computer from mine."

"That sounds particularly easy," Stella says. "I hope it's more complicated than that?"

Jazz says, "Trust me, the technical explanation would put you all to sleep. What you need to know is that now, every keystroke Peter makes, every image he pulls up, I can see too," Jazz says. "I can get into his emails, his socials, his texts. I can even take command of the computer's camera and mic and use it to spy in real time. Plus, I'm in their Ring system, so I could view what's on the other side of any of their home cameras. One quick clicked link later and here we are. Booyah!"

"Should we be more afraid for our online privacy?" I ask.

"So freaking afraid," she confirms. "Hey, you guys wanna see what the good doctor is up to right now?"

"No!" I exclaim at the same time Frankie and Stella vehemently agree. "That is so far over the line. Ugh, we shouldn't be a part of this. What are we doing? What kind of can of worms are we opening?"

"Yet you're okay with him balling his fist in a bartender's face? And being cruel to animals?" Frankie asks. Frankie has zero tolerance for bullies, which proves exactly how much he's grown since getting together with Gavin. He's starting to understand his own worth, finally.

I relent. "No, you're right. But this is a moral gray zone at best. Can we at least try to be as *not terrible* as possible here? Jazz, you should take the lead. Why don't you poke around his computer, maybe report back? You've gotten us this far."

"I don't mean to be obtuse, but I still don't understand—how did y'all even know what to say in the email to make him click? How did y'all determine what would appeal to him?" Stella asks.

Jazz takes a Zyn from a pack and sticks the tiny cheesecloth bundle between her cheek and gums. She's not trying to quit smoking, she just loves the nicotine rush. (I know, *I know*, I've tried talking her out of them. At least it's not vaping anymore.)

Jazz shrugs. "I didn't. Carmen did."

"You *hacked*, Carmen?" Frankie seems impressed. "You didn't even know how to use WhatsApp last time you went to PR!"

"I didn't hack his computer; I hacked his behavior," Carmen replies.

"And she was a fucking champ! She and I wrote and sent a bunch of different emails. I figured the key was redundancy, and I used a couple of his email addresses and I spaced them out so it didn't feel like a sudden attempt. I didn't need them all to work; I only needed one."

"How do you *know* this?" Gavin asks from the background. "No, wait, don't answer me. I'm not here. You don't see me. I'm just some guy in the background making Bolognese à la Gavin."

"Hold up, lemme check which one it was." She scans her screen. "Oh. Innnnnn-ter-est-ting," she says, drawing out every syllable.

We're all silent, waiting for her to explain as she reads and nods to herself.

"Care to share with the class?" Frankie asks. At this point, Gavin is right over his shoulder, expectant. No one loves hot goss more than Gavin, Bolognese be damned.

"Big yikes. This is the one I was rooting against working. It's the gross one, Carmie."

"Yuck," says Carmen. When she frowns, I barely even recognize her, it's so uncommon.

"But not surprising," Jazz says, making tsk-tsk noises with her tongue, which utterly confuses Luna, causing her to blink her one good eye.

"Jazmin Farah Ahmadi, we need you to be less cagey right damn now," I say.

"Oh boy, everyone's in trouble when Eli busts out the government name," Frankie says with a laugh. My kids always said they knew I meant business when they'd hear Henry Truman or Margo Rochelle.

"You're not gonna like it. Who else had their money on . . . *horny Slavic teens*?" Jazz says, her expression full of mirth until she has an unpleasant realization. "Oh. Shit. Diana's really not gonna like it."

"No, that had to be a mistake," I say, not wanting to believe this. "He couldn't have meant to click on that one. He must have fat-fingered it."

"Yeah," Stella says. "Orthopedic surgeons are *notoriously* butterfingered."

"Carmen, when you were in practice, and you were doing your research or on the stand delivering your expert testimony, how often were the criminals there by accident?" I ask.

Carmen gives us a sad shake of her head. "Almost never."

Ugh, I was really hoping for a different outcome. "People make mistakes?" I offer. Why am I the one vacillating here? Even Carmen is on board.

"Really, Pollyanna? Really?" Jazz replies, tapping furiously. "Okay, let's prove me wrong. I'm going to share the screen while we look at his Google history together because that will give us a taste for who Peter Pulaski really is. Give me a sec. And . . . we're live."

Our screens fill with Peter Pulaski's recent searches.

Oh, sweet baby Jesus. Each entry is worse than the one before it.

"*Hot nude Ukrainians*," Jazz reads, as though we couldn't see it ourselves in black and white. Even if I wish we couldn't. "Yep, who called that? Your girl here called that. *Best international dating sites.* That motherfucker. He's gonna go overseas to date when Diana's been dying to see Europe her whole adult life? *Mais non.* Also, uncool. *Halle Berry naked.* Eh, who among us? *Create effective Tinder profile.* Jesus. That definitely means he's not only dating but trying to be better at it. He's such a prick. *How to hide credit card entries.* That would make sense if he's dating. I bet he has secret cards she doesn't know about. That's how what's-her-name Streep found out that Jack Nicklaus was screwing around in that stupid old movie Gavin made us watch."

"Please use respect when you speak about Meryl," Gavin insists. "And it was the actor Nicholson, not the Golden Bear golfer."

"Babe? Great sentiment, excellent notes, wrong time," Frankie tells him.

"Okay, but we *are* watching *The Witches of Eastwick* together before Halloween," Gavin says. "If kids today don't learn about the classics, where are we as a society?"

And of course we will watch it together, because we support Gavin's passions.

"Whatever. Okay, what else? *Best offshore banks no US oversight.* Yikes, what are you into, Peter Pulaski? *Millie Bobby Brown naked.* Oh, come on, she's a child! *Gonorrhea?* Eww, the question mark particularly concerns me. He's a doctor, shouldn't he know? *Hold on to assets in divorce.* Oh, Diana, do you have any clue what this assclown is doing behind your back? *Why is my son fat?*" I don't know if it's a trick of the light, or if steam is literally pouring out of Jazz's ears right now. "I'm sorry, what? Ethan? My little buddy? No. Fuck, no. Okay, where's my shovel? This son of a bitch is going down."

Jazz clicks off screen-sharing his history and reverts to the regular screen. "I take no joy in saying 'I told you so,'" Jazz says. "Well, a little joy, but only because I was right. I feel awful for Diana, just so bad. So . . . are we agreed that we're all leaning more toward 'scare,' and less toward 'embarrass'?"

Every single one of our faces looks like we just received a fatal diagnosis. Frankie and Gavin are clasping each other and holding tight to a wild-eyed Kevin who has no clue why he's suddenly sandwiched between his daddies. Carmen is projecting so much disappointment and Stella can't stop wincing. As for me, I can see on the screen that my face has gone white, and I feel like my hangover has come rushing back. My stomach churns and my head pounds. The bile is rising in my throat.

Earlier today, when we were sitting at the restaurant table, reviewing cases involving men who killed their wives, everything seemed theoretical. My God, that now feels like a lifetime ago. Yet it was like we were conducting more of a thought experiment than anything. It didn't seem real, like something any of our group could experience in our actual lives.

But seeing that Peter has an entirely separate online existence? One that's sinister?

That isn't dissimilar to so many of the cases that we've pored over, examined in depth. My mind immediately goes to Susan Powell. She disappeared from her home in Utah, and her husband claimed he knew nothing because he'd taken his boys on a spontaneous camping trip to Joshua Tree in the middle of the night. In December. Not only was Susan's body never found, but it gets even darker from there, culminating in a murder-suicide involving her husband Josh and his children in the worst possible manner.

It may be the most horrific story we've ever covered, outside of Devonte Hicks, especially as it was preventable.

That Peter is hiding so much from his wife is an enormous waving red flag, and it makes every one of my senses tingle.

"How did she end up with someone so awful?" Gavin asks. "I feel like she should be with someone . . . different, you know? Someone who appreciates what she brings to the table."

We all nod in agreement.

"Actually, for funzies, let's turn on the camera and see what Peter Pulaski is doing with his day while his loving family is up in Sconie picking apples," Jazz suggests. "I'm going to guess he's not pruning Diana's roses." Before any of us can stop her, Jazz switches the screen again to a live view inside the Pulaski home from the camera on Peter's computer.

Oh. *Oh, hell no.*

I'm going to insist we go with "scare."

Chapter Ten

Diana

August 2001

"It's only August, Di! Classes have barely started. No one's even giving homework yet," my roommate Dorie says. "How can you need to study? It's Dollar Beer Night and going alone would be weird for me. As your best friend, it's my job to tell you when you're being a total buzzkill. Hate to be the bearer of bad news, but you're being a total buzzkill."

"You're not going to be alone; you're meeting everyone from the house there," I argue. Literally, all of our sisters can get into KAMS, even the minors. If you're under twenty-one, you're not supposed to have alcohol, but you're still allowed to be in the bar. Of course, Dorie got a ticket for underage consumption there a few years ago. The cops came in and it didn't occur to her to put down her Miller Lite. The officer looked her right in the eye as she was lifting the bottle to her lips. Even he said, "Are you kidding me right now?"

The police took Dorie outside and gave her a ticket. She had to go to court and pay a fine and everything! Her parents laughed it off, saying, "Girls will be girls." Mine would have killed me, or worse, been disappointed in me, so until I was twenty-one, I stuck to Diet Coke in the bars. Point is, I've been going to KAMS for four years, so it's not a big deal to stay home.

What is a big deal is that I have clinical rotations this semester and they're grueling. I've always been a good student, but I need to be great if I want my pick of jobs at graduation. I'm determined to keep my options open, even though I already have a pending offer for the nurse residency program at Northwestern Memorial Hospital, where I interned last summer. A lot of the other interns got an apartment together in the city, but my dad said it didn't make any sense. Why would I need an apartment when I could be door-to-door in thirty minutes on the Metra, living at home? I couldn't argue with his logic, even if I had the nerve to do so.

I want to keep my options open because I'm excited at the prospect of living someplace new. A friend a year ahead of me in the program was able to pick from job offers in cool cities all over North America. I'm obsessed with the idea of a change of scenery. She ended up in Quebec, which sounds so glamorous. I've lived exactly four places in my life, and in just two towns. First, my parents' house in the suburbs (not even the city proper), then my dorm room, then my sorority house, and now here off campus. What would it be like to live in a warm climate, like LA or Miami? Or someplace with a real outdoorsy culture so I could hike and learn to ski, like Denver? Or someplace historical and happening, like Boston or New York or DC? Or a beach town? Or the Painted Desert? (Not even sure what that is, but it sounds magical.)

Even better, what if I could live overseas? I've never been overseas. I've never been out of the country. My dad prefers national parks or our family place in Wisconsin, so that's where we've always gone. My mom hoped to go to the Bahamas for their honeymoon, but my dad said the Florida Keys were basically the same thing.

I'd love to live somewhere new, somewhere unknown. I want to meet folks who are different from me. How nice would it be to not run into the same faces I've seen my whole life? Half of my high school is here at U of I, as are the kids in the neighboring towns whom I met playing varsity volleyball or at parties. In the beginning of college, it was comforting to have a deep pool of familiar people, to have a small-town feeling on such a huge campus. But I've never been given the chance to go somewhere different, to see if I could be someone different if I had the blank slate of anonymity.

I always had to maintain a certain image growing up because everyone knew my family. There was pressure on me to preserve our good name, although I'm not sure how I could have sullied it. Still, I never broke the rules or cheated or skipped school, because I knew that would reflect poorly on all of us. I tried to be kind to everyone. But what if I went to a place where no one knew I was the beloved Doc C.'s daughter? Where they weren't all, "Your dad delivered my son!" Or "Martha is your mom? What an amazing woman!" I'd love the chance to make friends who have no preconceived notions of who I am and what I'm supposed to be like. No one had to worry about me drinking and driving or shoplifting or fooling around with boys; my reputation preceded me. Like it or not, it felt as though the whole town was involved in securing my chastity belt. Even on the rare instances I wanted to misbehave, my friends would stop me: "We can't do this; your parents would kill us."

Why couldn't I be the potential bad influence for once?

Why couldn't I be mysterious?

Why couldn't I be considered a little dangerous?

So many of my buddies took a semester abroad, but my dad explained it was a bad idea because some of the credits might not be accepted by the nursing board of whatever place I end up in. A boy I dated went to Amsterdam on an exchange program, and not only did he dump me a week into his stay, he came back with his own boyfriend. I acted like I was heartbroken, although the truth of it is, it explained a lot. *A lot.* Mostly, I was jealous that he was free to see the world and figure out who he really was. What a gift.

Dorie studied in Paris last year. When she told me she was accepted into the program, I stood in the mildewy shower on the third floor of our sorority house and cried. Yes, I was happy for her, yet it still hurt my heart. I want to see Paris so much, to practice all four years of my high school French education. Mademoiselle Murphy said my accent was spot-on, but I've never so much as even met a French person, so I wouldn't know. Dorie's just so lucky. Once she was back on campus, she'd wear a beret and smoke filterless cigarettes in the hopes that someone would ask her about her time in France. (I'm glad now that we're in an apartment together, she's cooled it with the smoking.) I've yet to hear her not work "Gay Paree" into her conversations ever since. It's a little annoying—likely because I am green with envy—but I'd never tell her that.

My point is, I love Chicago, I love being from Chicago, and I love being a few hours from Chicago here at school, but there's got to be more to life than what Illinois has to offer. So if I want to write my own ticket to go anywhere, I have to have the best GPA. Ergo, I need to keep on top of my workload.

"I can't go to KAMS alone. It's not like in Paris where it was chic to sit at the bar by myself with a book. I mean, when I'd hit my favorite café in the tenth arrondissement, I would meet the most interesting people, especially the European men." She kisses her fingertips and then splays them. *"C'est magnifique!"*

Every. Darn. Conversation.

"Do you know how big of a loser I'd look like if I went to KAMS with a book? Oh, my God, could I be any more of a social pariah? And what if I get there and the girls aren't there yet? What am I supposed to do? Dance by myself? Please, please, please," Dorie wheedles. "Just come for one beer. Come on, Diana, I never ask you for anything!" That makes me laugh, as Dorie literally asks me for everything. Just today, she borrowed my car, my small brown leather Coach crossbody bag, my butterfly choker, and then she wolfed down the rest of the smoked turkey I was saving to put on a chopped chef's salad for dinner. I had to make it with only cubed ham, and it wasn't very good that way. Sooo salty. Dorie realizes what she's said and amends her statement. "I mean, I'll never ask you for anything again."

We both know that's not true, and we also both know that Dorie will argue with me until she gets her way. (She's pre-law. It's exhausting.) In the time it takes for me to convince her why I can't go for a drink, I could have just had the drink, made sure she met up with our sisters, and come back here.

"Fine," I say, giving in.

"Great!" says Dorie, visibly cheerier. "I'm going to wear my new low-rise bells and a seafoam-green silk cami."

"You don't have new low-rise bells. Or a silk cami," I say. Dorie pisses money away and can never manage to save up for anything. I mentally scan the closet that, in Dorie's mind, we basically share, and I realize where she's finding the outfit.

"Then I guess I'm wearing yours."

We laugh, but I can't help thinking that sometimes I don't like my friends.

❧

This was a terrible idea. I don't want to be here. The bar smells like sweat and pizza and bleach, and a whole lot of other odors I care not to contemplate. It's so hot that the walls and windows are damp with condensation. Except where it's not condensation, because I just saw a frat guy pee directly on the floor. I'd heard of this happening, which is why I never wear flip-flops or sandals here, but I'd never seen it myself. I guess he didn't want to fight his way back to the bathrooms, so he just whipped it out. Yet I'm trapped because Dorie asked me to hold her purse—which is my purse—while she went to the bathroom twenty minutes ago. I can't leave because I have her keys, money, and ID. I don't know if she's stuck in line or somewhere on the dance floor gyrating to Destiny's Child, and now I am acting as her official purse valet instead of back at the apartment, studying organic chemistry so I have the option to get the hell out of Dodge when the time comes.

Stuck at the behest of someone else, story of my life.

I mutter, "*Putain,*" which is French because, unlike some people, I actually am fluent, thank you very much. From a spot at the packed bar beside me, I hear a rich, melodic laugh, enveloped in Acqua di Gio cologne, which is mercifully supplanting all the bad smells in this place. It's a lovely respite from the BO and spilled Budweiser.

The guy next to me says, "*Dis-moi ce que tu penses vraiment.*" Tell me what you really think.

"Oh, my gosh, I'm so sorry, I didn't mean to swear in front of you," I say, mortified, and I smack my hand over my mouth. The guy talking to me is so cute, with kind brown eyes, symmetrical white teeth, and a teasing grin that takes up half his face, yet the first thing he's heard me say is "For fuck's sake." For a second it feels exciting, because I'm not someone who curses in public; it's never the first impression that I give. Still, my mother would die.

"Considering I just saw a guy take a leak in the corner, I don't think we're standing on a lot of ceremony," he replies. He holds out a hand. "I'm Justin, by the way. *Et tu es . . .*?"

I take his hand. It's cool and smooth and his nails are neatly trimmed. "*Je m'appelle* Diana. My gosh, your accent is immaculate." He's able to pronounce everything with that nasal/guttural flair and soft consonants, even though his accent is different from any I've ever heard. I bet his French teacher's last name wasn't Murphy.

"I would hope so. French is sort of my native tongue . . . which sounds like a creepy expression now that I've said it out loud. My folks speak French, by way of Cameroon, so it's different from European French. Ironically, I was born in Indianapolis, where they ended up for my dad's work, so I'm trilingual."

"Really? What languages do you speak?"

"I speak French, English, and Hoosier."

"What? That's not a real thing," I say, and I give him a flirty little shove, which is never something I do. Wait, what is happening? Has a body snatcher taken me over? Who am I right now?

"Disagree. And alls I know is this place needs cleaned. Have you got your guyses' drinks yet? If not, we can go to the grocherys and get some pop."

That impression makes me bark with laughter. My sorority little sis is from Fort Wayne and he just nailed her syntax perfectly. *How do I not know this guy,* I wonder. I feel like I've met everyone on campus at this point. "Are you Greek?"

"No." He says this like he needs to explain a difficult concept to me. "I'm from Indianapolis." He pronounces each syllable really slowly, pointing to his mouth. Then he sees I'm genuinely distressed at my faux pas and he adds, "Kidding. Yes, I'm Greek. I'm an Alpha Phi Alpha. You look confused. Do you not know the Alphas? The men of distinction? The ice-cold brothas?"

We only have functions with the white fraternities, so I don't know the people in the Black houses, which suddenly feels super exclusionary. Why aren't we throwing mixers with everyone? I feel like I need a word with our social chair.

"I'm a Delta Gamma," I tell him, and I give him our goofy upside-down salute where my pinky touches my forehead before I can stop myself. "Do you know us? Our symbol is the anchor. Our motto is 'Do good.'"

Justin rolls his eyes and picks up his bottle, making a motion like he's got to go. "Oh, I'm sorry, I've gotta leave you now because I only wanna talk to people whose motto is 'Do bad.'"

"Oh, shut up." I nudge him with my shoulder.

He nudges me back. "No, you shut up. Actually, don't shut up. Tell me everything about yourself, Diana," he says. "Where are you from?"

I start to say "Chicago," but I catch myself. "I'm from a suburb of Chicago called Burr Ridge."

He nods enthusiastically. "Yeah, cool. I've been there. Do you know Lamar Mahoney? He's one of my brothers. He's from Burr Ridge."

"Oh, my gosh, yes, he was in my calculus class!" I say, clapping my hands together. "He was so smart."

He laughs. "Beg to differ. I went through pledgeship with him, and this fool got us in a lot of trouble. A lot. My arms still hurt from all the push-ups. Check it out. Biceps of steel. Thanks, Lamar." He holds his arm out with his muscles flexed and I can't help but touch it. Impressively firm.

I feel like there's something about Justin, something new, something different, and it's allowing me to be a little different. Like maybe I could be more of the myself that I strive to be. Like I could let down my guard and be honest and it wouldn't be weird or off-putting. "Hey . . . do you ever feel like for how big this school is, it's actually a really small world?"

"If this world got any smaller, we'd all have to lose weight to fit on it." Yes. Exactly. "Tell me more. What do you study?"

"I'm in the nursing program."

"I heard that's hard, so you've got to love it, right?" When Justin talks to me, he looks me right in the face and not down at the scoop neck of my top. Refreshing.

"No one's ever asked me that before. My dad's a doctor and I've helped out in his office for years, so going into the medical field seemed like a natural choice. It never occurred to me that it's something I should or shouldn't love," I admit. "It's just what's expected of me."

"Then tell me what you like about it."

It's not that nursing isn't my passion, I was just never encouraged to consider anything else. My dad thought this was the right path for me and it made sense to listen to him. But I have been enjoying it more than I expected. "I like taking care of people and being helpful, so nursing's not a bad fit. Although there's probably a lot of professions where there's a big 'people' element."

"Most of them, actually, unless you're a forest ranger, and even they run into people in the woods." He gives me an appraising look. "Hey, how old are you?"

"I'll be twenty-two next month. Why do you ask?" I say. "Are you an excise cop?"

He rewards me with another one of those brilliant smiles that make his eyes crinkle behind his cool Malcolm X Clubmaster-style black-and-gold glasses. He has such long lashes for a boy—that always feels unfair, and yet they work for him. "No. I'm just saying, you're only twenty-one. You don't have to make up your mind about the rest of your life yet. You have all the time in the world to figure out who and what you want to be."

I'm afraid if I let myself go down this line of thinking, I may not like where I detour. I may ask myself some questions I can't answer, like why I refuse to ever question authority, so I shift the attention back to him. "What's your major?" I ask.

"I'm studying architecture."

"Whoa, speaking of smart. Do you love it?"

He says, "Absolutely."

"Turnabout's fair play, so tell me why." I am flirting! Just like that!

"The cool thing about architecture is that it combines creativity with problem-solving. If form follows function, it's an interesting challenge to come up with a design that's beautiful but also useful. Imagine being given a giant jigsaw puzzle and making all the elements fit together to create a cohesive end product. And you level up the challenge working within a set budget. I love the idea of my vision coming to life in a home or building that could stand for hundreds of years, you know? Like, I'm creating a *legacy*. Something that says, *I was here.* I want to improve how folks live by creating spaces that are comfortable and functional, yet with an eye toward aesthetics. That just seems really satisfying." He stops to reflect on what he's just said. "All right, level with me, on a scale of one to ten, how uncool was that answer? One being Lenny Kravitz and ten being Carlton on the *Fresh Prince*."

"Easily an eleven. You sailed past Carlton straight to Steve Urkel," I say, vaguely shocked at the banter coming out of my mouth right now.

"Nice. Yay for me. Overachiever right here." He holds up his bottle and gestures to the bartender. "Can I get you another?"

You know what? Why not? "Amstel Light?" It's only August. I don't have to study right this second.

"Done." He orders and pays and tips well, and I'm already more impressed with him than every other man I've met on this campus. Most of the frat guys I know will fork over their $2.75 for their beer and hold their palms out for the quarter change. It's embarrassing.

I ask him, "Can I ask you something? Where do you see yourself in five years?" The harried bartender cracks open our beers and slides them across the bar, which is distressingly moist.

"The hell out of the Midwest. Possibly Europe. There's got to be more to life than cornfields."

His answer gives me a rush of serotonin that makes me feel tingly from the top of my head down to my feet. I raise my bottle and he raises his as we clink them in a toast. "Amen to that." Then in a pique of mischief, I deliberately knock the top of his bottle with the bottom of mine so the foam rises up and he has to chug it to keep it from spilling all over the place. This is one of Dorie's signature moves when she's flirting. It's bratty and nothing I've ever done before, but it just felt right.

He swallows and blots the foam from either side of his mouth. "Miss Diana, I think you might be dangerous."

That is the most erotic phrase I've ever heard.

Chapter Eleven

Eli

"First up, we need to find out where Peter's going and what he's doing," I say. "We can't make him pay if we don't know where to find him. Jazmin, what's the most expedient way for us to accomplish this technologically?"

We've been on our Zoom for quite a while. The dogs got so exhausted by hanging out during our marathon conversation that they simply went to lie down in the other room. In my next life, I want to come back as them. I'd be fibbing if I said I wasn't truly looking forward to pajamas and an early bedtime myself. Today has been a lot, and for once, I am feeling old and fragile.

Jazz gestures with one hand while she scrolls on her phone with the other. "We have so many choices, and I am not even kidding. Obvi, I can track him on his phone. That's a no-brainer and I've already started that," she replies. Her screen background is currently the track at the Indy 500 since Frankie mentioned how much he disliked NASCAR. The Indianapolis race actually isn't NASCAR at all, it's IndyCars—a friend owns one of the teams—but I feel like this info would disappoint them both.

Now that we've decided Peter has to pay, I'm treating this endeavor like I used to when I was managing projects on my way up the corporate ladder. Oh, is there anything more gratifying than whiteboarding a plan? (Spoiler alert: no!) I wonder if anyone in the yakuza (or whomever it actually is) felt this way when they were planning their hits?

Any executive worth her salt knows there are five stages to managing a project to its end. Obviously, we've already initiated the project—which is inflicting some pain/fear/humiliation on one Dr. Peter Pulaski. That means we've defined the project and identified the stakeholders. There aren't a lot of roles to determine yet, again because our plan is still amorphous and dependent on where he is and when. Our goal is to course correct his behavior and the budget is . . . clearly not a problem. I'll make sure of that. I don't like to be all Richie Rich, throwing around money at will, because it's not something everyone can do. That's why I want our group to meet membership growth organically, instead of me swooping in with a checkbook to save the day. We won't all feel like stakeholders if I'm the one who seems to be holding all the stakes.

"Is there a way for us to add redundancy? For example, what if he's using a burner phone and leaves his regular phone at home or in the office?" I wonder aloud. "If so, then how do we keep tabs on him?"

"Oh, shoot. Y'all, my family just got back from their day. Is it a big problem if I dip off? If not, they're gonna be hollerin' in the background," Stella asks. The chaos level in her town house just went from zero to sixty in three seconds, the precise amount of time it would take an IndyCar to accelerate to that speed. I also don't share this info.

"Honey, please go!" Frankie insists. "Thanks for being with us as long as you did and send our love to Uncle Cracker!"

"Do text me and lemme know what's going down!" Stella says before her Zoom square disappears. "I am up for whatever y'all need."

In terms of project management, our approach is more waterfall than agile, meaning it's a linear approach in sequential phases, so we're going to initiate, plan, execute, monitor, and control. I feel so in my element right now that my hangover symptoms have magically disappeared. Also . . . I did have a private nurse come over to give me a banana bag after my nap and second shower. I'd never tried this before, but a hangover has never been an issue before. Those fluids and vitamins made me feel less like death, and I'm no longer the color of Elmer's School Glue. Progress.

"Do we need to bring in reinforcements?" I ask. "Like a PI to follow him? I can call a friend and make that happen."

"Whoa, we're getting into losing plausible deniability here," Carmen notes. She's been a real trouper to stay on the Zoom as long as she has, considering her computer is in a closet that she made an office nook. She says it's the only quiet spot in her house. "The fewer people who know what we're doing, the better."

"Hear, hear," Gavin says from the background of Frankie's square. The Bolognese has been cooked, contained, and stored, and now he's on to cleanup.

"Honey, I thought you insisted on not being a part of this," Frankie says, turning toward the now-spotless kitchen to face Gavin.

"Nope, nope, I'm not, carry on," Gavin says, pulling up a seat at the table behind Frankie, where he pretends to dust.

"In terms of tech, we don't need to go overboard. It's actually super easy and inexpensive to stalk people now." Jazz says this as though it's fantastic news and it's going to make stalking a lot more affordable to the average Joe.

"That doesn't feel like a selling point," Carmen says.

"We just need to put an AirTag on his car. They're, like, twenty-five dollars. See? I already have one on her collar," Jazz says, showing us the quarter-sized medallion hanging from Luna's neck. "They're super functional. You can pinpoint their location on a map, it can give you directions to where it is, and it can even play a sound to help you find it. We won't need that for Peter, but we could for this pwecious widdle bebe." She buries her face in her cat's neck and Lunatic's purrs resonate through my speakers.

"Jazz, please never do that voice again, it's freaking me TF out," Frankie says.

"Yes, back to this," I say, trying to keep us from yet another tangent. "Then next, we're going to need to develop a work breakdown structure, create a project schedule, identify the risks, and—"

"Eli, I say this with love. We're going to figure out where he is and find a way to embarrass or frighten him into behaving better. I don't think we need a Gantt chart if we're going to, say, film us pantsing him," Frankie replies.

"Since when do you know about Gantt charts, babe?" Gavin asks.

"Since I listen to you when you tell me about your day, babe," Frankie replies. Come on, Frankie! Recognize what a good thing this is!

"Aw, that touches my heart," Gavin says, clasping his hands to his chest.

"I'm sorry, are you here or not, Gavin?" Jazz asks.

"Nope, nope, not here," he replies, backing up so he's only mostly out of view of Frankie's camera.

"So this is my proposal . . . I am going to make the appointment with Peter about my 'injury' and I'll procure the AirTag and stick it on his car. Frankie, you and Carmen are going to brainstorm on a creative yet satisfying way to make him pay that will not hurt him—"

"Much," Frankie says.

"Much," I agree. "But will serve to teach him a lesson and get him to fly right. And Jazz, you are going to dig into his emails, his DMs, his texts, et cetera and find out what we can use against him. Our goal is to accomplish this by the end of the month so we can circle back to our declining membership and make sure we get a good showing at DoomCon. Everyone, does this sound like a plan?"

"Absolutely," Carmen says.

"I mean, yeah, of course, obvi," Jazz adds.

"OMG, I live for when you lady boss," Frankie says.

"All I'm saying is that Diana is very lucky to have you guys looking out for her," Gavin adds.

"You're not *here*, Gavin!" Jazz shouts, exasperated.

"Nope, and I never was!" he replies, grinning and waving at us all.

We exit the Zoom and I find myself looking at a dark screen. I feel good that we have a plan and we have a way to execute this.

We're going to get this all straightened out, not to worry. I've yet to fail at a project and I don't intend to start now.

Chapter Twelve

Diana

"Hello? Earth to Mother." Lilly is snapping her fingers in front of my face, yanking me out of my thoughts from years ago. My first instinct is to swat her hand away, but we don't believe in corporal punishment in this house. I have to stop myself from thinking, *And it shows.*

"Let me ask you again—where is my uniform? I've got a game tonight and I need to pack my bag before school." Lilly stares me down as it takes me a second to regain my bearings. I don't know why I was just lost in a memory of August 2001, but I'm suddenly nostalgic for a time when everything felt possible.

I tell her, "Sorry, Bunny Rabbit. I'm not actually sure. Did you give them to me to wash? I don't remember seeing any of it in the laundry room. Or did you toss those pieces down the chute? If it was in the chute, it should be clean now. Let's go check." We both head to the laundry room and look in the dryer, but the uniform's not there. We open the door to the chute, but it's empty.

"If it's not in there and it's not in the washer or dryer, then where is it?" Lilly huffs.

"Have you looked in your gym bag? Or on your floor?"

Without another word, Lilly sprints up the back stairs and she returns in a full lather, uniform in hand. "My uniform was on my floor and it's still dirty! If you knew I had a game tonight, why wouldn't you have helped me out and just done it for me?"

"I didn't know you had a game because it's not on the family calendar." Wait, why am I the bad guy here? Because I couldn't read her mind? You know what? I am not in the mood for this. "Lilly, the rules are the rules—on the calendar or I don't know, and in the chute or it doesn't get done. But I can wash it right now and then drop it off at school for you, or meet you at practice after school, your call." I do have a hundred other things to do today, including a list of errands for Peter's family, but I can figure out a way to make it work. I always do.

"Oh, my God, you're impossible!" she hisses, banging the laundry room door shut behind her.

Peter pokes his head in, with a wry smile and a fresh shave. When he got his deviated septum fixed last year, it seemed to have eliminated the little bump in his nose. I'm still getting used to his face being different from how it always was. "What's with all the yelling?" His proclivity about not liking women to raise their voices apparently does not apply to our daughter.

"Oh, Lilly's upset because she forgot to give me her volleyball uniform to wash," I say.

"Then why didn't you just ask her for it? Her season has started, so it stands to reason that she'd need her uniform cleaned after every game. She's busy with all her AP classes; you can't expect her to keep track of everything," he says. "I mean, Jesus, Di, try to keep up. Also, did you call my mother?"

Peter has been on edge lately with work stress, so the last thing I want to do is set him off again. If he someday decides he's not happy with me, then what? What if he suddenly gets chatty about private family business? I can't risk that. So I nod and say, "Yes, of course, and you're right. I'll take care of everything." Then he exits to the garage without kissing me goodbye.

Someday I will figure out how to be a little bit dangerous again, after having to play it so safe after . . . the thing we don't discuss.

But it's not going to be today.

Chapter Thirteen

ELI

"Your problem is obvious," Dr. Peter Pulaski tells me, completely matter-of-fact, just supremely confident in his place in the center of the universe, where entire solar systems orbit around his gravitational field.

Wait, is this how deep space works? I haven't been in a science class since sophomore year of college. Granted, I could optimize a mid-tier manufacturer's supply chain processes in my sleep, from identifying bottlenecks to demand forecasting, but maybe astrophysics analogies aren't my thing. Of course, as an electrical engineer for He Who I Try Not to Name's aerospace company, Margo would know. She'd likely take a great deal of pleasure in correcting me. And I'd let her, because it would make her happy. (How old do I have to be before I stop being an embarrassment to my children? I look forward to that birthday.)

Regardless, Peter holds himself like he was a pharaoh in a past life and his body retains that muscle memory. He is his usual degree of spit shined and slicked back in his impeccable white lab coat with his name embroidered on the breast pocket. Everyone else in his office is wearing scrubs and Danskos or Crocs, but he's sporting suede Gucci loafers and no socks.

That's trouble in my book.

I always knew the road ahead would be rocky when I'd meet with a C-suite male executive in a business suit sans socks. It's an odd barometer, I know, but one on which I could rely. Ninety-nine times out of one hundred, that naked-ankle exec would prove to be rash and impulsive, more concerned about his own needs than what was good for the company he led, and bringing him around would always prove a heavy lift.

Peter has a distinct widow's peak in his hairline, a feature I have hated for years for obvious reasons. (Also not a fan of those *widow's* walks on homes in the Northeast or black *widow* spiders, FYI. I don't even like to say the W-word.) As I peer at Peter, I notice there's something vaguely changed about his face. Is . . . his nose different? I recall it having had a small bump. No, now I'm sure of it. That flaw was why Stella argued he couldn't be up to no good; he didn't have the nose for it. Literally.

However, I can't judge lest I be judged, given my close personal relationship with beauty treatments. Every day when I see my turkey neck in the mirror, I think, *I'm putting this on my list.* I haven't gone under the knife yet, largely because I don't want to waste all that recovery time just lying around. I loathe being cooped up or laid out, a fact made clear when I was vaguely disabled by my hangover on Sunday.

I'm saving having real "work" done (more than fillers and Botox) until something important goes awry, like a hip or a knee, or God forbid, a vital organ, so I can get the vanity bits done at the same time. My Margo says mine is a ridiculous plan, but I do not recall soliciting Margo's opinion. Also, Henry promises his family will come stay with me if I have to recover from a major surgery. Not the selling point he imagines it is.

"I mean, I can't believe it took you this long to make an appointment," Peter says, flashing a smug grin. "Your shoulder is in terrible shape."

I never thought about him as being handsome or not, as I rarely find myself thinking in those terms, but if I were looking at him as a stranger, I'd say he was classically pleasant looking. Maybe even a little dashing. He's tall, he's fit, and he's fastidiously groomed. He does appear to have all his own teeth—before the engagement party, that wasn't anything I'd considered as a selling point. Regardless of how symmetrical he might be, now that I've seen his ugliness at the party, all of his perfectly attractive features suddenly seem off, or maybe sinister. It's like his aura is dark.

There's something vaguely unctuous about Peter, despite his impeccable tailoring and the pristine white of his lab coat. I feel like he's about to slip me a bogus charge for my car's undercoating, but I am not so easily fooled. Thirty years of being the sole provider in the family taught me how to spot a huckster right quick. I remember when I bought my first car after I lost Hank. This was in the early days of the internet, but I did the research on exactly what I should pay and I promised myself I wouldn't leave the dealership until I got what I wanted. The used car salesman thought I was an easy mark. He was mistaken. By the time I was done with him, I left with zero percent financing, an extra set of floor mats, and free car washes for a year. That oily salesman learned a valuable lesson that day about not making assumptions or underestimating.

I'm in Peter's office, across from him in a bucket-seat plastic chair, the kind you'd park yourself on during a wait at the DMV. Meanwhile, he's behind a carved wooden Resolute-type desk in a seat that's shaped more like a throne and elevated a good six inches above me, presumably so he can look down on everyone.

Why is this room styled like the Oval Office, considering how sparse and low rent the rest of the office is? There was a spot of rust on the side of his exam table and cobwebs in the slats of his overhead light. The magazines in the waiting room are a year old. I know firsthand that JLo has been through multiple breakups since the one on those covers. Plus, there's a thick coating of plexiglass separating the patients from the staff. I can't tell if it's bulletproof or just an old COVID protocol. Either way, it could use a squirt of Windex and a quick toweling. What's petty to mention is that my ortho's waiting room has a waterfall feature, a gratis coffee bar with Nespresso pods, and an atrium built around a koi pond flanked with Japanese maple trees. It's like visiting a day spa, not a check-cashing facility.

Peter has luxe light-blocking damask drapes flanking his windows and all the furniture in here has been meticulously buffed to a glossy sheen. Did Diana decorate this place? It doesn't feel like her taste at all; it's too fussy and flashy. She's all about quiet elegance, and this office is shouting, *Look how much money I make!* The walls of his inner sanctum are paneled in a polished wood that looks more appropriate for a law office than a doctor's office in a medical complex. His diplomas and certificates are displayed in matted, gilded frames and his bookcases teem with family photos . . . yet I notice none of them are of Diana.

Why does this not surprise me?

"I'm curious," I ask. "Did Diana decorate your office?"

"What? This? No. This was all me," he replies proudly.

As part of our plan, I'm here for an "appointment" as a way of digging for information. The irony isn't lost on me that in attempting to make him pay, it's me who's coughing up the specialist copay. We agreed that I'd come in, get a lay of the land, see how he conducts his business, and obviously, plant the AirTag on his car.

This all seemed so smart theoretically, but now that I'm in front of him, I've lost a bit of confidence. A small part of me wishes we hadn't started down this path because I believe the only way off it is through it, so I feel obligated to push on.

For the millionth time, I wish Hank were still around. He was a beacon of reason and he always knew the right thing to do. Margo tells me that I romanticize my relationship with Hank, choosing to forget those moments that were irksome or annoying. Of course I remember them, but they're irrelevant now. What I wouldn't give for one more of his volcanic sneezes that were so loud they woke up sleeping children and made me jump out of my skin. His unrinsed oatmeal bowl in the sink. The half glasses of water he left everywhere because he'd lose track of them. Treasure, all of it.

As I've been watching Frankie and Stella get deeper into their relationships, I've been reflecting on the Chicago Young Professionals gathering where Hank and I met in the 1980s. I'd just received my marketing degree at UW-Madison and he was fresh out of B-school at the Kellogg School of Management. He'd printed up his own batch of business cards before the event, since he didn't yet have a job offer and was hoping to network.

As we chatted that night, he explained how he'd gone to Kinko's to chop them into individual rectangles with one of their sharp industrial paper cutters. He said he almost lost a pinky in the process. I liked how he wasn't purposely trying to be cool, acting like a future Master of the Universe, which every other guy was doing in the mid-eighties. He didn't try to convince me he was something he wasn't. Instead, he thought his home-run swing would be to come as himself: a decent, hardworking young man with a quick wit and a sense of humility. And he was the only B-school grad there who'd assume you meant a soft drink if you were to offer him some "coke." He had an innocence that seemed out of place with all the other sharks, and yet he didn't come across as a pushover either.

Hank was so funny and self-effacing that I took a shine to him that night. Feeling bold and like we'd connected after hours of effortless conversation, I asked him for his card because I didn't want to risk him not asking me for *my* number. He explained that he wasn't sure he should give me one because they cost him a whole dollar each, not insubstantial in 1984.

I must have charmed him because, in the end, he relented and spent the rest of his life telling me it was the best dollar he'd ever spent. I worked this story into our wedding vows a few years later, and I still have that card, framed and hanging on the wall in my home office. It is a prized possession.

Peter's been yapping the whole time I've been lost in thought, but I hear him say "You're going to need surgery" in a tone so confident that it borders on condescension.

"I beg your pardon?" I ask, as my rage at his terrible behavior toward his wife is temporarily supplanted by my confusion. Did he say "surgery"? Me? I thought I'd have trouble convincing him I had a problem, as there's nothing wrong with me. I did have a rotator cuff injury a few years ago when I was a little too enthusiastic on the pull-up bar. That was when my own ortho told me that if I continued to do CrossFit, great, he'd likely be able to put a deposit down on that beach house. That was hard to hear, but he was right, I was probably overdoing it, largely because I overdo everything.

I had to endure eight weeks of grueling physical therapy, but the injury did heal nicely, and that's when I switched to walking, and then running. So my shoulder is absolutely fine, something confirmed by a recent physical and also by not being in the kind of screaming pain that I'd previously experienced. Yes, I have a twinge now and then, especially when I'm loading almost a quarter ton of dogs into the car, but that's just age. The moment you turn forty-five, it's like your body flips a switch and then nothing ever feels quite right again. Carmen threw out her back a couple of years ago while she was reading on the couch. Just reading! As for me, one wrong sleep and my neck can ache for two weeks. Believe me, I *know* what a bum rotator cuff feels like.

I came in here confident that I had enough information to fake my way into a conversation, but I assumed he'd tell me I was overreacting. That he'd discount my symptoms and diagnose me as "fine," as happens all too often with women in physicians' offices. I recently read an article in *The Washington Post* about how many doctors have a gender bias when it comes to women describing their pain. They just don't believe us.

Honestly, I assumed—no, I'd banked—on him saying I was being dramatic, patting me on the head, and sending me on my way, *little lady*.

Yet Dr. Peter Pulaski begs to differ with what I'm confident is my real condition. "Oh, yeah. I need to get in there. At a minimum, we're looking at a tendon transfer, if not an entire shoulder replacement. I'm surprised you're not taking Oxy by the handful. Of course, since you're finding it excruciating, we could try some pain management before we get you on the table, but we'll need to cut you open sooner rather than later."

Wait, did I say it was excruciating? I'm pretty sure I said "sore." And did he just offer to go all *Drugstore Cowboy* for me? Or is my anger at him clouding my judgment and I'm looking for the worst in him?

Before I can reply, his harried receptionist Barb, with the tall gray updo and the cartoon kitties on her scrubs, pokes her head into the office. "Doctor P.? There's an Isaac Arthur on the phone for you again. He says it's important he reach you and he's going to stop by if you two don't connect."

Peter's eyes narrow into little slits that make him look almost reptilian. "Barb, I decide what's important. Take a message. Go, thank you, goodbye," Peter instructs before returning his attention to me. "Now, there is some good news about your shoulder."

Oh, good news outside of unnecessary surgery and an offer of unfettered opioid access? "And what's that?" I ask.

Peter rewards me with his most magnanimous smile as he leans back in his throne chair and clasps his hands behind his neck. "I'm aware that you're a person of means. A lot of my well-off patients prefer to pay cash instead of going through insurance because I can give them a substantial discount. Of course, we can always use your Medicare plan. They're great, they pay for *everything*."

Every single one of my internal alarm bells is chiming right now.

"Um, yes, I'd like to get a second opinion. Surgery at my age is always a little scary," I say. If it weren't, I'd have the neck of Selena Gomez. Fact. And damn it, I'm not even eligible for Medicare for two more years! "So I just want to be sure."

He gives me one more toothpaste-model grin and stands as though to dismiss me, and I notice the sunlight glint off his watch, which is different from the Submariner he was screaming about last weekend. I try not to be obvious while checking it out, taking in the stainless steel, complicated gears, and green alligator-leather band. He gives me a laugh that rings as insincere. “Well, now I’m offended. See you soon.” This comes out as less of a salutation and more of . . . a warning?

“Hold on,” I say, staying planted in my seat. “I’m sorry, I’m just such a watch aficionado. You have a magnificent timepiece. What is it, if I might ask?” Obviously, it’s a Piaget—I’d know that style anywhere. There’s crystal on the chunky watch face as well as the watch back, so I can see through it to the skin on his wrist. It’s interesting in that all the internal mechanics are visible, but I’m not sure I appreciate the aesthetics. If I were wearing one, I’d perpetually be distracted by trying to spot the gears turning. But I want to keep him talking because I believe I’ve just stumbled into something.

“Please. You can’t call yourself a watch person if you don’t know this one.” He proudly holds his wrist up to my face. “This is a Piaget Polo Skeleton. It’s rare. Obviously.”

He pronounces the silent *t* at the end of “Piaget.” Of course he does. While I have a ballpark estimate, I’m curious as to the exact cost, which I will google the second I finish planting the tracking device in the wheel well of his car, still so new it has temporary plates. And why does *he* get to upgrade to one of those awful Teslas when Diana drives a ten-plus-year-old minivan with a ding in the fender from that hit-and-run in the Target parking lot last year?

“Obviously,” I reply.

“You can talk to Barb on your way out. She’ll coordinate your pre-authorizations and get you on my surgery schedule. You’re going to want to get on it because my calendar is filling quickly.” He gives me more happy smiles and then escorts me out, just the perfect gentleman, but it feels like such a facade. Like I’m not seeing the real Peter Pulaski.

He closes the door behind me, but I can still hear him as he buzzes Barb, who winces as she picks up her line. “The next time you interrupt my appointment is your last time,” I hear him hiss over the intercom. Ah, there he is.

I suddenly feel a lot less guilty about the AirTag.

Chapter Fourteen

Jazz

"All that Jazz!" Frankie exclaims as he answers his phone. I've caught him while he's walking down Halsted with Kevin on his leash and a coffee in his hand. "Hey, girl! My phone rang and I was all, 'I didn't know I got oncoming calls on this thing.' What is shakin'? It must be big if you've actually connected and want to talk to my face instead of just texting."

Here's the thing about excelling at finding info—no one tells you what to do with the kind of shit you wish you could unsee. That you'd give anything to unknow. Like, there are a lot of ignorant people out there, so it makes sense that they're so happy. Ignorance is bliss. They didn't just have an anvil dropped on their head, you know? I had to talk to someone and I had to do it now.

"I found out more Peter dirt and I don't know what to do with it and I knew if I talked to you instead of everyone at once, I could just be fucking furious first without having to temper my emotions for the normies," I explain.

"Rage away, girl. I gotchu." For once, Frankie's not teasing me like he's a pesky older brother, so I must seem as panicky as I feel.

"Zlata," I say.

He's quiet for a second, and sort of confused. "It's z'lot of what, exactly?"

"No, Zlata. It's a name. Specifically, it's Peter's *girlfriend's* name."

There's a shriek and a *thunk* and Frankie's face disappears because he's dropped the phone. I see some sky and a streetlight with a Boystown flag hung from it and I hear a string of curses so long, loud, and profane that they actually make *me* blush. (Ironic, because I'm an artist who considers four-letter words her medium.) After about a minute of NC-17 content, he picks up the phone and I notice the veins are bulging out on his forehead and neck.

"Okay, now *you* feel like I feel," I say.

"Lemme take a breath and get myself into a space where I can listen," he says. He takes a handful of deep breaths in through his nose and then lets them out through his mouth until it doesn't look like his veins are about to burst. "Start from the beginning and tell me everything."

❦

"Eli, you tell Carmie and Stella. I can't go over the story again, I'm fucking spent," I say, resting my temple on my palm. Frankie let me get the bulk of my fury out, but then he suggested we tell the rest of the group because they had to hear. We met up with Eli for an emergency in-person lunch after the FaceTime call and we showed her all that I'd uncovered. Like that one Real Housewife who was quoted in Congress says? I got receipts, proof, timeline, screenshots, *fucking everything*. None of us could even eat.

Now that the whole group is assembled on Zoom, Eli looks as exhausted as I feel. "We were afraid of this and our fears were founded," she says.

"I hate him, I hate him, I hate him," Frankie fumes as he paces back and forth. I can hear Kevin's collar jangling off-screen, so he must be following him. Gross. Cats are so much better than dogs.

"Ditto," says Stella, and she hasn't even heard any of it yet.

Eli tells Carmen and Stella, "First, we found out his online paramour's name is *Zlata*. She lives in Ukraine."

"But why? Why Ukraine? If he wants to cheat, why not cheat with someone local?" Stella asks. "Is he too cheap to buy her dinner? Or what?"

"He's probably trying to build up to that," Carmen says. We can always count on her for a peek inside the human mind. "It's common for men to engage in online infidelity before they do it live and in person. Often, online relationships feel less consequential and they can be more anonymous and have lower risk. All of the pleasure, none of the guilt, *cachai*? A way of getting their feet wet, like a full-on adultery gateway."

"I jus' want to wring his neck," Stella says, taking her aggression out by stirring her sweet tea so hard with her straw that it creates a vortex in her glass. "So who is this person, exactly? What is she like? Because she cannot hold a candle to our Diana, I know that much right now."

Eli sighs. "If the pictures are any indication, she appears to have an allergy to any and every article of clothing, save for the scraps of satin and lace I barely classify as underwear in her boudoir photos."

"I can just screen share," Jazz offers and everyone quickly declines.

"No, if I see it, it will feel too real. I can't," Stella says, clutching her head between her hands. "Please, no, I beg of y'all."

"Why not send nudes?" Frankie asks. "I've sent nudes to *everyone*. It's not a big deal. I mean, not recently, obvi. But why bother with a couple of triangles of fabric that leave nothing to the imagination?"

"I imagine there's a financial incentive tied to full frontal," Carmen replies.

"Ugh, she is *not* cute," Frankie says. "She's a hot mess, actually. She's got a bunch of horsehair sew-ins, which are just flat black and dull and dry and they reach her waist. The color doesn't go at all with her vacant, pale eyes. She just looks off, almost like she's created by AI, but not great AI."

"Is it the skin tone, do you think?" I ponder. "It's fucked up, but I can't put my finger on why."

"Describe it," Carmen suggests.

"Do you guys remember those kids in your class who were just ballin' and had the 120 pack of crayons?" I say.

"I had the 120 pack," Frankie says.

"Yeah, you were rich," I reply.

"What's your point?" he asks.

"You mean, outside of you recognizing your crayon privilege? My point is, remember that color burnt sienna? Like a terrible brownish orange? That's what color she is, except she didn't even apply that color evenly, so it's really splotchy," I say.

"If y'all are gonna spray tan, exfoliate and use the mitt, otherwise it's just a disaster," Stella tells us.

"She has the lips a drag queen would kill for. Like, she can look at her mouth without using a mirror. They are so overinflated that they take up half of the real estate of her face. If she were to bump into a wall, she'd suction to it," Frankie says.

"I'm not trying to looks-shame, but I am trying to understand the appeal," Eli says. "That's what I fail to comprehend. Diana is the best person in the world—she'd give you the shirt off her back. She's beautiful outside, like a young Martha Stewart, but even more so inside. Why go shopping for expired hamburger when you have Wagyu at home? I don't get it."

Carmen says, "Why did Scott Peterson cheat with Amber Frey when he had Laci at home? Or Michael Roseboro? Or David Mark Temple?"

We did a whole month on men who cheated and then killed their wives. We never thought the subject could be relevant to any of us, though!

Carmen continues, "There can be a lot of reasons, even if they don't make any sense at first glance. Maybe Peter's unhappy with certain aspects of their relationship. Maybe they don't communicate well, or maybe he's looking for a challenge. Maybe he has low self-esteem or they don't have a lot of emotional intimacy. Here's what you have to understand—cheating is not necessarily a reflection of the caliber of the relationship or the love he feels. Most likely there's a lot of contributing factors and it's probably too complex for us to grasp, knowing only what we know."

"What does he get out of it?" Stella asks.

"He might get to feel like a savior to her," Carmen speculates. "Don't discount that."

"From what Jazz uncovered from their chat feed, sounds like she needs a lot of money for her 'sick mother,' which Peter has cheerfully been supplying for a few years now," Eli says. "Here's what gets me. Are *we* a tiny bit at fault? Obviously, it was his decision to start a relationship outside of his marriage, even if it's only been online thus far. Yet Peter blamed 'my wife's friends' for monopolizing her time."

"No!" Stella shouts. "That dirty dog!"

"Unfortunately, yes. He spends a surprising amount of time complaining about his wife and life in a place I'd imagine would be mostly sexy talk," Eli replies.

"Stupid question, but wouldn't therapy have been a healthier alternative?" Frankie asks. "And they're usually on chat on Friday nights when Diana's busy with us. I wonder what the time difference is?"

"Just add Ukraine to your World Clock on your phone and you can see for yourself," I offer.

"Well, that is just infuriatin'. Isn't Diana allowed to have a single moment to herself? I mean, Carmen's husband took up building model trains when we began our meetings. My Abe volunteers as a Big Brother. Gavin stays late at the office. Missing one night with your SO shouldn't be a reason for starting a relationship outside of your marriage," Stella says. "Lemme ask y'all this, why are we not in a car, on our way to murder that sumbitch?"

"Oh, no, we haven't even gotten to the twist yet," Frankie says.

"There's a twist?" Carmen says. "I'm afraid to ask."

He nods. "Yeah, the only thing keeping me from putting Peter in a chokehold right now is that there's a high likelihood that Zlata is a Nigerian scammer."

"What??" Carmen and Stella say in unison.

"Believe it," I say. "After I read everything, I started doing reverse image searches. Get this—I'm 99 percent sure that he was whacking it that day to a fake photo and the words of an internet Yahoo Boy."

"I don't have a clue as to what that is," Stella says. "Should I be laughing or not?"

"Go ahead. They're basically Nigerian scammers who catfish stupid fucks like Peter. I'm not *positive* positive, but my sources are currently pointing to Peter conducting an emotional affair with a forty-nine-year-old named Adedayo in Abuja. Ironic because one of his complaints about Diana is that she's gotten too old for him. So this dude is actually older. Also, he's a dude," I explain, in case that wasn't clear.

"Explain to me again how you know this," Eli says. "I want to make sure we're not making any wrong assumptions."

I try to talk them through the rabbit hole I've been going down. "So, 'Zlata's' original IP address is being masked. Obviously, they're using a VPN, but there's also a chance that they're using a Tor network, which anonymizes online activity to bounce the data, and—" I notice that everyone's eyes start to glaze over and the finer details probably only matter to me. I say, "I guess the bottom line is, does it make a difference for us if she's a catfish even though he thinks she's real?"

"Yeah, now that we know, does this change our plans?" Frankie asks.

"I don't follow," Stella replies.

"Well, we're faced with the dilemma over whether we tell Diana the whole painful truth. How would we explain what we learned, or the invasive way we discovered it? What he's done is gross, but what we've done is a gross violation of her family's privacy. The ethics are so muddy. We were poking around in places we didn't belong, but we did it to protect her. Do our ends justify our means? Especially if this isn't information she wanted? Would she ever speak to us again? I don't know that I would," Eli says.

"You make a great point," Carmen says. "Would making him pay even mean anything if we blow up their marriage and our friend group? The only one who pays in that scenario is poor Diana."

"Yeah," Frankie says. "We don't want to lose her, but we also don't want her to be played for a fool or have her health endangered in case he takes his online cheating offline. Also, he's given her/him/them a shit-ton of money. Peter and Diana seem pretty bougie, but Zlata's been milking him forevs. Where is he getting all those stacks to send to her? Is he tapping into their kids' college fund? Is it coming from legal sources? It's like every thread we pull leads to more loose threads. What do we do?"

These aren't questions any of us necessarily want to answer, yet they persist.

Chapter Fifteen

Eli

While we debate our game plan, we've been following Peter's movements for a couple of days, easily identifying most of the places he goes. He frequently travels to his office in the medical complex, as well as the hospital on surgery days, and he also hits the gym and the golf course at his country club. I can't help but notice he doesn't assist with school drop-offs or pickups or Lilly's volleyball practice, or basically anything that looks like an errand or could be useful to Diana. (Go figure.) But there's one place he keeps going that confuses us. When we pull it up on satellite, it appears to be a run-down strip mall out by the airport.

Why would he need to go there? What is that place?

I reasoned that maybe if we know more about what he's doing every day, our path will be made clearer. Everyone in the group agrees, and we've talked about doing recon together, but they all have jobs or responsibilities during the week. I'm the only one with unlimited free time, and there's no time like the present. I had to drop off the boys at the groomer, and there's only one place I trust with them, even though it's a bit of a haul from my house. Because they have impenetrable double coats and a penchant for rolling in coyote poop, I'm at Carol Anne's Canine Coiffures in Park Ridge every other Wednesday.

Today, after camping out at Panera like usual while the boys get their wash and blowout, I decide to skip my second coffee and take a little field trip. I don't tell anyone what I'm doing because they'll try to talk me out of it. Yes, I realize I am violating the true crime golden rule of always letting someone know where I'm going. But it's a parking lot, not a dubious Tinder date or a horror movie, so I'm rolling the dice. I put the mystery address into GPS and see it's only twelve minutes away. Who am I fooling—I'd be furious with myself if I didn't check it out, regardless of what the Crew thinks. Plus, I carry Mace and a stun gun and there's an SOS button in my car, so I feel like I have my bases covered.

I arrive at the strip mall before Ashley Flowers of *Crime Junkie* even gets to a commercial break, it's that close. Yes, this is definitely a strip mall, but it looks largely abandoned. This area is a bit of a no-man's-land, due to its proximity to O'Hare. Everyone says they like to live close to the airport, but no one wants to be close enough to read the tail numbers on the planes. One plane swoops in so low on its descent that it makes me gasp before I remember I'm basically on the other side of a runway. The vibration from its powerful jet engines rattles my entire car, but it doesn't seem to faze the flock of seagulls milling around a shallow puddle a few yards away.

What is it with seagulls and random parking lots? Shouldn't they be on a beach? I never understood the draw.

The strip mall has patches of weeds punctuating spots in the asphalt on the far end of the lot, and most of the big-box stores are empty, with heavy brown paper taped on the inside of the plate glass windows and faded *FOR LEASE* signs. There are only two functional businesses here—one is a temporary Spirit Halloween store housed in a former Toys "R" Us and the smaller one right next to it doesn't have a sign. While this area doesn't seem completely innocuous, it's not so downtrodden that young moms with plastic shopping bags and toddlers in tow aren't going in and out of the costume store.

I recall those days fondly, when the most important thing in the world was creating the right costume for the big day, like it was a make-or-break proposition. Things were tight for us then, so the kids and I poured all our creativity into breathing magic into scraps of felt and cardboard. My favorite was when we took a couple of saucer-shaped snow sleds and made them into respectable Ninja Turtle costumes with some glue and some love. (And in Margo's case, sequins. "Why can't Donatello be fabulous?" she asked. I couldn't argue.) They even allowed me to don a shell and accompany them. I was so sad when they decided that trick-or-treating was "for babies"; it was too soon. *Of course* Henry's children don't trick-or-treat. Ramona forbids sugar in their home, which feels like cruel and unusual punishment to me. But considering how hyperactive their brood is without sugar, that might not be the worst idea. I recall the day when I took Henry and Margo to Great America and I let them have ICEEs, churros, and cotton candy; the ride back to the city was my own personal Vietnam.

I can't imagine Peter's been putting this much thought into a Halloween costume, especially in September, so I'm going to assume he's been stopping at the smaller storefront with the dirty vertical blinds obscuring the view inside. *Why*, Peter, why?

I park about ten spots from the door and begin my watch. An older sedan pulls up and a man who looks down on his luck gets out and limps to the door, starting a queue. Over the next few minutes, a few more people arrive and line up behind him. One person is using a walker and another has a sling around her shoulder.

Is this a free clinic? I wonder. Is Peter actually volunteering? Do we have him all wrong?

After about ten minutes of waiting, I see the blinds crack open and someone unlocks the front door from within. The piled-up gray hair seems oddly familiar. Wait, is that Barb from his office? What is *she* doing here? I roll down my window for a better look, but I can't see inside, so I hop out and circle the long way around my car to approach the business from an angle.

I scoot around a minivan that's covered in stickers telling everyone exactly who these people are and what they love. There's a stick figure of a mom with a space where the dad appears to have been hastily scraped off, leaving part of his left foot, along with two child stick figures and a cat. Another reads *My Child Is an Honor Student at East Maine School District 63*. A third says *I'd Rather Be at Orangetheory*. Ugh, I hate this. Do you know how easy it would be for a stranger to go to the children's school, tell them their mom talked to him at Orangetheory, and that she sent him to do a pickup because their cat was at the vet? Or what about when people have USMC or army stickers, essentially announcing they have an active-duty partner who isn't home for long stretches of time? I wish people were savvier, especially when they have kids.

"Why are there so many seagulls?" I hear someone say in what I'm guessing is a Russian accent. A man about my age has just exited a shiny black Escalade and he's gazing at the gathered flock, shaking his head, bemused. He seems to be talking aloud to himself, not to me. I've noticed I've been doing this more and more often. I'm not lonely, but sometimes I like to hear sounds in my house, rather than just the echoing silence, so I tend to externalize my inner monologue. The dogs' nails do tap a cheerful beat on the wood floors, but only when they need to be trimmed. The house will be deadly still for at least a week until they grow out after their grooming today, so I'll likely just leave CNN on in the background.

"Hey, hello, you birds. Why a parking lot? Is there no water or green space nearby? Maybe a nice forest preserve?"

I can't help myself but answer him. "I was just wondering that myself."

The man looks startled to hear someone answer what he probably thought was *his* internal monologue, and that's when I get a look at his face. The man's hooded eyes are dark and sad and he has lines carved in his forehead and a series of scars on his cheek. But when he spots me, he gives me the kind of crooked smile that warms my heart and his whole face softens. Sometimes, it's nice to be heard. I notice his rough, worn hands, like he's worked with them his whole life.

"Do you think maybe they are hungry? I have some beautiful *pirozhok* filled with apricot jam. I think I will offer some to them. There cannot be much to eat here, just garbage." He goes back to his car and grabs a pink bakery box from his front seat, untying the string and scooping out a handful. "These are for my mama in the assisted living home, but she will be angry if I were to leave a creature hungry. This is not what we do."

The few small crescents of yeasty dough he removes truly do define beauty. The pirozhok are golden brown domes, but not so symmetrical that they don't look homemade. They flake into a million shards when he tears them into little bites, which tells me exactly how buttery they are. Panera doesn't carry *anything* that looks like these and I am suddenly ravenous, despite the slice of pumpkin bread I ate while I was there updating my TikTok. He tosses the handful of little bits in the seagulls' direction and I watch the pieces fly with some longing. One bird notices the bounty and begins to peck and the man and I exchange a shy smile. Then another bird notices and the creature gobbles it down with enthusiasm.

"Yes, very good!" he says. "Breakfast is the most important meal of the day, even for you."

What should be a nice moment turns into a scene from *The Birds* the second the rest of the flock notices the source of the food and they signal their cohorts on the roof. We're both suddenly swarmed in a dive-bombing seagull feeding frenzy, entirely surrounded with wings flapping and earsplitting squawking. We have to run for cover and we're both laughing when we get to safety.

"Okay, very bad call on my part. Not smart," he says, brushing a stray feather off his windbreaker. "I am so sorry. You are fine, please?"

"Oh, I'm fine," I assure him. "But I have to ask you, where did you get that pastry? It looks delectable. Is it somewhere close?"

The man stands up straighter and beams with pride. "They are mine, from my bakery. I am Yuri, owner of Russkaya Pechka. The name translates into 'Russian Oven,' which my son always said was a little too 'on the nose.'" He taps the slightly bulbous tip of a nose that would likely send Stella into peals of joy. "But it is literally a Russian oven. What would be a better way to describe it, I would ask him."

I have to laugh. "You also have adult children who question your every move?"

Sadness clouds his eyes and he suddenly looks weary. "Yes and no. I did. I do. But my boy Konstantin, he is gone now. Much too soon. He made bad decisions, and I would do anything to turn back time and stop him. But what can you do?" His defeated shrug breaks my heart.

"Oh, my God, I'm so sorry," I say. I feel terrible for saying anything that reminded him of his pain, as it seems particularly fresh. The feeling of loss is like a tidal wave, crashing down on you again and again, relentless. Grief is a riptide that pulls you under in ankle-deep water to remind you of its presence, especially when you do dare experience joy again. The pain of loss never goes away, and it doesn't get better, but it does get different. It mutes, whispering where it once screamed. As with any open wound, scar tissue eventually forms around that void. That protection allows you to keep on swimming.

But I don't know how to explain any of this to a stranger in a parking lot.

The man is quick to apologize for exposing me to his pain. "No, no, please, I didn't mean to share that. I still have two perfect daughters, who don't understand how I manage to crawl out of bed every day without bumping my head. They say, 'Papa, how do you get by?' Oh, I don't know. Maybe it was with the same skill that allowed me to come to this country with almost nothing, to build a business, to pay for your liberal arts degrees and your weddings with the champagne fountains. Not Korbel either. Nice stuff. Small bubbles. Very bougie."

"I run marathons and my son recently asked me if I might need a home health aide to help me 'take baths,'" I say. "It was insulting."

"How many children do you have?" he asks. I can't help myself—I take a peek at his whole sock situation. He's wearing sensible Rockport shoes and what looks like a pair of Smartwool socks. Nice. I always say if you take care of your feet, your feet will take care of you.

"Two, a boy and a girl. One's in Texas, the other in Florida." I am not normally one to give out personal information, so I'm not sure what's come over me. But what if that's my problem? What if I'm so safety conscious, so closed off, that I've made it impossible for myself to connect with someone?

"Mine live down the street from me," he tells me.

"Then that's a blessing," I say.

He lets out a small burst of laughter. "Is it? I don't retire, because then they would never leave me alone."

His answer delights me. I find myself telling him, "My daughter sent me one of those phones that types out the words that people are saying because she thought I was hard of hearing. Turns out my hearing is perfect and she just needed a new set of earbuds."

"I have one better for you. My girls, they bought me grab bars for my toilet for Christmas. 'Oh, Papa, you need these.' I said to them, 'This is how you see me? I haul fifty-pound bags of sugar and flour all day, every day. My mother in the home does not even need the bars yet.' My girls forget they have this nice life in America because I was tough. I came here with money I won from wrestling a bear."

"No!" I protest. I can't tell if he's teasing me or if he's actually serious.

He points at the scar on his cheek. His hands are large enough to palm a basketball, with broad knuckles that must have come from years and years of dough kneading. "This was my souvenir. But you should have seen the bear afterward."

I peer closer. "Really?" The gouges do seem to match the business end of a bear's paw.

He holds up a hand scout's honor–style. "Yes, not a hair out of place. I lost quite badly. Don't wrestle bears, they are worse than birds. There may have been some vodka involved."

Being charmed by an age-appropriate man is the last thing I had on my bingo card today, and I'm not entirely sure how to react. I haven't flirted since Reagan was in office, and I have no idea what to say or do next.

Then, it's like the universe offers me a sign.

A harried mother cruises past us and gets into the minivan with all the identifying stickers on it. Yuri points at her taillights. "No. No, no. Why would you do that? Why tell the world all your business with tacky stickers? One look and I know she's divorced, she has at least one smart kid and a cat, and she likes high-intensity cardio. Don't do this. It is unwise," he says. "Too many bad people in the world. Don't broadcast your business to strangers. You do not know what they will do with your information. Here is a hint of what they will do—nothing nice."

"You took the words right out of my mouth," I say. We watch as another beater car squeals up and a young man practically runs from his car into the office where Barb works. He looks strung out and vaguely desperate and I recall why I'm there. "I'm sorry, do you have any idea what that business is?"

Yuri gives me a measured look and then says, "No, I do not, I am sorry. I am here to buy ladybug costumes for my granddaughters." He gestures toward the Spirit Halloween store.

A light bulb goes off in my head. "You know what would work so well? See if you can find some of those flying saucer discs for sledding. You could spray-paint them like a shell and they'd be way better than what you could buy at a party store. Plus, no one else would have anything like it. Homemade costumes are always better than store bought," I say. "It's the love. And the duct tape."

Yuri nods slowly, warming to the idea. "That is a good idea. Thank you, yes. Smart. Then this winter, I could take the girls to sled on them. Two uses, not one, very smart. I would be a very popular papa. Thank you, kind lady who I accidentally made birds attack."

I glance down at his hands again, looking for a wedding ring, a sign that he's been claimed by someone else, but there's no trace. I don't know what comes over me, but before I can overthink it, I ask the one thing I haven't even considered asking in forty years. "Um, Yuri? It's Yuri, right?"

He nods encouragingly.

"Do . . . do you happen to have a business card?"

❧

Frankie would know exactly what to do here. I could pick up the phone and in ten seconds I'd have total and complete confirmation on how to dress myself, including a first, second, and third choice. He knows my closet better than I know it. He'd say, "What vibe do you want to project? What mood do you want to establish?" Then he'd find the perfect thing for me to wear and I could check this to-do off my list.

However, I'd have to tell him what I was doing and why I was doing it, a day after my big recon mission. I can already picture his reaction. I suspect he'd carry on so much, just so excited, that I'd lose the tiny sliver of confidence I have and I'd end up not going.

So, what do I put on to meet a nice man for a cup of tea? I am headed down to Yuri's bakery because yesterday I very casually said that I would stop by to get some things for the upcoming club meeting, and then he told me what time would be best, when the shop was the quietest so that we could have a proper cuppa and conversation. My stomach twists when I think about doing that, but it doesn't feel like fear.

Is it . . . anticipation?

My closet isn't nearly as expansive as Frankie tells everyone it is, largely because I've simplified my wardrobe since I retired, donating the bulk of it to a charity that helps homeless women find jobs. I'm not sure they can use my things from the early days, with all the power suits and the linebacker shoulder pads, but they said they could resell them in their charity shop. I did have more sophisticated, tailored pieces in the 1990s, and then all the norms were broken at the advent of the dot-com era. I recall meeting Sergey Brin for the first time—luckily I'd done my research on him (ironically, before I could have googled him) so I was prepared when I walked into his office to find him in a T-shirt and jeans. Eventually, as I worked with more and more tech companies, I could count on the scruffiest person there in the dirtiest hoodie being the one in charge. Even after all the norms changed, I preferred to wear items that felt professional. Toward the end of my career, the only people who'd regularly wear suits and heels were lawyers and me.

I guess I could wear a more feminine St. John knit. I have quite a few of those pieces because I thought I'd become one of those philanthropic ladies at the luncheons, so I leaned into making sure I fit the part. My God, were those events boring. So much posturing. So much small talk. So many of the same people. I decided I was better off just writing a check and finding something more useful to do with my lunchtime.

Maybe not dating is why I was able to make my business into the success it became, because for thirty years I never had to worry about what to put on my body to consume a hot beverage with a man. This is already exhausting! There's a pile of tops and jackets and trousers ten deep on my bed, and dogs are looking at me as though I've lost my mind. And maybe I have. But after we talked and laughed yesterday, I came home feeling different. Like maybe I declared the factory closed a little too soon, like there's a bit of life left in it. Is that ridiculous? Is it a trauma response from confirming that Peter isn't what he seems? I don't know anything except that this sort of feels right, despite no longer knowing how to dress myself.

You know what? For better or for worse, I should just show up as myself. While I refuse to believe I'm old, I have far too many miles on me to worry about how others feel about my choices. I go with some Libertine boyfriend jeans, accented with colorful studding, my Basquiat mandrill tee, and a pair of Vans that Frankie painted for me. They have a white windowless panel van on them, with *FREE CANDY* painted on the side of it. I laughed for five straight minutes when he gave them to me. They're a little twisted, but they give me such joy.

I also grab a soft cropped cardigan in case it suddenly gets cold, even though it's been particularly warm all month. This is the time of year that Chicago lulls everyone into a false sense of security because it's so damn beautiful. The weather tricks us into believing that winter isn't actually coming, and it's always going to be sunny and in the mid-seventies. But one day in the next month, it's going to drop thirty degrees, get dark at 4:00 p.m., and start raining sideways (until it starts snowing sideways) until April. Of course, the only people who are happy about this are Gavin and Frankie.

I check myself over in the mirror and I notice that there are high spots of color on my cheeks. I look . . . happy? Excited? I give the boys a kiss and a couple of large marrow bones so they don't eat yet another ottoman (what is the appeal, I wonder) and I'm out the door.

As I'm cruising down the Edens Expressway, I see that Margo's calling. I press the Phone button on my steering wheel to connect through Bluetooth. "Margo, hi. Nice to hear from you. What's happening?"

"Hey, Mom, I was wondering if you—hold on, are you in the *car*? I feel like I can hear traffic." Sometimes I think she and Henry call me just to see if they can catch me doing something they can worry about.

I adore my daughter, despite the fact that she is a bona fide energy vampire. "Hands-free, honey. I'm safe as kittens right now."

"I'm not worried about your hands, I'm worried about the distraction," she says. "Your reaction times are probably degrading."

I can't help it; I have to mess with her. "Margo, don't worry about the distraction. Worry about the three Manhattans I had at lunch."

She shrieks "Are you kidding me?" so loud it makes my speakers vibrate.

I can feel the smile spread across my face. "Yes. Of course I am." Especially because I am not drinking anything with ABV for a while. It took me days to fully recover from Stella's party. "Would you feel better if I called you when I got home?" I ask.

"Definitely. I'm gonna go right now, watch the road, bye!"

Not five minutes later, Siri reads me the text I've received from Henry: *margo says you're driving recklessly! pls stop!! hire a driver!*

I do not give him the courtesy of a reply. But every time my kids do something that makes me feel infirm, I make note of it. When I feel like I've reached my tipping point at their age-shaming, I dive into something that would give them palpitations, which is why I learned to free solo climb. If they keep it up, I swear to God I'm getting my pilot's license or learning to scuba dive.

I arrive at Yuri's bakery and the scent of what's inside hits me before I even open the front door. The yeast, the cinnamon, the vanilla—intoxicating. This legitimately smells like a mother's hug feels. The space is small but absolutely spotless, and there's an A rating by the Board of Health in the corner of the plate glass window. It's obvious that he takes a great deal of pride in his shop.

As I look around, I spot Yuri condensing the few remaining baked goods into a crystal clear glass showcase by the register. Our eyes meet and his face lights up. Yep, another stomach twinge, with a side of heart flutters. This is why I wouldn't tell my children what I'm doing—they'd send me straight to a cardiologist. And yet I believe Hank would likely be thrilled. Had it been me who'd perished without notice, I'd be furious if he'd put any part of his life on hold in my honor. I'd hate if he'd thrown all his passion into building a business and not a life outside work.

So why did I do it?

The kids have been gone for more than a decade and the last thing I need is their approval now. Maybe it's been more out of habit than anything else, as there's no rational reason.

Instead of my usual degree of overthinking and forecasting, why don't I just let go a bit, see where the day and the conversation lead me? I smile at Yuri and he returns it twofold.

"Looks like you've been busy today!" I say. "You're almost sold out of everything!"

"The bird lady! Miss Eli! You came! I am so happy. I saved a few boxes of special items for you—I was afraid it would all go before you arrived. Please sit." Then he opens a swinging door into the back and says, "Mason, I am going to talk with my friend. You are in charge of the counter. Please listen for the bell in case a customer comes in."

He arranges a teapot, cups, saucers, spoons, and a plate of absolutely gorgeous pastries on a tray and he brings them to me.

Every single baked round and square is a work of art, whether mounded with glazed fruit or topped with powdered sugar and crushed nuts or drizzled honey. I gasp at their perfection. "I'd say that you shouldn't have, but I am thrilled that you did. They're almost too pretty to eat."

"No, they are so pretty, you must eat them," he replies. "It would be a crime to waste them."

A teen boy with floppy hair holding an iPhone pokes his head out of the back. "Papa, my mom wants to know what kind of friend."

"My grandson. He is very busybody," Yuri says. "You. How about less spying and more sweeping, yes?"

Mason eyes me and then half-heartedly pushes a broom around our vicinity, but the floors are already sparkling.

"Long ago in Russia when I had a misspent youth, people feared me. I had reputation for being strong and scary. Now? I am explaining myself to a fifteen-year-old so he will not tell on me to his mother," he says in an amused voice.

"Have you ever considered taking up skydiving?" I ask.

"I have not, but I am intrigued why you would ask the question."

"When my kids make me mad enough, I take up a new hobby they'll hate," I explain.

He laughs from deep within his belly. "You and I are going to get along very well, I think." And to Mason he says, "You. Keep your lip zipped."

❦

I stayed at the bakery so long that dusk is starting to fall as I drive home. There's absolutely no way my ottoman hasn't been violated at this point, but replacing it will have been worth it. I had the loveliest time connecting with someone in a way I've not considered in decades. Nothing physical of course (I suspect Mason would have imploded), but there was a bit of chemistry that I would be interested in exploring.

I forgot how nice it was to connect with another person like this, where there's the potential for the possibility of . . . I'm not even sure what there's the potential of. I think I've lived vicariously through witnessing Stella and Abe fall in love, and Gavin and Frankie. Watching the predictable and unshakable rhythm between Juan and Carmen gave me the chance to imagine where Hank and I might be right now. What kind of grandfather would Hank be? I suspect he'd have secrets with them like Yuri has with Mason, and that warms my heart. And I guess that's why I've not been able to let go of the idea that Peter isn't treating Diana well. I assumed that kindness and mutual respect was their default setting, and now that we know it's not, it's cause for alarm, for action. While Diana's problems serendipitously led me to meeting Yuri and cracking open a door I thought long since boarded up, I don't want to lose sight of the notion that we need to help her.

Yet I have to appreciate that their circumstances brought me to that parking lot, which led me here today. And to so alter my mindset that now I might possibly not have the next twenty or so years of my life so meticulously plotted out.

What a glorious conundrum that is to contemplate.

Yuri truly touched my heart when he told me about his son Konstantin. The pain of his loss was palpable. Being with him was a gentle reminder to remember to appreciate my children for who they are, to meet them where they live, rather than expect them to be different.

As I pull down my drive, Siri reads me a new text from Henry: *its dark where are u?*

This may be a work in progress.

Chapter Sixteen

Diana

I remember once when my Uncle David and Aunt Nancy and their kids were coming down for a visit, my mother insisted we spruce things up a bit. Their family was legitimately wealthy, so my mom always took extra care of our house when they'd come. Even though our home was really lovely and well kept, their place was so much grander, with a sweeping staircase and an original Tiffany chandelier in the foyer. I wasn't sure what a Tiffany chandelier was when I was a kid, but I knew it was a big deal from the way my mom went on and on about it to her friends. She was the one who was the most impressed, even though they were on my dad's side of the family.

Before the visit, Mom and Dad were hanging a gallery wall. I guess because my aunt and uncle had a gallery wall, *we* needed a gallery wall. While they were putting up a picture, my mom was holding the nail so my dad could eye it. Of course he measured twice first, but he wanted a visual confirmation that it was in the right place, so he had my mom put the nails in position and he'd pound them in. They hung the whole wall, save for one last family picture. As my mom was holding the final nail, my dad accidentally missed the nail and smashed her thumb with a claw hammer with full force.

We all felt the impact, that's how hard she was hit. Yet my mom barely made a peep, even though she'd been bashed so badly that tears streamed out of the corners of her eyes. Then her thumbnail turned black and Dad had to puncture the nail to relieve the pressure. A geyser of blood spouted out, but she was quiet the whole time. So stoic. Once the fingernail fell off, it never quite grew back properly. Yet my mom refused to complain, though she'd have to learn to hold a pen differently even after it healed. She'd make little jokes like "My goodness, this is going to end my professional hitchhiking career!" if anyone asked her about her clearly damaged digit.

Smile and move on, that's what we did, and that's what I've grown up to do. And that's why I never quite know what to do with myself when Peter yells at me, as it was never *our* way until recently. That's why I wanted to—and was ultimately too scared to—talk to Frankie that night I walked him to his car. Everyone else comes from such lovely families that I believe if I were to share anything less than perfect, they might not get it. Yet given Frankie's upbringing, I feel like he's the one who'd understand how you can love people with your whole heart and yet still feel profoundly disappointed when they let you down.

"How hard would it have been to just do what she wanted?" Peter says after he hangs up the phone. He'd just been speaking with his sister Kelty, who I thought was calling to thank me. Way off on that. Apparently she wasn't fond of the floral displays that I'd arranged for her anniversary party last night.

I just freeze up when he raises his voice, because even after so long together, I never quite know how to handle his little tantrums. The first few years of our marriage were absolutely paradise, back in the days when we only had to worry about ourselves. Peter was my very best friend and we would share everything. I truly felt like he was my partner in every aspect of life, and he reveled in being the center of my universe.

Once we had Lilly, I couldn't lavish all my attention on him anymore; I had a baby to worry about. As much as he loved her, it was almost like he was jealous. That's when he started getting a little snappy here and there, so I made it my job to make sure I made everything just right to keep his stress at a minimum.

Sure, he still has the occasional outburst—like at Stella's party—but fortunately, no one saw and I was able to hustle him into a cab and calm him down. When we arrived home, we opened a bottle of wine and watched *Saturday Night Live*. Just business as usual. I've found that the easiest thing is to act like the dustups never happened, because that restores his equanimity the quickest. The last thing he wants to do is talk about his feelings, and I try not to dwell on mine. He wasn't raised like I was, so his default is yelling, and I've just had to learn to deal with it over the years. It's no different from him being a Sox fan, while I'm loyal to my Cubbies; our families just did things differently. At some point, do I need to stop sweeping this under the rug? Everything in my life is starting to feel a beat or so off—not just my family, but even with my friends. It's like they suddenly have inside jokes that I'm not a part of, or that they're looking at me differently. But why would things be off with them?

Am I being hypersensitive, like my old roommate Dorie used to say?

"She said the flowers were 'vile,'" he barks. "She said, 'They had messy stamens that spat yellow dust everywhere and they smelled like a funeral home.' What the fuck, Diana?"

He wasn't even there so he didn't see how beautiful the arrangements were. Everyone else said they were incredible, so much so that I wonder if she's mad about the attention I received. Plus the scent—it was like walking into a wall of perfume. It felt magical to me.

"Honey, they were lilies. I love lilies! The aroma, the intricate patterns, the symmetrical lines—I think they're mesmerizing!" I say. Honestly, I love lilies so much that they inspired my daughter's name. And had I known his sister had such strong opinions, I'd imagine she'd have pitched in more with the planning instead of dumping it on me. With as off as everything's felt lately, I relished the chance to throw myself into something I was good at, just to get that dopamine hit.

"Well, she was not mesmerized. Far from it."

"You know, she didn't even thank me." I don't mention that she said nothing about reimbursing me. Mind you, I wasn't expecting effusive gratitude or anything, but I thought maybe she'd at least say *something* gracious about my efforts during her toast? I ran around all week for her! I spent most of the day Wednesday driving from Bolingbrook to Schamburg, as neither IKEA had enough of the rattan place mats she wanted. There was construction on I-290, so it took forever, although fortunately I was behind on my episodes of *True Crime Obsessed*, so I made the best of it, like I always do. I looked on the sunny side because if I didn't I'd drive past my exit and keep going until I hit a coastline.

"Diana, don't be stupid. Why would Kelty thank you when she wasn't happy with the result?"

I could fight for myself here and end up with his sour mood for the next week, or I could accept responsibility so we can quickly sprint past this. I hate to challenge him because he's held my secret like an oath after all these years, when he didn't have to. That counts for a lot in my book.

"You know what?" I say. "I respect that she had a vision and I didn't fulfill it. I will make up for it with the table decor at Thanksgiving. I'm planning an actual cornucopia with gourds and mums and sugared fruits. I've already put samples and a mood board on my Pinterest; it will be epic. But I'll make sure she loves them first."

"Great. Was that so hard?" he says over his shoulder as he leaves the room. He's definitely defused, and I let out a sigh of relief. He pops his head back in. "By the way, you'll want to call her and tell her you're sorry. Spoiler alert? You're probably going to get an earful."

I smile and nod blandly, which seems to actually defuse him. And that's a relief because every time I challenge him, I worry that someday he won't be so loyal.

That someday he'll spill all the tea, and then what?

Chapter Seventeen

Diana

August 2001

I wish I hadn't promised to come back to my parents' house and watch my brother Mark's first home football game this weekend, because I could be at a party with Justin right now. He was such a gentleman—not only did he insist on walking me back from KAMS after Dorie finally materialized without apology or explanation, but he asked for my number and tried to make plans with me on the spot. He didn't play it all nonchalant and wait three days, he wanted to cement a date in the moment. It's like he's getting instructions from an entirely different manual than the other guys on campus, and I'm not mad about it.

Dorie had the nerve to try to give me grief about going on a date, hemming and hawing about what might be wrong with him, even though I saw past her subterfuge and it boiled down to the fact that he isn't white. She was all, "What will people think?"

I stiffened my spine. Instead of placating her as usual, trying to look at every side of the argument, I said, "They'll think that it's 2001 and it's completely normal to date someone different from you. And anyone who feels differently is small minded and racist." Then she backpedaled, but the whole interaction with her bothered me; it felt so parochial and it made me more anxious than ever to get out of Illinois.

So, instead of hanging with a very cute and intriguing Man of Distinction, I'm spending my Saturday night in the TV room with my parents on either side of me watching *Mission: Impossible 2.* I feel like I'm fourteen years old all over again. My parents opened a bottle of Riesling at dinner and they didn't even offer me a glass, like it never occurred to them that I was a legal adult who could buy her own wine. They went on and on about how good it was too, about its apricot notes and floral bouquet. I said, "Wow, that sounds delicious," and they agreed without even suggesting I have a sip. Argh.

I wanted to drive back to campus this morning, but my mom said it would hurt Mark's feelings if I didn't stick around for the whole weekend after seeing his game last night. Yet he's too busy being the big senior starting quarterback to make time for his sister. He's at a dance right now! Of course, Stevie wasn't summoned home from IU for the game and no one guilted him, probably because he's pre-med and they think his major is more important than mine. Yeah, I'm sure prepping for the MCAT is the top priority at the Phi Psi house tonight, especially considering he's still a sophomore.

Tom Cruise is busy speeding away from yet another bad guy when we hear a knock at the door. "Hmm, seems awfully late for a visitor," my mother says. She clutches her bathrobe closed as my dad springs up from his seat. "I wonder if there's an emergency with a neighbor?" That happens more often than you'd think, so my dad always keeps his packed doctor's bag by the door.

We're in the back where the den is, but I can hear my dad's voice booming from here. "Hey there, stranger! This is an unexpected surprise! What brings you to our neck of the woods?" If anything, he sounds thrilled. Aw, I take it back. If Stevie's here to surprise his brother, then I misjudged him and he's not a spoiled little punk. But why would he knock?

"Martha! Diana! Come on out, you'll never guess who's here for a visit. He finished up some business early in the city and thought he'd swing by. Isn't this great?"

My mother and I come out to see the guy who's practically my dad's twin standing in our doorway. We kids call him Uncle David, although he's not my dad's real brother. Instead, they're cousins, but you'd never know they weren't brothers because of how similar they are. They grew up on the same street up north and all of their mannerisms are the same because they were best friends for the longest time. They're still so alike now, both pillars of the community, both beloved by all, both with perfect families—and both with hair loss that has left them with the exact same horseshoe-shaped fringe.

I'd say this is a nice surprise, yet something about this impromptu visit feels off. Dorie read *The Celestine Prophecy* over the summer, so lately she's been talking about feeling the energy of a place, like how the "vibrations" were off at Zorba's, so we had to go to Custard Cup instead. At the time I assumed she just wanted dessert instead of lunch and was trying to justify the indulgence. But what if she's onto something? If there are vibrations here now, they're making the air feel stagnant and close, like the bathroom no one wants to use on the third floor of the sorority house because of the poor ventilation. I hate to say it, but as much as I love my Aunt Nancy and the kids, there's always something that gives me pause about my uncle. I can't put my finger on why, but he always makes me feel vaguely uncomfortable. Yet when I told my dad, he was so peeved that I never said anything else again.

When I hug my uncle, I notice he smells not of his usual citrus aftershave, but slightly rank and vaguely of rot, so much so that I take a step back from him and run into my father.

"Careful there, kitten," my dad says.

Who comes to visit at 10:00 p.m. on a Saturday night? And where's my aunt and my cousins? And why does he seem off? Not anxious or nervous, just not his usual self. Sort of disconnected and spacey.

There's something not Kosher about this, but my parents don't notice. My dad's too busy slapping him on the back and declaring, "Davey, my boy! It's been a dog's age!" Then he's opening more of the Riesling—still none for me—and sending my mother off to her immaculate kitchen to throw together sandwiches and snacks, all in celebration of this special and unexpected guest.

We do a cursory catch-up while Uncle David eats somewhat ravenously. I soon beg off because I'm exhausted. I'm a night owl at school, but being back here makes me feel like I'll be in trouble if I'm not tucked in with lights out by 10:30 on the dot.

After following my mother's instructions to put fresh sheets on Stevie's bed for my uncle, I wash my face and brush my teeth. I know I'm completely safe at home, but I can't shake the feeling of something being amiss. Intuitively, the vibrations feel wrong. When my mom comes up to kiss me good night, I tell her as much.

"I just think it's weird that he's here," I say.

I'm in my room, tucked into my brass queen bed with its lacy bed skirt and the layers of tulle woven around the bedposts. This room hasn't changed one bit since we did the big remodel when I was in eighth grade. I was allowed to splatter-paint one of the walls with my friends. We got sodas and chips and made the whole thing a party while we listened to Ace of Base on my jambox, flinging the drops with little artist's brushes. I chose to splatter in shades of purple, lavender, and pale yellow, and the colors are so harmonious together. My eyes have traced all the dots and slashes a million times over the years, looking for hidden patterns that might reveal something fascinating, some profound truth or prediction about my future, but they've never looked like anything but dots and streaks. My mom bought me new Laura Ashley bedding in a lilac print after the paint had dried, and I loved it so much. For a few years, I thought this was the most beautiful space in the world, like it should be featured in a magazine. But now with the wreaths of silk flowers and all the splatters, it feels sort of chaotic and oppressive, like I'm choking on dust, even though it's immaculate.

"Oh, Diana, you're being ridiculous," my mom says, but I wonder if part of her agrees with me, because she sounds worried. She smooths my hair back from my face and then brightens. "It's a blessing to see family unexpectedly! Why would you say anything different?"

I fiddle with the satin edging on my blanket. "Uncle David owns an accounting firm. What kind of business is he doing on a Saturday, especially here in Chicago? None of his corporate clients would be in the office. He's literally never once done this in the twenty-one years I've been alive. It doesn't feel right."

"I'm sure it's perfectly normal." She looks vaguely perturbed with my observation, yet I can't seem to let this go.

"It's still strange. And why wouldn't Aunt Nancy and the kids join him if he had to come down here? They could go shopping or to museums while he was busy. They've done that every other time, for years and years. Why waste a trip all the way down here and not invite everyone, especially when they love the city so much?"

"I'm sure the kids are busy with sports and activities. Or they could still be at their vacation house, because they may not go back to school until after Labor Day," my mother says, yet she wraps her robe around herself more and more tightly.

"He has a car phone. Why wouldn't he have called first?" I ask. Uncle David was the first person I ever saw with a car phone, and he got it back when only doctors (like my dad) had them.

"Honey, you need to stop watching that awful *Unsolved Mysteries* show. It's warping your thinking and you're suspicious of everyone now. He's one of Daddy's oldest friends, in addition to being close family. I promise you it's just as simple as a pleasant surprise." She kisses me on the forehead and then flicks off the overhead light. She pauses in the doorway and then pulls my door shut behind her, so the noise of the family reunion doesn't keep me awake.

I lie here for a long while, staring at the splatters, looking for truths. Then, for the first time ever while living in my parents' home, I lock my bedroom door before going to sleep.

I wake up in the morning to the low tones of tense conversation in the hallway.

"I'll just drive her back, then, Martha," I hear my dad say. His tone is terse, which is super surprising. "It's fine. I'm sure there's an explanation. We'll figure it out."

My mother sounds worried. "But what if—"

More forcibly, he says, "We'll figure it out."

Drive who back? *Me?* Why would my dad drive me back to school? I drove myself here, taking the most boring road in the world. I-57 is two straight hours of cornfields, punctuated with truck stops, fast food, and tiny towns no one's ever heard of. I could do it in my sleep. I pad into the hallway, which is directly across from Stevie's door. The bed is still as neatly made as I left it last night, and I feel a flash of fear.

Why wasn't it slept in?

"Where's Uncle David?" I ask. Both of my parents have odd looks on their faces, and if I didn't know better, I'd say I interrupted a fight. But that can't be. We don't fight.

My parents exchange glances. "He had to go," my mom says.

"Already? He was barely here," I say.

Mark emerges from his room, tousled-haired, red-eyed, and if I'm not mistaken, smelling like the inside of a keg. Wait, was he out *drinking* last night? He's in high school! How is no one calling him on this? And why couldn't I have a glass of wine? I'm actually legal! "What's with the loud-ass family meeting? Some of us are trying to sleep," he says. Why is he allowed to curse?

"Markie, honey, your sister is going to be taking your car back to school today," my mother says. She gives his shoulder a motherly rub. It seems like she's trying to avoid my dad's gaze, as he suddenly seems pissed.

"What? Why? What am I supposed to drive? I'm a senior. I can't take the bus. I'll be laughed out of school," he says. He's not wrong.

There's a long pause and finally my father says, "You can take your mother's car."

"Ooh, the higher-roller Corolla. Sweet. But what am I missing here?" he asks. I'd like to know the same.

"Your uncle had to borrow your sister's car," my father says. He says this in a way that does not encourage additional questions, but I can't help myself. The flickers of anxiety I had been feeling ignite into a full-blown bonfire. This is *all wrong*.

"Why lend him mine? Why didn't you lend him yours? Shoot, I had some of my textbooks in there! I need those!" I say.

"It's not a big deal, we'll just replace them," my mother assures me, yet the panicked look in her eyes doesn't match her placating tone. What is going on here?

"My org chem book was $125 alone! You're just going to replace it?" I say. "That's unbelievable! Where's Uncle David's car? Did he leave it here?"

My parents exchange another look, communicating something that I can't interpret. "Diana, Mark, why don't you both shower before church and we'll have a nice breakfast." This is not a question from my mother; it's a command, and it's the end of the discussion.

At church, we're in our regular spot, in the third row from the front, on the right, on the interior aisle beneath the stained glass window where Jesus is hanging out in a meadow with a bunch of lambs. Years ago I named the lambs Larry, Curly, and Moe, which my father said was blasphemous. I never did understand why, so I just started calling them that only in my head.

My dad sits on the end closest to the center aisle, then my mom, then me, then Mark. We've been sitting here in these exact same seats my entire life; only, Stevie goes on the end next to Mark when he's here. Seats aren't assigned, but woe to any newcomer who thinks they can just park themselves anywhere.

No one's acting distressed about our uncle being gone with my car, yet his car is nowhere to be seen. How did he get to our house? He has one of those big diesel Mercedes in a pale gold color that he calls "champagne"—it's very flashy. I looked for it all the way from our place to the church and I didn't see it parked anywhere.

When the offering plate is passed, I reach inside my bag to grab a few dollars. My parents tithe a straight 10 percent and they pay the church directly, but I don't want anyone raising an eyebrow at me, all, "Doc C.'s girl was home and she didn't put anything in the offering!" Again, it's a tight-knit community and I'd never hear the end of it.

I open my wallet to the slot where all the bills are always neatly faced in denominational order. But they're not here. Wait, did I put the money back somewhere else when I stopped at McDonald's on the way home for a Coke and some fries? That's not how I do it, but maybe I was too daydreamy about the "ice-cold brotha" Justin and I wasn't paying attention. I look in the other slot while the folks down the aisle wait in a rather unchristian way for us to pass the plate. My brother takes the plate from me and keeps it moving. I'm confused; this isn't right. I look in the other slots and open the coin zipper in the back, but my money's not there. There's nothing there.

"Mom," I whisper. "All my cash is gone. Even the money Dad gave me for rent yesterday."

With a smile plastered to her face and her eyes straight ahead, she hushes me under her breath. "Not now," she whispers through gritted teeth arranged in a smile.

"No, Mom, you don't understand," I say more insistently. After digging around more in my handbag, I realize that's not all. "My credit cards are gone too." The debit card from my bank is missing, as are the Visa and gas card my parents gave me for emergencies.

"Diana, no."

I start to say "But—" and she hushes me again and then pinches me in the soft part under my arm. Ouch! She's still sitting here with a smile pasted on her face, like she hasn't a care in the world, but her eyes are darting toward my father, whose jaw is clenched. There's a fat vein throbbing in his forehead. I notice Dad's clasping Mom's left hand with his right, not in their usual perfect-family-at-church sort of way, but a real firm grip, like he's trying to keep her quiet.

Something right now is very wrong with my family.

Something is especially wrong with my uncle, John Davidson Karlsson.

Chapter Eighteen

Frankie

We're all settling in for the usual Friday night board meeting at Eli's house, each of us claiming our places on her elegant new outdoor furniture. OMG, the chairs are *amaze* and now I have something new to be obsessed with in her house. The pieces are made from curved gray wicker, each chair, chaise, and couch topped with a cushion so soft that it feels like being suspended on a cotton candy cloud. If there's a Heaven, it's outfitted with this furniture.

After we pose for a couple of shots for Eli's Instagram, she tells us, "These pieces were made in Belgium by Manutti."

"Hun," I reply, "you say that as though it were a brand that mere mortals would know or could pick up at the Home Depot," and she gives an embarrassed laugh. Sometimes Eli forgets that she's in an entirely different socioeconomic class than the rest of us, and yet she still clips coupons and frequents thrift stores with me. (Obvi, the Goodwill in Northbrook is far superior to the one in Glenview, but neither can hold a candle to the Salvation Army in Mundelein, FYI.)

"Oh, Eli got something else new. Fun," Diana says. I think she's trying to tease Eli, but it comes out sort of bitchy and Jazz pokes me in the thigh. I poke her right back. Our vibe is off tonight—way off. It's like none of us are saying what we're actually thinking, and our usual chill lovefest feels stilted and weird, like we're a bunch of strangers trying to fake familiarity. Gavin predicted it might feel strange tonight because we've never had secrets before. I thought he was way off, but now I owe him a Coke.

"Explain to me how you forget that you're rich. Or is that why you're rich?" I ask, which causes Eli to chuck one of her pillows at me. We're trying to front like it's biz as usual tonight, but we're all on edge because we don't know how to approach Diana. We've been making a lot of meaningless small talk, which is so not our way.

"How is it that each of these roses is the size of a durn softball?" Stella asks. Eli's backyard is—spoiler alert—absolutely OTT. The blooms in her English rose garden are as big as a fist (heh), so heavy with petals that her landscapers have to brace some of the bigger branches with supports.

"It's the time of year," she explains. "They're best in the late spring and early fall because the temperatures are lower and that keeps them from peaking prematurely like they do in the height of summer."

Her backyard, on a craggy bluff overlooking a slice of Lake Michigan, is a riot of color, and it smells like a Taylor Swift concert out here, so many competing scents. The air is so fragrant I can almost taste the cherrywood smoke from the firepit and the earthy, sugary musk of the overripe grape arbor leading to the gazebo. When we leave tonight, we can count on her cutting armloads of the best blossoms and sending them home with each of us, wrapped in wet paper towels and butcher paper, like she always does. That's the brilliant thing about Eli—whatever she has, she shares. This whole scene makes me want to whip out a canvas to capture the colors. We're on the patio and the setting sun streaks the water with a sheen of gold against a dusky pink horizon. The weather right now? It's nice, but it doesn't hold a candle to when the wind whips off the lake at 40 mph, causing the surf to crash over the seawall like the mighty Atlantic. Gavin and I will don our down and multiple layers and sit on the rocks at Foster Avenue beach and just vibe. Who knew a delicate kid from Nashville would be so into Yankee winters?

Tonight isn't Eli's usual turn in our rotation, but she thought it would be better if she hosted today because her dogs were groomed earlier this week and we're less likely to need lint rollers afterward. The boys do look especially fluffy and fresh. They smell like shampoo, instead of like musty sponges, which always happens after they take a forbidden dip in the lake or the neighbor's pool. Right now, their manes are so full and thick, Eli was like, "Don't they look like Def Leppard?" but Jazz, Stella, and I were all, "Who?"

And then Carmen chucked a pillow at us for not knowing whatever obscure reference she was making.

Anyway, we're all here and the vibe is *not chill.* We're anxious, knowing what we now know, but we're trying to fake that we're not. Stella is taking her arty backlit selfies by the grape arbor, but even her heart's not into it because she didn't even ask for my help. We've mostly just been having drinks and snacks and talking about nothing. We spent ten minutes discussing traffic. Traffic! Like, who TF cares? It's a fact of life and so not interesting. It's like there are volumes being said in what we're not saying. Although I am laughing at how Eli's clutching her LaCroix so hard, because the smell of wine is giving her flashbacks to her hangover.

"So, anyone see that new Nicole Kidman show on Netflix?" Carmen asks.

"No," Stella replies as she looks through her snapshots. "Should we?"

"Eh, it's okay," Carmen replies. "Not anything must-see."

Television? Really? We're talking about shows on streaming? We weren't even this formal with each other in the early days of Zoom. It's like we're strangers seated together at the loser cousin table at a colleague's wedding.

"Did you guys catch the Bears game on Sunday?" Eli asks. "The new QB looks promising."

"Watch a sportsball game? Not unless I lost a bet," Jazz replies.

The atmosphere here is kinda heavy, like how in the summer the skies will blacken before all hell rains down. The rest of us have been in such close contact this week about the making-Peter-pay business, so we're struggling not to exchange meaningful looks or blurt out something Diana shouldn't hear. Our energy is off and we all feel it. The vibe in our group has shifted, like we're snapping a half beat too slowly for the song. Even Diana, who's usually so ebullient, is taciturn. She didn't even react when I told her how her new blouse really showed off the girls. Usually, she'd laugh and blush, but tonight? Nothing.

"So, crime, yes, let's discuss," I say, trying to pull us out of the strangeness. "Should we revisit Scott Peterson in the wake of the new documentaries?" If nothing else, sleuthing will bring us together. I mean, except when we're sleuthing someone's husband.

"I would love to see us cover this," Diana says. "People are always interested."

"The LA Innocence Project decided to take on his case, and that is not insignificant," Carmen says. "But it's a tricky one. On the one hand, he was found guilty not only by a jury of his peers, but especially by the media—we're looking at you, Nancy Grace. But the Innocence Project doesn't take on cases that they don't believe they can win, and that gives me pause."

Stella has been listening the whole time she's been posing, and she asks, "What do they know that we don't? That's my question."

Eli isn't convinced. "This feels like a rehash, so maybe it's not the best choice."

"Hard disagree," says Diana, which takes us all aback. "There's a chance he didn't do it, and I think we should talk about it. What if we all had it wrong? What if it wasn't what it seemed? Why not give him the benefit of the doubt?"

"Seriously? Given the preponderance of the evidence, and unless he's the unluckiest motherfucker in the world, it's hard to argue that he didn't kill his wife, even for me, you know?" Jazz says. "He showed up close to the Mexican border with bleached hair, a fake ID, stacks of cash, his brother's credit cards, *and a bottle of Viagra*! Come on! And he ordered a porn channel *the day after Laci disappeared*."

Diana's never quite been on the same page as us when it comes to Scott Peterson. He was one charming psychopath that always seemed to have her snowed. Like she couldn't believe such a suave guy could have bad intentions, and that if he wanted to do her harm, Laci would have known. She'd have mentioned it to her friends and family. I always attributed this to Diana's naivete and only now does this opinion give us pause. Does she have monster blindness?

"All I'm saying is that people grieve in different ways," Diana says, and I have to stare at my hands so I don't give everyone loaded looks. I notice I didn't get all the phthalo green out of the creases around my knuckles.

Jazz snorts audibly, ironic because she's a phenomenal poker player, just top notch. And I can't disagree with her assessment.

"Di, love you, but these are hardly the actions of a man concerned about his missing, pregnant wife. And don't even start me on the nonsense about the umbrellas and boat anchors in the back of his pickup truck," I add.

"We're still losing members, and the Peterson case doesn't seem fresh or new enough," Eli says. "Let's keep ballparking to see if we can find something better. Why don't we table this for a beat. Maybe we'll be inspired by something else. By the way, I have interesting news. I was attacked by birds this week."

"Okay, random, but interesting," I say. "Are you okay?"

"Right as rain," Eli replies brightly. Okay, something is definitely different with Eli tonight, and it's not just a brush with potential bird flu. She seems lighter, more joyous, which is strange considering what we're all dealing with. I'm too concerned about Diana to pull her aside and grill her. But I will. Count on it.

More tense silence.

Why is this night so freaking awkward? I hate this. *Hate.* If I wanted to make stilted small talk where we avoid the elephant in the room, I'd go back to Nashville for Christmas.

Then, out of nowhere, Diana asks Eli, "How's your shoulder?"

Granted, we all helped plan Eli's "sting operation" this week at Peter's office, but Diana doesn't know she'd seen him about a fake shoulder injury. And she *shouldn't* know either.

"My shoulder?" Eli asks, pausing in the middle of a bite of smoked-salmon crostini with a smear of cream cheese and basil pesto. Both Herman and Pee-wee have their eyes trained on the mound of fish, with rivers of drool pooling at their giant paws. The menu tonight has a bit of a Russian flair, which is a fun change.

"Yes, Peter said you came in this week. Said your rotator cuff was in bad shape, and he's concerned that he doesn't see you on his surgical schedule yet," Diana replies. In a gently chiding voice, she says, "You can't let these things go. Level with us—are you secretly doing CrossFit again?" If Eli were sneaking into a garage to flip tires, it wouldn't be the first time. In her head, Eli is still the exact age she was when she lost Hank, and no one can convince her—or her body—otherwise.

While we collectively hold our breath, cautiously, Eli swallows her bite and replies, "I wasn't aware you knew of my appointment. Also, I overreacted. Turns out, it was just a twinge and it feels fine now."

"Eli, you don't get bonus points for pretending you're Superwoman," Diana clucks. I can see Eli bristle because this feels dangerously close to Diana questioning her physical abilities, which is a no-fly zone. There are a few hard and true facts in this world: The sun will rise tomorrow, Uncle Sam demands his cut, and Eli is an absolute beast when it comes to health and fitness.

Carmen immediately homes in on the fact that Eli didn't authorize Peter to share this info. Even though she's no longer a practicing psychologist, the laws about doctor-patient confidentiality haven't changed. "Eli, did you give Peter permission to discuss your visit with Diana?" Carmen asks.

The air is electric with tension.

"Erm, no, we did not discuss Diana. I didn't tell him to mention to her I'd seen him. That's not because it was a secret but because I didn't want her to worry," Eli says, fidgeting with the embroidered edge of her linen napkin. (So posh!) A key justification for allowing her to do a covert mission to Peter's office was that he wouldn't be allowed to share that information with Diana, yet here we are. But the whole thing is, Diana isn't supposed to know. She's not supposed to know! We did not plan this out! This is not according to the script we discussed! And now Diana knows what she's not supposed to know and she's being all Diana about it, and I'm worried that this is about to end badly. She needs to be in the dark so we can protect her.

"Let me get this straight," Carmen says. She stands and begins to pace, something we have never once seen her do, although Juan says he calls it a "walk and think" and when her kids see it, they call it a "run and hide." Carmen holds up a finger for each fact. "Number one, you did not grant Peter permission to tell Diana about your visit. Yet, two, he told her anyway. In addition to mentioning seeing you, three, he also disclosed the nature of your injury. And, four, he speculated with her about your course of treatment?" Carmen holds up four fingers. "Do I have this correct?"

Nope, nope, nope. I am giving Carmen *abort* eyes. We're not supposed to lean into this. But Carmen is just staring down Diana, who is staring at her right back. It's not supposed to happen like this! We role-played scenarios on how we'd approach our suspicions about Peter, but this is way off script. *Way* off script. We wanted to have a calm, supportive conversation—not a confrontation about medical ethics. Yet the two most chill members of our group are leaning forward in their seats, with rigid posture and clenched fists.

Mutely, Eli nods, visibly uncomfortable and taking it out on that poor napkin. I think Carmie's latching on to this breach because we've been in such an ethical gray zone all week and now we're actually getting to something that is truly black and white.

"Shit, meet fan," Jazz mutters, while sneaking an osetra-topped blin to Pee-wee, who inhales it in one fell swoop. Luna is turning her into a pet person.

Stella raises her arm as though seeking a teacher's permission to speak, causing her delicate cloisonné bracelets to clink merrily as they slide down her wrist. "I'm sorry, I don't follow what's happenin'."

"Woo, you're getting a little spicy there, *mamacita*," I say to Carmen, fanning my face. I'm trying to defuse the situation by leaning into being a big queen, just a silly dancing monkey, what I do when I'm uncomfortable, hoping that my dramatics will take everything down a few degrees.

No such luck.

"What's happening is a *clear ethical violation*. Diana, as a nurse, you should know better than anyone that discussing a patient by name and condition, even to a spouse, is against HIPAA," Carmen says, nodding with herself to emphasize her point, eyes flashing as strands of curls escape her topknot.

What Diana can't realize is that Carmen's anger is less about the HIPAA violation and more about . . . everything else we know, so Diana interprets this as a personal attack against her husband because that's what it has to feel like.

Oh, shit.

"Well, that just can't be true," Diana replies in a tone so sharp it snaps the dogs out of target-staring at the snacks. "My Petey would never violate HIPAA."

"Gurl, I know you did not just talk smack about her mans," I say, affecting an accent and mannerism to deflect Carmen reading Diana for filth. Jesus, what am I doing? I'm a caricature of my true self, just defaulting to defense mechanisms because I feel like it's all about to blow wide open.

"Except he did," Carmen argues, enunciating every syllable.

Shit.

Diana clenches her jaw. I can see the muscles in her temple working and she balls her hands into fists in her lap. "I don't believe it. You are mistaken. And I expect an apology." This is terrible and awful and I am powerless to do anything but let it unfold because sometimes you cannot unring that bell, no matter how hard you wish for it to stop reverberating.

"I'm sorry to say it, Diana, but I didn't give him permission," Eli says, sounding like she regrets even having gotten involved. "I generally keep my medical information close to the vest. Remember after I mentioned my cholesterol results to my kids? They came up here at Christmas and went on a rampage, divesting my fridge of every scrap of red meat and anything processed, as though I were no longer a sentient adult capable of moderation. Now, please, Di, I'm not mad, but I do want you to be informed so you can help educate him that that was not okay. I'm sure it was just a slip of the tongue. No harm, no foul on my account."

"No. He doesn't *need* to be educated. *You* must have given him permission. You just don't remember. Maybe your memory isn't what it once was," Diana insists as her skin flushes and color appears on her neck and chest.

"Boom goes the dynamite," Jazz whispers, more to her drink than anyone else. If Diana's kryptonite is Peter, then Eli's is anything to do with inquiries about her age or speculation on her capacity. Her dad was recently diagnosed with early-stage Alzheimer's, so she's been particularly sensitive lately.

"So, what were you saying about the Bears, Eli?" I interject, but they all ignore me. The straws, I am grasping for every one of them.

Eli is visibly upset, and she also rises from her seat. "Diana, I didn't forget. I wouldn't have said anything, but it's you who brought this up. But now that we're talking about this, you should know that Peter diagnosed my injury without any testing. No MRI, no ultrasound, no X-ray, nothing. He just poked at it and told me I needed surgery.

It feels somewhat irresponsible to not have tangible support for a diagnosis first."

Especially when we all knew her going there was a ruse! Before Diana got here, Eli told us that when she opened her statement this morning she saw that her insurance had been billed for an MRI. She did say she hoped that was in error, but what if it was intentional?

"No," Carmen says slowly, her brows knitted and hands planted on her hips. "That feels like medical malpractice."

In the history of wrong things to say, that may well have taken the cake for Diana.

Big mistake. Big. Huge.

Diana flies out of her chair like she's been ejected by a spring hidden underneath her cushion and positions herself directly in Carmen's face. At this point, I can't even catch my breath, because I don't know what to do. I want to protect Diana, but what Eli and Carmen are saying is the truth, and ultimately, the truth is what she needs. But it all sounds so harsh, not at all what we planned. Honestly, we were sort of going to hint about things and hope Diana took that bait. I didn't think we'd go *Full Metal Jacket*. Everything about this moment feels dangerous, like we're on a precipice, about to plummet into pure chaos, where we take a breath before we begin the downward plunge on a roller coaster.

Diana launches into a white-hot rage, the likes of which we haven't seen since her neighbor helped himself to the zucchini in her garden, saying they were growing over *his* property line, so they actually belonged to him. It took us weeks to talk her down, and they were just zucchini! And thanks to her special soil mix and serious green thumb, she always grows so much she can't even give them all away—it's actually one of our running jokes. Trying to be a kind neighbor, one year she placed little pyramids of zucchini on local porches and people were so freaked out, they started a Facebook post about "The Zucchini-ing," reacting as though it were a crime or a Banksy installation. People thought their homes were being marked by gangs. After that whole thing blew up, Diana was too embarrassed to just admit she was trying to be sweet.

The event made the Police Beat column in the local newspaper, because some people dialed 911 about the unexpected bundles. (Not a lot happens in her suburb, FYI.) We call her the Zucchini Bandit when we want to tease her, but this is clearly not the time.

Instead, Diana is reacting like a wounded animal who bites the hand of the one trying to administer aid. "Oh, *please*, Carmen. You're not even in the medical field anymore. You quit the minute the pandemic hit because you couldn't hack it, so I guarantee you're ill-informed. And who do you think you are, *Elinor*, to spread damaging lies about my husband? It's not *my* fault that you're jealous of what we have. It's not *my* fault that you're unhappy and alone, up here in your ridiculous castle with your ugly made-in-Belgium furniture where *you* know everything and *we peons* know nothing. Now, if you'll excuse me, the stench of your ostentatious roses is giving me a migraine, so I'm leaving." With that, she sweeps up her handbag and stomps out of the backyard, slamming open the heavy iron garden gate and banging it shut behind her.

That was definitely not in the playbook.

Chapter Nineteen

Diana

I am so . . . I don't even know. Embarrassed? Enraged? Out of sorts?

I haven't felt this angry for a long time, not for many years.

I hate this feeling and I do everything in my power to avoid it. I never want to feel like I'm powerless, like I have no say, hence my overreaction. Because it draws me back to one of the worst times of my life, one of my greatest losses. Because it was so unfair back then, and it came out of nowhere. I felt so powerless.

"Diana, that's preposterous," my dad said. "Absolutely not."

"But why?" I asked. "What's preposterous about it?" I genuinely believed it was a good idea and I had spent months putting together a plan. I wanted to get all the pieces in place so my parents would understand that I'd considered every aspect of what it would take to move abroad. I figured out how to apply for the Tier 2 visa and I made contacts over there about my Nursing and Midwifery Council registration and competency assessment. Because wasn't that what I'd been working for my entire college career?

"You can't live in England," he said. "It's out of the question."

"It's not completely without merit. She does speak the language," my mother replied. My dad gave her such a poisonous look that I instantly knew that was the first and last time she'd advocate for me.

"But I have enough money saved for my ticket. I've socked away all the money from my summer job and I have savings for at least three months' worth of living expenses, plus there's the option for me to take loans if I need them. I've already talked to recruiting agencies and I've got housing lined up. I'd be in a dorm situation with a bunch of other new nurses," I explained. I'd made a plan. I'd been meticulous. I wasn't asking for permission; I was explaining my decision. Plus, how could they blame me for wanting to get away? After everything?

"This is a pipe dream and it's out of the question. This conversation is over," he said, and then he raised his newspaper to continue reading. Because that was what we did, we just stopped talking about it. I remember trying to swallow my disappointment and vowing to myself that I'd come home after graduation, I'd study for my boards, and I'd take the job at Northwestern. I'd do it for six months, really, really save up, and then, regardless of what he said, I'd move to London because no one was getting in the way of my dream. Except they did.

I never yelled back then, never lost my temper. But maybe I should have. Maybe my parents would have had more respect for me, would have treated me like an adult. Maybe I'd be different in my adult life.

Tonight was not how I normally handle any interaction. But I felt like everyone was suddenly dogpiling on me because Eli misunderstood or misremembered a situation and no one had my back.

No one gave me—or Peter—the benefit of the doubt. Oh, no, it *had* to be that Peter got it wrong, that Peter violated his medical ethics, as though that was the most logical conclusion, the only possible explanation. Because of course The Great and Powerful Eli never makes a mistake because she is *perfect*. Elinor, the patron saint of doing everything a million times better than everyone else. She couldn't just get a damn job to support her family, nope, she had to found a public company and get a column in *Forbes*. She couldn't just be a working mom, no, she had to be the voice of working moms on *Today*. And now, she can't just run a TikTok, she has to be the social media superstar of the senior set. Why can't she simply go on walks like anyone else in the

AARP? Or do water aerobics wearing a silly rubber flower-petal bathing cap? Why is she running stupid marathons, trying to break her personal best instead of moving down to Dallas to bond with her grandchildren?

I never really thought about it before, but now that I'm allowing myself to feel my anger, I feel like the blinders have been lifted from my eyes. Suddenly, Eli's actions all seem so selfish, not as in greedy, but as in centered around *herself*. It's like her whole vibe is *Look at me*, with the loud T-shirts and the garish nail polish and the dogs that are as big as the nameless lions that flank the Art Institute entrance. She even posed them that way on the masonry columns at the front of her house and put that picture on her Christmas card. *That* was all anyone could talk about, despite my sending that gorgeous card of my whole family in front of our rental in Florida in the golden light of the magic hour, wearing those dark wash denim jeans and white shirts. Every single kid, all my nieces and nephews, were looking right at the camera and smiling, like we were pulled from a toothpaste ad! Do you know how long it took for me to get everyone in that shot? And how much effort I had to employ to seamlessly Photoshop myself into the back row when the tripod broke and I had to actually aim the camera? All Eli had to do was wave a Milk-Bone and those beasts were putty in her hands. It's not fair for me to not get the credit for having put in the work.

I've never really thought about my friends in a negative light before, but I've also never been ganged up on. I guess this is new for all of us. It never occurred to me that they wouldn't have my back. It's like, the game has all changed. Like they're suddenly playing by a different set of rules.

My mother would be quietly aghast if she had witnessed my scene. Not only did I raise my voice, but I took the Lord's name in vain. My mother was probably in the middle of a friendly game of couples' bridge at the retirement village, a cup of decaf at her side along with a couple of mint Milano cookies (one of her few indulgences), yet I bet a chill traveled down her spine.

I don't know that I've ever stormed out of anywhere before, but in an odd way, my exit made me feel . . . strong? Like a force to be reckoned with? I wonder, did I look dramatic, sweeping out of the backyard into the sunset like that? Did I leave them all with their mouths agape? Did they try to chase after me to appease me but I was too quick and too wily for them?

Why does this feel vaguely exciting?

What are they saying now? Did I render them speechless? Did they even continue their night? A part of me hopes they didn't, that they just could not function without me. I feel like it would serve them right. The vibe has shifted, and all of a sudden, I'm being excluded. The askew glances, the little touches they don't think I see. But I saw.

I've never allowed myself to wallow in my anger, but now that I've cracked the door, it's all I want to do. Like I'm having a reckoning with myself.

I love the group with my whole heart, but lately it's trending more and more to being The Eli Show, like, *Let's give Eli all the attention on Instagram* and *Let's discuss the cases that Eli approves* and *Let's bring awareness to causes Eli likes*. I mean, I know she spent a lot of years being the head honcho at her company, but someone needs to inform her that she is not the boss of the group. She is not our superior. We are an autonomous collective. This isn't *Animal Farm*; no pigs are more equal than others.

I'm just so mad that they're all jumping to Eli's side and not giving Peter the benefit of the doubt. I know he's imperfect, but I don't *cast aspersions* on their significant others. I don't accuse Gavin of malfeasance when he works late with yet another "IPO." I don't denigrate Juan for spending all that money on his odd model railroad passion, especially now that Carmen isn't even bringing in an income. Are the overalls and the conductor's cap really necessary? I suspect they aren't. I don't fault Abe for fanning the flames of Stella's narcissism. And Jazmin? I don't laugh at her dream of finding love on what's *literally the worst show on television*! *Love Island* is where the contestants go when they flush the toilet on other reality TV programs. Yet I support them all wholeheartedly; where's the reciprocation?

How dare Carmen accuse Peter of wrongdoing without any of the facts? Medical malpractice? Them's fightin' words! Carmen thinks because she's the quiet one that she's *so* much more observant than the rest of us, that her still waters run so much deeper. She didn't even observe *anything*, yet she's so blinded by what she perceives as her own keen intuition that nothing else could possibly be true. If A, then B. That is reckless in my book.

Maybe *she's* the one who's malpracticing.

What's more is that *this is not what we do in our group*! This is not how we pursue a hypothesis. We gather evidence and we pore over each kernel of information and form the outer skeleton of the puzzle before we try to fill in the center. We don't bash a random piece into a spot that sort of looks like it *could* fit. It's not how jigsaw puzzles work! Did Nancy Drew or Trixie Belden go around accusing everyone before they had their facts straight? Absolutely not! Even Scooby-Doo and the rest of the gang in the Mystery Machine had worked out the entire timeline before they pulled the mask off the person who'd have gotten away with it had it not been for those meddling kids!

I know deep in my core that Peter would never behave in a way that wasn't professional. If he weren't trustworthy, I'd have never unburdened my soul to him. He's never once brought it up either—never once. He's had my back, so now I need to have his.

He's worked too hard to get to where he is, and he's finally now reaping the benefits of that sweat equity, so I certainly don't begrudge those little luxuries he's been buying himself. He has earned them. When he asked me if I wanted to upgrade my car, I said no because status isn't important to me, unlike some people, *Eli*. You know what? I'm not even going to ask him about the "alleged" incident because it will seem like I don't believe him and I don't want to put him into one of his sulks.

And the last thing I want him to do is question me, not after all this time.

I have been in such a lather since driving away, so deep in my thoughts and feelings, that I almost miss my exit at 79th Street. Ha! Wouldn't *that* be something, getting lost on the way back home? Peter would laugh so hard at me! He already thinks I'm such a scatterbrain, and he may not be wrong. Like when those new credit cards arrived in my maiden name last year? I was like, *Is this identity theft?* But Peter explained how I must have applied for them when I was taking that prescription sleep aid when perimenopause was keeping me awake all night. I finally stopped taking the pills, thinking I would rather be tired than reckless. What if I'd tried to get behind the wheel? I've read stories about people on Ambien taking themselves to the grocery store! How dangerous would I be on the road? And . . . what if I were to accidentally talk about things in the past that I would rather keep quiet? Who hasn't made a mistake or been forced to make a call that they came to regret? What a fine kettle of fish *that* would be if I suddenly started blabbing! There's just some stuff that should stay in the vault for everyone's benefit. What's done is done and I can't change history, even if I wanted to.

I realize that I've been gripping the steering wheel so hard that my knuckles are white. I take my right hand off the two o'clock position and shake it, and then I switch sides to get the blood flowing again. I feel a rush of relief.

I always felt such peace when I'd pull onto our block. Serenity would wash over me. Like, no matter what else is happening in the world, it would be so good to arrive at my oasis of calm, my happy place. This is the kind of block where we rope off the street, set up folding tables, and gather with potluck dishes a couple of times a year. But woe betide the *next one* who puts raisins in the potato salad, *ahem*, Amy S. *That* is a crime in my book. This abomination isn't the only reason Amy S. and her husband Drake don't receive my world-famous tray of hot cross buns at Easter, but it's definitely a contributing factor.

If they truly wanted to be better neighbors, they wouldn't flout the HOA rule about dragging out their bins so early. Sometimes they'll do it two days before pickup! And they're not even on vacation! And why do they even have so much recycling? If I wanted to look at garbage cans all day, I'd move back to that terrible condo in the city.

And right now, as I cruise into what should be my happy place, I don't feel anything, and *that* feels like a problem.

I click the opener for the garage, which yawns open at a leisurely pace, and I'm surprised to see that Peter's car isn't here. I let myself in through the garage door and I'm immediately swarmed by the cats demanding a second dinner. I'm glad that Jazz applied to adopt Luna, but she was such a sweet kitty that I'm sure I'd have been a foster fail yet again with her. Even though I know they're such little liars, I open a can of extra stinky Blue Buffalo and portion it out into all of their dishes in the mudroom, and they immediately dive in, completely forgetting me, which doesn't hurt my feelings at all.

"Why are you here?" is how Lilly greets me. She's digging a soup spoon into a jar of Nutella and spreading the paste on saltines, which are flaking all over the place. She's clad in a pair of Lululemon Align high-rise shorts, a sweatshirt with the neckline cut out so it bares one shoulder, and the kind of ultra-scrunchy socks that I thought went out of style in the 1990s. But everything comes back eventually, right? Sometimes it's a little disquieting looking at her, because it's like seeing myself thirty years ago, from her long legs to her bee-stung pout to how the edges of her eyes tilt up, although she's taller and thinner than I ever was. (Peter says that's his genetics, despite having no idea what I looked like at fifteen.) She even has highlights in all the places that I had mine, particularly at her temples and along her center part. ("Never a side part, argh, God, Mom," as Lilly would say.) People used to ask me, "Who did your hair color?" since there were so many shades of blonde melding together, from dark honey to platinum, and I'd always say, "My parents!" That would be *my* Scandinavian genetics, thank you very much.

"Hey, Bunny Rabbit, I'm glad to see you too," I say, going in for a hug that she neatly sidesteps in one fluid movement. Is there anything worse than when your kids grow out of welcoming your hugs and kisses? At least Ethan is still amenable to a quick squeeze, but I make sure I never do it in front of his friends. "Where's Daddy?"

She rolls her eyes. "I imagine *your* daddy is at the old people home with Grandma."

I'm too spent to engage her. "Fine. I mean, where is Peter?"

Through a mouthful of saltine shards, she says, "Out."

"I gathered that." I grab a paper towel, dampen it, and sweep the crumbs into the sink. "Did he say where he was going?"

"He said he was going somewhere. He was in a hurry."

Why is she so obstinate with me? I feel like I did everything right with her, giving her boundaries but also space. Being interested in her life, but not showing exactly how invested I am, lest that cause undue pressure. I go along with her ideas and I support her every interest, even though she's quick to abandon them, especially if she thinks I'm too enthusiastic. The garage sale I could have with everything she couldn't live without and now couldn't care less about. But God forbid I try to sell the acoustic guitar, the Rollerblades, those creepy marionettes that scare me every time I run across them in the basement. And do not even get me started on the faulty ant farm that necessitated not one but two visits from Terminix and her screaming that we were murdering "her babies!" the entire time. Yet when her dad asks her a question? He gets a dissertation in return. I'm lucky if I get a thumbs-up emoji, which Jazz insists is aggressive.

"That is very useful info, thank you," I tell Lilly with a wry shake of my head. Someone somewhere has a magical formula to get details out of their teenage daughters, and whoever shares it is going to get quite rich. For me, talking to Lilly is like trying to pry secrets out of the Taliban.

"He had a bag with him."

Hmm. He must have another medical emergency. Sometimes he does have to scoot off with no notice, like when there's a bus crash and he has to stay at the hospital. When those bleachers collapsed at that soccer game a few years ago, he was gone for three days. It was harrowing! I never bother him when he goes, because he says I'll hear from him when I hear from him and that's just the on-call life of a doctor's wife . . . isn't it?

Then it dawns on me that the kids are home alone. Lilly is old enough to be by herself, but not when Ethan's here because I'm afraid she'll be her usual degree of mean to him and he's pretty sensitive. I like to bring in a neutral third party. "Wait, did he leave you guys with a sitter?" I ask. "Who's in charge?"

Lilly gives the spoon a lick and me a withering look. "Are you freaking kidding me? You do know I'm almost sixteen, right? There are girls in my class on the pill."

"Uh-huh, and they don't have mothers who care so much about their well-being," I reply, sweeping her hair out of her face. I'd like to think they're on birth control because those girls have difficult periods, but even I'm not that naive. "Do you want me to make you a real dinner?" Lilly shakes off my touch.

"This was a real dinner. Since you're home early, you can be in charge of the mutant upstairs. I'm going to Mara's. Bye-ee." She drops the dirty spoon next to the sink and saunters off, leaving the jar uncapped, the silverware drawer open, and a half-empty sleeve of saltines on the counter. She slides into a pair of battered Birkenstock Bostons (because showing your toes is apparently "disgusting" to Gen Z and should be "preserved for selling feet pics") and leaves out the side door before I can get in another word.

"Sure," I mutter to myself as I tidy up. "Let me get that for you, Bunny Rabbit."

Lilly used to want to be around me. We'd have such fun mother-daughter times where we'd leave the boys together and we'd go shopping or get our nails done. Oh, the matching outfits we'd don! We'd go to that place she liked for crepes and hot chocolates. Now she says that chocolate is "disgusting" (spoiler alert: Everything is "disgusting") despite the dent she just made in the Nutella jar. When she hit her tweens, that was it, I was *out* like yesterday's sushi. I don't know what changed between us. That's why it was so gratifying to connect with the group. They filled an emptiness I didn't realize I'd had.

But now who knows what's going to happen with me and them? We've never had words, never once, and I feel vaguely nauseated about it. I need one safe space, one place I can just *be*. My home was that until it wasn't, and then the group was that. At this point, I feel like Sandra Bullock in that astronaut movie, just launched into space, untethered, and it's terrifying.

I have to do something to ground myself, so I'm fixing myself a pimento cheese sandwich on toasty brioche bread—the ultimate comfort food—when Ethan pads down the back stairs. He rewards me with a grin that lights up his whole freckled face. His cheeks are still round and he has a layer of baby fat that I'm in no hurry for him to outgrow. I don't know what I'll do when he finally gets taller than me. (Therapy, probably—ha!)

"Hey! Mom!! You're home so early. Did you not have fun with your friends?" He sweeps me into a side hug and he smells like that fabric softener I specially order from Amazon because it's a Le Labo dupe. When he squeezes me, it feels like my heart just got a full recharge and it's at 100 percent again.

Ethan is the definition of what any mother would call a "good boy." He's the kind of kid who not only knows when it's his school bus driver's birthday but also will bring him a cupcake and a card. Peter insists Ethan's "socially awkward" because he's not one of the popular kids like Lilly, but I vehemently disagree. While he's not athletic—Peter was mortified by his whole T-ball performance a few years back—his social IQ is off the charts. That is why he's so good talking to other adults. Sometimes I have to remind Jazz that he's not her peer and to please cool it with the swearing. Ethan will look every grown-up in the eye, ask them questions about themselves, and actually listen to their answers. He has a deep empathy.

I often worry about Lilly, like I'm afraid she'd literally get into anyone's van for the promise of Taylor Swift tickets, but I never have a moment of doubt about Ethan. If anyone's going to make this world a better place, going to make good decisions, it's him. He's not one to follow the herd. When every other boy his age is shivering in their basketball shorts and soccer slides in the winter, Ethan is smart enough to don a down parka, snow boots, and heavy jeans. When I remarked that it's Ethan who's truly "sigma" among all those freezing cold lemmings, Lilly forbade me to ever use that word again.

"Tonight was an off night," I tell him with a casual shrug. "It happens." While he's a willing ear, he's still my son and I'm not going to burden him with what's weighing on my mind. Your children are not your friends, and if you treat them that way, they end up never moving out of your basement, *Carmen*. (Hmph, still mad.)

"Since you're home, do you want to watch *Dancing with the Stars*? It's jive night and I've been saving it for you-ou," he singsongs as he does a rock turn and extends a hand, inviting me to join him on the dance floor. I take it and he spins me around once and we both collapse with laughter.

Ethan isn't great at catching or throwing any sporty-type projectile, but he did excel in ballroom dancing when they taught a section of it in gym class. Obviously, that kind of extracurricular activity was never going to fly with Peter, so Ethan is resigned to being a fan and not an active participant. Yet given how smooth that spin was, I suspect he practices moves with YouTube videos. While I argued that Peter was crushing Ethan's spirit by not letting him pursue lessons, Peter was so adamant that he'd be ostracized by his peers that I finally had to admit he might have a point.

"Shall I make us some popcorn?" I ask.

"You just read my mind," he says.

"Sweet and salty, spicy, or savory?"

"Dealer's choice," he says. He scrolls through the TV guide and I notice there's a new Idris Elba show and I make a mental note of it. I like Idris Elba. *A lot.* He reminds me of Justin. He thought I hung the moon. He always treated me like I was a prize that he couldn't believe he'd had the luck to win. He went off to London to study architecture when we graduated. For a hot minute, I thought I'd follow him, figuring I could be a nurse anywhere, but my dad was not having it, and I wonder exactly how much rage I've suppressed about this over the years. Justin broke up with me shortly afterward. It didn't make sense for us to stay together if I wasn't going to move there. It took me a long time to come to peace with being stuck in the States. Four years to be exact, and only because I met Peter and finally had a reason to revise what I'd foreseen as my life's plan.

❧

Justin and I are Facebook friends now. Every year, he remembers to wish me a happy birthday before the notification system has to remind him. He married an elegant French lady and his family is stunningly beautiful, so I'm confident it all worked out like it should have. I never picture the life I might have had in London, which I try to convince myself is way too far from home, even though distance is probably just what I've always needed. Instead, I'm exactly where everyone else thinks I should be, living how they'd anticipated. No surprises is what everyone wants, or at least that's what I have to tell myself. Sometimes I wonder if I were to start letting it out, if I were to really act out, would I get into my car and just start driving? For so long, Peter was my escape, yet now in the dark hours of the night, I worry that he's what I need to escape, yet it's not anything I've been able to put into words.

But I can't let myself go down that path; it feels too dangerous, so I decide to focus on the moment in front of me, being appreciative of what I have and where I am.

Ethan and I chat while I make my famous savory buttered popcorn, which includes a generous heap of shaved parm and a sprinkle of paprika. Decadent! I serve it in a wide, carved wooden salad bowl and carry pint glasses of ice and cans of Orange Crush to the coffee table, a beverage that appalls Peter and Lilly. They say it tastes like chewable children's vitamins, which, yes, is exactly the point of it.

Ethan presses play, but before the show starts, he pauses. "Hey, will you please do me a favor?"

"Anything for you, pal!" I settle into the pillows and I click on the remote to our gas fireplace. It starts with a tremendous whoosh. It might get a little warm in here, but it makes the room so cozy, and I just want to be in the moment right now because everything else feels chaotic, between Peter's moodiness and now my fight with my friends. Lured in as though moths to the flame, the cats materialize and arrange themselves on the hearth, their fuzzy bellies aimed toward the heat source.

Ah, I need this. I relax into the couch and exhale.

Eyes focused on the screen, he asks, "Mom? Do you mind picking me up some more athletic socks? I seem to be running low for some reason."

Nooooooo!

Whatever happened at the hospital must have been a big deal because Peter still isn't home and it's getting pretty late. As of now, I still haven't heard from anyone, including Peter. I don't expect him anytime soon, because his bag is gone, but it would be nice if he'd actually reach out and tell me all was well.

As for the group, I guess I expected that the apologies would be coming in hard and fast, especially because I feel like I was the victim there. That has to be the case. Peter wouldn't have done something unethical . . . right? I wouldn't be surprised if Carmen were to drop off her "please-forgive pasteles" tomorrow, something she always makes for Juan when they have a squabble. (Probably about the overalls, ha!) I'll be magnanimous and forgive everyone, of course; that's what I do.

Almost as if on cue, the doorbell rings and I feel a small rush of excitement. How should I play this? Most likely I'll end up being the one who apologizes, even though I'm not entirely sure I did anything wrong, but that's just how I am. (Okay, maybe I had some mean thoughts right afterward, but I didn't share them.)

Lilly says I'm so much like Grandma, that I throw "I'm sorry" around like a high-rolling Vegas gambler on a hot streak throws around tips. She got so mad at me for apologizing when that lady sideswiped us in the Target parking lot last year. She was all, "Stop being a doormat, Mom, God! Why won't you just speak up?" She was so disgusted by my lack of fight, but she doesn't understand that making a scene changes nothing. It only serves to ruffle feathers and makes everything harder. And it didn't seem worth it to me to fight or collect that driver's insurance info. That poor lady seemed so harried and I didn't want to add to her burdens.

But with the group, I simply reacted like someone does when they're cornered and unjustly accused. As my dad explained after . . . everything with my uncle, sometimes people are desperate and they say or do desperate things and you have to extend them some grace, some benefit of the doubt, even if you find out later that was the wrong call. Maybe you were trying to be kind and you didn't know the extenuating circumstances until it was too late. As a penance, you spend your whole adult life trying to atone, trying to be so good that your bad decision doesn't matter. That can't be so unusual. I may even be willing to tell Carmen that we should move on, so we never have to revisit the incident. Honestly, my mother's method has merit and I'd rather the unpleasantness be in the rearview mirror, even if it does leave me with a metaphorical dented fender.

I try to arrange my face into an expression that's welcoming and willing when I open the front door, anticipating seeing Carmen's wild hair, somber expression, and a foil-wrapped platter. She must have gone directly home to make them. I bet if I ask now, she may actually feel so contrite for being harsh and accusatory that she finally gives me her recipe. I've tried to deconstruct the pasteles, but there's something complicated about the masa base, a flavor I can't quite decipher, and I even went to a Latin market to pick up the achiote oil she uses. Mine are pretty good, not to sound boastful, but if I had Carmen's recipe, they could be great, especially because I would make my knots around the banana leaf more decorative than just a basic, boring tie closure. I take a breath before turning the knob, then I swing it open to—

A guy in a suit who looks like a Fed.

What is happening here?

Chapter Twenty

Eli

I can't stop thinking about what happened earlier.

None of us moved as Diana hurled open her car door and peeled out down the driveway.

"Oh, my stars and stripes," Stella said. "Should we go after her?"

"Please, the way she screamed out of here, she's already on the Edens," Frankie replied.

"Just me, or did she react like a rat trapped in a coffee can?" Jazz asked as she fed Pee-wee a piece of sausage, which he took gently and chewed more delicately than his brother, because *he* is a real gentleman.

"That was not our Diana," I said. "She must be under so much stress to react like that. It was like she was possessed. Please don't be mad at her, don't judge her—that's not who she is. We need to be empathetic."

"*Mierda*, I need to calm down before I talk to her again. Denigrating my credentials? That was below the belt. I stopped working because I thought it more important to help my boys get through virtual high school. And that's not stress she's showing us, that's *delusion*," Carmen said. She was clearly still furious, which was just as disquieting to see as Diana losing it. "And however it is we're planning to make Peter pay?

We need to make a decision. Whatever this is must stop because she's being triggered by something he's doing."

Stella raised her hand again, waiting for someone to call on her. When no one did, she said, "Wait, we're not shootin' him, right? You did say 'trigger.'"

"Of course not!" I exclaimed. "That would make us as bad as the criminals we discuss. And how is that an option? No one here even has a gun."

"Right. Right, right, right. Of course we don't," Stella said, sheepish, eyes cutting over to her enormous tapestry handbag at her side.

"Stell-Belle . . . do *you* have a gun?" Frankie asked.

"Well, I don't *not* have a gun," she admitted, and I think we were all floored. "What? Don't give me those left-wing looks. I've been hunting with my daddy since I was knee-high to a grasshopper. It's like having a bicycle where I'm from, or carrying a spare tire in the car. Y'all won't know when you need it until you need it, so y'all better always have it."

"Can I see it? Can I hold it?" Frankie asked, sliding into the seat next to her.

"No, you may not see or hold it," Stella said, grasping her bag to her chest. "You're not licensed, you're not trained, and you're not sober."

"Gurl, please. I've had, like, three White Russians," he replied.

"Exactly my point. I am not going to be responsible for y'all shootin' off a toe and then complaining about not being able to wear cute shoes anymore," Stella said. "Don't want to be hobbling around in Chucks all the time, no offense meant, Eli. You know how fussy this one is." She gestured to me with a raise of her chin.

"That is the least of my worries tonight, Stella," I replied, and I realized I was wringing my napkin for all it was worth.

Jazz's laugh came out like a bark, so loud it scared the dogs. They galloped off toward the house, still managing to leave piles of fur in their wake despite their fresh grooming. "Hold up. Stella, you brought a *gun* to a *garden* party. You're assuming a dubious slice of moral high ground right about now."

"Well, I'm not *shootin'* him," Stella reiterated, as though it were a legitimate strategy that we'd been debating.

"Of course we're not shooting anyone," I said. "But what *are* we doing?"

As it turns out, we spoke a little too soon about not shooting anyone.

❦

"Honestly, I'm glad she left. Now I can tell you guys the full extent of what's up. No more dancing around it and you're not gonna like it," Jazz says, whipping out her laptop, plonking it on my quartz-topped breakfast bar, and rolling up her sleeves. "It is *fucked* to the *up*. You guys don't even know the half of what I found out this afternoon. This is an episode of *Dateline*. We have kicked a hornet's nest, and the hornet with the biggest prick is Peter."

"Ugh. Ironically, I have zero interest in Peter's prick. That is how unattractive he is to me," Frankie says, curling his lip as though smelling sour milk. He stress eats a slice of the dense brown pumpernickel bread I bought at Yuri's place, spread with a generous topping of the vibrant orange shredded carrot and cheese salad he sells. The combination is far more delicious than it should be, given its humble ingredients. "Look at all the carbs I'm inhaling. This is dire."

Carmen wipes away a fat tear, smearing her mascara. "All I want to do is go after Diana, I feel awful. I hate seeing her upset. Should I call her? Should I text her? What if I made her my please-forgive pasteles? I can't have this. I can't have her feeling like we ganged up when we're trying to protect her. Can we just level with her, give her all the information, let her judge our actions, and allow the chips to fall where they may? I would rather lose her as a friend than see her hurting." Carmen always feels everything the most deeply, although I'm right there with her now. Maybe this is why I've avoided romantic entanglements—anything even vaguely smacking of a breakup is just terrible.

That's what this feels like: a breakup.

"Honey, I know it's temptin' to say sorry and to make it all better, but we have to fix the problem right now. We've gotta cauterize this wound or she's gonna bleed plumb out. There's no getting past this if we don't stop him in his tracks. If this were truly a *Dateline* episode, then you know good and durn well there's a legitimate chance our girl is in some danger. We've studied too many people like Peter to not know that this could get real ugly real easily. *That* is what bad men do. They don't face the consequences, they make their inadequacies everyone else's problem," Stella says, pulling on Carmen's sleeve to stop her pacing. Stella pulls out the barstool next to her and pats it, coaxing Carmen to sit down.

Stella's not wrong. I swear, half of the cases we follow are where the husband screws up and the family pays the price for his greed or hubris. Addiction, financial ruin, indiscretions, it's *never* the wife's fault but *always* her problem. That's how we got here, meaning becoming a group, thanks to the whole John Davidson Karlsson business. It's almost *always* the husband. "Jazz, please enlighten us," I request.

"So we've been trying to figure out what that storefront is, right? Well, I tapped into some records—"

I stop her. "If you explain, are we accessories to a crime?"

Jazz nods vigorously. "Oh, 100 percent, so let's just say I 'took some liberties.' The little storefront is a medical supplies facility. At first glance, it makes some sense that Peter's involved in selling wheelchairs and walkers, right? People have hip replacements, people have their ACLs repaired, and then they need durable medical equipment to help them be mobile. Crutches and shit. And it even makes sense that he wouldn't do this out of his main office because DME is totally down-market. It's the unsexiest part of health care. If surgeons are the quarterbacks in the whole medical hierarchy, medical supplies are the freshmen picking up everyone's sweaty jockstraps in the locker room to run them to the laundry."

"That is quite the visual," Carmen says.

"It's a gift. Anyway, what's weird is that they don't move a lot of wheelchairs or walkers, according to records I found through *entirely legitimate sources*. Ahem. But they move a shit-ton of catheters. You know, the stuff that goes up your blowhole to help you pee?" Jazz clarifies.

"We're familiar," I say, even though Stella seems confused. I tell her, "You do not want details."

"Cool. Guess how much they billed the government for catheters last year? No, don't guess, it will take too long. Let's just say there's a lot of zeros. A. Lot. Peter's rolling in fancy watches now? This is why," Jazz says.

"How is he cornering the market on catheters?" Frankie asks, stuffing more bread in his maw. "He's not a urologist. Or a gynecologist. I mean, that hole is not in his purview."

Jazz whips off her nonprescription cat-eye glasses that she wears specifically so she can whip them off when she wants to make a point dramatically. "Right. That's why he's billing for catheters, but he's not *providing* catheters."

Now everyone looks confused. "He's committing Medicare fraud?" I ask, seeking clarification. I thought that could be the case when I saw what I was billed for, but I was so hoping to give him the benefit of the doubt.

"Ding, ding, ding! And Medicaid. He's suckling off the taxpayer's teat. But wait! There's more!" Jazz says. She spins her laptop around so we can see the Excel sheet she made, detailing the bogus charges. She scrolls and the numbers go on for pages and pages. I feel my stomach lurch. Oh, Diana, you don't deserve this if it's true. The evidence is damning if it's true, and the dollar amounts are staggering. But how do we really know?

Frankie clutches his head and cries, "Ugh, no! Damn it, Diana! Wait, how are people not checking their bills? No one's going to be like, 'Why do I need a catheter when I have strep throat?'"

Jazz puts her glasses back on. "When was the last time you opened an insurance claim and scanned the CPT codes? Let me answer that for you, you didn't because it would give you boredom cancer. Your insurance covered most of whatever you had done and then you just paid your deductible because you figure they know what they're doing, right? They bank on you not looking, and if you do look and it's wrong, they're all, 'My bad!' But they're counting on it just getting paid. In your case, you probably just handed your bill over to Gavin. You're on his insurance now?"

Frankie nods. That was a big step for him because he's so commitment shy. When Gavin offered to put him on his coverage as a domestic partner, Frankie freaked out. He almost broke up with Gavin because he said signing his name on that paperwork made him feel confined. Poor Frankie was so conditioned to being in bad relationships that it didn't occur to him that one could be good. (I wonder if I haven't been just as commitment phobic as Frankie, only because it was so good before that I can't imagine it ever happening again.)

Moving into Gavin's loft felt like overcoming a major hurdle, and he didn't fully unpack for the first six months. He lived out of suitcases and boxes instead of sharing the space that Gavin had made for him. It was Diana who helped Gavin navigate their tenuous relationship, saying to treat Frankie like you would a rescue cat and slowly entice him and introduce new things so he wouldn't get spooked and hide behind the radiator. And that's just one of the million things that Diana has done for all of us, which is why we're vehement about having her back. I say, "I mean, *I* check the insurance and I look up the codes. That's why I questioned being billed for the MRI, as well as the hour consult when it was maybe ten minutes. But I also dissected financials for a living and I may be an outlier."

Jazz boops me on the nose. "Oh, Eli. It's so fun that you think you're typical of anything. Point? Medicare typically loses $60 billion per year due to fraud and abuse. With a *buh* and not a *muh*. Given what we know about Peter, it stands to reason that he'd get tired of following the rules, tired of not being the exceptional snowflake his mommy always told him he was, and he'd find a shortcut. Diana said by the time he graduated, he had something like $300,000 in school loans."

"You know what?" Frankie adds. "You might be onto something. When Gavin and I were talking about maybe looking at bigger places, she mentioned that they overspent on their house because they got one of those special doctor's mortgages where they ignore your student debt and they lend you a boatload because they assume you're good for it. Big house, close to the city, highly rated school district? That's a lot of checks to write every month, you know?"

I do some back-of-the-envelope math. "Let's run the numbers. We'll say he owed $300,000 in loans. He probably initially borrowed in the early 2000s when he started med school, and I think the interest rates were around 8.25 percent, give or take a point or so. Maybe he was able to defer the loans until he finished his fellowship ten years later, which means he'd end up paying back an extra $141,000 because the interest would keep accruing."

"That's where they get ya. They just bend y'all right over," Stella adds. "For a ten-year loan, that'd bring the total payback amount to about $441,549. We're looking at about 32 percent interest, 68 percent principal, give or take."

Frankie blinks at Stella. "Sometimes I forget you're Math Barbie."

I grab a pen and scratch pad from the kitchen desk to record my figures, as Stella and I work this out together. I say, "So we're talking about a monthly payment around $3,679, straight off the top, before they pay a single bill, buy a load of groceries, gas up the car, splurge on a kid's camp, or cover the cost of their mortgage. Oh, and we didn't even talk about all the renovations they did, so they have a HELOC too."

"Mmm-hmm. Gourmet kitchen, three top-o'-the-line bathrooms, finishing the basement. Probably another $200,000, and if that's spread over ten years, we're looking at a little under $270,000 after 3.5 percent interest, adding another $2,244 each month. Oh, my gosh, I sure do hope they refinanced everything when the rates were so low during the pandy," Stella adds.

I say, "Okay, then you look at the capital expenditures to start up a private practice, which can run anywhere from $100,000 to $300,000, although the interest rates were a lot lower when he'd have borrowed those funds, as opposed to the student loans."

Stella nods. "Don't forget medical malpractice insurance, which I believe is higher for his specialty."

"And of course, will depend on his claims history," I add. "But let's say it's $200,000, although I bet it's more like $250,000 if he ever does spines. Does he do spines? Eh, doesn't matter. Who'd pay for this? Him or his practice? Or are the funds comingled? Regardless, until all their loans are satisfied, I'd say their monthly nut is a minimum of $25,000, and that's without a cent put toward savings or investments."

Dead silence, but not surprising. That kind of debt does feel like a heavy burden.

"I'm sorry, did you two just do that math in your heads?" Frankie asks, blinking hard.

"I wrote it down," I say, holding up my pad.

"I did it in my head." Stella shrugs. "What, like it's hard?"

Jazz insists, "My original point remains—sounds like he's leveraged AF."

"Should we set up a GoFundMe so they can keep livin' indoors?" Stella asks, helping herself to the piece of the layered honey cake that Yuri promised would be life-changing when I'd tried it at his shop. He was right. She takes a bite and closes her eyes in ecstasy. "And what is this and why have I never had it before? I would leave Abe and marry this durn cake right now, and I am not kidding."

I try to play devil's advocate, even though every fiber of my being is convinced Jazz is right about Peter being in over his head financially. I dealt with companies in trouble every day, and he's exhibiting all the same signs of stress as the execs I tried to help, only now I don't have the luxury of being a detached professional about it. "Having a lot of debt doesn't make you a criminal. If that were the case, all of Gen Z would be out pulling bank jobs. The real crime here is what you kids are having to pay for an education these days. One of the only reasons I made it after I lost Hank is because college was cheap in the 1980s and no one graduated with debilitating debt. Our current system is broken."

"Put *that* on the words of wisdom you post on your mornin' *Elinspiration*," Stella says, licking the tines of her fork after finishing her cake.

Jazz says, "Not gonna argue that. But, listen, remember when Peter bragged to us about cheating on his taxes, laughing about all those fake deductions he claimed? He went on and on. And when he talked about shaving those points off his handicap? Why would that even matter? But it did somehow. Point is, the man has a tenuous relationship with doing the right thing. Right thing? Never met her. And if he's willing to admit the quiet things out loud to people who are essentially strangers to him, what is he doing behind closed doors?"

"Zlata?" Carmen gasps and slaps a hand over her mouth. "*Mierda*, that slipped out. I'm sorry."

"What he's doing behind closed doors is burned into my damn retinas," Stella grumbles, scrubbing at her eyes.

"He is untethered and that makes him unstable, and unstable is scary AF for a spouse or domestic partner," Jazz insists. "That's our thesis statement. And I haven't even told you the worst part."

I glance down at my pad and I brace myself against the breakfast bar. "There's more?"

"Oh, girl. You're gonna wish you were the you from ten minutes ago when I tell you this next part," Jazz promises. She stretches her arms out in front of her and cracks her back, warming up for the big reveal as she pulls up a new screen. "Lemme tell you a little something I learned on the dark web. Spoiler alert? It involves the Russians. Lemme tell you all about the pill mill Dr. Peter Pulaski has been running."

❦

CEO mode engaged; it's time to take out the trash. As decisive as I feel, I am having trouble shaking the coincidence of meeting a Russian guy outside Peter's storefront. Wouldn't that be something, if I finally meet someone and it turns out he's a criminal? Then my kids really would put me in a home. I'd like the luxury of replaying our meeting in the parking lot again and again, but there's no time right now. I have to silo that off, compartmentalize, and focus on the problem at hand.

No matter what, our decision is made. We must stop talking and start acting. We've hemmed and hawed enough. We've only been together a few hours tonight, but it already feels like a lifetime has passed. I tell the group, "We cannot keep saying we're going to make Peter pay and not follow through. Our poor Diana is imploding, if tonight's behavior is any indication. That man is going under and he's trying to use her as his flotation device. We need to roll. We know where he is. We know what he's doing."

"We know who he's doing," Carmen says and then gasps. "Augh! I have to stop saying this stuff! What is wrong with me?"

"Follow me to the garage," I say. I start walking and notice they're still sitting there in the kitchen, shocked, taking it all in. "I meant now, please."

"Should I bring the bread?" Frankie asks, looking at the counter full of delicious Russian snacks. "Yeah, this is a lot to process. We need more carbs. I'm going to bring the bread."

We weave through the breakfast nook, the butler's pantry, and my house manager's office before we get to the mudroom that leads to the garage. "This place is big as a durn shopping mall. Sometimes I forget you're rich," Stella says. "You're just too normal."

"Thank you? I don't know how to respond to that. So, this is part one of our plan," I say as I start unfastening straps and tugging at the canvas car cover on the vehicle on the far end of the garage by the workbench. Oh, would Hank have loved having a garage with a workbench! The worst part of his aneurysm is that we had no notice. I would never have wished him to be sick, but if he'd had an illness, we'd have had some emotional runway. We'd have been a little more prepared. We could have braced ourselves. We could have said our final words. As it was, I handed him his travel mug of coffee, kicked around the idea of a pizza for dinner, and then kissed him goodbye and never saw him alive again. Even now, it feels so wrong. His death was so sudden, so unfair, that I've spent the last thirty years trying to accomplish his goals as well as mine.

I guess that's made me a bit of a machine.

"Um . . . what the actual hell is this?" Frankie asks, his eyes as round as saucers as I finish removing the dustcover from my second car.

"Have you never seen an automobile before?" I ask. "They have a gas combustion engine and they go zoom zoom, thanks to all that dinosaur juice."

Dead silence. Sometimes I worry my sense of humor is too esoteric. (I should work that line into a social media post and see if anyone else gets it.)

I continue, "I was thinking, my SUV is in desperate need of a vacuum, and Jazz's and Carmen's cars are too small for the five of us, so I thought we'd be most comfortable going to confront Peter in this." After we headed inside, we came up with a plan to go down there and threaten him enough to make him fly right. We're not going to be violent, but our plan is to imply the violence, like when you see people pretend to have a gun in their pocket when they rob a donut shop. We want to intimidate him and catch it on video so we can use that footage against him, posting his humiliation on the internet. Stella and Jazz gamed it all out for us, and it seemed plausible and immediate, like her life could be in danger right this minute, so here we go. There's no Chris Watts on our watch.

As I unclasp, I notice four sets of eyes staring back at me. "I can see from the looks on your faces, you require more explanation. The short of it is, I am solving a problem that none of you yet realized we might have. That's kind of my forte. It's why all of *this* exists," meaning the perceived excesses of my life.

"Yeah, no, I'm familiar with the concept of a motor vehicle. What's giving me pause is you *whipping out the car that Kennedy was assassinated in*," Frankie replies, running a paint-stained fingertip down one of its long, shiny fins. "Poof. Out of thin air."

"Why is this a surprise? This thing has been garaged the entire time I've known you guys. If you've ever come to the fridge out here for a Fresca, you've walked past it. I've had it for years, I just don't drive it very much. And FYI, Kennedy was assassinated in a Lincoln Continental," I reply as I wipe a chamois across the wide bench seats so we don't get dusty. Full disclosure: I've become a bit of a gearhead in my dotage. "*This* is a Cadillac Eldorado. Entirely different manufacturer and entirely different decade, for that matter."

"Y'all weren't alive for the Kennedy assassination, were you?" Stella asks. "Mee-maw still talks about it. She said one day she turned on the TV and saw the president get shot, so she never turned it off." In sotto voce she adds, "It's kind of a problem, if y'all want to know the truth."

"Of course Eli wasn't alive. That was, like, eighty years ago," Frankie says. "She's not that ancient."

"Unfortunately, I am," I say, and I feel every year of it at the moment, after everything we've learned tonight. I actually would like a Werther's Original followed by a nap, but that's not an option right now. A cardigan and a low-stakes game of *Wheel of Fortune*? Sign me up. "I was a toddler and I don't have much, if any, memory of it, but I was around. Growing up, the assassination was very fresh in everyone's mind. That truth was a constant presence, as it changed everything. Then it was RFK who was killed, then MLK Jr. Really, Stella, no one could take their eyes off the news for a while."

"Bad time to have a *K* last name, it sounds like," Stella says.

"You know it was the Russians behind it, right? You don't buy that Lee Harvey Oswald shit," Jazz says. She opens a package of Zyn and offers them around. No takers. She shoves one in her mouth. "Two words—grassy knoll."

Carmen laughs. "Jazz, that's who you blame for *everything*. And while you may be right about most of it, including maybe Peter, in the case of JFK, the Warren Commission begs to differ."

"Who?" Jazz asks. I have to smile to myself—kids.

"What confuses me is, why was there a building there to deposit *books*? Was it like a bank? For books? Isn't that called a library? That never did make a lick of sense," Stella says. "Y'all ever seen a book depository elsewhere? I feel like we should be suspicious of its very existence. That's the kind of fake business you see in a bad movie. Like they couldn't pay for writers who were smart enough to come up with something more credible."

Frankie clears his throat and tries to wave off the cloud of dust that I raised in taking off the cover. "Again, we're all missing the point here. *Elinor*, why in the actual eff do you have this parade float hiding under a tarp in your garage? How did we not know about this?"

"Honestly, I never thought about it. It's just something I have. I mean, I don't know about everything hiding in your garage," I reply.

"And thank God for that," he says with a bark of laughter. "But now we need an explanation, and make it girthy." He holds out his palms as though indicating the size of a very big . . . fish he'd caught.

"Gross," says Jazz, after she high-fives Frankie, delighted.

"I feel like Ferris Bueller is about to have his day off in this thing," Carmen says in a tone tinged with awe.

"Again, different manufacturer, different decade," I say. I really do love this car, so I'm happy to elaborate about it. "This is a two-door Coronation Red 1972 Cadillac Eldorado convertible, but if you want to call it cherry red, I won't argue. I even took a picture of it once to the Elizabeth Arden counter at Saks and said, 'Give me this color lipstick.' You'll note the white vinyl roof, the gleaming chrome accents, and, you can't see it, but there's an entirely rebuilt V8 engine. Oh, she purrs like a kitten! I can pop the hood if you'd like to take a peek." I pause, waiting for takers, but they're all quiet. "No? Okay. The tires have those pristine whitewalls and a fender skirt, which is a nice detail you just don't see anymore because it adds so much weight, but no one was talking about gas mileage in 1972 because the oil crisis didn't hit until 1973, and *that* I recall quite clearly. The gas lines, the even/odd days for fill-ups. It was a nightmare. Do you realize this bad girl weighs over five thousand pounds? They don't make 'em like her anymore, probably because she gets ten miles to the gallon highway. And of course, her interior is white leather, obviously." I sweep my arms in front of each of its attributes like a car show model.

"She's a lady?" Stella asks.

"Isn't it obvious?" I say. "Ooh, and pay attention to her iconic V-shaped grill and its pencil-thin steering wheel. This car was *the shit* in '72. They didn't name her after the City of Gold for nothing. The Eldorado boasted the smoothest ride known to consumers at the time, probably because of all the weight—it's incredibly well stabilized. I am talking about the pinnacle of American engineering. The only upgrade I made was to her sound system. I added Bluetooth and satellite radio. I struggled with the addition, but then I realized it's not like I have a bunch of eight-track tapes sitting round, and you need the right tunes for when the top is down," I explain. "That's just hard fact."

Stella rests a warm palm on my shoulder. "Honey, I don't believe the question we were askin' was about its mechanical specs. It's more about its very existence in your garage."

Oh. Of course.

"This was Hank's dream car. It's not something we could have afforded when we were young, but it was always his 'someday.' Well . . . he didn't get a someday, but I did."

I notice that Frankie sweeps what looks like a tear from his eye with his cuff and Jazz reaches for Carmen's hand. I am not always comfortable with the emotional stuff, so I plow on. "The Eldorado was his passion, and over time, after he was gone, it became mine. When I finally started making money, I found her at auction, and I slowly had her restored in his honor. I don't take her out much because she's almost nineteen feet long and it's virtually impossible to find a parking space. Also, I cannot keep the influencers from trying to pose all over her when she's out in public. No offense, Stella."

"None taken. I'm already figurin' out my angles," Stella replies, appraising it hard.

"Does she have a name?" Carmen asks gently.

"Maybellene, obviously," I tell them.

"Maybe she's born with it," Frankie mutters as he eases himself into the luxurious back seat. "Oh, my God, the leather! The legroom! I'm going to have a hard time cramming myself back in the MINI Cooper after this."

I tell them, "This is the time of year I like to drive it around because it's not too hot. Yes, she does have air conditioning, but the whole point is to have the top down. So, now that we've completed today's episode of *Car Talk*, I suggest we get going because Peter may not be at that storefront for long. And it's high time that bastard *paid*."

Chapter Twenty-One

Jazz

"All I am saying is this doesn't *not* feel like *Ferris Bueller's Day Off*," Carmen says, cutting waves through the airstream with her hand and forearm as we fly down the expressway.

"I don't know him," I say. "He in the club?" These guys love talking about people I don't know. Maybe that's why I always feel like I have to show them what I can do, demonstrate my worth.

"How do you *not* know who Matthew Broderick is?" asks Carmen.

"Same reason you don't know who Jake and Logan Paul are," I counter from where I ride shotgun. They are always coming at me with old-people shit.

"Touché," says Carmen, struggling to make herself heard against the wind tunnel this boat of a convertible creates as we make our way to Peter's storefront.

I can't entirely hear her, but I get the gist. "Oh, yeah, they are sort of douches, so I guess you do know them," I say. "My bad."

Carmen's hair has escaped the confines of her scrunchie and it's hitting Stella in the face and tangling in her fake lashes. Eli has a large patterned silk scarf tied around her head and neck. Frankie says she's serving 1960s glamour, but she has a print of a baboon's butt on her T-shirt, so I don't see it. Frankie's hair doesn't move, even at 60 mph, which is impressive. He gives it tentative pats and leans out to look at himself in the side mirror, sucking in his cheeks and tilting his head left and right. He really is most at home with the top down.

Per my app, Peter's still there at the storefront, so we're banking on arriving in time. Our plan hinges on not trying this at his house, because Diana would immediately recognize us (even disguised), and also stop us. And probably never forgive us, because she'll fail to grasp that what we're doing will ultimately benefit her the most. Our plan is kinda haphazard because we spent so much time discussing *why* we needed a plan that we failed to make one that was terribly cogent and we've had to figure out the specifics while driving, so it's been a bit of a game of telephone. Eli wanted to hash out a more specific plan, but I convinced her we have to act right this second, so we're basically gonna scare him and film it. We feel like we have to jump on this because he's making Diana so volatile right now; she's behaving so out of character. I don't want to see her snap, you know? Go all Susan Smith? Smith snapped and did the unthinkable, so maybe Diana could be close too? Yeah, well, not with my Ethan. So I insisted we stop planning and start acting because analysis paralysis will get you every time. Fingers crossed that what we've cobbled together is effective. Sometimes you have to leap and believe a net will appear. Eli grudgingly agreed and then everyone else followed suit. This feels like a win to me. Maybe they're finally respecting my credibility as a leader.

As for specs, we're planning to put on army stuff, paint our faces in camouflage, and lie in wait in the shadows of the clinic. When Peter comes out, we're going to act like we're armed. We'll ambush him and steal whatever bougie watch he's wearing today. (Like why would you spend so much money on something that *only* tells time? How do you not opt for an Apple Watch??)

Obvi, we're not keeping it, because he'd just file a claim and a police report, and this is about making *him* pay, not his insurance company, although no one GAF about *them* right now. We'll eventually get the Piaget or Rolex back to him because theft is not our goal, and also, no fun. I mean, I have the ability to get into systems and take whatever I want, but I don't. For me, it's not about the *taking*; it's about the *ability* to take, the *option* to cause chaos. That's where the power is.

Our plan is to *shame* him. Carmie says we're taking our marching orders from a quote by Margaret Atwood, who said, "Men are afraid that women will laugh at them. Women are afraid that men will kill them." Is she the Handmaid lady? Doesn't matter, because we're going to film him presumably screaming and crying because we're convinced that's how he'll react when confronted with five masked baddies.

If he were to wet his pants? All the better.

Are we sure this will work? No, there's a lot of margin for error. So much.

Here's what we are sure of: Men like Peter Pulaski are bullies. Thugs. They never threaten or harass those they consider their equals. They're not looking for a fair fight because in the recesses of their pathetic little souls, they're weak. If they were strong, they'd never punch down. They pick on subordinates, their kids, service workers, anyone who's not positioned to take a swing back at them, because it makes them feel powerful to win a fight that's weighted in their favor. This is why you should run from any man who claims to be an "alpha"; true alphas don't have to tell you because it will be obvious.

That's why *we* don't need to fight fair either.

So today, we're using our strength in numbers to take what's most precious to this pathetic little man—his watch and his pride—and to frighten him enough that he's forced to look inward. Carmie says he won't like what he sees. Then, we'll edit the video of him groveling for maximum humiliation, leaving him with the message that there's more where this came from if he doesn't change his ways, *bitch*. My mind's still racing as I try to figure out where we'll post the footage, but I'll figure that out once we have it. Maybe we'll even try to blackmail him about it?

We don't know, we're still workshopping it.

Traffic's light, so we're fucking flying to our destination. But in terms of an incognito vehicle, we may have been better in Eli's black SUV, regardless of all the fur. Not only are other drivers on the road gawping at us, some are even filming video. "I hope it's not an omen, but does this feel like *Thelma & Louise* to anyone else?" Carmen asks as she attempts to wrangle her curls back into submission.

"I don't know them," I reply. "Are they in the club?"

"No, they're—never mind," Carmen says with a sigh.

"If that Spirit Halloween isn't open, our plan may not work," Stella says. "Otherwise, we're just dressed up like ourselves and he'll recognize us."

"I'm sure they're open. It's a month before Halloween; it's not like they're keeping bankers' hours," Eli replies with a confidence the rest of us do not feel. I don't know what's crawled up Eli's butt all of a sudden, but whatever it is, I like it. She's suddenly way more amenable, even to the stuff I suggest.

Don't ask me why, but I feel like it has something to do with the Russians.

We exit the expressway and make our way to the strip mall via side streets, so it's easier to hear each other now. "Who's going to do the talking?" Frankie asks. "It can't be me, my voice is too distinctive."

"Heh, ditto," drawls Stella.

"English as a second language, *chicas*," Carmen says.

"Me, I'll do it. I am so great at accents. Remember when I took that improv class at Second City?" I ask.

Listen, I know how it is. You find out your bestie has joined an improv group and you're obligated to see them perform. Ugh. What no one tells you is that improv *is only funny to the people on the stage*, at least when they're novices. Sure, stars like Tina Fey and Amy Poehler make it look easy and hilarious, but they've been doing it for decades. Anyone's first day of anything is generally their worst day, regardless of their talent or natural aptitude. You think Yo-Yo Ma was a virtuoso on the cello on Day One? I guarantee his folks were like, "Is the cat in a blender?"

That's why they're so lucky I'm actually really great at it.

Improv performers live and die by two words, which are "Yes, and . . ." The whole point of improv is coming up with bizarre scenarios and then playing off the other people onstage, no matter what it is that they bring up when they throw the scene to the next person. It's like, "You're zombie George Washington back from the dead to cross the Delaware? Yes, and . . . ," then they go into whatever scenario was in their head. Comedy comes from the unexpected turns.

Truth, I don't like it because all I want to say is "No, but . . ." I just feel like it's funnier to watch them squirm, you know? And why would George Washington be a zombie? He'd be a ghost, if anything. Plus, I think it makes you much better at improv if your partner "no, buts" you. Then you really have to think on your feet.

"Ve haf vays of ma-kink him tolk," I say, cracking my knuckles with an evil cackle.

"Darlin', is that supposed to be a German accent?" Stella asks, using the side-view mirror to powder her nose. "Hmm, maybe pull a different one outta your improv hat."

"No worries, I have plenty more," I say, unconcerned.

I am legitimately so good at this.

❧

Two things are working in our favor. First, Peter's car is still right up front in the parking lot. This shit stain has the nerve to be parked in the designated accessible spot, despite this vast lot being virtually empty. They always say that morality is doing the right thing when no one's looking, so what does it say about him when he's perpetually doing the wrong thing when out of sight? Such an asshat, I can't even.

We watch as the final patients/customers leave his storefront, noting that no one's carrying a bag larger than a McDonald's sack. He's obviously not moving wheelchairs or walkers today. Then we watch as some lady with a big beehive hair-*don't* shuts the blinds and locks the front door before basically sprinting to her car. She really does not seem to like her job or being here.

Second, Eli was right and the Spirit Halloween is open.

"So we're definitely going with camo? Are we married to that idea?" Frankie asks as we peruse the costumes. He and Stella are drawn in by items with feathers or sparkles and Stella is currently draped in a rainbow of boas as she smiles and purses her lips at her screen. Typical. "I'm just noodling here, but if this is going to be on film, I feel like it would come off better if we did more of an elegant cat burglar thing. I'm thinking chic black turtlenecks, black tights, a pencil pant. Very *Thomas Crown Affair*. Maybe a wide belt at the midsection. Oh, and thigh-high boots? I'm talking crime but make it *fashion*."

"For fuck's sake, Frankie, we're not going for *lewks*," I argue. Why am I always the voice of reason? "We're not headed to a party. We just need something to conceal ourselves. Everyone in the same army outfits—"

"They're called fatigues," he replies.

I continue, "With masks and camo paint under them. I think that's our best bet. The whole reason the military puts people in uniform is so they look *uniform*. They're harder to distinguish that way and easier to replace when there's casualties."

"*Mierda*, that got dark quick," Carmen says.

"Hey, war is hell. Don't even start me on the military-industrial complex," I reply as I check myself wearing the "Pink Pony Club"–type spangled cowboy hat in a mirror. I feel like my Goth phase could be concluding. This pink is *working* for me.

Stella says, "You know what would be a fun group costume? If we went as a BLT. Now y'all hear me out—someone could be the slice of bread, someone could be the bacon, the lettuce, the tomato. We'd all stand together and just be the whole sandwich. That would be a laugh riot. Someone would need to be a Duke's mayo jar. Has to be Duke's. I love me some Duke's on my BLTs, so that's the one I'd choose because I look amazin' in cream and mustard colors."

Carmen's attention has been diverted and she's clucking over all the skimpy offerings. OMG, she's such a mom sometimes, even more proper than mine. "Okay, sexy nurse? Yes, I could see that. It has a role-play vibe and that is a healthy expression of human sexuality. Sexy devil? I understand that kink too. There's a lot of psychosexual baggage around religion. Same sort of thing. But sexy hot dog? *Jesus Cristo.* You can be sexy or you can dress as a hot dog. It is a Venn diagram where the circles do not overlap. It does not compute."

"Shit," Eli says, slapping her palm to her forehead. "I just thought of something. Who has cash?"

"Like, in the bank?" Stella asks. "Well, that'd be you, Melinda Gates."

Eli says, "No, on their *person.* Who has cash with them? I don't think we should pay for this with credit or debit. We're already standing out enough, given our group and our ride. We need to draw the line at creating an *actual* paper trail."

"Cash is gross," I say. "Apple Pay all the way."

"Carmie drove tonight so I didn't bring my wallet because I don't like to sit on it in the car," Frankie says. "It ruins the line of my pant."

"Call them '*pants,*' for God's sake," I insist.

"And Jazz gave me so much shit about my satchel that I don't carry my bag now, which is why I only have my ID and credit card," Frankie says, patting his breast pocket.

"Yeah, you're welcome," I say. "Someone's got to save you from yourself. At least you're not *beskirted* tonight."

"I have seven dollars!" Stella offers, digging through her massive carpetbag, after discarding a set of earphones, an umbrella, and what appears to be an overripe banana.

"Carmie? Any cash?" Eli asks.

"I put everything on my credit card for the points," Carmen says. "Do you realize that we have not paid for a trip back to Puerto Rico in years? Thank you, NerdWallet, for recommending the Capital One Venture Rewards card!"

"What about you, Scrooge McDuck?" Frankie asks Eli. "You always have coin on you."

Once we had dinner at a place that was cash only and none of us realized it until it was too late. Eli told us not to worry about it, and she pulled out a roll large enough to choke a horse. When she saw us gawping, she said that cash is always good in an emergency. In our heads, that meant, like, a flat tire. But in her world, it's apparently enough to leave the country and assume a new identity.

"I got so wrapped up in telling you about the Eldorado, I left my bag in the garage on the workbench," Eli admits. "Everyone, check your pockets and let's see how much we have, and I'll figure out what we can get for it."

We produce a grand total of . . . eleven dollars. Fuck.

"Do we just want to rethink this?" I ask. I mean, it was me who was pushing so hard for us to jump on this, but now I'm starting to second-guess myself.

"Jazmin, did you not tell us that he's supposed to meet up with Zlata in person next week?" Carmen demands.

"I did," I say.

"Then it needs to be now," Frankie says. "Eli, you're the planning queen. What say you?"

Eli looks at the pathetic pile of singles, coins, and a bottle cap (from Stella, ironically from a Stella Artois), deliberating. "You know what? Sometimes you have to take a leap." Then she snaps her fingers. "I know exactly what to do. Go outside, I'll meet you there."

Having Eli take charge is always kind of a relief. So we follow her instructions, waiting in the hulking shadow the car casts. She joins us carrying a small Spirit Halloween bag minutes later.

"Problem solved. We have a crude but elegant solution," Eli says. First, she hands us five black surgical masks. "These were free at the door."

"Did you bring any hand sanitizer?" Frankie asks.

"Why would we need that?" Eli asks, vaguely puzzled.

"Well, that was free at the door too," he replies. "I thought if you were taking stuff . . ."

Then Eli removes five Hefty contractor bags, and for the first time ever, I question Eli's judgment.

"Darlin', what exactly are we supposed to do with these?" Stella asks, holding her bag with her fingertips, trying to make as little contact with it as possible.

"We'll punch eye and air holes and we'll put these over our heads," Eli replies. "They're ninety-six-gallon contractor bags, so they're about sixty inches long. They'll conceal us from the knees up. These, coupled with the masks, will hide our identities nicely."

"I guess we're not gonna make it fashion," Frankie says, despondent.

"For eleven dollars, we had to be creative," Eli replies.

"They charged you eleven dollars for some trash bags?" Carmen asks.

"I bought the bags for a dollar and the clerk's silence for ten. Oddly enough, she gave me the impression this wasn't the first bribe she's taken," Eli says. "What a strange store."

We quickly get to work. Stella blackens the area around all of our eyes with an Urban Decay kohl pencil that she warms with a lighter, then she uses her nail scissors to cut holes so we don't suffocate. What does that bag not hold? One by one, we help each other don our Heftys. Of course, as the brains of the operation, I have the genius idea that we sit crisscross applesauce by the door, all piled up against each other so we look like we're actual loads of trash so we don't attract any attention from anyone doing late-night costume shopping. Although, fortunately, it's kind of a ghost town out here. The last thing we need is witnesses.

"Just me, or are these giving Balenciaga Winter 22 Collection?" Frankie asks, hopeful, referring to that fashion moment where the runway style seemed to be inspired by sheets of plastic and rolls of duct tape. I feel like everyone could tell the difference between that and this, yet I tell him they totally are. He seems to need this boost.

We arrange ourselves on the sidewalk, our legs tucked under us, and we suspect that from a distance we actually do look like bags of trash. "This is a legit costume," I say. "Throw in a few stuffed rats and a pizza crust and we could say we're going as a New York City street."

We're close enough to the entrance to hear if there is a conversation happening inside, and we believe Peter is alone.

Now all we have to do is wait.

❧

"Not to be indelicate, but I am sweatin' clean down the crack of my ass," Stella tells us. "I'm turning into a virtual puddle under here."

I guess we thought that once we were in position, Peter would immediately come out and we'd jump him. It has to be after 10:00, because the Spirit is closed and it looks like everyone has left. We must be as inconspicuous as I thought, as none of the few straggling customers even glanced in our direction. I fucking told you so! In fact, one Spirit employee tossed a few bags next to *their* front doors instead of in the dumpster I assume is out back. That's only to our benefit.

Fortunately, if everyone's gone, there's no one to film us for the Citizen app; we'll control all the media taken. Unfortunately, we've been sitting here long enough for the unseasonably warm temps and our body heat to turn our garbage bags into sauna suits. We're practically cooking ourselves sous vide.

Stella adds, "I think I've lost five pounds. I don't want to lose five pounds. I will get a ration of shit from lah-di-dah-di every-freakin'-body. They'll be all, 'Lady, why is your face thinner? How can y'all say you're about body positivity when you're secretly on a diet? Is it Ozempic? Don't lie to us!' It's bad for my brand."

"No worries, hun. It's just water weight," Frankie says. "All you have to do is drink a Gatorade or eat something salty and you'll put it right back on. Trust me, I know. High school wrestler. Ironically, this is not my first time cutting weight wrapped in plastic."

"Wait, you were a jock?" Carmen asks. "I saw you more as the rebel, or even the basket case, not as the brain, but maybe the homecoming queen. Definitely not the jock." Carmen is obsessed with '80s movies, as I guess that's when her family came to the US. Watching TV is how she perfected her English. It's not unusual for her to define things in what she calls *Breakfast Club* terms; she says John Hughes made a huge impression on her.

(I don't know who he is.)

"Carmie, think about that. I rolled around on mats with hot, fit men in skintight leotards. It was right up my alley," he replies. "In fact, it was a *revelation*."

"Ha!" Carmen replies, delighted. "Did you ever tape anyone's buns together in the locker room?"

"I have no idea what you Boomers are talking about," I say.

As they get into some random squabble about the true greatest generation or the genius of Anthony Michael Hall (?), I see the lights inside the storefront go dark.

"He's coming," Eli whispers. "Everyone, get into a crouch so we can spring into standing position."

Peter comes out with a janitor's ring of keys, securing the door's multiple deadbolts. *Awful lot of security for a bedpan store,* I think. As he works the locks, we leap into position, or at least try to, because only some of us have young knees.

"The hell?" Peter says, alerted to our presence by some minor crackling, groaning, and straining, likely exactly the sounds he hears when he's trying to diagnose someone.

"Put-ta you hands-a up, this-a is a robbery!" I shout in my best *Super Mario* impersonation.

"Oh, God, oh, God, oh, God," Frankie mutters under his breath. "If we decide to conduct an after-action review—and we should—we're going to want to assess if a video game Italian accent was our home-run swing."

But he's wrong. My accent is *molto bene.* I studied Italian on Duolingo for a month; I'm golden.

"Huh?" Peter is less afraid and more confused.

"Give-a the monies!" I shout.

"No. No, no," Frankie hisses. "We weren't going to take his wallet. This has nothing to do with his wallet. This is why you were bad at improv: bad instincts. You're 'no, butting' this whole thing."

"I was awesome at improv," I hiss back.

"English, motherfucker, do you speak it?" Peter calmly asks.

"We can add xenophobia to his list of crimes against humanity," Stella grumbles.

Carmen has her phone aimed at Peter so we can capture all the action. We didn't trust Stella with the job because we suspected she'd have her camera view flipped around and she'd end up filming herself instead. (This will definitely be part of the game tape that we review.)

"Give-a me-a you timepiece-a!" I demand. That asshole has the nerve to laugh at me. So do Carmen and Frankie.

"Give-a you my timepiece-a? You mean my *watch*? Or what?" Peter scoffs. "I'm sorry, is this an attempted robbery by the California Raisins?"

"Who-a are they-a?" Why is everyone so old?

Eli takes over. "*Zdravstvuyte*, comrade," she says, her voice pitched low in a mid-realistic Russian accent. She made some offhand remark about talking to a nice Russian guy at a bakery this week, so she must have been inspired or something. "We need discuss business."

Peter's countenance changes. But instead of shifting into fear and compliance, now he's furious, definitely not what we were expecting. Okay, I didn't anticipate this and it's making me kind of anxious. I generally see a half dozen moves in advance and right now I don't and . . . it's kinda freaking me out.

"No, this isn't the deal. I give you guys your share every month. I have been more than generous. We have an arrangement. This is not how you negotiate, you fucking savages. This is pathetic. You're just a bunch of low-level thugs trying to shake me down. I mean, you're wearing *garbage bags*. Could you *be* less threatening? Probably not. Now get out of my way."

Where's the fear?

Where's the begging?

Where's the pants-wetting?

This isn't what we workshopped in the car *at all*. And what is he talking about with shares of money? Is this Mafia shit? Wait, is the *actual mob* involved here, like I speculated? Honestly, I sort of thought I was wrong because sometimes I go a little fabulist.

But I'm not sure now that I was. The Crew thought my story was far fetched when I explained that Peter's malfeasance went far deeper than just generic Medicare fraud. I was super clear that he was into a much darker business model, that his storefront was really a "pain management clinic." In true crime terms, that's a pill mill. I figured that he's been writing scripts for dangerous controlled substances in exchange for cash. He probably has to deal with a criminal element to launder that much cash, so naturally, I'm gonna assume a Russian connection.

We actually covered a case like this on our platforms. We spoke about Texas physician Dr. Oscar Lightner, who operated Jomori Health and Wellness. What a piece of shit. His operation was freaking insidious. Not only was he prescribing meds to those without a legitimate medical purpose, his office manager was recruiting homeless people to come in and pose as patients to receive bogus prescriptions for controlled substances and opioids. So gross. These fake patients would then go to legitimate local pharmacies to fill those scripts, and then runners would sell the drugs and give the office a cut. Both the doctor and the office manager were convicted a couple of years ago on multiple drug counts by a federal jury.

This is what I've thought Peter was up to. Poor Diana. Does she have any idea of who she's married to?

Since a criminal connection is appearing more and more true for Peter, this loser needs to pay in ways more than just being embarrassed on the internet. Screw taking away his pride or his watch. He needs to be charged for trafficking, for fraud and conspiracy. He needs to lose his medical license. He needs to go to jail. And God help him if any of his patients overdosed. I will rain down hellfire my damn self. I saw what opioids did to some of the kids I learned to program with at camp. They should have gone to U of C and instead they went to the morgue. We can't let this happen, we can't let him get away with it.

"Now get-a out of my way before someone-a gets hurt," Peter says. He uses the giant satchel he's carrying as a battering ram and he shoves Eli as he rushes to his car. She stumbles into the plate glass window and I hear a terrible crack. I'm not sure if it's a bone or the windowpane, but either way, it sounds gnarly. She cries out in pain before crumpling to the ground. Hey, no! No one's getting hurt on my watch, especially not one of the best people I know. I don't let a lot of people in, so I don't have many to lose.

Frankie's high school wrestling past must have awakened inside him at seeing Eli manhandled, and he makes a flying leap at Peter before he can open his door. However, Frankie's too tangled up in his trash bag to effectively get his arms out so he can grip him. Peter slithers out from underneath Frankie's plastic-clad form, still clutching the satchel, which he uses to knock Frankie's head into the cement.

Frankie's shriek of pain turns Carmen into a mama bear. She runs up to kick him, but she's wearing a pair of those ultrasoft mom-style Kizik marshmallow sneakers, so it probably feels like being popped with a bag of cotton balls. Peter catches her foot and uses her energy against her. He takes her heel that he caught and lifts it through the air with the motion of the kick and now she's flat on her back too, landing with a terrible thud.

We are so bad at this it would be laughable if we weren't the walking wounded. Not only is this asshat going to get away with his malfeasance if we don't get it together, we're getting seriously hurt.

When it seems like despite our best efforts we have been bested by this douchebag, I hear the sound of the safety slide being disengaged on a Smith & Wesson.

Holy shit, Stella pulled out her gun.

I have to Kegel so I don't wet my own pants. Whatever we're doing right now went from a potential misdemeanor to a serious felony. We went from low stakes to all the damn stakes.

"Didn't your mama tell you it's not nice to push people?" Stella asks. She's pulled her garbage bag up enough to reveal the gun resting so comfortably in her grip that we're reminded of that Turkish guy who won the silver medal at the Olympics. (FYI, I insist he's an assassin and I'd wager a whole bunch of rubles on who he works for.)

The situation must finally feel real to Peter and his disposition changes yet again.

"Wait, wait, wait. There's no need for guns. We can work this out. I'm sorry. Please, let's be levelheaded here. What do you want? Let's be reasonable," Peter says, adopting a placating tone. "Whatever you want, I can do it. You want my watch? Take it." He slips his Rolex off his wrist and places it on the ground, kicking it toward Frankie, who has the presence of mind to stuff it in his pocket. "You need more scripts? No problem. Looking for a cut outside of your boss? We can figure it out. Here, do you want my wallet? It's yours. Let's just all get home safely tonight, okay? There's no call for violence. We're businesspeople; let's come up with a business solution. We don't have to resort to violence like a bunch of animals. And think about this—I'm worth way more to you alive than dead, right?"

What the fuck is he into if this is the defense he pulls out of his pocket? Did we just bite off way more than we can chew? But then I think of that cool girl Portia who was in my cabin that year, and her friend Darrin. They were nice to me when a lot of the others weren't. We got tight after my sophomore year, but by the end of my junior year, by the time I got to camp again, they were gone. Because of people like Peter Pulaski, who made it so easy.

"Problem is, we didn't introduce the violence, now, did we? And my associates are banged up pretty good because of you. How we doin' over there, friends?" Stella asks. We're impressed that she remembered not to use anyone's real name. I'm impressed. Maybe we can still get away with him not knowing this is us. Eli can only offer a guttural moan in response and clutch her left arm. Frankie shakes his head under his bag, as though trying to clear the cobwebs, while Carmen manages a feeble thumbs-up.

We have to get Eli to a hospital. Probably Frankie and Carmen too.

Staring down the barrel of Stella's gun, Peter is suddenly amenable to the point of being obsequious. "Please, let's just keep the peace right now. I mean, I have children." Peter begins to cry. Fat tears run down his face, cutting paths through his tinted CC cream and causing his mascara to run. Okay, so we didn't know Peter is wearing makeup now. Did not see that coming. The whole thing is a little too J. D. Vance for us. Oh, I hope Carmen has the presence of mind to capture this—it's the exact begging we'd hoped to film. I can make this viral on TikTok within an hour.

I can feel myself unclench a little bit, like we just pulled back from the precipice of something un-take-backable.

The floodgates open and now Peter is bawling like a baby in the next seat in economy on a cross-country flight. A river of snot pours from his nose, which he brushes away with his shirtsleeve. Gross. "My daughter can't lose her father. I'm her whole world. Do you know what happens to girls who grow up without a dad? They end up on the stripper pole."

"Oprah Winfrey begs to differ," Eli mutters.

"Yeah, but Oprah got fat. She's hardly a role model," Peter replies through his sobs. Probably the wrong thing to say to the fabulous plus-size woman holding a gun on you, so he quickly realizes his error and changes track. "I have patients who depend on me. I'm an important member of my community. I'm a *healer*. I make people better. Please, you don't want to do this. People love me. They depend on me. They need me. Their sick mothers in Ukraine need me." Peter's voice is getting higher and shriller as he tries to negotiate from his position of weakness.

His girlfriend? He's bringing up the person he's cheating on his saint wife with as a reason to spare him? Oh, hell no.

"And what about your wife? Does she need you?" Frankie asks, his voice strangled. Seems like he got his bell rung pretty hard and his movements are tentative, but his thoughts are in the right place.

"Her?" Peter asks. "Meh."

Wrong answer, pal.

Fortunately for all, and stemming from his disdain for our girl, this is when I remember my mixed martial arts training. It's time for me to join the fray, save the day, make him pay.

With a "Hi-yah!" I throw a perfect roundhouse kick at Peter, putting in all my might, not just for Diana, but for Darrin and cool Portia who taught me how to do a French braid. She should be here still.

So . . . okay.

Fine. When we review the game tape, I'm willing to own up to a few problems with my strategy. First, I gave him ample warning with my war cry. That was kind of a fuckup and it's on me. Also, even if I'd had more than a month of mixed martial arts training, I didn't think about our simple size disparity. I'm five foot one to Peter's six foot two. Complicating matters further is that my spin was so incredibly powerful that I didn't have a lot of control over it. I was kind of in beast mode. So instead of connecting with Peter's throat, which I am too short to do, my foot bashes into Stella's trigger finger.

The gun goes off and Peter goes down.

Shit.

Chapter Twenty-Two

Eli

"We have a situation to manage; now is not the time to fall apart. First, everyone take a breath," I say as I unfurl to a standing position to survey the scene. Everyone is shell shocked, most of us splayed out on the blacktop. "This is going to calm your central nervous system and help you focus. We're going to fix this but I need you to focus on me and do exactly what I say."

This is not my first crisis management rodeo. I was in the business of coming up with solutions when everything seemed dire. I dealt with what felt like life-and-death situations every day. From a high stakes negotiation with the Teamsters to avoid a labor strike to navigating through a denial-of-service cyberattack to keeping my team from physical harm when there was an active shooter two floors below our Loop office, I maintain my wits and focus on the solution. Everyone comes through safely on my watch. I can—and will—melt down later in private, but right now the Crew needs me to be strong.

About fifteen years ago during a terrible summer storm that was itself as tumultuous as the state of my fledgling company, my late flight to Dallas was diverted to Omaha for an emergency landing. We'd been hit by lightning and the skies were too dangerous for us to continue our journey. Like the old FedEx slogan goes, I absolutely positively had to be there overnight because my company was at a crossroads. The fate of the company I was building depended on making it to and nailing a pitch because we wouldn't continue to make payroll without it. So I rented a car and drove all night over backcountry roads, through tornado warnings and the worst weather I'd ever experienced in my life. The rain was so hard that I could barely see the white line in the center of the road. But I arrived at the client's office, acted like I'd spent the night at the Ritz and not white-knuckling through a hailstorm, and I won the pitch. I compartmentalized what was hard, what was scary, and I focused on what I knew to be true—that I was their best and only choice. That win set success after success in motion. Failure was not an option then and it's not an option now.

Fortunately, the crack I heard was the window spiderwebbing and not a bone break, so that's working in my favor. I try to move my arm and I yelp as I feel an electric bolt of pain that's so intense, my knees buckle and I have to right myself. Okay, that's not so great. There's an element of irony that now I likely do need to have my rotator cuff repaired, as I felt something tear when my shoulder bashed against the window. I guess my ortho is getting that beach house after all.

I can't tell who's crying the loudest among our group, but there's a real cacophony out here. I have to raise my voice to be heard. Carmen is sitting up, head poking through her bag. She's trying to stand, but she hurt her hip or leg when Peter laid her out, and she groans when she tries to move her right side. Frankie has fully pulled off his trash bag and he appears to have had his bell rung. He's shaking his head like he's righting his perspective, trying to extricate all the cartoon birds flying around his bruised melon of a skull. The side of his face is scraped and bloody. I'm concerned he's concussed yet impressed that his hair still hasn't moved. I know I'm focusing on the small details, but they're helping me keep my cool. If I looked at the big picture right now, it would be game over.

Jazz is in hysterics, clutching her midsection as though *she* were the one who'd taken the bullet. She's absolutely sobbing, utterly inconsolable. "We killed him! We killed him! I wanted him dead in theory, but not in reality!!" I can't say I'm surprised she's the one who's crumbled. It's easy to be a badass behind a screen, when you don't see firsthand what you've wrought. And in my experience, the one who talks the toughest is the first to show their soft underbelly. I'll need to pay special attention to helping her through this. I forget how young she is because she feels like such an equal to everyone.

Stella is the most stoic of the group. She seems rather resigned about the whole thing. "Y'all know you can't pull a gun if you're not intendin' to use it. Guns aren't for scarin', they're for hurlin' bullets. If you aim one, you have already accepted the consequences of having pulled that trigger. I rolled the dice, I really did. I made my choice and I stand by it. Jazz, you didn't do anything. This is on me. I . . . Oh, shoot. I just realized, if I go to prison, that's gonna ruin the weddin'. Abe's gonna be so sad. We were gonna release doves right after we stomped on that wineglass. It was gonna be glorious."

"Crew, we don't have time for reflection. We need to clear the scene. We can regroup, but that hinges on our getting away from here. I'm sure someone has already reported the sound of gunshots, so we have to leave *now*," I instruct them. "Take your trash bags, pick up your masks. Leave nothing here. Now, what is Peter's status?"

None of them can even look at the heap into which Peter's collapsed, so it's on me to assess his condition, to assess our condition as a whole. With the benefit of only one functioning arm, as the other is clutched to my side, I give him a thorough once-over. Blood is gushing across his face, but head wounds always bleed the hardest. I give him a thorough scan, checking for a pulse to verify my suspicions.

I am correct in my assessment. He's going to be fine, but I don't have time to explain the specifics of why to everyone; I just need to get us all out.

In the distance, I hear sirens. I delegate because we only have minutes before this goes even more wrong, and I am determined to not let that happen. My team gets out of this, hard stop. "Here's what we're doing—Frankie, Stella, Jazz, I need you to carefully load Peter into his trunk. Throw his bag in too." Most likely, this is his medical kit and it's stuffed with supplies, which we can use. And if it's not, we still don't want to leave a trace of him having been here. Fortunately, I don't see any blood that we need to clean up.

"Oh, my God, we've killed him and we're just going to stick him in his trunk? Like a deer you hit on the highway?" Jazz wails.

"Wait, why would you put a deer in your trunk?" Frankie asks. I suspect he banged his head hard, as I already see a goose egg forming. "I didn't think *your* people mounted deer heads on your wall. I thought that was just ours."

"What are you talking about? You put him in the trunk so you can take him to the emergency vet, obvi!" Jazz replies. That cat really is making her a pet person.

"My Uncle Cracker once hit a twelve-point buck. Mounted that head like the greatest trophy ever in his front room, like he was the mightiest of hunters and not just drivin' his truck with a bit of a bourbon buzz," Stella tells us.

And *this* is who they wanted me to date? No. "We need to focus. Tasks, now!" I demand. They all seem to be in shock, so I'm giving them grace. We just got very lucky but it won't last if we don't go.

"This is like the sloppiest mob hit ever! We're not even wearing gloves! We're going to get caught in, like, five seconds!" Jazz says. Her voice is hoarse and quavering from the intensity of her crying. "We've left so much DNA on the scene, just from our sweat puddles alone! We're so screwed!"

"Stop. Breathe. Focus. *We will be fine if you do everything I tell you.* I need you to trust me," I say, remaining calm, even though my shoulder is screaming in agony, as opposed to everyone else, who's just screaming. "Stella, grab the shell casing. Carmen, don't try to get up, just flip over and crawl to my car and lift yourself in. Go. NOW."

I pitch my voice at a shout, which I hate. Compliance should never come from intimidation; it should manifest voluntarily when feeling empowered. But we don't have time for that. Too stunned to disobey me in full lady boss mode, they fall in line and follow my orders. Finally.

"I don't know how to open the hatch!" Frankie says, tapping all around the back end of the glossy Tesla in search of a latch. *Of course* He Who Must Not Be Named made a stupid design choice based on how cool it looked rather than how functional or intuitive it would be. (My fight with Musk is a story for another day.)

"Or wait, isn't this the kind where you can use the hood as a trunk? I think it is. Oh, fun!" Frankie paws at the front. "I can't figure out how to open this either!"

"Put him in the back seat!" I instruct Frankie. "Strap him in. Use your belt."

He taps at an indent in the door handle and instead of swinging open, the door rises up like its namesake, the falcon wing. "Whoa. This is the coolest thing I've ever seen!"

Carmen glances back over her shoulder as she drags herself to my car and hauls herself into the front seat. "*Dios mio!* It's like the crane kick scene in *The Karate Kid*! Sweep the leg, Johnny!"

They are losing focus; again, this has to be shock. This is on me to right the ship. "Car! Now! Go!" I yell, using my old CEO voice. That gets their attention. (It certainly got Musk's, back in the day, but I can't think about him now.) Frankie secures his own belt around Peter's arms to lift him and he props Peter in the back seat. Frankie gives the door a wistful close. Yes, we definitely need to get him checked for a concussion.

"Now, Frankie, Jazz, hop in and make sure Carmen's comfortable. Check if anything's broken. My guess is there's going to be a contusion, but we have to verify. Stella, listen closely because I'll only say this once. I need you to take Peter's car and follow me back to my house. We're going to fix everything there. No time to explain, but I need you to trust me that it's all going to be okay. Let's move." I have a plan, but time's of the essence and I don't have the spare moments to explain it.

"But I don't drive!" Stella protests. "Or have the durn keys!"

I say, "You do today. There's a card or a fob and it's obviously on Peter's person because the car is unlocked. If he's in the car, *he* is your key. Listen carefully, this is what you do—get in, step on the brake, which is the one on the left. Pull down on the stalk, which is the handle to the right of the wheel. Let go. Driving is nothing but left pedal to stop, right pedal to go. This beast is going to go zero to sixty in less than three seconds, so watch your acceleration. Turn the wheel in the direction you want to head. Don't argue. If that eight-year-old on the news could steal her family's car to go to Target last year for a shopping spree, you can do this. I believe in you."

Stella nods like a boxer on the side of the ring who's taken too many punches *not* to listen to their coach.

I say, "Pull out of this lot and get to a safe place. Then, watch a TikTok on how to put this monstrosity into autopilot if you're too afraid to drive it all the way back to Winnetka. I promise you, do what I say and this will save your wedding. Don't freestyle, don't second-guess, don't be cute. Be my brave soldier and follow my orders." Much as I hate all things Elon, Margo insisted on renting one of these stupid cars on our last family vacation, so I learned how to operate it under protest. Give me gas combustion any day.

"Yes, sir," Stella says with a mock salute.

I climb behind the wheel of Maybellene and I pull her out of the parking lot. In the rearview mirror, I see that Stella is doing a passable job getting away from the scene with only a modicum of lurching stops and starts, so I accelerate. We'll be out of the immediate vicinity before the police arrive, and that is key. All they'll see is a cracked window, if they even look that closely, which isn't exactly the same as capital murder. They likely won't even stick around long enough to file a report, as they'll chalk up the noise to a car backfiring. And lucky for us all, the shopping center is too low rent to have cameras.

I exhale. The most immediate portion of our mission is accomplished.

I pull into an apartment building parking lot a few miles away where we can stop the car so I can put the top up. Jazz is still hyperventilating. Carmen is next to me in the front, sitting at an angle to accommodate a bruised hip, staring intently at her phone. She may be in pain, but she's more focused on whatever she's looking at.

"Oh no, you're putting the top up?" Frankie asks. I'm assuming this is the head injury talking and he's just defaulting to what he'd say if his brains hadn't been scrambled on the hard pavement.

"We just killed a man," Jazz shrieks, "and you're worried about fresh air? Really, *Franklin*? You'll get plenty of fresh air in yard time when we go to prison! We offed Ethan's daddy! We're the worst people in the world!" She begins to cry again. All of our eyelids were already ringed in kohl to make up for the eyeholes, so with her copious tear flow, her face is now covered in black streaks and she looks like the little girl from *The Ring*. If we weren't in these circumstances, this image would likely delight her.

"No, I don't think so," Carmen says, eyes trained on her phone.

Jazz says, "Can we please not have your toxic positivity right now? We just killed a man, okay? Cold fucking blood. And guess what, it did not feel like I was just offing zombies with melee attacks like in *The Last of Us*, and that game is a lot of fun. Given the option, I always 'killed' instead of 'spared,' and offing everyone gave me joy, but in real life, it doesn't work that way. Didn't see that coming. I am not a cold-blooded killer; I am a *coward*. I am scared and I am embarrassed and I might throw up."

"Please use this if you have to," I say, handing her one of the Hefty bags. "But knot the top because of the eye and mouth holes. We want to contain any liquids."

"You say not being cold blooded like it's a bad thing. We actually don't want you to be a monster. We like the softer side of Jazz. Come see the softer side of Jazz," he sings, parodying those old Sears commercials. He needs to be checked, stat.

"Peter Pulaski was a total douche canoe, but that doesn't matter in the eyes of the law. We should have spared him. I didn't want him dead, I just wanted him to not be a dick to his wife and kids and cats," Jazz says, pounding a fist onto her flattened palm.

"We didn't kill him, *chica*," Carmen says, placing a placating hand on Jazz's shoulder.

"She's right," I say, but before I can elaborate, Jazz begins shrieking.

"We all saw it, Carmen!" Jazz protests, twisting and batting her hand away. "Don't tell me I didn't see what I saw."

Carmen launches into psychological mode, and just in time. "Of anyone, you should know that eyewitness accounts can be fallible. There's memory distortion, there's the weapon focus effect, there's perspective skewed by stress and anxiety. You heard a shot, you saw him drop, and you thought you saw blood. You thought that A, then B, then C, so you assumed D. However, there is no D this time. You made a logical assumption. But that's not what happened. Look, I was filming. I caught the video. Let me play it back in slow motion and you'll understand," Carmen says.

She holds up her phone and confirms exactly what I didn't have time to explain when I was trying to exfiltrate us from the scene. A bright flash whizzes by Peter's ear and he swats at it, confused. He swats again, feeling something amiss. We watch as he draws his hand down, sees a tiny smear of blood on his hand, and then passes out. His knees buckle and he goes down fairly easy. Instead of a grave injury, the bullet barely grazed the tip of his ear. The bullet didn't drop him; his fear, and likely guilt, did.

"He's not dead?" Jazz asks. "You swear to God?"

"At the moment, yes, he's alive, but he's still in the car with Stella driving, so . . ." Carmen trails off.

"She will rise to the occasion," I predict.

"So we're not murderers?" Jazz confirms. Her tears stop flowing and she brightens. "We didn't do it? No Nancy Grace coming after us, no podcast about us, no documentary about the Doom Crew Five? We're free and clear?"

"I wouldn't say that. We are technically kidnappers, but we're not murderers," I say. The kidnapping is the closest alligator to the boat, but at least it's not a murder.

"He's okay?" Jazz persists. "Peter Pulaski will live to be a garbage person another day?"

"He'll need a bandage and some bacitracin, but otherwise, he should be fine. His head landed on his bag when he passed out, so I imagine Frankie's actually in worse shape," I reply.

"Thank you!" Frankie says. The moment we arrive at my house, I'm calling my concierge doctor. Frankie needs immediate testing.

"Can we see the video again?" Jazz asks. Carmen plays it again and the results don't change.

"Hey, Eli, can I ask you something? Why did we have to put him in his own car?" Jazz asks.

"It made the most sense in the moment," I reply. There's no reason to tell them the rest of the truth—partly because of evidence, but mostly because I didn't want any blood on Maybellene's white leather seats. It feels selfish, now that I think about it. If they grasped the pains my mechanic went through to restore the leather to its original finish, they'd probably understand, but now is not the time to overload them with information.

"Hey, do you guys want to know the silver lining?" Frankie says.

"What's that?" I ask, cutting my eyes to the rearview as I pull out of the parking lot.

"We did catch him wetting his pants on film," he replies. "So there's that."

Chapter Twenty-Three

Frankie

I always knew Eli had the skills to guide us—we just never had a crisis to this degree before, so I didn't know how competent she could be, even with one arm behind her back. She evacuated us from the scene of the crime, she kept us calm, and I believe she'll come up with a way to make everything better. I could not be more grateful for her leadership. We are totally electing her president again next time we have to choose officers.

I feel like today has already lasted a week, but it's only been a few hours since Diana departed dramatically, setting this all in motion. The kitchen is as we left it, save for the two fluff monsters having helped themselves to the snacks they could reach at the periphery of the counter. I note, "It's a good thing we brought the bread with us."

Eli offered to have her concierge doctor come to look us all over. We think we're largely okay, especially now that we're back here in her house. Carmen has a full range of motion in her hip after resting in the car, albeit the diagnosis is tentative. While Eli's shoulder seems painful, she's holding it—and us—all together. She currently has me seated on a barstool and she's run cognitive test after test. She already made me try to balance, and then follow her finger with my eyes. She asked questions to test my memory and concentration. That one was inconclusive, as those were not my strongest suits prior to hitting my head. Nothing seems to have degraded, so knock wood, I am none the worse for wear, relatively speaking.

"Ow, that's way too bright," I say, wincing and trying to bat her away from me. "Can we be done, please?"

Carmen hands me a bag of frozen peas. "Put this on your head." I place it atop my immobile hair, as though it were a fashionable chapeau. "No, baby doll, hold it up against your bump," she clarifies.

Carmen is managing to be upright, with a bag of frozen spinach ravioli shoved down the side of her yoga pants. She says she feels better now that she's had a handful of ibuprofen but makes no promises about the ways in which her body will protest tomorrow. As for Jazz? She's admiring her über-Goth visage in the bowl of a sterling serving spoon, her mind spinning with ways she can re-create the look.

The consensus is we're far superior at dissecting crimes than committing them.

"What are you doing to me now?" I ask Eli as she shines the beam directly into my eyes.

"I'm trying to determine if your pupils constrict because that will show me if you have intercranial pressure," Eli replies.

"I was once in a band called Intercranial Pressure," I say, and I crack myself up.

Eli says, "Your sense of humor certainly wasn't damaged."

"Please, he's definitely broken," Jazz says. Once she learned Peter wasn't dead, she brightened considerably and understandably.

"Ha!" I say, flipping her a double bird. "Joke's on you because I was *already* broken."

"Frankie . . . what's our rule on negative self-talk?" Eli admonishes as she clicks off her flashlight and places it in a neatly organized and labeled drawer. "Do you remember? I want you to say it and I want you to believe it. Come on."

I give her a petulant "No." I should be allowed time to wallow.

"Frankie." Eli turns my name into a command. There's no way I can't comply.

"Fine. 'Instead of self-doubt's pressing weight, let my positivity find its gait. Embrace my worth, my skills, my might, and let my light shine extra bright,'" I say with a sigh.

"That was a test and you passed," Eli says, giving me a peck on my nonscraped cheek. "Here, have a treat." She unwraps a platter of pastries and hands me one. I snatch the napoleon right up with both hands and tear into it like a raccoon ravaging a campground garbage can. Kidnapping is hungry business.

"What happens when Stella gets here with Peter? Just spitballing, but I'm going to suggest we do not shoot him again," Jazz says. "Really did not care for it. I mean, you think you know yourself, right? I need to completely readdress strategy if there's ever a zombie apocalypse because I am not a firearms person. Am I more of a minefield kind of gal? I suspect I am. Overall, I'd say this has been a big day of growth for the whole Crew. Lot of self-discovery."

"That's good to hear, Jazz. Now, at this point, Peter is aware that it was us and he has to be fairly confused. Our element of surprise is gone. Not only did he hear us, he saw us," Eli says. "I can't imagine what's in his head right now, but we're going to have some explaining to do on all sides. We don't have the benefit of anonymity anymore, so we're going to need to do some spinning."

Eli clears away the empty plates that held the snacks that the dogs devoured. But because Eli is always prepared, she pulls out fresh offerings from the fridge and we dive in. Everyone else is ravenous too. The boys must be full, as they're both splooted across their beds, which are each the size of a twin mattress, four paws spread in all directions. They look like two bear rugs.

Eli tells us, "Our best bet is to confront him with what we know. The goal was for him to stop being awful to our Diana and treat her like the queen she is. Obviously, it wasn't intentional, but we did shoot at him. So, in my estimation, we have made him pay already, and then some. The good news is that we have the video evidence that we can use to shame him if he doesn't start acting right. We have the leverage to force him to change his behavior. Bottom line, he must behave like the partner Diana believes him to be. Yes, she's delusional, but we have enough dirt on him to force him to comply with her delusions. Beyond that, whatever he's into, we demand he stop, and if possible, make amends before it's too late. I can't believe the fraudulent billing hasn't already caught up with him. Medicare and Medicaid have whole teams devoted to sussing out fraud. Plus, the fake scripts. He's extremely fortunate it's us who found him out, and we're going to explain that to him so he doesn't come after us."

"Wait, I don't understand. What's our leverage? We didn't collect any of our information legally, so it's not admissible in court. Any decent defense attorney can and will argue against evidence obtained via a violation of Peter's constitutional rights. *Mierda*, even a public defender could," Carmen says as she scoops up a bite of beet caviar. "We have leverage, but our hands are tied with it. If we're coming at this from a moral standpoint, we have the upper hand, but thus far morality hasn't had an influence on him. He's yet to do the right thing; why would he start now?"

"If he doesn't stop, we have the information to help guide a formal investigation that's not a violation of Title 18, US Code 1030," Jazz says.

"I have no idea what that is," Eli says.

Jazz says, "It's a bunch of bullshit that makes it a 'federal crime' to gain 'unauthorized access' to 'protected computers.'" She makes air quotes with her fingertips on the words she finds distasteful. "Pain in my asshole is what it is. Basically, I can go behind the scenes to blow the whistle without implicating us. Remember last year when that crooked mayor stole that money from her village and took all those vacations on the taxpayers' dime? Who do you think created that legal paper trail that allowed investigators to pursue her within the bounds of the Constitution? Heh. You're welcome, Cicero, Illinois."

"Sometimes you terrify me," Carmen says.

"Aw, that's really sweet of you to say," Jazz says. We don't explain to her that wasn't meant as a compliment. Let her have a win; it's been a rough night for all of us.

"But what about Zlata?" I ask. I gingerly move the frozen bag to my goose egg and then quickly pull it back because it's too cold.

"Frankie, bag, now," Carmen instructs. "It will be chilly at first, but then it will feel better."

"The second he finds out he was sending money to a Nigerian Yahoo Boy and not some hot, horny Slav, he's gonna stop," Jazz replies. "She's not real. Who knows, she may even be AI."

"Did something change? Are we 100 percent confirmed?" Eli asks. "I thought we were still checking on that."

Jazz shrugs. "You're big on dotting your i's and crossing your t's, Eli. I'm taking a logical shortcut here. It's Occam's razor. We have not 100 percent confirmed that Zlata's fake, but it's the most likely scenario, like 99 percent, especially in a country that's probably too busy fighting a war to catfish sad old guys. Let's just assume I'm right."

Honestly, it does make the most sense to us.

The sound of an enormous fart rips through the night. "Oh, my goodness! Herman! Pee-wee! Not nice," Eli gasps. She grabs a dish towel and covers her nose and mouth. "We may want to consider gathering in another room. I'm concerned we're all going to pay for the cabbage rolls they ate." None of us move. Eli claps her good hand on the counter. "Sense of urgency here, people!"

I sniff the air. "Uh-oh, I must have lost my sense of smell. Nothing's hitting me."

"Or me," says Carmen. "And I'm not potentially concussed."

I hear the fart again and again, and now the dogs seem affronted by the unjust accusation. "It's not them," Carmen says, pointing toward the driveway. "That farting noise, it's coming from out there."

"What fresh hell is this, I wonder," says Jazz with a degree of enthusiasm that indicates some excitement over the prospect of fresh hell. We hustle out the front door where we find Stella behind the wheel of Peter's Tesla. She's honking the horn, which inexplicably sounds like wet flatulence.

"Fucking Elon Musk," Eli mumbles. She's yet to share her issue with him, but I suspect it's juicy and am dying to hear the story. The only thing more interesting than Eli's mysterious wealthy friends is the notion of her having a powerful enemy. Eli's almost as relentlessly positive as Juan is, so it's odd for her to have any sort of rival.

I notice that the car is more than a little worse for wear, with a number of fresh dings and scrapes and what appears to be the better part of a shrub sticking out from underneath the front right wheel well.

"Is that a boxwood hedge?" I ask.

"Is that *my* boxwood hedge?" Eli asks.

"This thing really accelerates through the curves. And sorry about your mailbox, Cinder-Eli," Stella says.

"No worries," Eli replies. "I'm delighted to see you here in largely one piece."

"Well, I thank y'all for believing in me," Stella replies. "I drove! I didn't even have to use the autopilot. I figured it out because *I can do hard things*, just like that neon sign says in my town house."

"Oh, wait, shit, you don't know," I say, snapping my fingers in an a-ah moment. "We have to tell you, Peter Pulaski isn't dead."

"Yeah, I gathered that when he sat up and began hollerin' at me," Stella says.

"I wonder why he didn't try to hop out and escape?" I ask. "I did put my belt around his arms to lift him, but not that tight because I thought I was touching a dead guy and it gave me the squigs."

"Because I'm not letting you lunatics shoot me *and* steal my car!" Peter screams. White bits of spittle fly out and hit the car's window. "What in the actual fuck is wrong with you people? Talking about crimes isn't enough, you want to *do crimes* now??"

"The word you're looking for is 'commit,'" Jazz says, breaking out her handy air quotes again.

Stella clucks her tongue. "He's been like this for a good twenty-five minutes, ever since he came to. Kinda messed up my concentration, if y'all want to know the truth. I was doing pretty good before the shoutin'."

"You stole my watch, you shot me, and then you stole my car! Now you've constrained and kidnapped me! What kind of cult are you all in?" Peter yells. We ignore him.

Eli smooths a stray lock of Stella's hair. "Stella, I had full faith in you. I wouldn't have put you in this situation if I didn't believe you could handle it. I felt in my bones that you would rise to the occasion."

"Well, I am peachy keen, thank you very much. Because I quickly reminded Mr. Shoutypants back here which of us is a lyin', cheatin' sack of dog shit," Stella says. "And which of us still has the gun she has demonstrated that she is not afraid to use."

"You're the worst driver in the world!" Peter screeches from the back seat. "Look at what you did to my beautiful Tesla! My face is all banged up from when you kept stopping short!"

"Told y'all to put on your seat belt."

"My arms are bound!"

"Well, if you're so mad, then give me zero stars on Uber. Now hush your durn mouth, the grown-ups are talkin'," Stella tells him. To us, she says, "It's not his fault his mama didn't raise him right." She casually exits the car, one hand on the weapon trained on Peter.

"Nope, nope, nope, I do not fuck with guns," Jazz says, and she dashes back into the house. Her little feet pound up the stairs to the second floor, where she peeks out the window of the front bedroom at us.

"Peter, we'd like you to join us inside," Eli says, opening the car's back door. "We want to come to an understanding with you."

"Aw, I wanted to open the door!" I say with great dejection. It's so fun! I kick at the bluestone of the driveway. A few pieces skitter and ping against the car.

Peter is apoplectic. "New car, new paint, you troglodytes!"

"I don't know what that word means, but it felt like a hate crime," I say, metaphorically clutching my pearls.

"If you want, you can close the door," Eli says, which cheers me considerably.

"Where is this bizzarro world you've taken me?" Peter demands as we pull him out of the car.

I close the door with a "Whee!"

"This is my home, Peter," Eli says. "Welcome to Winnetka. I can't believe you've never been up here. You've been invited a number of times."

I grab the back of the belt and I march him inside while Stella keeps him in her pistol's sights. "How are you making *me* sound like the rude one here, Eli? Assault with a deadly weapon, theft, theft again, kidnapping. Sorry if I missed an RSVP, for fuck's sake," Peter says. His rage and indignance has gone on for so long that he's starting to lose steam, like a toddler who tantrums themselves into a nap. That will only make this confrontation easier on us.

"Peter, I find it odd that you haven't yet asked about Diana. Aren't you curious as to where she is? What her involvement might be?" Carmen asks. "You've got to be wondering, right? She's not a part of this, by the way. She's probably never going to speak to us again, and that weighs on my soul."

"And mine," Eli adds. "I don't know what we'd do without her. We're desperate to make sure this sits right with her."

"Great! Because you are all bananas here! You people are batshit, bugfuck, ham-sandwich crazy!" he says, but he's definitely losing steam. He barely said that louder than his normal speaking voice.

As soon as we step inside, we're hit with . . . wow. It's less of a smell and more of an olfactory event. We walk into a wall of the pungent aroma of old gym socks, raw sewage, and an entire Easter basket full of rotten eggs. The sulfuric stench is a full-on sensory assault.

Peter begins to choke and his eyes are watering. "Are we adding poisonous gas to your list of crimes?"

Eli pulls her collar up over her nose. "Oh, that? No worries, it's just cabbage rolls."

❧

"Is this really necessary?" Peter says in reaction to the exercise bands and bungee cords we've used to strap him to the grape arbor. Until the first floor airs out, we've relocated to the backyard to question him. Eli's place is on a few acres, so it's doubtful anyone can hear us.

"Yes, it is! You've injured all of us!" Carmen huffs. "You bashed Frankie's head into the ground, you made me fall, and you tore Eli's rotator cuff."

"Number one, I was reacting to an armed robbery, by, if my memory serves correct, the Super Mario Brothers. And number two, your cuff was already torn," Peter scoffs.

"You know goddamned well it wasn't," Eli says evenly. She is unflappable when all the rest of us are still good and flapped.

"And I broke a nail!" Stella says, shifting the gun to the left hand and splaying her fingers. Her index nail is jagged and missing the diamanté accents. Not demure, not mindful.

"You broke it when you pulled the trigger to shoot me!" Peter replies. "You are not the victim here; I cannot stress that enough!"

"Potato, po-tah-to," Stella says. "Point is, I had a full set when we started and now I do not. I'm gonna have to go in for an emergency fill, and my girl does not like to have to squeeze me in like that. She's very particular."

"Well, she's fine," Peter says, pointing his chin at Jazz. "I didn't touch her."

"*She* has PTS-fucking-D," Jazz says. "I am anti-gun now. Thanks for that. I'm going to start a petition."

Carmen grips Peter's jaw to hold him still. "I need you to stop squirming so I can bandage your ear," Carmen says. She's already cleaned his wound and applied an antibiotic from Eli's first aid kit.

"You're sticking a pantyliner to it!" he says.

"Yes, because it's clean and absorbent," Carmen replies as she folds it over the top of his ear and arranges it so the sticky sides come together.

"I'm gonna look like an asshole!"

"Darlin', I'd wager that is the least of y'all's problems," Stella says.

"And who'd have thought your medical supply bag was full of cash and fake IDs and not doctor-y shit," I add. "Pack some gauze next time, Dr. Douche Canoe."

"Can we get to the point here? What do you people want from me? You're well aware that the second you let me go, I'm calling the police. Jail, every one of you," Peter says. He eyes me. "Oh, they're gonna love *you* in prison. Hey, OUCH."

"Sorry, was that too rough?" Carmen deadpans, having just pinched his damaged ear.

Eli drags a chair over to Peter with her good arm. She's since repurposed her scarf as a sling and damn it if she didn't make her injury *fashion*. That is *my girl*. "Peter, friend, what we have here is a case of mutually assured destruction. Yes, you could call the police about our temporarily picking you up," Eli says.

"You shot me, you stole from me, and you kidnapped me! Felony, felony, felony!"

"Potato, po-tah-to," Stella repeats.

Casually, Eli crosses her legs, just a full-on boardroom predator. Damn, I wish I could have witnessed her in action at her company. Gavin says she was brilliant, but I'd have loved to have seen it for myself. "Yet you seem to not understand what we know about you. First, we know about Zlata and—"

"You can't prove that," Peter protests, but he's already sweating. He did not anticipate this. "And it's a crime to have an online friend? Isn't that what all of you people are, for Diana?"

"I have never sent your wife a dick pic," I say, then I eye Peter up and down. "Spoiler alert? Not impressed."

"Pfft, you would know," Peter says.

Calmly, Stella aims at Peter again. "Cast aspersions on his sexual orientation one more time, I implore you. I will sacrifice the rest of this nail if I need to."

"You do realize that Zlata is a Nigerian Yahoo Boy, right?" Jazz asks.

Peter goes a shade paler and he fights against his restraints to no avail. "You don't know what you're talking about, but it doesn't matter. You're all going down for this!" Peter promises.

Eli tells him, "No, we're not. We've evened the score, or we will have once you comply with—"

"I'm not doing shit," Peter says, and Carmen slaps him in the ear. He yelps in pain and Carmen looks sheepish.

"I couldn't help myself," she says. "I guess we do crimes now."

He says, "You're gonna hear from my lawyer and—"

Eli shuts him down and just takes over, just being a real boss here, shifting all the energy of the group. *Obsessed.* "Peter, I'm speaking and I will finish. I need you to understand that we know everything about the scam you're running with Medicare. The facts, the figures, the paper trail—we have it all and we will not hesitate to use it against you. So, your catheter kingdom?" Jazz quickly backs Eli up with a few more air quotes. "You're shutting it down immediately. You're returning as much of the money as you still have. And the business about inflating your own CPT codes and the false billing of your legitimate patients? You're doing this to senior citizens? On fixed incomes? Violating your Hippocratic oath? Shame on you. Peter, you're better than that and it ends here."

"What are you, my mother?" he spits.

"If I were your mother, you'd have been raised with a moral compass," Eli says evenly. "By the way, I have her number. I met her at a luncheon a few years ago." Eli holds up her phone. "I'm happy to loop her into this conversation."

"No! No, that won't be necessary. Don't talk to my mom. Please. But what if I don't comply?" he asks, trying to find some wiggle room.

Nothing strikes more fear into a mama's boy's heart than said "smother" turning on him.

"Then we have the receipts," Jazz says. She cracks open her laptop and shows him. "Pages and pages and pages. And how gross—are you putting your crooked shit under Diana's maiden name? Stella should shoot you just for that."

"Mmm-hmm," Stella agrees.

Eli explains, "What she means is, all of our evidence will get filtered through the proper channels to the attorney general—who happens to be a friend—and the FBI. You stand to lose your license, your freedom, and most likely, your family. Including your mother. You're still young and skilled and you can make plenty of money without having to take shortcuts, like writing bogus pain scripts. Maybe you're not going to earn Piaget money—the *t* is silent, by the way—but you'll be able to continue to provide for your family. And speaking of your family, we're going to be watching you. If we get so much as a whiff of your not being your kindest, most loyal, best self to your wife and your children—"

"And your foster cats, you son of a bitch," Jazz adds, doing a fake lunge at him. She seems pleased with herself when he winces.

"And your foster cats, then this is a small taste of what's to come," Eli finishes. "What you need to realize, Peter Pulaski, is that I have two things on my side. I have unlimited time and unlimited funds, which means I have unlimited access to power, should I choose to employ it. If I decide you must pay again, then pay you shall."

"Period," I add, throwing an amen hand in the air, like Eli just took us all to *church*.

"Exactly how do you intend to make me pay again?" Peter asks. He knows he's been bested and he's far less defiant than he was a few minutes ago.

"I'll make the video we have of you pissing your pants go viral," Eli says.

Peter swallows hard. This one sticks and leaves a mark.

Eli stands. "So we're all clear, here's what's going to happen. You are about to become husband of the year. No more online affairs, and God help you if we find out you've physically strayed in person. And we need you to be more present for your children."

"I go to every one of Lilly's games!" he protests. "We have father-daughter day at least once a month! She actually talks to me! A few weeks back, when she ended up at a drinking party, she called me in the middle of the night and I went and got her, no questions asked. I didn't tell Diana because she'd freak and that would break Lilly's trust. Whatever else you people think of me, I'm a good dad."

"Yeah, well, you have two kids, Captain Fatherhood. Stop telling Ethan he's fat and uncoordinated. That's just hurtful," Jazz said.

"And if he wants to ballroom dance, you sign him up for lessons and sit in the front row at his performances," I add. "You don't single him out for being different, you celebrate it."

Peter rolls his eyes. "Whatever."

"Not 'whatever,'" Stella says. "We need compliance."

Peter takes a long pause and I can see the rest of the fight leave his body. "Fine. Agreed."

"Next steps," Eli says. "You will shut down the storefront and you will stop the fraudulent billing immediately. You rectify what you can. Believe me, this is the path of least resistance. And won't a part of you feel better at not having to live a double life?"

We studied one school shooter story in our group and it was far too much for any of us to handle. Too dark, too tragic, so we never covered another. But during the course of the discussion, we learned that most of these shooters—especially when they're young adults—are actually looking for someone to stop them. They often don't want to do what they're planning. They want guardrails. Maybe Peter was looking for someone or something to give him permission to stop? Like he couldn't slam on the brakes himself, and maybe our confrontation is a tiny bit of a relief.

Peter won't look at any of us. "*No.* No. Well . . . maybe."

"I'll take that as a *yes*," Eli says. "Now, here's what's going to happen next. We're going to undo you and you're going to come inside and get yourself cleaned up. We're not sending you home to Diana like this; you look a fright. Also, are you hungry?"

Peter is wary from the sudden change in temperature. "A little. Why? Are you people going to eat me or something? Is this all the punch line to a cruel joke where you end up being cannibals?"

Eli says, "No, I ask because we have plenty of food inside, and I can't send you home without a proper meal. It's late and you have to be starving. Also, I wasn't raised by wolves."

We loosen the restraints and he doesn't immediately run away, even though he's free to. He seems to be torn between escape and unburdening himself, so he comes inside with us and immediately pounces on the spread. Terror makes you ravenous, we've discovered. We watch him eat in awkward silence until Carmen can't take it anymore.

"Peter, can you please tell us why?" Carmen asks. There's no accusation in her voice, only curiosity.

Peter swallows his bite of bialy. "I don't know."

I am extending less courtesy. I can feel myself glowering a hole through Peter. "Yes, you do."

Peter takes a sip of water. "I guess . . . I guess I was bored, okay?"

"No!" I shout and smack the countertop. This is a bullshit answer and it enrages me. "You're going to blow up your life and your family because you're bored? No. Wrong answer." Life is good now, but when Kahlen, my ex, cheated on me, it wrecked me. I didn't think I'd ever recover. Finding out the person you thought was your everything was something to someone else? That's a tough pill to swallow. And it's a pill that's made me bitter about my future, too gun shy to commit to the perfect person who's begging for me to spend the rest of my life with him.

"What is this, therapy now?" Peter asks, but not nearly as defensively as I'd expect. I wonder if he wouldn't like to get some of this off his chest.

"I mean, I am a licensed psychologist," Carmen says with a shrug.

Peter scrunches his eyes together and rakes his hands through his hair. "Truth? Fine, I was scared. The pandemic was pretty fucking rough. My business took a big hit because people weren't coming in for anything other than urgent treatment and my bills started to pile up. My monthly nut is *a lot*."

Eli is always right, isn't she?

"You guys seem to think Diana doesn't ask for much, but there's a shitload of unspoken expectations for her to re-create the kind of life she had growing up. We needed *that* house in *that* neighborhood so our kids could go to *that* school. And then she needed the upgraded kitchen, the renovated bathrooms, the finished rec room. All the money for kids' camps and her causes, plus I still had to keep up appearances, you know?"

Carmen nods at him, using her silence as a way to encourage him to talk. That's an old police trick we've learned from true crime stories. People are too uncomfortable with silence; they have an urge to fill those gaps, and that's often where you find the truth.

"And then she works for her brothers and doesn't even allow them to compensate her. Like, we could have used that money, especially when I was still paying off med school. There we were, living paycheck to paycheck and she was taking what we had and blowing it on stupid shit to impress the neighbors."

His perspective is so different from Diana's. Have they ever even sat down and compared notes? Do they even, like, *talk*? My God, that's what I discovered when Gavin and I got together. Kahlen had so many secrets from me. But Gavin? We talk about everything, even the smallest details. He knew he had to earn my trust and he did it slowly but surely by telling me everything, to the point I couldn't not trust him.

"Then she was all, *Why are you working for someone else when you could run the whole show?* So she sort of forced me to go into private practice, which was so much capital expenditure. So much. She didn't understand how different it was for me to set up an ortho office as opposed to her dad's family practice, which basically just entailed updating the stupid Norman Rockwell prints in the waiting room. So the pandemic hit and I was stuck at home all the time, getting deeper and deeper in debt, and I looked around at the walls closing in on me and thought, 'Is this it? Is this all I worked for?'"

"Nope, nope, no," Jazz says, crossing her arms over her chest. "Not you making me empathize with you. Today has been traumatic enough."

He's not winning us over, not by a long shot, but he is proving that there's always another side to a story. He's actually making me realize exactly how good I have it with Gavin, and I'm wondering now why I've been so hesitant to make our relationship legal. He hasn't asked me to marry him in a while, but if he did now, I wonder if I'd just say "yes" instead of "someday."

Peter takes another bite, thinking while he chews. Then he says, "All of a sudden, Diana had other stuff to do when she met you people. Whatever, fine, she should have friends. But being a part of your group consumed her whole personality. It changed her. Even though I was in a house full of people, I got lonely. So I made some bad choices. Sue me."

In no way, shape, or form are we excusing Peter. We were scared and lonely during the pandemic too, not to mention stressed and, in some of our cases, for those of us who were waiting tables, in trouble financially. Until the moratorium, I was about to be evicted from my apartment because I couldn't pay my rent when the restaurant where I worked closed. That fear and stress bonded us together to form something positive. But I can see how someone else could have found solace in other ways, even if the ways went against our ethics. Desperation comes in a lot of shapes and sizes and there's no one reaction to it.

"Did you ever tell Diana any of this?" Eli asks.

"Pfft, Diana only hears what she wants to hear," Peter says.

"You take that back," I say, shaking a fist at him.

"No, think about it. She's my *wife*. I was really in love with her until it felt like she was starting to ruin our lives with her quiet demands. You think I didn't try to talk to her? Like I went from zero to asshole for no reason? Like I'm one of the psychos you guys talk about on social media? You don't even know what I know about her, and yet I've stood by her. I get no credit for that. What happens when you tell Diana something she doesn't want to hear?" Peter rakes his hands through his hair. "I'll tell you. She does that 'la la la, I didn't hear that' stuff and then she changes the subject. I've never met anyone more uncomfortable with being uncomfortable, and less willing to look at hard truth. She is Diana-patra, the Queen of Denial. Guess what, it gets old real fast. Shit, even if Zlata is a Yahoo Boy, she or he or whatever—this is not about pronouns—*they* really listened to me. They said stuff like, 'It sounds like this is hard for you.' Certainly didn't ever get that from Diana."

"Devil's advocate—if you're the victim here, then why do you allow your family to walk all over her?" Carmen asks.

Peter lets out a bitter laugh. "I'm sorry, do you think that's on me? She fucking insists on inserting herself into everything, and when everyone doesn't do it exactly her way, she martyrs herself. But she's so saccharine sweet about it that *you* end up apologizing."

"Please. She doesn't do that," I insist. I won't hear anything against my Diana. Nothing.

Carmen and Eli exchange a look. "The dishes."

Jazz raises an eyebrow, and exhales hard through pursed lips. "What about the backlog?" Um . . . wow. This is a new perspective Peter is giving us. I can't help but remember the to-do last year over our fundraiser when we wanted to expand our charitable reach.

"I don't follow. What do you mean?" Peter asks.

Eli explains, "We wanted to give to the DNA Capacity Enhancement for Backlog Reduction Program, because it would help labs process more DNA samples. It's important to us because these samples would be added to CODIS."

"That's the name for the FBI's Combined DNA Index System," Carmen adds.

"If we donated our DoomCon proceeds, we could help them hire more people, buy better equipment, et cetera, and they could process more evidence that way and likely solve more cold cases. We thought it was such a win-win for everyone. Yet Diana, politely as could be, fought us tooth and nail about diversifying our donations. Ultimately, we let her win because she had the strongest feelings about it," Eli says.

Another laugh escapes Peter. "No surprise she'd be against DNA evidence."

"What's that supposed to mean?" I ask, my ruff still up. But maybe a little of what he says is getting through. "Listen, this is yours." I reach into my pocket and I hand Peter back his watch, which he immediately slips onto his wrist.

Peter gets up from his seat and slaps the front of his thighs, in the universal Midwest "let's get this show on the road" gesture. "Listen, that's her story to tell, not mine. But maybe you don't quite know your friend like you think."

"Again, what's that supposed to mean?" I ask.

"I'm gonna let your *bestie* fill you in on that," Peter says with a bitter laugh. "Eli, you said something about having a pair of your son's pants I could borrow? I need to go."

"Let me grab them," Eli says. She quickly returns with a pair of new black sweatpants, tags still on them, and hands them to Peter.

While we are not ending this night as one big, happy family, I feel like we've established a beachhead. Peter Pulaski has paid. I believe Peter's heading back on the right track, and he'll be better to Diana and Ethan because he won't have to act out as a way of trying to get stopped anymore. He's actually given us some understanding of his world. He'll start abiding by the law because he knows our threat is hanging over his head. Lucky for him, we dispensed our version of justice before he got a taste of real consequences.

I do wonder what he meant by the DNA business, but my bell's still a little rung, so maybe I misunderstood. I look around at everyone else, but I think they're all too punch drunk to have caught it.

Eli says, "Here, wait, before you go, why don't you guys dig into that other box of pirozhok? I was saving these as a special treat for us.

I can't be left alone with these, they're too good." She slides the pink twine-tied box across the counter.

All the blood rushes from Peter's face and he looks like he's seen a ghost. "Did you go to Russkaya Pechka?" Peter asks slowly and deliberately. "By the airport?"

"I did! I met the owner. What a nice man," Eli replies, a faint blush rising in her cheeks. OMG, there *is* more to this story, and I can't wait for this to be over so we can download everything.

"Tall man with a scar?"

"That's him."

"How did you meet him? And where?" His pupils dilate and his hands begin to tremble as he takes quick, shallow breaths. Okay, weird. What is going on with him?

"Literally by accident. Actually, since we've reached a new level of honesty in our collective relationship, I was following you. So I can tell you it was by your storefront earlier this week," Eli says.

Like a flash, Peter drops the sweats and books out the front door.

"Hold on! You forgot your pants! Where are you going?" Eli calls after him. She swings back to see what we're all doing to have caused this reaction.

"Don't look at me, I'm not holdin' a gun to him for once," Stella says. Peter screeches out of the driveway like a bat out of hell, despite the shrub's encumbrance.

"What is it with the Pulaskis and their dramatic exits tonight?" Carmen asks. "This is exhausting."

Jazz looks at all of us and shakes her head, disgusted. "When are you guys going to start to believe me about the Russians? It's so freaking obvious."

"Now what, Jazz?" I ask, resigned. "What are you trying to say?"

"I'm trying to say that Peter Pulaski is a dead man walking."

Chapter Twenty-Four

Diana

I always expected this day to come, the official at the door, demanding answers about what I know and when I knew it. But I never anticipated that I'd be asked about Peter's secrets and not my own.

What the investigator tells me about Peter horrifies me, although I have to admit it would account for the changes I've seen in him. Plus, I don't know how much is speculation and how much is proof. I wonder if I'm not so grateful that this man is not here to grill me about JDK that *any* conversation would be better than that. While I feel sick, it's nothing compared to how I felt that September day when my parents called me.

"We need you to come home now, Diana." The order came down from my father via an early morning phone call. From his tone, it was a command performance, and not up for negotiation.

America had woken up the morning he called in a very different world. Before I knew why, I didn't blame my dad for wanting me back in Burr Ridge. Classes were canceled for the rest of the week, and I didn't know how long it would be after that. Justin had already gone home to Indianapolis because he wanted to be around his family. We didn't even say goodbye—he just left me a voicemail because the draw of being with his people was too strong, and I understood that.

All Dorie and I had done the day before was stare at the television in fear, fury, and disbelief, watching the planes crash and the Towers collapse, the first responders running toward trouble, the people fleeing covered in ash. It still feels surreal today, decades later.

The day my dad called, we had no idea what was going to happen next, or if the attacks were even over, so I had no issue packing a bag and going home. Home sounded pretty good to me. I recall getting into my mom's car, and the next thing I knew, I was home. I was in such a daze that I couldn't even remember the drive up there, except that it was a bright blue, sunny day and that the roads were empty. I recall wondering how the weather could be so perfect and temperate when the most horrific thing anyone can imagine happened just the day before. Sunshine felt obscene. The weather should have been in mourning too. There should have been pounding rain, thunderous skies, tornadoes, something to mark the day that the world stopped making sense.

When I arrived home, I flew into my parents' arms and I was so glad they'd made me come back. I needed to be here, needed to process my grief with the people I loved.

My parents sat me down in the front room, a space reserved for guests and condolences that day. "Diana," my mother said. She was pale as a ghost, without a lick of makeup, still wrapped in her dressing gown. She appeared to have aged ten years since I saw her last, but that was to be expected. As sad as it was, and while I was praying for the rest of the nation, it hadn't happened here. We had a degree of separation. We weren't New Yorkers, not Pennsylvanians, not from DC. The attacks impacted us, but not directly.

I couldn't stop thinking about my friend from New Jersey who lived in my dorm freshman year—her dad worked for Cantor Fitzgerald. She woke up to go to class and by the time she finished breakfast, her entire universe had come to an end. The whole drive home, I wondered, *How do you deal with that? How do you get past it?*

We'd talk a lot about grief in my classes back then, because we were training to be on the front lines in a hospital. We knew that while we'd do our best, not every outcome would be favorable, so we were taught to show empathy and compassion but also to do it in a way that we didn't lose ourselves. We had to learn to set boundaries to protect our own well-being.

As my mother sat across from me, she dabbed at her eyes with a crumpled Kleenex. "We received some terrible news."

I can still feel how my heart dropped down through the floor. I thought, *Did we have family on one of the planes? Was someone we love visiting New York, unlucky enough to be in the most wrong place at the most wrong time?*

"Wait, where are Stevie and Mark?" I broke out in a cold sweat, my stomach twisted, and my adrenaline spiked. I felt an electric jolt pass through me and I couldn't catch my breath.

"They're upstairs, they're fine," my mother said.

"Thank God, thank God," I said as I started to cry. I wasn't even sure who I was crying for, save for everyone. She and my father exchanged a look that I couldn't interpret.

"It's about Aunt Nancy and the kids," my father said after a long pause.

"And her mother," my mother added. We called Aunt Nancy's mom "Nana Banana," as she wasn't our actual grandmother, but she was close enough, especially while we were growing up. I remember how my mother was grasping her Kleenex so tightly that her knuckles were white and all the veins were sticking up on the top of her hands.

I swallowed hard, trying to form my question for which I did not want an answer. "Were they on one of the planes?" I asked.

"They're gone," my father said, and I sobbed harder. We were really close when I was younger. They came down here all the time for our big Sunday suppers. My cousins Clara, Shelly, and Davey Jr. were so much fun. Davey was the ringleader and he'd always insist we put on shows for our parents in the garage. I wonder if one of the reasons I feel so close to Frankie is that he reminds me of what Davey might have been like. All our cousins would share a room when we'd go on family road trips because my father and Uncle David loved hitting national parks together.

"What happened? Where were they?" I asked.

They didn't say anything. I recall the silence was thick, suffocating, deafening.

I had to ask again, "Where were they?" But I felt deep in my gut that whatever it was that happened to them was not an accident. Years ago when I told Peter my secret, when I shared all the details of what happened that day and what came after, I thought confession would make it better, would make me feel like I had absolution, but it didn't. If anything, I felt worse. Hearing it out loud made it real. To Peter's credit, he didn't react poorly. He was so loving in those days, and he used to listen. Yet I still felt like a monster.

But I can't think about that right now. That is not the biggest problem at hand.

Mr. Arthur, the investigator, is empathetic, considering the news he's broken to me about my husband. He's laid out the government's whole case and the evidence seems damning. But I cling to the notion that maybe he has it wrong.

For being the bearer of very bad news, he does have kind eyes. He doesn't seem to be taking any pleasure in telling me what he believes Peter has been up to.

Maybe he doesn't believe it?

Could he have it wrong about Peter's practice?

Or am I just being delusional, overlooking the obvious?

My mind is racing to try to find any other explanation, just like I did that September morning, despite my innate feeling of knowing it was the truth. But this is my husband and my life now, so I owe it to Peter to not assume the worst, even though all of this tracks.

I play devil's advocate in my own head. Could there be some confusion with his office staff? I have never been entirely confident in his staff's abilities. Poor Barb is always so frazzled, so scattered. I even offered to train her in office management and billing, but she wanted no part of me in her books and Peter supported her, not me. (That did hurt my feelings.)

This has to be a simple case of oversight. It has to. Surely there's some confusion. And when was the last time any government agent or agency was efficient? Or got it right on the first try? I mean, I've been to the Illinois Department of Motor Vehicles; it should not take an hour and a half for a safe driver with perfect vision to get her license renewed. And yet this would neatly explain Peter's recent expenditures, which I've not called attention to, because they seem to make him happy.

Mr. Arthur—although he told me to call him Isaac, that doesn't seem right—somehow felt familiar at the door. He looks like Idris Elba, which is who Justin grew up to look like.

A part of me was relieved that he was just here on a fact-finding mission, and relieved that Lilly isn't home and Ethan is upstairs in his room, having already gone to bed.

But then he started telling me about Peter's fraud, and I was disassociating so hard it was like I'd left my body for a minute. He must deal with this all the time, the clueless spouse who's looked the other way, who never questions anything.

As he's leaving me with way too much to consider, I notice a little gold boxing glove charm on his keychain and I find myself doing what Frankie calls my nervous talking thing. The charm has worn, raised writing on the back and a shiny little stone in the palm of the glove, so it caught my eye, especially as Mr. Arthur seems like a no-nonsense sort of man, yet here he has a tiny piece of flair that states otherwise. The dichotomy interests me and thinking of anything but the reality in front of me seems important.

"What is that?" I ask. I can't help myself.

He takes a beat, like he's trying to consider the wisdom of telling me personal information. But he must not consider me any sort of threat because he says, "That is my good luck charm."

"Is there a story behind it?" I ask.

This question seems to throw him. "Sure, but it's a long story."

As does my answer: "I don't mind long stories."

"My goodness, I've taken up enough of your time this evening, Mrs. Pulaski. I've given you a lot to digest and I should leave you to the rest of your night," Mr. Arthur says, rising from the armchair in the front room where we've been talking. Of course I'd served a plate of cookies and coffee. I'd probably offer a cheese plate to my executioner.

"Please, I've had so much caffeine, I won't be sleeping tonight," I say with a nervous laugh. I want to try to get a hold of Peter, but he's not responded all night, even though I see he's getting my messages. I can't imagine he'd answer my call now, if he didn't the first few times, and I suspect he's not at the hospital. Maybe he's trying to get away, to get to a place where he has the time and space to prove his innocence.

If I keep talking, maybe I can buy Peter the time he needs?

I say, "I'd love to hear a long story right about now."

Mr. Arthur seems to be fighting an internal decision. The side that allows him to tell me his story prevails. He sits down again. "Okay. Let me go on record saying this is not exactly appropriate, but far be it for me to be rude. So, when I was sixteen, I was falsely accused of an armed robbery. It was mistaken identity that eventually got cleared up with DNA evidence, which was pretty new back then."

I nod and swallow, as I feel a stab of anxiety when anyone talks about DNA testing. Someone gave Peter an Ancestry DNA test for Christmas a couple of years ago, and he thought it would be fun for the whole family to take one. I demurred, saying I thought it was a waste of money. My family is Swedish for hundreds of years and I didn't need a test to reinforce what I already knew. At no point did I mention that familial DNA is how they found the Golden State Killer, though it was top of mind.

Knowing what he knew of my secret, it suddenly bothers me that he tried to goad me into it.

Mr. Arthur continues, "I still spent six months locked up in juvie because of it. I had the same sad story as everyone else there. See, I grew up in the Robert Taylor Homes, single mother, government assistance, the whole nine yards. I was not someone the court cared to invest in. I would not be missed. None of us there would. And everyone claims innocence anyway, right? If you asked them, there wasn't a guilty guy in the joint. Here's the thing—I was lucky that my Uncle Gene was a Baptist minister, I mean salt of the earth. He was the kind of person who'd stop traffic on 54th Street to make sure a family of geese could cross the road safely."

"I love that," I say. That's the moment when Snowy, my deaf, fluffy white former feral rescue pokes her square head out from under the dust ruffle on the chair. She presses up against his leg as he speaks. She generally dislikes everyone, yet she leans into his hand as he scratches her behind the ears. "Oh no! She's going to get her fur all over your dark pants!" I say.

"Then that's the price I'm willing to pay," he says as he rubs her under her chin, causing her to absolutely melt. "Anyway, Uncle Gene didn't write me off, even though everyone else thought I was just another kid with a dead-end future. He fought for me and he believed in me. I still don't know the favors he called in."

He laughs and nods, remembering. "I may not want to know. But he was able to get that DNA evidence introduced and I was eventually exonerated. The only thing he asked of me was to stay out of trouble, so he set me up with a friend who ran a boxing gym. That changed my whole trajectory because I found something I was good at. I'll be honest, I didn't do what I'd been accused of *that time*, but I was headed down that path before boxing. Boxing changed my life. Eventually, I won an amateur Golden Gloves title before I enlisted in the army, which got me into the all-army boxing program. Between the GI Bill and a boxing scholarship, I was able to go to college, and then to law school, and the rest is history. Here I am. Anyway, I've carried this charm ever since then because it reminds me to fight for the people who don't have someone in their corner. When it comes to victims, I want to be their Uncle Gene. Now, I really do have to go, so thank you for listening, especially given the circumstances of our meeting."

How is it this stranger in my home had more time to share something with me than my own spouse?

I'm afraid if I start examining this, really digging in, I'll start screaming and I won't be able to stop.

Then he gives me his card and adds, "Please, it's imperative I speak with your husband. If you can, have him get in touch as soon as he gets home. Doesn't matter how late. My goal is to get him to *come* in before we're forced to *bring* him in, if you understand what I'm saying."

I nod. I do understand what he's saying. He's been honest and forthright, and gentle in the way he addressed me. What I don't understand is the roiling mix of emotions I'm experiencing right now, from hurt to confusion to shame to rage.

He says, "Again, thank you and sorry for the circumstances. I've left you with a lot to think about and I am truly sorry for that."

We shake hands and I thank him—why do I thank him?—and he leaves before I'm tempted to blurt out the secret I've carried for so long.

My God, what is wrong with me today?

After Mr. Arthur leaves, I call the hospital. Given what I've learned this evening about his potential fraud and secret double life, I know in my heart he's not there, but I have to check anyway. I'm passed around from department to department, and no one seems to have seen him and he's not on a rotation.

Where is he? I don't so much as go to the grocery store without texting him, because it's so my habit, even though he stopped answering every text years ago. My mind begins to race. How is it that Mr. Arthur was saying the same thing the Crew tried to tell me about and I refused to hear them? Eli said she had the proof in black and white on her invoice from Peter, and instead of listening, I lost my temper, blind to the truth staring me in the face. How did I not believe the people who 100 percent have my back, all day, every day? Once is a coincidence, twice is a pattern. That's not the number one true crime golden rule, but it's right up there.

I just need to see Peter, to talk to him, to get his side of the story because we're missing some critical pieces to this puzzle. Both things can be true—that the Crew is right, and that Peter is a victim of circumstance. I try his phone and I'm routed to voicemail yet again.

"What was that all about?" Lilly asks, practically vaporizing out of thin air by the back staircase, and I jump. I thought she was still at her friend's house. She's hugging her arms close to her chest and she somehow looks very small, like when she'd creep down the stairs years ago after she had a bad dream. Now it's me having a nightmare.

"Woo, you scared me, Bunny Rabbit. When did you get home?" I ask, taking a few deep breaths to calm my pounding heart. "How was Mara's house? Did you have fun? What kind of trouble did you two get into?" Distract, distract.

She is not so easily dissuaded. "Who was that?" Lilly asks. "The guy?"

"That was no one and nothing for you to worry about. Don't even waste a single thought about it," I assure her, bright and cheery as can be. "He was just an old friend of your dad's."

"Didn't sound like it," Lilly persists. "Sounded like trouble."

"Then you didn't hear it right," I reply. "I promise you, it was nothing."

Lilly clenches her jaw. She's not buying it. "Are you trying to tell me that I didn't hear what I heard and I didn't see what I saw?" Lilly asks.

While, yes, that would be the Carlson way, I do not say this aloud.

"I would never do that. It's true, swear, scout's honor. No worries here." I will absolutely not let her get dragged into this, because the last thing I want is *her* hauling around a terrible secret for her whole adult life.

"Please never quote a Taylor Swift song again. And we're just going to gloss over it and not talk about what's really going on, like always?"

Again, *yes*. She doesn't know it, but it's a million percent kinder if I do.

"Whatever you think you saw and heard, you're mistaken. Why don't you head to bed; it's getting late." Then I do the one thing guaranteed to make her scatter—I go in for the hug, which she neatly evades.

"Whatever, good night," she says as she trots up the stairs. To herself, she grumbles, "We'll just keep on the fucking sunny side then, won't we?"

Ouch.

She knows and I know she knows and I feel powerless to do anything about it.

❦

It's practically dawn when Peter finally calls me back. I've been mentally retracing everything that he's told me about work for months. Now that I'm examining it, truly digging in, none of his stories make sense. Have I honestly been this foolish? And why was I too proud or stubborn to listen to those who've only protected me, who've never betrayed me?

At some point I must have fallen asleep, but it was deep into the night, and I wake at the first ring.

"Peter, thank God, I've been worried sick about you! There's a lot going on here," I tell him. It's so good to hear his voice, like a life preserver to cling to in a sea of chaos "Where are you?"

"I'm outside of Louisville," he says. I can hear the faint sound of traffic in the background. His voice has a sharp edge to it and I can sense the pressure radiating from him, even all these miles away. I feel like he's a heartbeat from raging at me and I brace myself, try to make my questions softer and smaller so I don't feel the brunt of his angry reply. But I'm not the one accused of doing anything wrong here, so why am I apologetic?

"What? Louisville? As in Kentucky? Why are you going to Louisville?" I ask. I ask and I don't want to know but I have to know.

There's a pregnant pause. "I'm not, and it's a long story."

"I don't mind long stories."

He snaps, "Well, I mind having to tell one. I'm fucking exhausted and I can't get into it right now. I need you to listen to me, okay? This is *very* important. I need your help."

"But Peter, what I have to tell you is important! Did you listen to my voicemails? There was an investigator here! He said they want you to come in *before they have to bring you in.* Arrested! Charged! That sounds so serious! Listen, we can fight this. I can get you an attorney first thing in the morning, but I'll need to hear your side of the story so I can help you. Of course I told him he was completely wrong. He was wrong of course, right, Peter? Right? I suspect if anyone, this is about Barb, but—"

"Was he Russian?"

"Sweetie, why would he be Russian?" I ask. The investigator didn't say anything about an international element, and somehow, the fact that this is what he asked sends a chill down my spine. *Peter, what are you into?* I can feel my nervous chatter shift into overdrive. "The oddest thing was, this Isaac Arthur gentleman reminded me of Justin, that nice guy I dated my senior year at U of I. I've told you about him—he lives in London? He's the one who—"

Peter barks, "Damn it, Diana, can we not reminisce right now? I need you to stop talking and start listening. Get a pen, write this information down, all of it." I scramble for a piece of paper and a pencil inside my nightstand. He rattles off an address in the Cumberland Gap area of Virginia. (Cumberland Gap, Virginia? Why?) He also has me write down the latitude and longitude, for some reason. "Go into the safe in my study and—"

This throws me. "You have a safe in your study?" What else do I not know?

He growls audibly before speaking, just a purely guttural sound that almost isn't human. "Just please *listen*. The safe is behind that framed landscape. The combination is 0-7-0-3."

"Aw, that's the date we met!" I say. I can't help it; I feel a rush of love. Then I realize that I shouldn't be flattered that he remembers; I should be furious that he's been keeping enormous secrets from me. I told him the worst of mine; why couldn't he reciprocate? Why couldn't he lean on me like I've leaned on him? I am a forgiving person but what I can't forgive is being shut out. Just give me the truth and we can deal with it together.

There's another long pause after he lets out a ragged breath. "When you open the safe, there's a thumb drive on the upper right shelf. Grab the thumb drive and take the kids to your brother's or parents' place and then bring me the thumb drive at the address I've given you. It's a matter of life and death."

I'm so confused. "What's on the drive?"

Heavy sigh. "It's a crypto wallet."

"Can I just download it and send it to you? And whose life?"

"Mine, goddamn it!" He's so loud, the whole phone vibrates and the panic in his voice stops me in my tracks.

I have to ask but I already know the answer, just like I knew it back in September 2001. "Peter . . . is what everyone is saying about you true? The Medicare stuff? Are you in trouble with the law?" My friends were telling me the truth. They cared enough about me to level with me, when my husband would not. I bet they've known about this for a while and it's why things have felt off. They have probably been agonizing over what to say to me and how, and instead of being open to them, I had terrible thoughts about all of them and said things I regret. I totally lost it on the Crew, when all they were doing was having my back.

My God, it's all so clear now. Shit, shit, shit. I've interpreted all of this wrong, haven't I? I feel deep in my gut that this is real, that he's been playing me for a fool. That he isn't who I thought he was.

How could he do this to me? How could he do this to our kids? What was he thinking? Why would he risk everything we've built for the past two decades? I can't wrap my mind around this.

"The government is the least of my problems, Diana. Get the drive, get out, do it now."

I agree and he hangs up and I grab the card the investigator gave me. I want to do the right thing, but it's not clear what that is. I don't want to be blindly loyal because deciding to do that the last time has haunted me my whole adult life. But maybe that was so difficult because it wasn't my decision. If I were to do this for him—and I wouldn't be doing this for him, I'd be doing it for Lilly and Ethan—then at least it would be my choice.

Chapter Twenty-Five

Eli

Given how our night has unfolded, it makes the most sense for everyone to stay at my house because we suspect we'll be called into action and we don't want to split up. Everything feels off and unsettled and I have a sense that Diana is going to reach out. In my heart, I feel like she has to, and if she doesn't, then we will. We're too connected not to.

Thanks to Jazz's intrepid research, we begin to piece together that our threat of turning him in isn't what sent Peter on the run; it doesn't make sense.

"With a good attorney, he could fight the charges or negotiate a settlement. Best-case scenario, he'd be barred from participating in Medicare for a period and he'd face civil penalties. He'd likely have to repay the government too," Carmen says. "Being caught doesn't have to be the end for him."

Stella nods. "I mean, worst-case scenario, he could lose his license, face criminal charges, and serve time. But he'd almost certainly end up in a white-collar, minimum security–style place. Like a country club, where he could work on his pickleball game."

Frankie adds, "If he were to get off on the lighter end of criminal charges, he could be sentenced to house arrest with travel restrictions and curfews, possibly with electronic monitoring. Basically, the Anna

Delvey treatment, minus the invitation to compete on *Dancing with the Stars*. And OMG, did you guys watch when she was cut and she was all, 'I didn't learn anything from this experience.' Icon." (Frankie has a soft spot for Anna Delvey that the rest of us do not share.)

I say, "None of this is the end of the world. Nothing that would make him chuck all he'd built and everyone he loved. That's what's so confounding."

We've spent all night parsing what Peter had told us in the heat of the moment. He seemed to indicate he had a deal with the Russians before he rushed off. We're all gathered on my custom California king sleigh bed, made extra wide and long to accommodate me and the boys. We're positioned like the grandparents in *Charlie and the Chocolate Factory*. Frankie's snuggled next to me, and the girls are across from us. I position myself in a way that I'm not putting weight on my arm, as it is smarting, but I keep that to myself. Ironically, my arm hurts way less than my feet did after those stupid shoes I wore to Stella's party.

"If he's taking in large amounts of cash in the pill mill, he needs a way to wash it," Jazz says. "You've seen *Breaking Bad*. Walter White had to set up a cash business where he could clean all that money, which is why he had the car wash."

"Like, physically scrub it?" Stella asks, perplexed. She must be tired, as she starts peeling off her lashes while we speak and we've never seen her naked eyes before. "I don't understand."

"Don't you guys remember when I suggested we cover the Wachovia Bank money laundering scandal? They laundered almost $400 billion of Mexican cartel money? And it was a huge deal? It was why banking laws changed, because they found that Hezbollah was also using Wachovia accounts?" Jazz prompts, her tone expressing even more frustration than her usual level of disdain. "But I was outvoted because you didn't want to do the research, Frankie? You said talking about a bank gave you 'boredom cancer'?"

"Yeah, yeah, yeah, I totally remember now!" Frankie says with a big stretch as he settles back into the pillows. "Because I didn't get it.

Money laundering didn't make any sense to me until Heather Gay described how it worked on an episode of *Real Housewives of Salt Lake City* when she was talking about Jen Shah's business. Stella, do you remember that?"

"Nope, I only watch *Potomac*, *Atlanta*, and *New Jersey*," Stella says.

"No *Beverly Hills*?" Frankie is incredulous. "Dorit's fashion is life."

"Nah, not a fan since Lisa Vanderpump left. And then they did Denise Richards so durn dirty that I was doubly done with them."

"*New York*?"

"Ugh, hate the new cast."

"I feel like you need to give Jenna Lyons more of a chance. Icon! But no *Orange County*? This last season was unhinged. I died. Dead. See, Shannon got dumped by long-term boyfriend John Janssen and then totes spiraled. She got drunk and drove into the side of a house. It was on the news. Complicating matters, they brought back Alexis Bellino, who—"

Jazz slaps the side of the bed for everyone's attention. "*Eli*, can you please explain money laundering to these nimrods before we go off track *again*? Life and death here? Tick tock, we're running out the clock? Yeah, we hate Peter but don't want him dead?" She massages my bedding. "Also, your sheets are like butter. No, like liquid suede, but that is beside the point."

"Okay," I say. I'm already under my Egyptian cotton covers to the shoulders. Even though it's still warm outside, I like to keep my bedroom cold enough that I can use my down comforters year round; it's just cozier. "Here's Money Laundering 101. Let's say you have illegally obtained money, like from selling prescriptions for cash. You can't just deposit large sums, it sets off too many alarm bells, triggers investigations."

"Thank you, Wachovia," Jazz adds.

I continue, "You have to set up a system to make the money look like it came from legitimate sources, meaning a cash-centric business, such as a salon or a restaurant. If you want to do something other than bury that cold, hard currency in your backyard, you need a way to introduce it to the financial system, by depositing it or buying assets. Basically, there's three steps. Placement is the first step and that entails depositing. Layering is when the money is moved from account to account to further obscure the origin. People will put it in an offshore account or a shell company."

"Is that why we think that Peter was creating companies in Diana's maiden name?" Carmen asks. "All those credit cards, ugh. If he ruins her credit on top of this, he'll *wish* he just had to deal with the Russians."

"I can't say but wouldn't be surprised. Regular guardrails of morality and ethics do not seem to stop him. Anyway, after that, the third step is the money is integrated into the legitimate economy. That could be purchases, like watches and cars, or investments. Obviously, this is illegal for a whole host of reasons, largely because of tax evasion. But more often than not, this money started off hidden because it's used to finance illicit activities for anything from human trafficking to funding terror," I explain.

"Then it's real bad," Stella says. "Wait, didn't I see something like this on the show *Claws*? It was about a nail salon."

"If you people had let us cover the Wachovia thing, we'd all be up to speed by now," Jazz complains.

"Bad is an understatement," I say. "So if Peter was talking about the Russians, they're likely the ones who have the cash business where he's washing the money. Sounds like they're already on the take, so there's a missing piece here, Jazz. Can you explain to us why his business partners would be after him? What may have changed? Is this because he's under investigation?"

"Thank you for clarifying for *some people*. Here's the thing—it's not about the business. I did some digging while you guys were dicking around, changing into pajamas and picking out bedrooms like it's a *Real Housewives* cast trip," Jazz says, pulling the comforter over her legs. "Seriously, what is this thread count? A million?"

Full disclosure—during the pandemic, I went a little stir-crazy in the early days. I stocked my house with everything I might need if a bunch of people had to stay with me unexpectedly, like if there was a terrible storm or . . . yet another global pandemic. So those weren't my son's sweatpants I tried to give Peter. They were from my stockpile. My son accused me of trying to lure people into my gingerbread house with all the extra luxury *everything* I have, but I think his feelings were hurt that I didn't particularly want *them* here. I did donate the lion's share of it later on, especially all the food, but if the Doom Crew needs to camp out for a couple of days (okay, weeks), I have everything they could require to reside here comfortably. If the unthinkable happens, the least I can do is make sure everyone has the basics, from toothbrushes to fresh undies to heavy coats.

"I've got some unfortunate news about your bakery lunch buddy, Eli," Jazz says. "It wasn't a coincidence that you ran into that Yuri guy outside of Peter's office. Pretty sure he's the head Russian, and I doubt Peter's ever met him. At that level, they never get their hands dirty; they're firewalled from their partners. Yet he was clearly watching the storefront, which is a big breach of protocol. You said he told you about losing his son?"

Oh no, I was afraid of that connection. I've been trying not to put those pieces together all night, just dreading that the lovely man who shared a pot of tea with me could be a monster. My God, if the first person I could even consider liking since Hank is what Jazz is saying, what does that say about me? About my judgment?

"When I went to his bakery yesterday, we really formed a bond," I sadly admit. This causes Frankie to shriek into his pillow with glee.

"Honey, not the time," Stella tells him.

I say, "I don't often discuss my loss with complete strangers, but he was such a willing ear that I told him all about Hank. He was so sweet, so empathetic. Then he told me about his son Konstantin."

"I don't like where this is heading," Carmen says.

Nor do I. But I have to force myself to bring it to the group.

"Really? Because I love it!" Frankie replies, now hugging his pillow.

I say, "As usual, your perception is dead-on, Carmen. Sorry, Frankie. This can't be a love connection if he's in the Russian Mafia, but you'll be glad to know that talking to him made me realize that I'm willing to consider pursuing a relationship with someone." He shrieks again. I appreciate that even when things seem grim, he's able to eke out a spot of joy.

I explain, "Konstantin was the apple of his father's eye, instrumental in helping him run his business. He was smart too, freshly graduated with an MBA from Northwestern. He was really trying to assist his dad in modernizing the place, like coming up with a better social media presence and online ordering. But Yuri was stubborn, he admitted. He fought change and wanted to carry on the old way, didn't want to put up the capital to expand and hire more personnel, so Yuri and his son did all the heavy lifting, literally."

Tears glistened in the corners of Yuri's eyes when he got to this part, and I was so moved by how emotionally available he was. Was it all an act? I got where I am in part because I'm a good judge of character. He felt real. His words felt sincere. His connection with his grandson was genuine; you can't fake that. Or can you and I've just lost my touch, my ability to discern reality from bullshit?

I say, "His son hurt his back unloading a pallet of flour. He really wrenched it and PT didn't help, so he went on pain meds."

Stella grimaces. "Uh-oh. Same thing happened with a couple of my cousins, and this story does *not* have a happy endin' if full sets of teeth are important to y'all."

I nod. "Like so many others, Yuri's son developed an addiction. When his doctor cut him off, he went doctor shopping. He never bought anything illegal or on the street, because he didn't have to. There were too many legitimate physicians who were happy to accommodate him, as well as a whole pharmaceutical industry."

"Fucking Purdue Pharma," Jazz says, scowling extra hard.

"Matthew Broderick is who played Richard Sackler in *Painkiller*," Carmen explains to Jazz. "*That's* who Ferris Bueller is."

"Oh, that guy!" Jazz cries. "I *hate* him."

Frankie cradles his face in his palms. "Dr. Pulaski, what the hell did you do?"

"Obviously, Yuri didn't tell me that part. But the pieces fit," I say, feeling existential dread creeping into my soul as Yuri's involvement starts to feel more tangible. There's no other explanation, is there? "That's the missing portion of the puzzle. Peter wrote the script."

"Y'all, this is a chicken or the egg conundrum," Stella says, gathering up her hair and knotting it into a bun without benefit of a hair tie. "Which came first?"

"I don't follow," Carmen replies.

Stella says, "We don't know what came first—if Peter got into the whole money laundering deal with Yuri and that's how Konstantin met him, or if he gave Konstantin the script that resulted in his overdose and Yuri sought him out to do a deal."

"But if it's the latter, why would he do that?" I ask. "If he wanted revenge, why wait? What's the benefit?"

Jazz looked up from her computer. "Maybe he was playing a long game? I don't know, that part's unclear. Here's what I do know from poking around on the dark web."

"Ooh, how do you get to the dark web?" Frankie asks, trying to peer at her screen from across the expanse of the bed. "Do you just google 'dark web' or is there, like, a password? Or do you have to be invited in, like a Soho House membership? Did you know Gavin's a member now? We should hang out at the pool there next summer."

Jazz ignores him and reads from her screen. "*Yuri Kharchenko emigrated to the United States after the fall of the Soviet Union. He was a low-level enforcer for the Russian mob, but he had quite the reputation for violence, and he was called the 'Butcher of Belgorod.'* Holy shit. You had honey cake with the *Butcher of Belgorod*, Eli. We were eating dumplings made by the *Butcher of Belgorod*. Big yikes."

I'm suddenly nauseated. How is it possible that the first man who's even caught my interest in decades could be so terrible? Is my picker so rusty that it's irredeemable? He just seemed so kind; it did not feel like an act. Yet sociopaths can mimic humanity, though it's not something they truly feel. We always look to Ted Bundy as someone who got away with as much as he did for as long as he did because he could *act* like he was a decent man when it was to his benefit. He could read a room and pour on the charm. But that's what it was—an act. Why didn't it feel that way with Yuri, though? When we said goodbye, he held my hand and looked me directly in my eyes and I *felt* something. Our connection was real, I'd swear on it. But this isn't about me. I need to compartmentalize those feelings and just listen.

Jazz continues, "*He gained power in the organization when he came to the US but ended up being sent to prison for racketeering in the early 1980s. Conjecture is he took the fall for someone higher up.* Looks like he did a nickel and got out in the late 1980s. Not much info about him until his wife passed away from cancer in 2016. Pancreatic, ugh, that's a rough one."

When he talked about caring for Ekaterina during hospice, the way he'd brush and style her wig and draw on her eyebrows for her, tears were full-on pouring down his face. How did he fake that? It doesn't seem possible. I got to where I am not just because of hard work, but because of a keen sixth sense about people. I can't see how the person I sat with is the same person Jazz is reading about.

"Oh, wait," Jazz says. "Here's something nice about him." I hold my breath, waiting to hear something, anything, that might redeem him. "He has fantastic Yelp reviews. Wow, five stars, across the board. The honey cake is a huge hit."

"Everyone, it's late. Why don't we pack it up for now?" I say. I'm bone tired and, for once, feeling every one of my sixty-three years.

Even though I have enough guest rooms for everyone, we end up sleeping where we all are, until Lilly's text rouses me.

"Guys? Wake up. We're going to Virginia," I say.

Chapter Twenty-Six

Diana

Ethan is in the back seat dozing as we drive the twenty minutes to my parents' fancy retirement village, where everyone has a golf cart. He's not used to being up this early on the weekend. I'm not even sure he knew what he was throwing in his backpack when I told him that I had to leave town on urgent Doom Crew business. He bought the reason for the sudden evacuation, never once questioning why I'd have an urgent out-of-town obligation for what's essentially a discussion board about old crimes. He's still so trusting, so I feel particularly vile that I'm about to be an accessory to a crime again.

This time, willingly.

He deserves a mother who's better than that. Then again, I deserved a mother and a father who'd have given me a choice.

"You're loud, you know," Lilly says. I get anxious about having the kids in the front seat—it just doesn't feel safe, but she insists on being up here so she can control the music and temperature. At least it's not a long drive. She monkeys with the controls and Sabrina Carpenter begins to play. An espresso sounds pretty good right about now—I am beyond tired.

"Okay." I am not up for fighting with her; I have far too much on my mind.

She cuts her eyes over toward me. "Do you think I'm stupid? I'm genuinely curious."

"Bunny, you're in four honors classes. That is the last thing I would think."

"I'm coming with you," she says.

I let out a bark of laughter, just imagining the absurdity of it. "You can't. It's boring club business with my friends. I wouldn't even know what to do with you," I say, conveying a cheeriness I do not feel. I need both of them out of the car and safe so I can call the Crew, make amends, and have them talk me through what to do next because I am at a loss here.

In Lilly's words, I am having a small "menty b," even though she is mortified when I use her generation's slang. Does she know what a luxury it is to have a parent who repressed what she wants and needs for her? I suspect not.

"Again, *you are loud.* If you want to keep a secret, I suggest that you take your calls off speakerphone. Don't try to blow sunshine up my ass—"

"Language!"

Lilly throws up her hands in frustration at my deflection. "Up my *butt*, okay, Mom? I heard the guy last night and I heard Dad. I know what's going on. If Dad's taking off because he's committed fraud, I need to say goodbye to him. So don't give me any bullshi—*bullshirt* about some made-up obligation with your stupid old nerd murder club. I don't know why it's against your and my grandparents' religion to actually address anything that's ever going on, but I'm done with it, okay? You always say you want to be closer to me. Well, that starts by you not candy-coating everything. By not ignoring anything that's difficult or uncomfortable. You don't have to childproof reality for my benefit. Jesus, the repression in this family is suffocating. The silence is killing me. So I'm coming. Say less."

I don't know what to say to Lilly because I have so many conflicting emotions right now. But what I feel more than anything is . . . pride?

Because I would be a different person with a different life if I'd been able to do the same, to claim my voice and state my case, once upon a time.

I glance in the back seat and confirm that Ethan's not only out cold, but wearing noise-canceling earphones. I can feel the bile rising in the back of my throat, and I want to do anything but have this conversation, and yet I am compelled to push forward. It's time. Our legacy of silence stops here. "I have a story I need to tell you."

❧

"Say nothing. That's what we were to do if anyone questioned us. We were to say nothing. We saw nothing. We knew nothing. We had no contact. End of story," I tell her.

Lilly's been sitting quietly, absorbing everything I've said. But instead of looking at me with her usual degree of contempt, her face is open and she's nodding. I can't believe she's not raging at me, or completely disgusted. Finally, she says, "You get that what they did was batshit, right?" Lilly asks.

"Language!"

She laughs at me. "Oh, Mom, we're so far past that now."

She's right.

"My dad must have known something was off that night, because it took him weeks to report my car stolen and cancel my credit cards. We saw Uncle David in late August, and we didn't find out everything until September."

"So Grandpa could have helped track him down? He could have called the credit card company and given that information to the police and they could have seen where he was going? I don't understand," she replies. "What about the stuff he charged? How did that work?"

"I think my father paid the cards, at least until we learned the truth," I say.

"So he literally aided and abetted a murderer? Grandpa? The guy who won't even let me sign in on the neighbor's unsecured Wi-Fi network? My mind? Blown."

"You have to understand, for the longest time law enforcement thought that my uncle had been kidnapped because he was missing. But no one put much effort into his recovery because local police forces were so busy with a post-9/11 response. Everyone was so spooked. The second I heard they were gone, I knew that the family died at my Uncle David's hand. I felt it in my guts. I have never been surer of anything in my life. I always felt like there was something off about him. He was my dad's doppelgänger, but a darker version somehow. He had the dominant, controlling thing, but he didn't have my father's loving edge.

"My parents couldn't have known that night. They couldn't have. My dad looked at the person he was closest to, outside of my mom, and he blindly helped him. I know in his mind he was convinced he was doing the right thing. So imagine how he felt when he realized how wrong he was."

A part of me wonders what might have happened if I hadn't locked my door that night. Or if my mother felt a psychic disturbance and stood guard. I don't share this part with Lilly. She already knows more than I ever anticipated her learning.

"Did you know?"

"This is the question that's kept me awake at night for decades. Honestly, I think we all felt that something was terribly amiss, but my father was too deeply in denial to admit it. Was Dad trying to protect Uncle David? Or himself and his reputation?" I say.

"Why didn't you ask them? Demand answers? That's what I would have done."

I give a sad little laugh. "I didn't because I'm not *you*, Lilly. I always wanted to get confirmation that my family actually helped my uncle with his getaway. Or were we minor casualties in the whole scheme of it? Did he steal from us or did we willingly give to him, aiding and abetting? The coroner was never too clear on death timelines, as

Uncle David had cranked the heat before he left, so that accelerated the decomposition. No one can pinpoint exactly when it happened. We don't know if Uncle David came the day it happened, or if he'd already been on the run. What if he left us and it happened after? We will never know."

"I'll tell you this—I am absolutely logging onto Grandpa's neighbor's Wi-Fi next time I'm over there. So explain this—you never asked them anything? You guys never talked about it?"

"We literally *never spoke about the murders again*. I had the feeling my mother wanted to discuss it, wanted to scream, *How fucked up is this?* but our home was my father's castle and that was that. We lived by his rules and we didn't question them. We were going to look on the sunny side, hard stop. In my heart, by not doing the right thing, by not going to the police with everything we knew, I felt like we were and are accessories to murder, and there's no statute of limitations."

"Jesus, Mom. This is so messed up and I'm sorry you had to deal with it."

Lilly's unexpected empathy takes my breath away. How long have I been waiting for someone to tell me that they *saw* me, that they understood what I was forced to bear? I never told anyone but Peter because I thought it would drag them down. But instead, I feel lifted up.

I tell her, "I've just pushed all of this down deep, so deep, over the years, that it almost doesn't feel real. That's why I've been searching message boards for years, seeing if anyone held any additional clues. It's how I connected with the Crew, yet I've never shared the crucial information I have with them."

"Well, that's just messed up. You have the greatest resource in the world, and you're not doing anything with it. That'd be like buying a Gucci bag and then never carrying it. Like, why? What is the point? You know you have to tell them, right?"

I do.

"Explain this—how did no one ever connect that you were related?" she asks.

"My family was never connected to Uncle David because of the different last-name spelling. See, when our grandfathers came to America from Sweden, one took the Americanized version and one left it as is. Carlson and Karlsson, the same, but so different. Even in casual conversation, we called him Uncle David, as his father had also been John Davidson Karlsson and my uncle went by his middle name, so no one put the pieces together."

Lilly pulls out a tube of lip oil and applies it while looking in her visor mirror. "I've gotta say, I'm a little impressed at how you've held your shit together for so long," Lilly tells me. "It explains a lot about you. *A lot.* That was a compliment, by the way."

Even though everything is chaotic and wrong right now, I still feel a flash of joy at finally coming to an understanding with this kid.

We arrive at my parents' place and Lilly pokes her brother. "Hey, Captain Underpants, time to wake up."

He's groggy as he comes to, yawning and stretching in the back seat. "Okay. Did I miss anything important?" I realize I've been doing Ethan no favors by not being fully transparent with him.

"Well," I say, "we talked about—"

"We talked about how much fun you're gonna have hanging out with Grandma," Lilly says. She cuts me a look that communicates that now is not the time. And she's right.

"You think she'll let me join her mah-jongg game?" he asks, suddenly excited.

"She will if you insist," Lilly says. Even though I am exhausted and anxious and completely out of my mind with worry, I suddenly feel like I'm not in this alone.

We get out and I give Ethan a tremendous squeeze, trying not to think about all the ways in which our family may change by the time we come back.

For once I'm glad my folks aren't ones to request a lot of detail, so we drop off Ethan and we're on the road.

"So where are we going?" Lilly asks.

"Cumberland Gap, Virginia."

"That's random. Why?"

I level with her. "I have no idea." Then say, "Do you mind if I make a call?"

Lilly stares out the window at the road ahead. "I'd mind if you didn't. You've got this, Mom. Go for it." She rips open a bag of Flamin' Hot Cheetos that she insisted we pick up (along with a lot of other junk food) before we started our road trip. She offers me the bag. "By the way, you want? Breakfast of champions." I take one. It tastes way too hot.

I use the car's Bluetooth to call Eli. She picks up on the first ring. "Diana? Hi. We're so glad to hear from you. Everyone's here." I hear everyone's voices in the background. "Lilly texted us. Are you okay? What's going on? How can we help?"

I cut my eyes over to Lilly. "What?" she says with a sly grin. "I thought it would take less time than it would for you to explain things. You seem to have your hands full here, Mom. I thought you could use some backup."

I can feel the tears welling in the corners of my eyes as I finally let down my guard and tell everyone the unvarnished truth, starting at the beginning, more than twenty years ago.

"No, I am not okay."

Chapter Twenty-Seven

Eli

"I need you to be goodest boys for Miss Yancy," I tell Herman and Pee-wee as I plant kisses on their majestic melons. Pee-wee headbutts my shoulder and Herman puts a giant paw on my back, as though to stop me. I already feel a pang of missing them. However, they'll be in great hands with my sitter while we're gone. The last time she was here, she threw a barbecue for them and then she brought her Labradors over for a playdate. All creatures involved slept for three days after that. "Now go see your Yancy," I instruct them. I hate to leave them, but Diana needs us.

We've all come clean about everything—from our involvement with Peter to Diana's tie to JDK. Every single one of us cried. We're just so relieved to have our friend group back together and on track. The uncertainty and subterfuge were wrecking every single one of us. Now we're going to do everything in our power to make sure that Diana and Lilly are safe. I'm not worried about Peter, but I am worried about who's after Peter and the impact it could have on the rest of the Pulaskis, so we've leaped into action.

With one heartbreaking glance back at me, the boys both trot off to where Yancy waits to distract them with treats and fun. I wish I could make them understand where I am going and that I'll return soon.

Honestly, I don't recall it being this hard to leave my actual children when I traveled, but I'd never tell them that.

I survey the scene as we gather on the porch before loading into the waiting Uber XL. "Does everyone have everything?" I ask. "Anyone need to use the bathroom? If so, do it now, please. I don't know what the restroom situation will be like on the plane." How is it that a road trip never fails to put me right back into mom mode again?

"I should probably go," Frankie says as he dashes back to the powder room. Sheepishly, Carmen and Stella follow him. Jazz is characteristically annoyed for about thirty seconds, before she scoots back inside too. I shake my head and have to laugh, realizing that I love these people as much as I love my own children.

"Whose plane is this?" Carmen asks, eyeing all the polished teak and plush leather seats.

"One of my friends. She's a neighbor," I say. I thought flying would be the fastest way to catch up with Diana and Lilly. We have no idea what Peter has planned, but whatever it is, Diana will not have to be alone for it. Given that she knows everything, we're not afraid she'll succumb to him, but we want to be there as her backup just in case. We'll still have a drive ahead of us once we get to Knoxville, and the weather is starting to turn. The early fall heat wave is breaking, with a cold front heading our way. If we'd waited for the next flight to Knoxville in three hours, there's a good chance of it getting canceled.

"You borrow cups of *sugar* from your neighbors, not Gulfstreams. But this is so much better than flying Southwest," Frankie says, taking a delicate sip of his champagne, served by Hannah, our perky young flight attendant.

"I didn't know it would be this nice. I thought it would be a little Cessna. This is unexpected." I wasn't expecting a G400, or a Hannah who keeps trying to ply us with sliced dragon fruit and Veuve Clicquot.

But my friend was a Fortune 500 CEO, so I guess it makes sense that she travels in style.

"The bathroom has a shower!" Carmen exclaims as she returns from the restroom. "Imagine showering at thirty thousand feet! I'm already clean, but I'm half tempted to take one just to say I did."

"We do have about two hours," I say. "Although our time would be better off spent figuring out why Peter is in Virginia, of all places." This will keep my mind off Yuri. How did I misjudge him? What we've read and what I've seen just don't jibe. I keep feeling like there's more to the story. I'm never this wrong. Am I losing my ability to discern? Is that the beginning of the end for me? Is it all downhill cognitively from here? Are my kids right to have concerns?

"But it's barely Virginia. It's right in the pocket of where Virginia, Kentucky, and Tennessee meet up. It's about four hours from Nashville," Frankie clarifies. "Wanna know the good news?"

"What's that, Frankie? Did you figure out what's there or why we're going?" Carmen asks.

"No, but when we land in Knoxville, we're only going to be an hour from Pigeon Forge!" he exclaims, making a ta-da motion.

His answer sheds no light on any sort of news. Carmen asks, "And that's important why?"

He claps his hands. "Because we could visit Dollywood when we're done! And I bet we're just in time for their annual Harvest Festival!"

"Frankie, let's put a pin in that and see what Diana needs first," I say, returning my attention to the business at hand. "I hate going into this blind. If we only knew why Peter was there, we could plan. Is he hiding? Is he running? Are Yuri and his people after him? Does Yuri even have people? Is there going to be a confrontation? I don't think he means her harm, but there's so much mystery around this that it would be irresponsible for us to not be by her side."

As of now, our plan is to stand behind Diana, in whatever way that entails. Diana was so sad on the phone, begging us for forgiveness, but I cut that off quickly. I told her that it's going to take more than a few harsh words spoken in the heat of anger—and one hell of a family secret—to shake us, a sentiment Lilly deemed "badass."

"Oh, shit, why don't we just check the source material?" Jazz says, slapping her hand against her forehead. "I forgot I still have access to all his stuff. Does this thing have Wi-Fi, Hannah?"

Hannah gives Jazz a small card of heavy paper stock printed with the login instructions and Jazz gets to work.

"I've gotta log in too. My feed's been sufferin' lately. Y'all know that riding on a PJ is like winning the Super Bowl for an influencer? Lotta people will fake bein' on a plane by holding a toilet seat up against the sky. Or they go to a place that's staged like the inside of a plane, but it's just a set they rent for seventy-five dollars an hour. Sorta pathetic," Stella says as she snaps away and Frankie assists by styling the shoot.

"I'm not finding anything," Jazz says, toggling from app to app. "Damn it. He's got a ton of unanswered texts, unread emails, but nothing that points to how or why he's in the Appalachian foothills. Looks like he hasn't even been online, save for viewing some Google Maps. Weird."

"Again, we're missing a piece," I say. "This feels off. He's talking to someone. He didn't just pick this place out of thin air. Did he have a second phone on him?"

"I frisked him pretty good," Frankie says as he prop styles a Hermès blanket behind Stella. "I'd have found it." Frankie doesn't look like he sustained a head injury yesterday, as he's parted the swoopy portion of his hair on the other side, hiding the cuts. Fortunately, the lump has gone far down, although I will admit I woke him up every hour last night in case we were wrong about the concussion.

"What about the site where he talked to Zlata?" Carmen says.

"What about it? He promised us he was done with her, probably because she's a Nigerian dude," Jazz says.

"Peter has had a tenuous relationship with the truth," Carmen observes. "What he says and what he does are diametrically opposed. He didn't just change his spots after one confrontation. Think about it—Peter didn't admit to making a single mistake. He made unethical decision after decision after decision. He's established a pattern of doing the wrong thing. There's no reason to believe he wasn't lying to us to get off easier."

"And what if she's not a man?" I ask. "What if there's an off chance she's actually real? Is that possible?"

"Possible? Sure. Probable? That's pretty sus, but lemme see." Jazz shrugs and pulls up the Ukrainian Adult Friend Finder site under Peter's profile. She scans the screen, shaking her head, and then she grabs Frankie's abandoned glass of champagne and downs it.

She says, "Holy shit, you guys. Diana is not gonna like this."

That's when Hannah tells us, "Please fasten your seat belts, it's going to be a bumpy ride."

Frankie is impressed. "Gurl, ten points to you for the flawless execution and timing of the *All About Eve* quote."

"I'm sorry, sir, I don't know what that means. We're going to hit some weather and I want you strapped in for your safety," she replies as the plane begins to pitch and roll.

We buckle up, unsure of what's going to happen next. The plane banks hard to the left and we all gasp.

I hope that's not an omen.

Chapter Twenty-Eight

Frankie

The plane pitches and lurches its way southeast. I am scared AF. Even the most seasoned of us (ahem, Eli) are white-knuckling it. She tells us we're lucky to be in a private jet. She says we'd feel the turbulence more in a larger plane because they don't fly as high as the Gulfstream.

I sure as hell don't feel lucky.

Even Hannah looks a little green around the gills as we screech onto the tarmac at the Knoxville airport, practically hydroplaning off the runway until we come to an abrupt stop that throws all of us sideways in our seats. The water's just pounding the top of the plane, relentlessly hammering a staccato beat. The wind's blowing so hard that we're rocking, even after we've taxied and parked in the hangar. The skies are ominous and angry.

The rain is sheeting and wind howling as we wait for our vehicle to arrive from the rental agency. When the cold rainwater comes into contact with the hot blacktop, it forms steam out on the tarmac. Auntie Em, are we going to need to go to the root cellar? These feel like the ideal conditions for a tornado, and our phones are sounding with multiple watches and warnings. While Eli talks to one of the jumpsuited employees, Carmen calls Diana on speakerphone. "We've landed. We're about two hours south of Cumberland Gap."

"Two hours!" Stella exclaims like a kid learning there's still a whole state between her and Disneyland.

"I'm on I-75, passed Lexington about forty minutes ago. According to Waze, we're also about two hours away with the weather being what it is," Diana says.

"Nobody uses Waze anymore," Jazz tells them.

"That's exactly what I said!" Lilly replies.

I try to figure out Diana's vibe from the tone of her voice, but how could her vibe be good? She's bringing her husband a crypto wallet so he can escape from the angry Russian mobster who blames Peter for his son's death because he was selling scripts after stealing from Medicare didn't prove lucrative enough. Carmen says this is basically the plot of a telenovela. And there's sure as hell no pony at the bottom of all this manure, no matter how much Diana tries to bright-side it. All I want to do is wrap Diana in a hug and tell her how much she's loved, and how she doesn't deserve any of this. And that's not even to mention the pain she's been carrying around about JDK. I swear, no one's done right by her, not for a long time, and that makes me see red.

"How are you at driving through the foothills in the rain?" Carmen asks.

"Not fucking great!" Lilly shouts.

"Language!" Diana admonishes, but her heart's not in it. She sounds scared.

"We're sliding all over the place and some of these hills are getting steep. The ravines are so deep, and they're right on the other side of the guardrail! Plus there are these places for runaway trucks to escape? It's terrifying," Lilly tells us.

Eli joins us and begins speaking. "Diana, here's what you do. Do not go directly to where Peter's waiting. I want you to meet us in the parking lot at the Daniel Boone Visitor Information Center. It's about ten miles from our destination. I'm renting a car big enough for all of us. Ours will handle the terrain better than your van. I don't want you to have to meet up with Peter by yourselves, because we don't know what's waiting there. Looks like we're going pretty deep in the woods up a fire road. I don't know what cell service will be like, so we need to arrive together."

"I can't have you guys do that," Diana protests.

"They just flew down here specifically to do that, so of course you can," Lilly says. The kid is the voice of reason and I have to respect that. "Please. Yes. Let's meet. I'll do anything to get out of this frigging van."

"Language!"

"Frigging isn't a swear, Mom!"

"Hi, we're still here, Diana," Eli says gently. "We'll see you in two hours. You drive safely and remember: We're your Crew and we have your back."

"I love you guys," Diana says, her voice catching before she hangs up. I feel myself tearing up again, just hating all of this for her. She should be with a partner who lifts her up, not drags her down into the muck. I feel very selfish in this moment for appreciating what I have with Gavin. She should have that.

With her usual efficiency, Eli says, "All right, time to load up." We follow her to the other side of the hangar, where we find an imposing black vehicle that looks like the result of a one-night stand between an army tank and a luxury yacht. OMG.

"I feel like y'all didn't rent this from Budget," Stella says, eyes wide.

"No, I called a friend," Eli explains. If I find out that her Nashville friend is one Taylor Alison Swift, we are gonna have *words*. "I figured we needed a specialty vehicle with a compass and slope assist, but also enough room for everyone. This one has the third-row seating."

The normally blasé Jazz is the most awed, taking it in. She breathlessly exclaims, "This is the coolest thing I've ever seen. It's a beast. It's like the Swiss Army knife of SUVs."

Eli seems a bit offended. "Not cooler than Maybellene?"

"Different kind of cool," I offer, but I'm lying. I would legitimately date this thing, it's so sexy and rugged.

"Um, Eli, if you've got friends with planes and assault vehicles that they're happy to lend you, why the hell do you want to hang with us?" Stella asks, genuinely flummoxed.

That stops Eli in her tracks. She's equally flummoxed. "Why wouldn't I want to?"

"'Cause you're basically an older, more feminine version of Batman?" I suggest.

"No. Stop that right now. You are all selling yourselves short. Are you going to make me have you say it?" Eli asks, hand on hip. "Yes? Okay, then say it with me: 'A masterpiece, I shine so bright. I trust myself, my worth is true. There's nothing on earth I can't do.'"

Dutifully, we repeat her mantra with her. She says this is something she started saying years ago to get through the day when she lost Hank. Later, she'd say it to herself as a pep talk every time she went in on a client pitch, as she just refused to ever take less than she believed she was worth. Now followers all over the world say it. If we end up improving society through the power of her positive thinking, I will pretend to look surprised.

"Now get in and buckle up, it's going to be a bumpy ride," Eli says.

"Eh, it was better when Hannah said it first," I say with a small moue of disapproval. She's usually more original than this.

Eli laughs. "That wasn't a quote, it was an instruction. I still need you to get in and fasten your safety belts. The weather's worsening, so it's going to be bumpy as we make our way north through the hills. The wind's blowing hard west to east and we're going to feel it on our broadside, so I wasn't sure how else to say it."

"How about 'The open road is calling and we must go,'" Carmen says, climbing into the back seat.

"Now *that* was profound," Jazz says.

"It's a quote from Ferris Bueller."

"Ugh, him again," Jazz grouses.

"We're burning daylight," Eli admonishes.

But we're not; it's already black as night out here.

Diana and Lilly arrive about fifteen minutes after we get to the visitor center, and I am deeply disappointed that there's no gift shop. "I thought I could get one of those hats with the raccoon tails. I feel like I could have made it fashion."

"Wait, wait, it's them, they're here! *Gracias a Dios!*" Carmen cries. Even though it's shitting down rain, she dashes out of the car to grab Diana and sweep her up in a bear hug. "I'm so sorry, my friend! I never wanted to upset you! We only wanted to protect you." I am in line right behind her, practically elbowing Carmen out of the way so I can get my hands on her. Hugging her feels like coming home.

"We are never ever going to hide anything from each other again," I say, holding her chin and looking in her eyes.

Diana replies, "Frankie, I'm so sorry I wasn't honest with all of you. It's just that—"

"Hey, maybe we could apologize to each other *out* of the rain," Lilly suggests, holding an empty Target bag over her head. "I just straightened my hair yesterday." The three of them scramble into the car.

"Hey, girlies!" Stella says, clambering into the third row to make room for the new passengers.

Diana is overcome with emotion. "I can't thank you guys enough. This is all so much; I don't even know where or how to—"

"Diana, it's okay. We're past it. We need to focus on getting there now," Eli says as she plugs the coordinates into the military-grade GPS. "And then what happens once we get there."

"I don't know why he's here," Diana says. "Why Cumberland Gap? Why Virginia?"

We already came clean about the fraud allegations and the pill mill, as well as our sting operation. But the worst part? We didn't want to be on the phone for this. We wanted to be with her so we could hold her and cry with her when the roughest part of the truth comes out: that his online girlfriend appears to be real and she's the one who's orchestrated the safe house. And that we believe he's leaving to meet up with her in Europe, taking all of his ill-gotten gains that are housed in cryptocurrency and accessible only via his crypto wallet on the flash drive.

How do we tell her she just risked her and her daughter's lives driving through a terrible storm, only to make it easier for this complete asshat to start a new life after leaving hers in ruins?

We don't know how, but we're hoping to figure it out as it unrolls.

With a grim expression on her face, Eli says, "I guess we'll all find out together."

"Um, what kind of car is this?" Lilly asks, taking in the cockpit-like dashboard and the reinforced doors, trimmed out in luxe leather and cherrywood.

"For our purposes," I say, "it's the Batmobile."

Despite being ten miles away, it takes us almost an hour to get to the cabin, as it's raining so hard, some of the roads are covered in debris and downed limbs. I don't know how badly this area was hit last year during Helene, but it's clear that the infrastructure isn't what it once was.

When we arrive at the small cabin tucked into the side of a hill over a steep ravine, the place looks abandoned. It's pitch black and appears uninhabited, but then I spot Peter's Tesla, shrouded in pine branches.

He has to know we're here. We just rolled up in a customized Range Rover version of a Sherman tank. Make no mistake, even with air-conditioned seats and surround sound, this thing is a monster. The way its tires grabbed the muddy incline and hauled it upward may even make Stella into a gearhead.

"What do I do here?" Diana asks. "Do I go up there and knock on the door? What is the protocol?"

"Not by yourself. Everyone, stay in the car, I'm going with her," Eli says.

"The hell you are. I'm comin' as well," announces Stella.

"Um, ditto," I say, springing up.

Carmen doesn't have to say anything; she's already flown from the vehicle.

"What? Like I'm gonna stay here by myself like an asshole? I'm in too," Jazz says.

"Honey, how do you not think we're all in this together?" I say, pushing my way through to her side.

"Do we have to keep having our dramatic moments in the rain?" Lilly asks, even though she's clearly moved by witnessing our love for her mom.

We all approach the door seven abreast as the rain comes down harder. Thunder booms in the distance, although it feels like it's been creeping closer, as the time between the thunder and lightning flashes is lessening. The sky lights up in eerie, jagged lines while the wind whips debris at our backs. A few yards away, a tree comes crashing to the ground and we all scream at its impact. This is the kind of hundred-year storm that shows you just how insignificant you are in the universe.

Carmen bangs on the door and it flies open. In the darkness, I hear a small voice coming from behind a piece of furniture.

"Diana?"

Jazz aims her phone's flashlight and we all follow suit, shining our beams on what appears to be an old hunting cabin. It smells of mold and rot and fear. All the lights must blind Peter because he stumbles toward us, arms out.

"Fun vacay vibes," I say because I can't help myself.

"Wait, you brought *them*?" Peter asks. "How are you people planning to fuck up my life now?"

"Language, Dad!" Lilly exclaims. I don't know what the ride down was like for Lilly and Diana, but they are now very much on the same team and it makes my heart smile. I have a feeling they're going to need each other when the final truth is revealed.

"Lilly's here?" Peter asks, incredulous. "What the hell, Diana?"

While we're establishing who is and isn't present, Eli pulls a couple of lanterns out of her bag, because of course she does. They cast a warm glow over the single room and now I can see everyone's faces in the wan light.

Eli places a hand on the small of Diana's back and pushes her forward. "Why don't you tell your wife why we're all assembled, Peter?" Lilly quickly follows and stands right beside her mother. She has her father's coloring, but her face is all Diana in this light.

"Did you bring the crypto wallet or not? Because I am a dead man if you didn't. Okay, you're going to be responsible for Lilly losing her daddy here, Diana."

"Nope. Wrong answer," Lilly says, totally and completely having her mom's back, much to both parents' surprise.

Suddenly feeling Lilly's unconditional support must be what breaks Diana, because she's lit from within with rage. "No. *You* did it, Peter. You did everything. You're the one who lied and stole. You're the one who ran an illegal operation. You're the one who allowed this to color your ethics and impact your family. It's *your* fault you're in this predicament. I didn't make you do the wrong thing. I had no idea. Even when my friends told me what you were doing, I didn't believe them. I fought them. I couldn't believe that you would do this to us, to our family. And for what? For a little bit of money?"

"That's a line from *Fargo*," Carmen whispers to Jazz, who nods approvingly. Jazz does love the Coen brothers.

"Tell me, Peter. Tell me what you did," Diana says so coldly, we almost don't recognize her voice. "Explain yourself. I need to hear it from you. No, *we* need to hear it from you."

"Well, you wanted stuff. Our lives were expensive. So I took some shortcuts. A few scripts here, a padded bill there. Everyone does it," he says. "You talked to the investigator. You already know. I did this because it's what *you* wanted."

"You're putting this on me?" Diana demands. "You decided to break the law because of *me*?"

"Oh, fuck him," Lilly mutters, her eyes glittering with fury at her father. I want to cheer, but it feels really wrong time, wrong place.

"Well, you're no saint yourself, Diana. Why don't you tell your good buddies what *you* did?" he counters. "You're not exactly Miss Innocent here."

"You know what? I've come clean. I've told everyone here, and when we get home, I'm taking what I know to the authorities. I'm tired of not living in the truth and you should be too. And if there are consequences, then I'll face them. I am done with hiding behind a lie."

The wind blows so hard, the door bangs open.

Carmen says, "Peter, what you fail to realize is there's not a thing this woman could do that we wouldn't forgive her for, including putting you in the ground. In fact, we'd help bury you. We brought shovels." (We didn't in actuality, but we're carrying them in spirit.)

"Whoa, Carmen!" I exclaim. "You tell him!"

The thunder rumbles and lightning strikes almost directly overhead, lighting up the whole room.

"Your friends are weird, Mom," Lilly says with more than a little admiration.

"Give me the flash drive, Diana. Please. He's going to kill me if I don't get out of here. He's probably tracking me right now," Peter says. Lightning flashes again and the thunder sounds like it's directly overhead.

"Who's going to kill you, Peter?" Diana asks. "And why?"

"Tell her, Peter. Give her the whole truth. Start from the beginning. Tell her about Zlata."

The Russian-accented voice makes all of us scream and jump. There's a man, older but still powerful looking, standing in the doorway. Then I notice he's brandishing a large pistol and I feel my blood go cold. Where the hell did he come from? Is he here to kill all of us? To make every one of us pay for Peter's misdeeds?

Eli takes a step toward him. "Yuri, I know you don't want to do this."

Holy shit, *this* is Yuri? What is happening?

"Miss Eli? My goodness, this is a surprise. I'm sorry you got tangled up in Peter's web. Everything he touches dies," Yuri says. "You should not be here. The weather is terrible and the roads are so messy."

"Amen," Jazz mutters.

"Who is this?" Lilly asks. I can't believe this kid's moxie. I am shaking in my boots and she's glowering at him, like a complete badass.

"The Butcher of Belgorod," Eli says, staring directly into his eyes.

I step between her and him, and the rest of the Crew follows me. When we do the after-action review of today, she's probably going to bring up trust issues, since the first guy she's appeared to like ever in my lifetime appears to be a Russian mobster. Is that on us for pushing her?

Yuri laughs—laughs? "Ach, they always get the translation wrong. The Baker. I was the *Baker* of Belgorod. Not the Butcher. I didn't butcher anything. But my son would call me 'the Butcher' when he was teasing me. So, yes, anyway, I've been a vegetarian for quite a long time now; it is better for the digestion."

"The Baker of Belgorod sounds a lot less menacing," I say, as if it will take some of the sting out of this for Eli.

"Potato, po-tah-to," Yuri replies with a shrug.

"Yuri, I want you to think about what you're doing," Eli says. I can't believe how calm she is, how utterly devoid of emotion. But that must be how she succeeded in the business world. She must have never let them see what she was feeling, even though I know she's got to be all torn up inside. For her to talk to someone that made her think that maybe alone wasn't the only way to go? That is *major*. "Another wrong won't make a right. You can't kill this man in front of his daughter."

"Killing him is the last thing I would do," Yuri says.

"But you have a gun," I point out.

"It's America. Everyone has a gun. Now, I have no intention of hurting your Peter, because I know he will comply. So give me the flash drive," Yuri says.

"Wait, how do *you* know about the crypto wallet?" Jazz asks.

"Because I am Zlata," Yuri says, like it's the most obvious thing in the world.

We all look at each other in the wan lantern light. What the actual fuck does that mean?

Then Jazz starts to laugh, hard. She literally doubles over. "Holy shit, Eli, I love this man. Oh, my God, if you don't date him, I will. I don't care if he has old balls. I don't care if he's in the mob, because he is *gangster*."

"No, no, you are mistaken. I am not connected anymore. I ended that affiliation decades ago," he says. "My daughters, my goodness, they would never let me hear the end of it. They did not even want me to join the Rotary Club."

My head is spinning. What is going on?

"You can retire from the mob?" Carmen asks.

"Of course you can. Remember? We did that feature on Joe Bonanno? He retired from the mob and then wrote a book about it?" I have to remind her. "It was a great read."

"Listen to your nice yellow-haired friend here, he is very smart," Yuri says.

"Thank you," I reply, trying—and failing—not to beam with pride.

"It is rare, but I made a deal. I took the fall for someone else and when I got out, I was free in all respects," Yuri explains. "I was able to start a legitimate life, got married, had children, started a business. American dream."

However, I am still completely confused, as is everyone else. "Then who was shaking Peter down for payments at the pill mill and laundering his money?" Carmen asks.

"Oh, yes, that was the Russian mob—but I wasn't a part," Yuri says.

Stella raises her hand. "Can y'all explain?"

"Don't you see?" Jazz says, wiping tears from her eyes. "It's brilliant. Yuri's been playing the long game, *exactly like I said*. Okay, Zlata's not a Yahoo Boy, but he's definitely a dude. Yuri here catfished Peter."

"I don't understand. This doesn't make any sense. So you're not in the mob," I clarify. Someone's got to make some sense of this mess.

"Not since the Reagan era," he says. "The Gipper's commission on organized crime? Pfft. You did not want to mess with that, especially having ties to the Soviet Union."

"But if you're not a criminal, why are you here holding Peter at gunpoint? Please make it make sense," Eli says.

Yuri says, "Dr. Peter Pulaski is why my son overdosed. Yes, my son had some responsibility, but it was Peter's script that ended my boy."

"Jesus Christ, Dad," Lilly says. "And you had the nerve to get mad at *me* when I told you one of my friends tried an edible? Double standard much?"

"But he said I had to keep supplying him with scripts because his dad was the Butcher of Belgorod!" Peter wails, as though somehow *he's* the victim here. "I tried to cut him off!"

"Yuri," Eli says with steely calm. "I need you to explain how you fit into all of this. You say you're not a criminal, that you're not involved with organized crime, but your actions right now belie that."

"I am no longer employed in the world of violence. Not for many decades. I had to do what I had to do to get to this country to establish myself, but my actions hurt my dear mama so much. I promise you, I never took a life, but I was an enforcer, usually to kneecaps. I had a crowbar; it was a whole *thing*. Mostly, the threat of violence was enough. I made people pay, but not good people. *Good people* don't need to be enforced. When I went to prison, my mama, I thought she would turn her back on me. But she loved me unconditionally. When I came out of prison, I started baking with her again, the recipes we used to make in Russia. That is my passion, my calling, other than my beautiful family, of course."

I can see the hard lines of Eli's face softening as he speaks. "So I baked. I created an honorable life. An honest life. But then this careless man took away something I treasure, and I felt the kind of rage I had not experienced in many years. So I thought to myself, *How do I take away what he treasures? How do I make Peter Pulaski pay?* Like yakuza does."

"Okay, so it's *definitely* the yakuza?" Jazz asks.

Yuri looks over both shoulders and then nods. "Yes, but you didn't hear it from me. Anyway, why would I possibly kill Peter Pulaski when I could make him suffer for long term, when I could ruin his business, impact his life?"

Eli is listening to his every word, her spine far less stiff and her eyes damp. I think she believes him. I guarantee that I believe him. And I suspect that she's going to forgive him. Maybe not today, maybe not tomorrow, but soon and for the rest of her life. (OMG, how proud would Gavin be of me quoting *Casablanca* right now?) It's probably not the time to mention how much the two of them have in common with the whole yakuza thing, but it's at the top of my list once all of *this* is over.

"But why do y'all have a gun?" Stella asks. She seems to want to give him some grace too. Carmen is nodding, encouraging him. So we're all Team Yuri? I feel like we might all be Team Yuri.

"Please, you don't bring a knife to a garden party," he replies, tucking his gun back into his waistband. "Plus, there's bears out here, and believe me, you do not want to tangle with one of them. It is fine, I'm not shooting anyone. Guns are very loud and not one of you has ear protection. Oh, the ringing!"

"Diana, we can go. We can start over. You've got the wallet—there's plenty for us to start over in another country. The three of us, let's go, I mean it," Peter begs. Jesus, I almost forgot about this guy. "He made his point, he's not going to hurt us. Let's just go."

Diana, who has been silent this whole time, finally speaks. "Who is Zlata?"

"It's him," Peter barks. "She's no one."

"But who was she to *you*?" Diana says, her words urgent and full of fire. "You know what? I can understand wanting to protect your family. I can understand making bad calls to keep us safe. But if there's someone else, then this was never about us."

"Looking out for family is the most honorable thing one can do," Yuri says with a wry smile. His face is giving Tommy Lee Jones and I am sort of here for it. "Family is everything."

"He thought she was real," Eli says. "It still counts as cheating because he thought she was real."

Diana takes a deep breath and puts her arm around Lilly, who curls into her, finally shaken by this experience. "I carried a terrible burden for years because it protected my family, even though I knew it was wrong not to come forward. Even though it impacted my whole life. So there's a part of me that gets why you'd cut corners and break laws if you thought it was going to move the family forward, if it was for us. If it was to keep us safe or happy." White-hot anger radiates off Diana. "But you didn't. You didn't do it for us. You did it for you and for some person who doesn't even exist. Now I need you to tell me one thing and I want the truth. Did you tell her you loved her? We can get a lawyer and make a plea for the other stuff. But if you told her you loved her, that is a bridge too far. We cannot come back from this."

She looks to Yuri, who shrugs sadly and nods, confirming exactly what Diana suspects, as he'd know—he was the one on the other side of the internet connection. Diana appears deep in thought, looking from Yuri back to Peter, on the precipice. Every single one of us is holding our breath. I will support her in whatever she chooses, but I hope for once she chooses herself.

Finally, Diana pulls the flash drive out of her bag. "You know you have a son too, asshole." And then she tosses the drive to Yuri. "This is for you."

Peter screams in agony as I let out an inadvertent cheer.

"What will you do with this money?" Diana asks Yuri. "It's all dirty. It's stolen."

"Hold on a goddamned minute, Diana. You do realize that the *real* Russian mafia is still going to be after me? They're going to insist I keep giving them their cut. I can't quit," Peter says. "That money was going to save us."

"No," Eli says. "It was going to save *you*, Peter."

"I send to help war effort in Ukraine. I am from town that borders Ukraine. My mama, my papa, both from Ukraine. In my heart, I am more Ukrainian than Russian. This is bad money, but it can be used to do good," Yuri says. "I need some good to come out of the poison Peter Pulaski spread in the world."

Eli is nodding at every word Yuri says. Weirdest first date ever? We have a contender.

"Ha! You can't do anything without the passcode!" Peter shouts.

"It's 0-7-0-3," Diana says, so matter-of-fact that I am completely stanning her. "Lilly, please say goodbye to your father. I suspect you won't see him for a while."

Lilly approaches him and gives him a perfunctory hug, yet she can't hide her disgust. It's hard to see your idol fall. "Oh, my God, Dad, how hard would it have been just to be nice to Mom? I am going to be talking about this in therapy *for years*."

"You should go," Yuri tells Peter, patting his waistband. "In case I change my mind. It is also possible my former colleagues are coming after you. They do not like when you stop paying. If you are lucky, all they have is a crowbar."

"But where am I going to go? What am I going to do?" Peter pleads. "That was my nest egg, my escape pod."

"You are a smart guy. Doctor. You will figure it out," Yuri says. "Of course, you do not need to escape. You could always go home, atone for what you have done. Confess and you no longer have a mob problem. Maybe the government will take it easy on you if you become informant. You get probation, maybe. Or they put you somewhere white collar, you learn to play pickleball. It is not so terrible. You will pay your debt. Living in the truth, living in the light, it is good. It will bring you peace."

Without a pause, without hesitation, without even looking back at his family, Peter picks up his bag full of cash and he takes off like a shot. He throws the pine boughs off his car and hightails it down the mountainous road.

We all look at each other, disappointed but not surprised.

I guess that Peter Pulaski has truly, finally paid, yet the price he extracted came from those he was supposed to love the most.

We all hug, for lack of knowing what else to do. Diana is being super stoic right now, but I know she's going to need us in the coming days, and we will be there for her. Count on that. Lilly begins to cry, and Diana pulls her even closer.

"Miss Eli, I have no regrets about my actions, save for the idea that this may have damaged my ability to know you," he says. "For that, I am profoundly sorry. I have been lucky in my life that I got a second chance to redo what I got wrong. I am not so bold to think I deserve a third chance."

I have to clap a hand over my own mouth so I don't start chanting "Third chance! Third chance!"

"I'm going to need some time to reflect," Eli says. "It could take a while."

"Then I will wait until then. You will know where to find me if you are ever ready," he says.

"Um, Yuri—it's okay to call you Yuri, right?" Jazz says. "The one thing I can't figure out is, why Cumberland Gap? Why are we *here*? I deduced so much, but not why we're here."

Yuri shrugs. "I just . . . always wanted a reason to visit Dollywood."

Epilogue

Diana

Six Months Later

I am still in my scrubs after working a grueling overnight shift in the ER. I'd forgotten how much I love nursing. When I was younger, I wasn't sure what I should do with my life, but now when I'm there on the front lines, being the smiling face that my patients need to see when they are on the brink, I feel like I am living my destiny. I help people through some of the most difficult days of their lives. I am exactly where I need to be.

It's almost Easter, so I'm out delivering my signature hot cross buns to all my friends and loved ones. I'm dropping them off a little early because we have a family trip planned to London and Paris and we're leaving the day before Easter! I don't know who's more excited, Lilly or me. (Spoiler alert: It's me.) I knock on the door of my neighbors, Amy S. and Drake—the folks who stole my zucchini. I figure that since I was given the chance to start over, maybe I should give them a second chance too. I knock again, but no one seems to be home. That's okay. I leave their buns on their bench, along with a nice note.

Détente.

I talked to an attorney about a number of things, from ending my marriage to my responsibility under the law regarding my Uncle David. He says the family isn't considered culpable because we didn't know about the crime when we let him get away with my car. And it's getting a lot of attention because I insisted we feature his story on the club's page, and our members are working to gather clues. If JDK is still alive, there's a possibility he'll be brought to justice once and for all, since our sleuths are on the case. That's what's important, but that it helped us with our membership dilemma is an added bonus. We're hitting our numbers and doing a lot of good, so I'm glad something positive has come from all of this.

Obviously, we're in family therapy, at least the immediate members. Telling Ethan everything wasn't easy, but he has his sister to rely on. Not only have they made peace, but they occasionally team up against me, which quietly delights me. They have their own secrets together now as their relationship has become close. She's teaching him to be more of a thirteen-year-old boy and less of a forty-three-year-old man. Kids his age, rather than just adults, appreciate him. I know the circumstances were less than ideal, but he seems so much happier.

Lilly is a trouper. I've started to call her on her behavior and she seems to appreciate that. I could live without her always joking that she's got daddy issues and she's going to end up on the pole, but her gallows humor seems to help. Jazz is teaching her to code, which only scares me a little bit.

My parents still refuse to talk about anything Uncle David–related. They act like nothing's happened, but I know that denial is no way to go through life. Obviously. And I've become closer to my own brothers as well. Our relationship was always superficial, but I have to say, being able to sit down with them and say "That was messed up" opened an emotional floodgate, for all of us and for the better.

Peter is still in the wind and his family blames me, as though this were somehow *my* fault. Can't say that I miss any of them. Once in a while, Peter sends an email from a burner address to Lilly *and* Ethan. I appreciate the effort, but I am a hell of a lot older and wiser now. I am not about to fall for Peter Pulaski's pleas again. Ironically, I don't look older, as I finally let Lilly talk me into tinting my grays a pale blonde. I . . . don't hate it. I'm still not Botoxing, but I feel like I'm at a never-say-never point of my life now.

Everyone else is exactly where they should be and that delights me. Things have normalized since last fall. Stella's wedding was the event of the season and we wept and wept. She was so beautiful. I don't know who was happier that day, us or them. Despite our urging, Eli did not bring Yuri as her date. But there's definitely something forming there, even though the progress isn't what Frankie is dying for. Don't think we didn't notice the honey cake she served at the last board meeting. Time will tell. Of course, the last time we were at her place, she was dog sitting a couple of enormous Russian wolfhounds "for a friend." Do the math.

His "brush with death" (Frankie's words, not ours) convinced Frankie that he should just say *yes* to Gavin already, so we have another wedding in our sights. Of course I am doing their flowers. Of course I am. My designs will heavily feature lilies because everyone loves them, save for Peter's spoiled sister. I don't miss being at his family's beck and call. Distance feels good.

Carmen's boys are still living in her basement, much to her delight. I swear, she is never going to let them go, and now I totally get it. I, too, want to keep my babies close, especially as Lilly and I have figured out how to communicate with each other. All she ever wanted was for me to be "real." Well, that and Eras Tour tickets, which somehow Eli miracled for us last November, along with backstage passes. (I suspect I know who owned that car in Nashville now.)

Jazz says she has big news to share at our next board meeting, but of course we already know what it is. What else could it be? There's only one thing in the world that she wants, so we imagine she'll be taking a small sabbatical from the Crew over the summer. But we'll be watching.

We'll all send her a bunch of bikinis so she has a tangible reminder of us while she's there.

As for me? Today's a big day. I've taken a major step.

I get to the Starbucks, order my drink, and select a seat in the corner by the fireplace while I wait for it. It's still cold out and spring has come late this year, much to Frankie and Gavin's delight, so it's nice to be by its warming flame. When he enters, I can feel the smile spread across my face.

Isaac greets me effusively, kissing my cheek. We've been in touch every time I've heard from Peter, and we're both committed to bringing him to justice. But each time we've talked, we find ourselves on the phone longer and longer; this isn't about Medicare fraud anymore.

"It's really lovely to see you in person, Diana. I'm so glad you invited me." We're breaking new ground here and we both know it.

He lays his phone and keys on the café table. The diamond from his charm catches the light.

"What would you like to drink?" I say.

"I'd like an espresso, but I can't let you get it," he says.

"Nope," I say. "I asked you on this date, so it's on me."

"It's a date?" he confirms, and I nod. Then we both grin at each other like a couple of teenagers and tentatively touch hands across the table.

"So tell me what you're drinking, and I insist." Because this time, it's Diana Pulaski who must pay.

ACKNOWLEDGMENTS

First of all, I have to thank all of my favorite true crime podcasts. Also, I want to be super clear that you *absolutely* should be able to make a living off your work. I made the Doom Crew not-for-profit only because I thought it worked better for telling their story. *True Crime Obsessed*, *Crime Junkies*, *True Crime Garage*, *Morbid*, *My Favorite Murder*, *Strange and Unexplained*, and every murder-y series on Wondery, I have nothing but love and respect for all of you. All of you handle the stories you cover sensitively and with the victims first. No notes.

Thank you to my editor Laura Van der Veer and my developmental editor Tiffany Yates Martin. Even though I thought the editorial process was going to, um, *unalive me*, every suggestion you two made was right on target, despite my kicking and screaming. Thank you for not letting me just coast.

As always, major gratitude to Erin Niumata and Steve Troha at Folio. This was a particularly fun one and I can't wait to see what we do next!

Many, many thanks to everyone behind the scenes at Little A—from sales, to marketing, to publicity, to the art department—you all make the trains run on time. And extra thanks to the copy editors because even after all these books, I didn't know what a comma splice was. Thank you for not letting me look like a d-word, and thank you to the sensitivity reader for flagging words like the d-word because I do want my writing to be as inclusive as possible.

Thank you to my friend and client Liz Elting for being that badass lady boss who actually lived through the real-life harrowing flight, drove through the night during tornadoes, and went on to land that business and build an empire. You are an icon who did indeed dream big and win.

Of course I have to thank Fletch for running the show when I realized that I had a handful of books due at the same time. I'd say I'll plan my time better going forward, but we all know that's a damn lie.

Finally, I want to thank the real-life Doom Crew, aka the Zoom Crew, for inspiring this story. I couldn't be luckier that you all have my back no matter what . . . and that you all have your shovels ready, no questions asked.

ABOUT THE AUTHOR

Photo © 2016 Jolene Siana

Jen Lancaster is *The New York Times* bestselling author of the novels *The Anti-Heroes*, *Housemoms*, *Here I Go Again*, and *The Gatekeepers*, and the nonfiction works *Welcome to the United States of Anxiety*; *Bitter Is the New Black*; *The Tao of Martha*; *Such a Pretty Fat*; *Bright Lights, Big Ass*; *Stories I'd Tell in Bars*; *Jeneration X*; *My Fair Lazy*; *Pretty in Plaid*; and *I Regret Nothing*, which was named an Amazon Best Book of the Year. Regularly a finalist in the Goodreads Choice Awards, Jen has sold well over a million books documenting her attempts to shape up, grow up, and have it all—sometimes with disastrous results. She has also appeared on the *TODAY* show, *Oprah*, *CBS This Morning*, Fox News, NPR's *All Things Considered*, and *The Joy Behar Show*, among others. She lives in the Chicago suburbs with her husband and many ill-behaved pets. Visit her website at www.jenlancaster.com.